THE
RECORD
KEEPER

Center Point
Large Print

Also by Charles Martin and available from
Center Point Large Print:

Send Down the Rain
Chasing Fireflies
The Water Keeper
The Letter Keeper

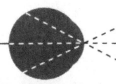

**This Large Print Book carries the
Seal of Approval of N.A.V.H.**

THE RECORD KEEPER

A Murphy Shepherd Novel

Charles Martin

CENTER POINT LARGE PRINT
THORNDIKE, MAINE

This Center Point Large Print edition
is published in the year 2022 by arrangement with
Thomas Nelson.

The text of this Large Print edition is unabridged.
In other aspects, this book may vary
from the original edition.
Printed in the United States of America
on permanent paper sourced using
environmentally responsible foresting methods.
Set in 16-point Times New Roman type.

ISBN: 978-1-63808-412-9

The Library of Congress has cataloged this record
under Library of Congress Control Number: 2022937414

For Bones
Because the needs of the one
outweigh those of the ninety-nine

PART 1

CHAPTER 1

Coastal Georgia

The plane touched down on an off-the-grid military runway in southeast Georgia. I hesitate to say airport because there was no tower and ours was the sole airplane. We landed, climbed into a rented Suburban, and in less than three minutes were accelerating south down the I-95 on-ramp. A few miles later, we turned east off I-95 at exit 58 and wound through two-lane highways to a map-dot fishing hamlet called Spellman Bluff.

Just past the Dollar General, two run-down bars sat opposite each other on the only road leading in. The marquis at the first read, "My favorite form of exercise is a beer run." The second played off it by responding, "Yeah, I have a feeling my check liver light might come on this weekend."

We pulled off the hardtop onto a dirt road that led toward the water. Bones wound through abandoned double-wides and dilapidated shacks where bamboo shoots spiraled out of rusty cars with no wheels and no engines and long-forgotten sailboats lay on their hulls, choked by vines, home now to cats and rats. This is ancient earth populated by old trees, some six feet in diameter, whose moss-draped limbs swoop down to kiss the ground only to rise again.

We cruised down a private drive and parked at what looked like an old fish camp. Well kept, unlit, and apparently empty.

"How'd you know about this place?" I asked.

He smiled. "I don't tell you all my secrets."

We stowed our gear, and Bones took me to a covered dock where he punched a button, raising the door, and then pulled the cover off a Zodiac Pro RIB—an extremely durable half-rubber, half-fiberglass boat about twenty-four feet long and just over nine feet wide. Powered by twin 350-horsepower Mercury Verados, it could carry a dozen people and do so quickly. It also would allow us to do this relatively unseen, as matte black rubber tends to blend into the night.

"Nice boat," I quipped.

"Thought you'd like it." He tossed me a line. "Get in. Let's go for a ride."

It was after midnight. Dead low tide and the half-moon shone on the oyster beds rising up like pitcher's mounds around us. If there were that many around us, then what lay beneath us was a bed of razor blades. Bones navigated through the shadows seemingly without thinking, turning the wheel via muscle memory. We ran dark. No running lights.

I asked but the question was rhetorical: "You been here before?"

He pointed to a bluff, the remains of a dock and what had been a home. "Grew up there."

I had no idea. "Really?" Our wake spilled gently over the few remaining dock pilings freckled with barnacles.

Bones smiled like a man who'd just returned home to the smell of fried chicken and hugged his mother.

We idled out of the tributary and into the larger waters that bled into the Intracoastal. The Southeast Georgia coastline is protected by hundreds of barrier islands, most of which were inhabited at one time. North of us sat St. Catherines Island, once home to several thousand Guale Indians. South of St. Catherines sat Blackbeard Island, named after the famous Savannah smuggler and pirate. Some think the island still holds his treasure. South of the Sapelo Sound, gateway to the Atlantic and entrance to the Intracoastal, sat Sapelo Island. A wildlife refuge.

I could tell by the look on his face that Bones was calculating distance and time. He pointed at the sound. "If she enters here"—I followed his finger south down the IC Waterway—"either she'll turn hard south and follow the coastline, or if she needs fuel or is picking up passengers, she'll head inland."

"How will we know?"

Another smile. "Local knowledge."

Inland waterways are charted by multiple engineers and experts before they are printed. The intersection of land and sea is literally measured with satellites, and thousands of hours are spent providing the best and most up-to-date information available. But inland waterways are not static and have a way of moving. Whether a result of hurricanes or time, the banks and depths change constantly, which can wreak havoc on captains. Given this uncertainty, every chart is printed with words like "Strangers should seek local knowledge before navigating this area." Or "Numerous submerged pilings. Local knowledge is advised."

Local knowledge refers to what the locals know by use. By being on the water. And few, if any, have ever read a chart.

Bones said, "There'll be a dozen. Nine to twelve years of age. Two pairs of brothers taken from Sweden to Switzerland. Blond hair. Fair skin. The traffickers wrote programs that sifted their parents' social media."

Disgust crossed his face. "Auction closed yesterday. Ten days and 130 time slots."

"That's a lot of money."

Bones nodded. "The *Sonshine* is eighty meters, and they'll board her east of Savannah. Four decks above the waterline. Three below. Her amenities include everything you can imagine.

Saunas. Massage parlors. Hot tubs. Bars. Couple of pools. Several dining rooms. Dance floors. Fitness centers. Suites. Quarters for up to forty crew." Bones shook his head. "It's a floating hell. And citadel."

"It's a floating hundred million dollars."

Bones continued, "She'll sail south along the coast, then turn inland just north of Cumberland and take on the first clients in the ditch. Either by helicopter or a thirty-six-foot Intrepid. And before you ask . . . four 400-horsepower Mercury Verados."

We studied the water for an hour. Talking through possibilities. What if she turned this way? What if she turned that way? Finally, at close to 2:00 a.m., we returned to the fish camp where Bones scrambled some eggs and I wandered around his two-bedroom home where I found no decorations. Only one small picture. Black and white. Two boys in the water. One holding a cast net. The other with his hand on the tiller.

"You come here much?"

He shook his head but didn't take his eyes off the pan. "Not much."

I had known Bones for twenty-five-plus years, and yet I'd never once heard about a home on the coast. Nor the fact that he grew up here. "You owned it long?"

A shrug. "Since before I found you."

13

Bones's silence struck me as strange, but I didn't push him. It was late and he'd talk if and when he wanted. We finished our eggs, I washed dishes, and Bones headed to the door. As he closed it behind him, he said, "Gotta check on a few things." He pointed at my room. "Get some sleep. Tomorrow we . . ." A chuckle. "Blend in."

"Blend in" was code for reconnaissance, but I asked anyway. "What for?"

He smiled. "Local knowledge."

CHAPTER 2

Colorado, 72 hours earlier

The morning air was chilly and thin, and I was breathing heavily before we set foot on the trail. Gunner jumped ahead, bouncing from rock to rock. I labored to put one foot in front of the other. Gunner had awakened me early at Summer's command. Neither was going to let me get fat and lazy, and any excuse about having been shot in the back had no effect on either of them.

We had ascended a thousand feet with another three to go when I finally gave up the fight, turned to my right, dropped to my knees, and hurled from my toes. Gunner sat, tail wagging. Amused yet waiting. Seemingly unfazed by the sounds coming out of me, Gunner circled and eyed my mess. He looked like he was about to lick my face, then thought better of it, spun, and trotted ahead.

I stood to my feet, willed one foot in front of the other, and tried to remember.

My recovery had been slow in the making. Six months had passed since Bones's brother sent his people to blow up Freetown and then paid someone else to shoot me in the back with my own crossbow. During that time, my body had spent itself fighting the infection that had occurred after I closed the wound in the cave. While I resembled my former self on the surface, save a limp and some abdominal scar tissue that made me look a little bit like the hunchback of Notre Dame, I knew inside I was not the same. My energy was low and strength even lower. Fatigue had become my unwanted companion. During my convalescence, Summer worked tire-lessly to feed me, rehab me, stretch me, and get me moving when I didn't want to. She started with a walk down the hall. Then Main Street. Then down and back twice. Then a mile. You get the point. In the last few days she'd been eyeing the Eagle's Nest. Four thousand feet above us. The trail beckoned. I knew it was going to hurt.

In truth the physical pain wasn't the deterrent. I'd been hurt before. Probably would be again. Pain came with the job. But as the weeks rolled by, I sensed there was something in me that was hesitant to climb back in the saddle. My problem wasn't so much my body as my heart, and I'm not talking about the muscle in the center of my chest. I'm talking about the place in me that holds my love—and just as important, my hope. I like to think it's down there behind my belly button. The place where you feel butter-flies. Maybe when the crossbow bolt passed through me, it nicked it. Allowing it to leak. My problem was further compounded by the fact that I'd had ample time to navel-gaze and consider my own problems. A luxury I'd never enjoyed before.

All of Freetown—and I do mean everyone—had rolled out the red carpet to get me healthy. I became their singular focus. "What do you need?" "How can I help?" "Is there anything I can do?" "How are you feeling?" Those were the first questions out of everyone's mouth, and each was well-meaning. Their intentions were beauti-ful. I'm not knocking the questions. And yet they produced consequences I never expected. This constant focus on me had an effect on me; it gave me time to think about me and what I needed, and did I really want to go through all of this again? That was a question I'm not sure I'd ever asked myself.

For the last fifteen years, I'd swallowed the pain of Marie's absence in my life and then dealt with it through David Bishop's fiction. But now, for the first time in my life, Murphy Shepherd was looking in the mirror and telling David Bishop to shut up. Don't write another word. Don't do that to your heart. It's too painful. When I could muster the courage to pick up a pen, I found my hope bucket empty and the page wordless. I, as much as anyone, knew that hope is what feeds us. It's the currency of mankind. The fuel of the soul. Without it, we wither and die.

My problem was twofold. One, even at my best, I could not protect those I loved. The events of six months ago proved that. And two, there was always one more. Despite over two decades of spending myself to rescue the lost, I'd made no dent in the cancer. Evil was no less evil. Some might find my longing to make a real difference idealistic. I don't. I don't do what I do for kicks and giggles. It's not a game. It's trench warfare. But somewhere, somehow, I needed to know that the sum of everything I'd done was having some effect on the guys in the other trenches. The war's effect on me was apparent. I was limping. What about them?

Bones had been patient. Me? Not so much. Summer would take me either way.

Gunner stared at me with an *Old man, what's your problem?* look on his face.

In short, I wasn't back to being me. I was glad to be in the land of the living but a long way from fully alive. That might take some time. I'd spent what will and energy I had staying alive in that cave. When they found me, I was on my way out. The forces pulling me down were stronger than me. Then I felt something pulling me up. Voices. Tears. Then the darkness returned. Then singing pulled me back to the surface. The tug-of-war lasted weeks. I shouldn't be here. Love won. That's all I know to tell you.

Which made it all the more difficult to get myself ready to do it all over again.

Truth was, I was stalling. Choosing excuses over sweat. Which included sleeping in and not training when I should or doing so halfway. Sunrise would find me sitting and staring at the mountain rather than climbing it. I'd pick at my plate rather than clear it when I desperately needed calories to rebuild lost muscle. Where a hundred push-ups was once routine, thirty was now the new norm.

For the first time ever, I wasn't doing what I knew I needed to—and the difference was not lost on Summer. My lax approach was dangerous, because those guys in the other trenches were doing what they needed to do.

Either unconsciously or not, I wanted out. When I asked myself why, the reason was simple. To make the bad man stop. Regardless of the success of Freetown and all those beautiful faces walking by us on the street or flashing across Bones's Planetarium slideshow, or the freedom known by all the names tattooed across my back, what I remembered most was the pain; the images I saw when I closed my eyes were those of terror and horror and heartbreak and pain.

Maybe this I-want-out place was what Bones encountered after a decade of doing the same and that's why he found me when he did. Maybe Bones chose to recruit, train, and then oversee me because he couldn't continue in this life any more than I wanted to now. Unless you've lived it, the life we endure is surreal. Unnatural. We walk about the planet waiting for the next text or phone call. We sleep with clothes laid out. Our phones never off. Always five minutes from boarding a plane. Not knowing when or if we'll return. We are tethered twenty-four-seven to "What if?"

Whatever my problem, I could not fix me. Summer knew this more than I. As I was about to discover.

During my convalescence, Freetown had rallied. Strengthened even. Our board is made up of many of the parents whose children we've rescued. From CEOs to scientists, from NYC to LA, these people are good at thinking outside the box and have the means to do so. They're also motivated because they've known the helplessness of waiting for the phone to ring.

When I woke up, Freetown was in the midst of a massive repair and renovation. The sounds of construction, from hammers to excavators, echoed into my room. The black scar caused by the explosion had been removed and new construction had taken its place. In years past we'd kept a low profile by being known as a private rehab and addiction facility. It was partly true.

We also never told anyone about those for whom we cared. We never shared a story. This created a cone of silence, which we valued. In fact, it was essential to who we are. We talk about no one.

That changed with Casey. When her book hit every bestseller list and movie rights were optioned, we did our best to protect not only her but everyone else. Admittedly, it grew more difficult with every copy sold because people wanted to know. Naturally, they were curious. As time passed, the cone of silence became more difficult to maintain, causing me to wonder if we shouldn't replicate the model elsewhere—and tell no one.

When the bomb went off, Freetown was home to sixty-three rescued girls and women. Include parents or siblings who made the trek with them, and that number quickly swells to over a hundred people housed in more than forty cabins tucked into the mountain. To care for those individuals, we employ north of two hundred people, from counselors to security to landscapers to ice cream shop and pet store workers. Our board secures donations from around the world, and as a result, our hospital has become sought after for neo-natal care, not to mention addiction and trauma recovery. Most of our girls stay with us for at least two years, during which—once healthy enough—they plug in and help where needed. Many work in the hospital. Some teach in the school. Some scoop ice cream. Others groom pets. We attempt to provide them with skills training in any area they desire. From art classes to nursing school to cosmetology to fashion design to completion of their college degree.

One of Angel's footprints at Freetown was the creation and development of several stores along Main Street that design and sell women's clothing, jewelry, and footwear. If they can think it and we can help them produce it, we sell it. Online sales are booming and at last count Angel employed more than a dozen girls, many of whom were either enrolled or applying to become enrolled in an online degree program out of New York.

One of the horrors experienced by trafficked boys and girls is that the world they live in becomes their box. The despair of their circumstances snuffs out any hope of ever stepping outside the confines of the cell in which they live, both physically and emotionally. They won't let themselves think outside that box because it's too painful. Hurts too much. When they come to us, we try to tear down the walls of the box and give them a reason not just to think outside it but to conceptualize the world in which that box is held. In our experience many trafficked women begin to believe they are not beautiful. They're taught by how they're treated—inhumanely, as less than an animal—that they are not only not beautiful but never will be. So why would they entertain the idea of fashion? They're convinced they're disposable and heinous, so why try to dress that up? The emotional warfare runs deep.

Angel suggested fashion design and the concept took off. Girls began wearing color. Bright colors. They created scarves, dresses, even designed shoes. If they could wear it, they could make it beautiful. Nothing was out of bounds. And their creations filled the stores along Main Street. They could shop every day of the week, the price was free, and they could return any item at any time, no questions asked. A wave of beauty washed through Freetown, much of which Bones captured with his Nikon.

As is the case with trafficked women, many had been tattooed. Most unwillingly. Several had been marked with a barcode like you'd see in a grocery store, the mark denoting ownership, a constant reminder that they were disposable property. Most tried to cover up those tattoos, so we brought in a removal specialist. Before long, girls were baring shoulders and necklines and smiles. Some of the girls even began studying to work as an assistant to the specialist.

Removal of the stain of that identity, along with the contagious spread of beauty, caused something else unexpected to happen. Girls decided they no longer wanted to be hidden, kept behind locked doors. They wanted to be seen. By each other. Their scars were no longer symbols of shame but signs of survival. *I made it. I'm alive.* Chins once resting on chests were now lifted high. Eyes once scouring the ground at their feet now stared two blocks down. We're not entirely sure what precipitated the change, but one night Summer convinced the girls to dance. Three hours in, they were sweaty and laughing so hard their stomachs hurt. Nightly dance classes ensued. From the electric slide to the macarena to ballroom dancing to Broadway acts, they couldn't get enough. Everybody wanted to dance with Clay, who first appeared in his wheelchair with oxygen tank in tow. The interaction did wonders for his recovery and nursed him back to health. Before long, he was standing tall on his own two feet and not only breathing on his own but wiping sweat off his brow, which only endeared him to them all the more.

Every night he'd show up wearing a new tux and penguin wing tips—given that the old ones burned up in the explosion—with a stash of handkerchiefs in his pocket. He'd give one to every dance partner, and he made a point of dancing with every girl. Wasn't long until every female in Freetown wanted only one thing: one of Clay's handkerchiefs.

I stood in the shadows and watched as an eighty-plus-year-old Black man reached deep into these girls' hearts without even knowing it. Clay was the gentleman they'd hoped for but never knew. He treated them like ladies of extraordinary value. He communicated to each one that she was worth the fairy tale. As a result, he became the singular reason many of these girls could learn to trust men again. The first night he returned dressed in a tux, Summer cued his entrance with the song "Staying Alive." True to form, Clay strutted in with all the charisma and charm of an inmate caged for sixty-plus years. A beautiful walk.

Given their dance experience, some of the girls asked Summer to help them put on a Broadway show. So Summer is now choreographing a couple nights a week.

And no, never in my wildest dreams did I think Freetown would become what it has become. Early in my training, Bones taught me that when a kernel of wheat falls to the ground, it dies alone. But if it is buried, watered, and fertilized, it puts down roots, spirals toward the sun, blossoms, and produces fruit. And what comes up is never the same as what was buried. It's exponentially more.

The residents of Freetown pay for nothing. It's free. They've earned it. A thousand times over. But getting here is not easy. The prerequisite to entry is slavery. Having been owned by another.

Until about six months ago, everyone here knew me as the guy who kicked down the door.

That's all. Just one of the employees. To ensure that opinion, I kept a low profile. I still do. Or at least I try. After my recovery—or better yet, after Summer nursed me back from the brink—they just saw me as the guy who wears a hoodie, hobbles down Main Street, sits on park benches, and sips oolong tea. Most afternoons I leave our home and limp to my bench, which gives me an unobstructed view of the pet store, clothing store, and salon. I feed the pigeons and the smiles feed me as the girls pass on skateboards, scooters, bicycles, or running shoes. In truth Gunner is far more the attraction than I. His ability to attract admirers and belly-scratchers is unmatched. And while I enjoy the smiles, I come here for something else. Something you can't touch. It's the universal sound of freedom. Laughter. On most days it echoes from one end of town to the other.

Possibly my favorite thing to do occurs most nights after dark. I'll shuffle to the Planetarium and park myself along one wall with a bag of popcorn and watch the girls enter and exit. It's one pajama party after another. Fluffy slippers, pillows, fuzzy blankets—they come to see Bones's latest pics. And because of Eddie's facial recognition software, their faces are "read" when they walk in so that the program shows an inordinate amount of pictures of them. Most of these girls didn't have any pictures of their growing-up years prior to arriving. Not their childhood. Not prom. Not graduation. Not anything. Few had any pictures of themselves whatsoever. Bones changed that. He documented life's beautiful moments, and he had an uncanny knack for snapping the shutter at just the right time. This ability led to requests for him to teach what he knew. So twice a week Bones taught photography to a dozen or so girls. He bought them each a camera and then taught them how to read and capture light. Now, every Friday night, when Bones releases his latest Freetown pics, most have been taken by his team.

The picture taking had unforeseen ripple effects. Having seen the moments of unadulterated happiness and laughter and wonder and beauty projected onto the ceiling of the Planetarium, more and more girls wanted their pictures taken. Having been hidden for so long, they now wanted to be seen. In color. And now that Bones's team was taking the photos, they felt free to capture images he never would have. In a natural and gradual transition, the Friday night slideshow began to include pictures of scars caused by needle, fist, razor blade, and forced caesarean. A big hit, which was always accompanied by raucous applause, was the before-and-after pics—damaged teeth restored, crossed eyes made straight, tattoos removed. Then there were the total body makeovers, which brought about standing ovations. It's not that their original bodies weren't good enough. They were. But for residents of Freetown, something in the process of the makeover was like thumbing their nose at their past. A revolt against their history. The transformations were astounding. And just as amazing was the fact that Bones had replicated himself and, in so doing, resurrected and redeemed memories.

Every girl in our care had walked into Freetown wearing some form and expression of shame. Across the board. It was true of all of them. It had been put there by someone else and wrapped around them like a blanket. Not only had it clothed them, but it had become their identity. But by nature and by design, life at Freetown swapped out that blanket for something new. Something that fit. Something they wanted to wear. Something that said, "I am beautiful. I am one in a billion. And I am priceless."

While I sat on my park bench along Main Street listening to the laughter, I kept my eyes open to the unexpected moment when any one of our girls willingly shed her rags of shame in exchange for her garments of beauty. Of new identity. On multiple occasions I watched as girls walked into any of our clothing stores only to walk out and carry a pile of old clothes to the bonfire we kept lit twenty-four-seven—and then watch in arm-in-arm silence as the old them went up in flames and the new them walked away. I'm not suggesting that simply changing clothes erased the horror that had occurred on the inside. That takes time—longer for some than others. But this exchange was a part of the process. And it gave them hope.

When each of us arrived at Freetown, our hearts and souls were held together by twine and tape and glue. Little more than a patchwork of pieces. Like a sweater with one loose thread, a simple pull threatened to unravel the whole. Each of us walked in with a singular need: to be known. I used to think the need ended there. Repair the tear and fix the person. Wrong. What I saw happening across the streets of Freetown, from fashion to dance to photography, convinced me there is one need deeper.

To be accepted in the knowing.

Maybe that's rescue.

CHAPTER 3

Through a confluence of geographic oddities I cannot pretend to understand, a sandbar surfaced just off Spellman Bluff at the intersection of three small tributaries and one larger arm of Blackbeard Creek. The sandbar stretched almost half a mile, and come lunch on Saturday, it was hopping with people, dogs, and charcoal fires. More than a hundred boats had either beached themselves or anchored at the water's edge, and close to three hundred people, in various stages of inebriation, modeled bathing suits that used to fit and many that never did. Two boats, one a pontoon and one a flats skiff, had been outfitted with stereos large enough to power a small rock concert. They were anchored just a few boats apart, and the stereo war had commenced with each playing their music of choice. The skiff was a Buffet fan selling Margaritaville, and the owner was screaming something about it not being his fault. The owner of the pontoon stood over a blender, actually making margaritas, while dancing to Zac Brown who had just put his butt in the water and toes in the sand—or something like that. The earsplitting mixture of the two made for one bad audible experience that I doubted either owner could hear.

Bones and I left the dock at his river shack in a small aluminum johnboat maybe fourteen feet in length and powered by a 20-horsepower motor. If we were trying not to attract attention, we were doing a jam-up job. Bones and I wore flip-flops and were dressed in faded cutoff jeans and T-shirts. Mine advertised a Hank Jr. world tour from the '80s, while Bones pushed an Aerosmith concert from a decade ago. My ball cap read, "I pee in pools," while Bones advertised John Deere. To complete the act, Bones held the tiller with one hand and a Busch beer in the other, which stood in stark contrast to my much more admired Pabst Blue Ribbon. When standing in the checkout line at the gas station and Bones had asked why, I simply responded, "When in Rome . . ."

Landing on the beach, surrounded by red, white, and blue cans, Bones applauded my decision, toasted me, and said, "Welcome to the Redneck Riviera."

We unfolded our beach chairs, placed the cooler between us, tipped our ball caps back, and blended in. Our assumption was simple—large yachts that leave New York and motor south usually take on fuel when they hit Intracoastal waters. It just makes good sense. Especially if you're running flesh and you're about to take

31

on paying customers. You never know when you may have to abort plan A and head out to sea. Or set the whole thing on fire to erase the evidence.

The first three hours included multiple football games between several armchair quarterbacks with well-insulated six-packs and a few ladies wearing dental floss bathing suits who looked like they could lift the couch with the guy still on it. The girls won twice. Guys once. This was followed by a whiffle ball game, which ended abruptly when an errant dog chased and ate a strong pop fly to left.

By late afternoon the sandbar had shrunk to half its size under the encroachment of a high tide. But by dusk it had swollen once again. I was tired of baking in the sun and really tired of drinking water—with which we'd filled our beer cans—when a new sound echoed from across the marsh. The sound was deep, throaty, and seemed to pulse below the third play of "Free Bird" emitting from the pontoon boat. Having run out of beer, the flats skiff had unbeached herself and departed for town.

The roar of the engines neared, turned south-west, and a black carbon and Kevlar hull came into view. Bones stared at it over his Costas. Didn't take me long. I'd seen that boat—or one like it—before.

When Summer had volunteered to use herself as bait to find Angel in the Keys, she was picked up by a trafficker in a rocket ship custom made in collaboration with Mercedes. These models were the *crème de la crème* of boats in this class. The 515 Project ONE was over fifty feet long, almost ten feet wide, and boasted a rum-runner's pedigree going back to Prohibition. Having tried to chase it, I could attest to this. Once used to smuggle rum and drugs, they were popular with the offshore racing guys from the islands to the mainland. Boats like this have a deep V-shape, making them comfortable in rough water. This particular version was custom-made from bow to stern, light and powered by a pair of Mercury racing engines producing 1,350 horsepower apiece. When racing fuel was used, the horsepower rose to a total of 3,100, pushing the boat to 140 mph. A waterborne rocket. From Key West, it could be in Cuba or Bimini in less than an hour. Even worse, it could be there and back in under two.

Staring at the hull, I felt my pulse quicken. The two tattooed men captaining the boat stopped at the far end of the sandbar and engaged some teenagers in conversation. Conversation finished, they turned to port or, in this case, east and idled toward the fishing village. When the boat turned away from us, the name painted across the back was *Daemon Deux*. Or demon boat #2.

I felt the hair rise on the back of my neck.

Bones left his chair and sauntered around the

sandbar, eventually chatting up the same teen-agers. A few minutes later, he returned. "They were asking about the nearest gas. More spe-cifically, a fuel boat." He pointed to the village. "Think we got our answer."

We spent the evening judging locations, esti-mating distances, and calculating the time of our approach and departure. The problem wasn't whether it could be done. It could. The problem was, could it be done in the time required? And given the number of boys, who were most certainly medicated, we'd have our hands full. Literally.

Our best guess was that the eighty-meter yacht would skirt the beach off St. Catherines and then turn west and enter the Sapelo Sound where, given its draft, it couldn't risk the shallow waters near the hamlet. Running aground would attract onlookers, and larger boats to pull her off, not to mention the Coast Guard. They wouldn't risk that.

Instead, she'd take on fuel in the sound—after having paid a hefty premium for tanker service in the ICW. Not uncommon for ships her length. What was uncommon would be the time of day, which we estimated to be after midnight because she'd want to be as invisible as possible. Tanks full, she'd cast off her lines, slip south under cover of darkness, and take on the first of her highest-paying customers.

Of course, this was all assumption—but educated assumption nonetheless.

The problem with boarding and rescuing kidnapped children off a flesh ship is that the owners are highly motivated not to allow us to do that. To protect their investment, they pay evil men to walk around with guns and shoot strangers. Security is high all the time, but security is code red anytime they interact with other vessels, because other vessels mean people, and unless those people have been vetted and are paying a considerable sum to board the ship, they keep their distance. Hence, boarding when she took on fuel would not be wise. But shortly after? Maybe. We wanted her crew comfortable. Resting. Drinking. Toasting the next few weeks, having let down their guard.

Knowing they had one night remaining before two back-to-back weeks of twenty-four-seven nonstop watches, Bones and I hoped they'd do just that.

The one exception would be the captain. His base salary would have been set, but incentives could multiply that times ten. He wanted that ship as profitable as possible, so we doubted he'd let down his guard. His goal was fuel and go.

But what time was the fuel rendezvous?

Bones and I finished our reconnaissance, returned to the docks, and moseyed up to the dirtier of the two waterside docks. Wasn't tough to pick out. The local shrimpers and crabbers had all docked in her slips. We figured if there was news to be found, we could find it there.

We sat at the bar, ordered beers, and listened to the four conversations around us. Wasn't tough to get what we needed. A midforties, sun-weathered, chain-smoking grease monkey hovered over several empty beer bottles, making no effort to conceal his excitement from the bartender.

"Yeah, that's what I said. 'You serious?' Those guys were all jacked and tatted, driving that sleek-looking boat and talking with their fancy accents, so I bowed up and said it just like that. Like, man, don't come in here and 'spect to push me around. This is my home. Ain't nobody pushing me around in my home." He emptied the bottle, and when he tapped the bar for another, the bartender happily complied. Evidently the previous six had lubricated his tongue. He swigged half of number seven and picked up where he left off. "Then they unfolded that wad of cash and started counting out Ben Franklins and I said, 'Mister, I'll be your huckleberry.' " He swigged, lit one cigarette with the glow-plug end of the other, and laughed at his own Doc Holliday reference. Proud of his accomplishment, like a man who'd picked the winning numbers, he pulled the wad of cash from his pocket and waved it in the air. "Twenty-five hundred to make a fuel run at 2:00 a.m.? With another twenty-five hundred promised after an on-time delivery?" He laughed, drained number seven, and slapped the bar with his palm. "Mister, for five thousand, I'll dress up like Little Bo Peep and dance a jig while the tank is filling."

Bones smiled, dropped a twenty on the bar, and whispered, "Local knowledge."

CHAPTER 4

Colorado

By the time I reached the Eagle's Nest, I was near to crawling. I climbed to the porch and collapsed while Gunner licked the salt off my face. When a shadow passed over me, I opened my eyes to find Summer staring down at me. A towel over one shoulder. Laughing.

Following my recovery, Bones had installed a hot tub atop the Eagle's Nest. To assist in my therapy. A carrot on a string. Although I'm not so sure that was his only reason. He seemed to spend a lot of time in it.

I pulled off my boots and hauled myself into the clear, hot water where Summer and Gunner waited. Gunner thought we'd made the pool just for him. He'd jump in, climb out, and then run in circles only to repeat the cycle moments later.

Whatever the case, step after step, the spring kept me climbing.

The warm water wrapped around me and convinced me I never wanted to climb that mountain again. Chairlift from here on out. Summer had been quiet this morning, and now she had that look on her face like she had something she wanted to talk about. Which usually meant I'd messed up.

I waited.

She edged closer. "You ready for tomorrow?"

I knew this was a trick question, but oxygen deprivation prevented me from seeing the answer. So I lied. "Yep."

A pause. "And you'll be ready?"

I used as few words as possible. Which meant less rope with which to hang myself. "Sure thing."

"And you remembered your part?"

I nodded, thinking the less noise I made, the less trouble I could get into tomorrow.

"And you're sure you got everything on the list?"

I had no recollection of a list. "I'm sure."

"And you're good on the time?"

I needed to get down this mountain and figure out what in the world she was talking about. Where was Clay when I needed him? "Great."

She did not look convinced.

My problem was me. Literally. I was once able to rescue imprisoned people. And that required that I fight bad men. Then one of them shot me. Infection set in and almost killed me. Actually, it did kill me, but something, or rather someone, brought me back. Then I woke up. Since that moment, my and everyone else's energy had been spent not only returning me to health, but getting

39

me back to me. Back to the guy who fights bad men. This pursuit required all my energy. All my focus. And it required most everyone else's as well. I had become the center of not only my attention but the attention of all of Freetown. My recovery had become all that mattered. Rightly or wrongly, everything else took a back seat. Even things that shouldn't. Like relationships. Because they required mental energy, I'd put them on a shelf. Told myself, "I'll get to that later." In a strange twist I'd started checking out. While my body was present, I wasn't.

I tried to persuade Summer. "Don't worry."

She swam closer and wrapped her arms around my neck. Cradling me. Whispering in my ear. "You have no idea what I'm talking about, do you?"

I shook my head, the admission freeing. "None."

She let go and turned me to face her. A wrinkle between her eyes. "You seriously have no idea?"

I wracked my brain, but nothing came to mind. I shook my head, the admission painful.

"Ellie's birthday? Fourteen? We're throwing a party?"

"Oh, yeah. That."

Summer closed the distance, her face inches from mine. "You want to talk about it?"

Admittedly, I was not firing on all cylinders, and the mental fog created by convalescent months on my back had not cleared. "I'll get it figured out."

She frowned and touched my nose with her index finger. "Your body is present." Then she shook her head and pointed at my chest. "Your heart is not."

Every word she said was true. My problem was simple: if I did what was needed to get myself back in shape, I was that much closer to leaving again. Healthy would equal absent. Which brought its own set of problems. Absent brought with it the possibility of being shot again.

A vicious cycle. And while Summer could pinpoint the fact that I wasn't all that present, I'm not sure she could see the storm clouds beyond. If I'd recovered completely and returned to my A game, to the me everyone knew and had come to expect, I'd have remembered the party. Engaged in the process. Joined her in the planning. Satisfying the short-term and immediate need of reminding Ellie how awesome we all believed her to be. Which I desperately wanted to do. But if I remained in my current condition as a limping, beat-up once-was, slightly disconnected from relational engagement, I could extend my stay here and delay the inevitable. Because while my current state frustrated her, my absence would hurt her.

Me becoming me came at a price. And while I could and would pay it, Summer would pay the higher price. Which hurt me more than being shot.

"I know."

Her voice softened. "You should take your own advice."

Truth was, I wasn't sure I wanted to fix the problem. And I knew what she was going to say. "Which is?"

Summer knew what I needed. "Write it out."

Months ago, I'd told Casey that very thing. And to her magnificent credit, she had. Summer was simply speaking my words back to me. Writing had always been my release. The thing I did to probe my own wound. Dig around. Unearth the shrapnel. Cleanse my soul.

Summer pressed her forehead to mine. "I know you are deep waters and there's more going on in here than you're voicing. These are broad shoulders and you carry all of us on them. And I love you for it. But she only turns fourteen once. It's a big deal and you need to up your game. You can be you and dance with your daughter . . . *and* be present in the dance."

She was right.

Summer kissed my cheek, climbed out, and stepped onto the platform awaiting the next chairlift.

I offered to ride alongside her, but she pointed at the trail and shook her head. "Just make sure you're showered and dressed by six. She's been practicing for weeks."

The chair appeared, Summer sat and pulled down the armrest and footrest, and then she descended the mountain. Gunner stared up at me, then returned to his bowl of food on the porch. After dragging myself out of the hot tub and drying off, I pulled a chair close to the railing, opened my laptop, and sat staring at the keys.

A blank page. Reminding me that books don't write themselves.

Two hours later, I'd not written a word. What had once come so easily now came not at all. While I wanted to tell more of David Bishop's story, the girls consumed my thoughts. What kind of dad had I become? Was I pouring in more good than not? What kind of husband? How about friend?

Maybe this was why Bones never married.

My thoughts, along with the empty page, suggested my problem was bigger than I would admit.

CHAPTER 5

At 11:29 p.m., we idled out of the hamlet in the Zodiac. Free of the no-wake zone, Bones pushed the throttle full and we began skimming across the surface with little more than the propeller in the water. When I last glanced at the depth finder, it read "0.5." Which meant six inches. Mind you, these were oyster-encrusted creeks. Not broad and deep rivers. Only someone who had been here before and knew exactly what they were doing would ever risk so much speed in such a small space. Twelve inches one way or the other, and we'd rip the engine off the transom.

I spoke inside the eye of the hurricane created by the center console: "Been here before?"

He smiled but didn't take his eyes off the water. Although I didn't know for certain, I had a funny feeling that while Bones's eyes were looking forward, some other part of him was looking back.

By 12:02 a.m., we'd reached our hide and tied up a few miles south of Sapelo Sound. The plan was to put ourselves in a position to watch her refuel, then wait as she approached our position. The key was to maintain a straight and clear line of sight. Which we had. The second key was to remove the captain and, in so doing, put the vessel on a collision course with something she could not navigate around—which we hoped would give us time to board her and remove her captives while the crew busied themselves with getting unstuck and not sinking.

Of course, you know what they say about the best-laid plans.

True to his word, our excited beer-slamming captain met *Sonshine* in the Sapelo Sound at exactly 2 a.m., where he filled her tanks and sent her on her way. We could only assume he was twenty-five hundred richer. Seeing her turn our direction confirmed our first problem. And it was not the half-moon night, nor was it the distance. The helm was well lit and stood nearly three stories off the surface of the water, and I'd shot that distance many times. Much farther even. The problem was estimating the forward travel of the 262-foot yacht as it motored upriver at six to ten knots. The difference between six and ten mattered a great deal. A knot is a unit of speed also known as a nautical mile per hour—which is equal to 1.151 land miles per hour. Six knots is a little over 10 feet per second. Eight knots is 13.5 feet per second. And ten is almost 17 fps. Seven feet can mean the difference between hitting and completely missing the target. And estimating that speed at nearly two miles away is nothing short of impossible, which is why I was thankful we had Eddie on comms.

I spoke into my voice box–mounted microphone. "Eddie, can you estimate the speed?"

Half a second passed. "Six point five knots."

I chuckled. "You sure it's not 10.970?"

A pause while I listened to keystrokes. Eddie was tracking the vessel via satellite. If it moved an inch in one direction or another, he'd know it before the captain. "Technically, six point five two."

My nautical chart translated that to eleven feet per second, which I then converted to meters in order to dial milliradians into my scope. Bones looked at my calculations and raised an eyebrow. "You want me to get you some more fingers and toes?"

The first clients would arrive in less than ten hours and would board the luxury yacht by either helicopter or tender. Our goal was to board *Sonshine* and offload the boys before that happened. Currently *Sonshine* sailed in Intracoastal waters just west of St. Simons Island in Southeast Georgia. One of the wealthier zip codes in the country. We'd studied topo maps on the flight down and found what we thought was a section of topography that would allow us to create circumstances to our benefit: a narrowing in the channel, along with an intersecting tributary where we could hide a barge. Step one was to remove the captain, and to do so quietly. Again, topography—most of which was either marsh or water—dictated distance. And having found where our narrow channel met a tributary, we then began looking for a suitable hide from which to make a long-distance shot with a rifle. Someplace I could lie prone, with an unobstructed and elevated view of the helm, and then fire the rifle unseen and unheard. Hence the distance.

The location of my hide was the roof of an abandoned river shack. Lying prone atop the shack, which had been built on a bluff, placed me almost eye-level with the captain. If anything, I was looking slightly down. Which was good. It would allow me to see what happened after the shot.

Yachts such as *Sonshine* navigated the well-traveled and well-plotted waters of the Intracoastal primarily on autopilot. Which meant, barring weather or traffic, the captain did very little. He stood at the helm, monitored the screens, and double-checked systems and redundancies. To some extent the boat drove itself. Which was exactly what we wanted.

Our plan was simple: remove the captain from the equation and then send something large and unavoidable across her bow that the autopilot would not expect and for which it would have no preprogrammed response. In short, what would happen when a two-hundred-foot barge crossed a 150-foot channel only seconds before *Sonshine* reached that same intersection—in the dark of night?

With the captain in control, provided he could see the barge, he'd reverse-all-stop, then decide how to navigate around it. And a good captain could probably do so without spilling anyone's drink inside the boat. But with no one at the helm, we wondered how well the autopilot could respond to the appearance of an unexpected barge with only seconds before impact.

We guessed not very well.

Our understanding of the autopilot system suggested she'd slam on the "brakes," spilling everything and throwing everyone into confusion. Thanks to twin screws and multiple bow thrusters, the boat could probably avoid the barge, especially with a favorable tide. But that would be her problem. She wouldn't have a favorable tide. She would have an outgoing tide and she would be traveling with it. Which meant, when she did actually throw it into reverse, everyone inside would think they were riding a bull, and no one was going to be able to hold on for eight seconds.

We had hidden the two-hundred-foot barge in a small tributary that joined the Intracoastal at a natural narrowing. The barge plus the forty-foot tug would more than close off the Intracoastal to north- and southbound traffic, giving vessels traveling in either direction nowhere to go. Plus, the barge was designed to work as a land bridge, loading and offloading large equipment. This meant it had a low profile and lay hidden below the tips of the marsh, which spread for miles around me. Hence, it would be difficult to see in the daytime, much less in the dark.

I lay prone, staring through my scope, the crosshairs steady on the captain. As I did, *Sonshine* slowly closed the distance between us. Two miles. One and three quarters. When it reached one and a half, Bones stared through his rangefinder and began calling the distance. A mile is 1,760 yards. Bones would range for me in yards, so we'd agreed he'd start at 1,900 and count down by ten. When he reached 1,770, I'd tell my brain to press the trigger—not jerk it—having already dialed in dope for 1,760. I was planning lag between brain and finger-press into the equation. A tricky balance. If the average man's shoulders were sixteen inches wide, and the pumphouse part of that was maybe half that, then what I was attempting to do was about like hitting an aspirin at a hundred yards. On cue and on the first and only try. On a moving target. Fortunately, our captain was a stout individual and a little more than average.

I'd zeroed the Berger .300 Win mag at one hundred yards, doing so through a Schmidt and Bender PM II—which, in English, is just a really nice scope with clear glass that lets you see far away as if it were close up. Shooting a 230-grain .30 caliber bullet at 1,760 yards would require me to dial in 20.75 MRADs, or milliradians, of elevation into the scope. In addition I had to account for a two-mile-per-hour east-to-west wind. So I held 0.4 MRAD left. An MRAD is little more than a unit of angular measurement defined in thousandths of radians. Scopes with adjustable elevation and windage, measured in either MRAD or MOA (another unit of angular measurement called minute of angle), allow shooters like me to shoot really long distances from a rifle using a single set of crosshairs held directly on the target rather than somewhere in the air high above. In other words, 20.75 MRADs took out the guesswork and eliminated the holdover. Basically, 20.75 MRADs meant I was aiming 1,342 inches, or 111.83 feet, above the target—the captain's chest—in order to hit his pumphouse from a mile away. Making my rifle shot more of a mortar and less of a zip line.

Bones and I had also agreed that when he reached 1,800 yards, he'd cue me by saying, "Zero." Then "Ninety," for 1,790, and so on, allowing him to use fewer words and requiring less time. When he reached 1,770, he wouldn't say, "Seventy." Because in a panic I might forget that "Seventy" means to shoot. He would use some other word. An agreed-upon one-syllable cue. In this case we chose "Box." Why? Because it was easy to say, and because after I pulled the trigger, someone would put this sadistic captain in a box and bury him at sea.

This brought us to the second-to-last hurdle. Timing. Estimating where the target was going to be when the bullet got there as opposed to where it was when I pulled the trigger. In brass tacks we were attempting to synchronize a vessel moving at six knots with a concurring four-knot current while one man, measuring and registering distance, then communicated that exact distance using words, which required minute amounts of time to articulate, into the waiting ears of a second man who needed to hear those words and translate their meaning in his brain and down through his finger, which then applied pressure on a sear, which released a trigger into a primer, which ignited powder, which exploded, which caused pressure, which propelled a .230-grain projectile down a twenty-six-inch barrel at a little over 2,800 feet per second, which would then cover a given distance—in this case 5,280 feet—in a given amount of time—in this case about 3.15 seconds—for the sole purpose of removing a target—the captain—so that we might board the vessel undetected and rescue thirteen innocent boys.

The variables were many, the possibility of failure high, and yet we'd done it before. Multiple times. And while not cocky, we were somewhat confident.

Yet even after all our mathematics and estimation, the last hurdle was the most difficult. Certainty. Before you punch a hole in a man's chest, sending him to the other side of the grave, you'd better make 100 percent certain that he is in fact siding with evil. That he's a bad guy and not just some rich dude on a joy ride in his shiny new toy. Was this captain a bad man? Did he know about his visitors below? Did he fully understand what evil was planned for each of them? Was he a willing participant or just a guy piloting a boat because the pay was good and times were tough? One of the things Bones taught me early on was that bullets are like words—once they've left the barrel, you can't take them back. And eternity is a long time.

Were we certain? Eddie had tapped into the video feeds on the boat via our satellite. And thanks to the more than two hundred cameras, we had more than enough video providing certainty. This was a bad man.

Bones lay to my left. "Eighteen hundred." Gunner lay to my right, eyes trained on me.

I disengaged the safety, pushing it forward to the fire position, and gently laid my finger on the trigger. Careful not to twitch. Gunner read my action and turned his attention to the lights downriver.

"Ninety."

I slowed my breathing, measuring inhale and exhale.

"Eighty."

I could hear my heart beating in my ears. The crosshairs hung steady in the middle of the captain's chest, just below his collarbone. I whispered to Gunner, "Easy, boy."

Bones spoke softly. "Box."

When the sound of the "Bo-" exited Bones's mouth, I pressed the trigger as he said "x," felt the recoil, and heard the suppressed percussion. Then, 3.15 seconds later, the windshield shattered and the captain disappeared from my field of view.

T-minus four and counting.

In the event of an oncoming obstruction, the ship's autopilot safety protocols would engage at eight hundred yards. Half a mile. It would act much like a car with adaptive cruise control. And at 6.5 knots, or eleven feet per second, that gave us exactly four minutes to get aboard that boat before the alarm sounded and she slammed on the brakes, bringing her to a halt before impact. Now, these autopilot approximations had been calculated using stationary obstacles. Something like a lighthouse or a beach or a bend in the river. But we needed more time. Four minutes wasn't enough. So how would the autopilot react to a barge appearing out of nowhere at nine o'clock on its port side, giving the 262-foot vessel a hundred meters at most to stop?

We weren't exactly sure but had to assume the difference would benefit us and give us more time to board and offload without detection.

Bones had told the owner of the tugboat to watch for my signal—the appearance of fire out the end of my barrel. From that second, *Sonshine* floated exactly a mile away traveling at 6.5 knots. The tugboat captain would then have to wait patiently as the luxury yacht crossed the mile to his bowline in approximately eight minutes. Given that the barge was stationary, the barge captain said it would take him about ten seconds to engage all engines fully and create momentum and, hence, forward movement. So he and Bones agreed to set a seven-minutes-and-twenty-seconds countdown timer from the moment he saw fire emit from my barrel. When the timer hit zero, he'd engage all full, placing him thirty seconds, or about 330 feet, from the oncoming and unsuspecting *Sonshine*. Provided he could get himself across the 150-foot waterway, thereby blocking the Intracoastal—which he said would be no problem. In truth we didn't care if he crossed it or not. We just needed him to act like he was, and we needed *Sonshine*'s computer to assume he was, which the safety protocol had been programmed to do.

In short, the presence of a two-hundred-foot

barge crossing *Sonshine*'s centerline just shy of eight minutes from now was going to light up every dashboard light she possessed and create the diversion we needed. Which was complete pandemonium aboard that boat.

In the millisecond before I touched the trigger, I wondered how many boys and girls had been lifted from their lives and relegated to a life of hell by this sick miscreant.

After I felt the recoil, I waited three seconds and saw the glass explode and the captain disappear, tumbling backward. Then I ran for the Zodiac while Bones waved at the tugboat captain.

Countdown started.

CHAPTER 6

Colorado

I left the Eagle's Nest and descended the mountain, then limped down the steps into my basement, sweat drying on my face. Every muscle in my body had tightened and I was tired. I had an hour until I needed to be ready. I came there thinking I was alone but I was not. The light in the cave was on and one of my three weapons safes was unlocked, door open. I leaned against the doorframe as Bones lifted an SBR—a short-barreled rifle—off the wall and slid it into a black carry case. Not the airline kind of hard case, but the soft, throw-it-over-your-shoulder or lay-it-in-the-back-of-a-boat-or-truck kind of case. Which told me a good bit. He followed it with a second rifle with a longer barrel—twenty inches.

He was wearing all-black BDU pants, boots, and no shirt—suggesting he was in the process of changing. We live in a relatively cold climate and in an environment where we work twenty-four-seven to respect the experiences of the girls in our care. Half-naked men can cause PTSD flashbacks, so we're overly careful. We don't walk around with our shirts off. Ever. Bones was midfifties but could pass for late twenties. Chiseled. No fat. Muscles on top of muscles. He took nothing for granted and had already returned down the mountain this morning before I set foot upon it.

The light shone on his back and lit the many scars spread across his skin. A few years before he'd found me in Jack's troller, he'd been carrying a young girl to a helicopter when someone shot him in the back. The buckshot pellets produced fourteen holes, a collapsed lung, the loss of about half his blood, and six hours of surgery. The years since had produced several other holes and one long scar under his right rib cage where he'd encountered a knife in close quarters.

His back was a road map of rescue.

As he turned, I noticed a bandage covering the soft tissue below his left rib cage and a puffiness to his left eye. Surrounded by shadow. He pulled on a black T-shirt, then a black tactical vest that included level-three body armor. Something I'd not seen him wear in a while. He wore his Sig 220 in a thigh holster, and about a dozen magazines on his vest for both the AR rifle and .45 ACP pistol. Tucked into its own bag along-side the magazines hung a tourniquet. Finally, he carried a scandium Smith & Wesson 327 in an ankle holster. It had a two-inch barrel, held eight rounds, and was considered a last-resort weapon. He called it his "get off me" gun.

When I tapped the side of his vest, he winced slightly.

"Going hunting?"

Bones was loading magazines and sliding them into a backpack. He laughed easily. Like a man who'd come to terms with his life. "No rest for the weary."

The way he said that told me this was not the first time he'd suited up during my convalescence. Making me wonder why he'd kept it from me.

"What's up?"

He handed me his phone. The message described thirteen nine-to-twelve-year-old boys held in a boat off Georgia. Making landfall in Florida sometime tomorrow. The accompanying pictures confirmed what they looked like. Blond hair. Light complexion. Taken without a trace.

Some reminders hurt. And some wake you up.

I scrolled through. "Going alone?"

"Figured you'd had your fill for a while."

Clarity started to set in. Bones had been doing double duty. "How many times?"

He laughed, zipped up the pack, and glanced at his phone. A pause. "Just because you took a vacation doesn't mean the bad guys did, or"—he pointed at his phone—"that thing quit dinging."

The recent wounds on his body convinced me

the time for feeling sorry for myself had come to an abrupt end. "How long?"

A quick glance at his watch. "Thirty-seven minutes."

I started grabbing gear.

He raised both eyebrows. "You strong enough?"

I inserted a magazine into my Sig, cycled the slide, and then press-checked it, physically confirming the presence of the round in the chamber with the tip of my index finger. More than half of all altercations involving a firearm occurred during low, altered, or failing light, so Bones had taught me long ago to confirm condition with my fingertips, allowing my eyes to roam elsewhere or, if needed, stay on target. I holstered the Sig. "No. But that's never stopped you before."

"Summer's been through a lot." The implication was clear. "You get hurt, and she'll never forgive me."

I nodded. "And thirteen 'fresh' boys housed in the belly of a luxury yacht hours from taking on wealthy clients won't be guarded by a mall cop."

He smiled. "They never are."

I pointed at the bandage and the swollen eye. "You want to talk about it?"

"Couple of weeks ago. Carlsbad."

"How come you didn't tell me?"

The look on his face told me the answer was obvious.

"What happened?"

He held up his phone, showing me the picture. "I brought her home."

Translation: "I did what was required."

I continued, "You know anything about this boat?"

He considered this, then reached into the safe and handed me the M4—telling me our engagement would be close quarters and a scatter gun might be helpful. It also told me that when push came to shove we would not be choosing the subtle tactic. The Benelli M4 was battle-tested and considered by many, if not most, to be the shotgun you'd take into battle if you could only take one. When fully loaded, it held eight in the magazine plus one in the chamber and could wreak unparalleled havoc when wielded by someone who knew what they were doing. Loaded with buckshot, it could blow a door off its hinges, while the right slug could pass clean through an engine block. It was also designed to cycle and reload whether it was mounted firmly against your shoulder or not—which made it incredibly reliable.

Point being, it went *boom* when needed.

I gestured to the boxes. Slugs or buckshot? He handed me both. "So glad I asked."

As we finished packing, he paused, stared inside the safe, then pointed at Jolene—my Bergara .300 Win mag. So named one night after she'd kept me company, and safe, in a Central

American town. Jolene was well-worn and accurate well beyond two thousand yards. "Better bring her."

Bringing Jolene meant we'd be sitting overwatch from a distance. Waiting for them to arrive and, if circumstances presented themselves, picking them off early, reducing their numbers and strength. Which told me they had a lot of both. Many times Jolene had been the great equalizer. Evening the odds. I shouldered both Jolene and the M4, turned toward the stairs, and paused.

Bones noticed my hesitation and glanced at the ceiling, which also served as the floor of the kitchen—where we heard shuffling. We both knew this moment was coming. He voiced it. "She deserves more than a phone call from the plane."

"I know. It's just . . . she's not in the best place with me right now."

Bones spoke as he passed me heading up the stairs. "It's the life we live."

"But convincing her is something—"

"Truth be told," he said, interrupting me, "she probably understands that better than you."

I began climbing the stairs, more aware than ever of the weight of my gear. "What makes you say that?"

He turned. "She's the one waiting."

Good point.

"But you ought to see someone else first." He glanced at his watch. "Nine minutes."

I found her on her bed, cutting pictures out of magazines. Pinning them to her corkboard. She spoke before she saw me. "You excited about my party?"

Then my clothing registered and her expression changed. The air let out of the balloon. I knelt next to her bed. Gunner jumped up, walked in a circle, and lay down next to her.

I set her hand in mine. As reality set in, her face betrayed the fact that the fear of "what if" was returning. Along with the fact that I'd miss her party. She shook her head and whispered one word. "Why?"

Words would not answer her heart, so I opened my phone and scrolled through all thirteen pics.

Each could have been her classmate. Her friend.

We sat there as she studied them. Expanding the screen with two fingers. After a minute, she returned my phone and sat quietly. Ellie had worn my Rolex since I had given it to her in the Keys. Despite the fact that it swallowed her wrist, she never took it off. Her constant reminder of me. And connection to me.

The clock was ticking. I had to go, so I stood and extended my hand. Palm out. She smiled, accepting my invitation, and I pulled her to me. Growing into the mirror image of her mom, she twirled, and we stepped silently to the choreographed dance we'd practiced, albeit without the Ed Sheeran song she'd selected. She moved seamlessly. A girl transforming before my eyes into a woman in bloom. My only wish was that Marie could be there to witness it. When the song ended in our minds, I held out my hand, fingers extended. Slowly, she did likewise. Touching her fingertips to mine. The watch dangling. I slipped my fingers inside hers, locking our hands, and asked, "Rain check?"

She curtsied, kissed me on the cheek, and whispered, "Rain check."

After they'd found me in the cave and airlifted me to the hospital, Summer never left my side. Twenty-four-seven. Regardless of the diagnosis. Each of which was worse than the prior. When they brought me home, having been told I'd never wake up, she stayed by my side. Tended my wounds. Bathed me. Sang over me. Slept alongside me. Talked to me. Wrapped her leg around mine like a vine.

Through all of this she had no idea if I'd beat the infection. If I'd live. I lay there dying, pus seeping from the holes in me, while Summer poured out her life and fought for me when I could not. She rescued me. Gave me life. Hoped when I could not.

I descended the stairs knowing both the price she'd paid and the one I was about to ask her to pay.

I found her in the kitchen. Apron. Hair pulled up. Sweat on her top lip. A beautiful mess. She was standing over a pot of lentil soup. Something she'd mastered during my recovery. When I set down my gear, she didn't turn. Didn't look. Didn't spin and twirl. There was no dance in her step. I was about to speak when she turned abruptly and pointed a long spoon at my face.

She'd been crying.

She pulled her shoulders back and lifted her chin while fighting another tear in the corner of her eye. "J . . ." She tried to speak but some unseen hand wrapped around her throat and choked off her air. She fought it back but it was too strong. The words wouldn't come.

I stepped closer. "I won't be long."

Her eyes narrowed, she stuttered again, and then she gathered herself. Her anger rising. But not necessarily at me.

Summer hadn't just cared for me. She wasn't simply my nurse. She'd become my very lifeline. She'd drawn the line in the sand and dared death to cross it, screaming at the top of her lungs, "If you want him, it will be over my dead body!" She was then and is now my defender. The lone figure who stared defiantly into the hurricane and sheltered me. Summer's soot-stained shield was grooved with scars meant for me.

I was caught between a love I'd never known before and a need I could not deny.

When she spoke, her lip was trembling and a roselike vein had popped out on her temple. "I'll . . . be right here." Then she turned and sank the spoon back in the soup, bracing herself against the countertop.

I placed my arm around her waist. She was trembling. Short breaths. Rapid pulse. After a moment, she faced me and tucked her arms inside the protection of mine. Her face flat against my chest. Ear to my heart. Listening. Her fear bubbling. We stood silently several seconds. When she spoke, her voice was raspy. "I know . . . this is the price I pay to love you. But . . ." She shook her head, speaking as much to my heart as my ears. "You are my one . . . and you outweigh the needs of all the rest."

Oh, how I love this woman.

Finally, she placed my palm flat across her chest where her heart felt like it was about to explode. Then she looked up, her eyes finding mine. She spoke through calm resolve. "David Bishop . . . I need you to bring Murphy Shepherd home . . . because I can't live without him."

I thumbed away a tear, kissed her, and Gunner and I made for the door.

As I approached the truck, they were waiting on me. The remaining two musketeers. Clinging to each other. Angel spoke first. "Don't make me come get you." She pointed. "And don't take any sh—I mean crap—from anybody either."

Casey was the last to speak. She placed her hand over her heart, tapped it twice, and bowed slightly. The gesture was purposeful. A reminder. Without saying a word, she'd articulated the elephant in the room. "I am what's at stake." Meaning girls like her. "So go get me and bring me back, because I can't rescue me . . . And I am not alone."

A second later, Bones put the truck in drive, and the lights of Freetown disappeared in the rearview. As he drove, Bones held out his right hand. "You dropped this in the cave."

In my hand he placed the worn silver coin he'd given me more than twenty years earlier. I'd been sitting alone at a café when Bones sat across from me and slid it across the table. I hadn't known it at the time, but he'd been the one to free me from a giant of a man named Jack after I'd tried, somewhat successfully, to free the girls he'd captured and tied up on his boat. I held the coin between thumb and index finger, reading the inscription like braille.

The eleven words that had changed me forever.

From that moment, little about my life had been the same. And as Bones, Gunner, and I boarded the plane, I felt another change coming. I just had no idea that it would start in coastal Georgia— maybe the only part of the world that really felt like home.

CHAPTER 7

With the throttle slammed to full, the Zodiac skidded across the top of the water. One minute later, we crossed *Sonshine*'s wake and pulled up along her port side. While Bones jumped onto the stern with our bowline, I cut the engine. We'd made the decision not to paint our faces black, because what kid wants to trust a man who's just scared him? Instead, we wore neck gaiters and skull cups pulled up and down to allow for the slits of our eyes. I told Gunner to stay, grabbed my gear, climbed up, and discovered that after a mile of travel and more than three seconds in the air, the bullet had done what I'd intended. Upon impact, the captain had made an involuntary backward somersault with what looked like a half gainer. The bullet-induced acrobatics carried him off the helm and three decks down, where the combination of the bullet and the gravity-induced collision with the deck rendered him no longer a threat. Bones slipped his radio from his belt, giving us access to their communication. Which was silent, meaning no one yet knew of the captain's fall.

On the spur of the moment, and because I

didn't have one handy, I skipped the box and buried him in the river. Then we moved inside and downstairs.

The hair stood on the back of my neck as we descended into the bowels of another flesh ship. Something about the eerie silence reminded me that every man has a basement. Some lay dark. Unlit. Concealed. Others sprawl like airport runways for all the world to see. The difference is determined by whether he is hiding something or digging it up. Hammer or shovel says much about a man.

My foot touched down on the bottom step. I looked around and whispered to Bones what he'd taught me in my training: "Hell is where the dead go to die. And these young boys will not be among them."

If the boys were medicated, chances were strong they'd be unable to walk or run, meaning we'd have to carry them. Six apiece.

We found the first cabin unlocked and the blond-haired boy asleep on the bed. We didn't bother checking his photo with those on our phones because if he was on this boat, our assumption was that he wanted off. No questions asked. The sight of the room—like those in the mansion in Montana—turned my stomach. It was appointed with multiple fetish options and floor-to-ceiling sound panels. Meaning a rock concert on the inside would not be heard on the outside.

Neither would the otherworldly depravity they'd planned for it.

We counted a dozen cameras. And those were just the ones we could see. It was the ones we couldn't see that would produce the money. They'd record everything that happened on this boat, and when these clients returned to their billion-dollar companies, their trophy wives, and their 2.3 kids, they'd receive an email. Just a taste. A snippet. A promise of more to come. Every single one of them would pay the blackmail. No questions asked. Silence bought by the tens of millions.

As for the boys aboard, by the time they reached the sunny shores of South Florida, most would want to die. Several would even ask for death. But their wish would not be granted because there was money yet to be made. Just off the coast, they'd be loaded into a barge and sold to a man who'd immediately post their availability online and then lock them in a roach-infested motel room with a needle in their arm, promising the next dose when they'd appeased the next client. Existence by the hour. A life span counted in months. Weeks even.

This was the beginning of the end. All that remained was the bleeding out.

Or so they thought.

Switching the M4 to my right hand, I lifted the boy onto my left shoulder and intersected the first unsuspecting crew member on the stairwell on my way out. Bones greeted him with a single round from his suppressed Sig, which while not quiet was quiet enough and reduced our chances of being detected. Despite the sound, the boy on my shoulder never stirred. He just drooled. Bones threw the crewman's body in the river while I set the sleeping boy in the Zodiac, leaving him in Gunner's care, and returned to room two, which we found much the same. Door unlocked and boy asleep. We cut his zip ties and I carried him to the boat while Bones covered me. In short order we cleared four suites on the lower deck, then four on the second. Eight down. Five to go. With Gunner standing watch, the Zodiac was starting to get cramped. Thus far, our appearance on the boat had been relatively undetected. We wanted to keep it that way.

Clearing the stairwell for the fourth time, I checked my watch. "T-minus sixty. Go time."

As I carried boy nine to the stern, the ship's alarm sounded, accompanied by angry voices and what sounded like grinding gears coming from the engine room, followed by a massive interruption of the boat's forward movement— all suggesting our hired barge captain had placed his two-hundred-footer across the Intracoastal and *Sonshine*'s autopilot system had only one response. All full stop. The effect on those of us inside her was both instantaneous and intense.

Under the reverse pull of the twin screws, the bow dipped, the stern bucked unnaturally, the 262-foot yacht rolled starboard under the torque, and the engines whined, followed by the smell of something burning. Our imminent collision was only seconds away.

Bones and I split up at the third deck and continued uncontested, suggesting the crew believed medicated boys proved no threat. Nor were they expecting one. I grabbed boys ten and eleven as Bones shouldered twelve and thirteen. Doing so required every ounce of strength I could muster and made me wish I hadn't climbed the mountain this morning. When I met Bones on the stairwell, he was smiling and not breathing heavy, while I was having trouble.

Our exit took us through the office, where we made a mental note of a locked closet all the more conspicuous because of a ventilation duct emptying into it—suggesting something that needed to be cooled. Like expensive electronics. Running through the office, I heard a faint and muted noise I'd not heard in a long time. The second time it stopped me. Bones likewise. There it was a third time. I pointed my muzzle in the direction of the sound.

Bones nodded.

"Engine room?"

"Sounds like it."

At the same time, we heard the unmistakable

hum of multiple high-output engines closing in on the stern of the boat. That meant company. And that meant a second boat. My guess was *Daemon Deux*.

We reached the Zodiac and the sound of Gunner's whining seconds before impact. I jumped in, Bones passed me each of the boys, and only then did we notice the *Daemon Deux* approaching our stern, proving once again that it was a rocket ship on water and returning my mind to our last meeting in the Dry Tortugas.

Gunner saw the boat and started growling.

Bones inserted a fully loaded magazine into his AR, grabbed his orange Pelican case, throwing the sling over his shoulder, and hollered, "Going for the drives."

That left the engine room and *Daemon Deux* to me. "Meet you in the engine room."

The only way the demon boat could board *Sonshine* was through the stern—which would be required as she would not be able to hail anyone on the radio and the Intracoastal channel was too narrow otherwise. With *Sonshine* having come to a full stop, the demon boat would be required to run astern at port and tie up. Tricky but doable.

Bowline in hand, the captain—the same guy we'd seen on the Redneck Riviera yesterday—shut off the engines, timed his jump to match the current, and landed in the stern, where he tied off the demon boat only to be greeted by me—and also a slug from the M4, which sent him overboard to join his friends.

I turned to Gunner and pointed at the demon boat. "Don't let anybody off that boat. And don't let anybody shoot at me either." With *Sonshine*'s crew busy assessing damage below, arguing with one another and screaming at the barge captain, Bones and I met at the door to the engine room. While he was carrying his AR, he was not carrying the orange Pelican case.

"Trouble?" I asked.

He nodded once.

We approached the engine room door, which had been fitted with a lock on the outside—which was strange. Why would anyone lock that door from this side? Smoke poured from around the edges, as did the screams of those on the inside. I hollered, "Back away from the door," then shot it off both its hinges with slugs from the M4. Bones kicked the door open and girls began spilling out. I quickly counted ten. And no, they were not listed on the ship's black market manifest or auction. With Bones forward and me bringing up the rear, we ran up two flights and then along an exterior walkway while I calculated what to do with ten more bodies. With the Zodiac full, Bones pointed at the demon boat and we nodded in agreement. He'd drive the Zodiac. Me the cigarette boat.

I was about to open my mouth to speak to the girls, who were whimpering and huddled together, when a furry flash darted from right to left across my peripheral. At the same time, I heard a radio communication emanate from the helm of the demon boat in a language not English, followed by the reflection of light off the optics mounted on top of an AK-47. The fact that I could see the reflection of the optics meant the barrel was aimed at me.

Gunner launched himself airborne and caught the second crewman at the neck as his finger contacted the trigger. The rifle fired high and to the right. Thereby missing me. I jumped onto the bow and ran to the helm as the bloody man on the floor bared a knife and began waving it wildly at Gunner.

Honestly, I had grown tired of people trying to hurt my dog.

With the second crewman now having joined his partner in the flowing current of the Intra-coastal, I returned to Bones and the ten girls, all of whom looked younger than sixteen. We loaded them safely into the cabin of the demon boat as multiple crew began firing down on us, followed by what sounded like the screaming of another girl. From somewhere inside *Sonshine*. Atop the forward deck of *Sonshine*, a rather burly crewman was dragging a half-dressed female by her hair along the walkway, and judging by her reaction, she was not excited about going with him.

Bones spotted the girl and jumped from the bow of the demon boat to the stern of *Sonshine*, only to turn and extend his palm, saying, "Zippo."

I tossed him my lighter and he began climbing stairs two at a time. I pointed to Gunner and said, "Follow him." Which he did while I covered him with my AR, emptying four magazines, or 120 rounds, as the two made their approach. Contacting the man dragging the girl, Bones quickly hip-tossed him overboard. The man flew Frisbee-like three stories to the water as I peppered him and the yacht with every remaining AR round I possessed. Cradling the girl in one arm, along with his orange Pelican case in the other, Bones returned to the steps and encountered two more crew, the first of which was met in the groin by Gunner. The second in the chest by me. I whistled, and moving more quickly than Bones, Gunner managed his retreat just as the stairs filled with more crew, blocking Bones's return. With no other way off the ship, Bones flung the Pelican case overboard where it spun out in the night, landing downriver a fair distance from any of us. He then climbed to the railing and, teetering on the edge, said something to the girl in his arms. As gunfire once again popped overhead, he lit and tossed my Zippo while simultaneously jumping. As Bones and the girl fell to the water below, my Zippo landed in what would have been the galley and evidently encountered something combustible, which, when lit, blew the top of the yacht to splinters and left a fireball in its absence.

Girl in tow, Bones swam to the Zodiac, pulled his frightened passenger inside where most of the boys lay sleeping, cranked the engine, and spun 180 degrees, only then to slam the throttle forward full. Bones was waiting on no one. I cut the bowline that tethered the demon boat to *Sonshine*, threw the engine in reverse, and cleared the stern just as a smoke-charred crewman jumped from the shadows into the helm and onto me. The smoking gorilla caught me across the chest and we tumbled backward amid the screams of the ten girls watching. The man was the size of a silverback and just about as strong. His bear-size paw latched a vise grip around my throat and stopped all air going in or out.

I didn't have long.

I'm not always aware of why I get angry when I do. Maybe it was having been shot by my own crossbow. Maybe it was the ensuing last six months. Maybe it was not having recovered entirely. Maybe it was just being mad at people in the world who think it's okay to own other people. To sell them with less empathetic connection than a deli owner selling a sandwich. Or a trash truck driver at any stop along his route. Maybe it was somebody trying to hurt my dog. Maybe it was the fact that Casey was still afraid to go outside because whoever had blown up Freetown and kidnapped her, Angel, Ellie, and Summer was still out there. Whatever the case, something bubbled up. I had become tired of evil men profiting off the innocent and unsuspecting, and when that emotion hit my brain, I brought my heel to my hand, unholstered my 327, pressed the muzzle to his chest, and told him to get off me. When he did, I shot him in the face and threw his body overboard.

Returning to the helm, I heard gunfire showering down on us, which was quickly answered by the same coming from our starboard.

Bones had returned and was covering our retreat.

With the welcome presence of two strong bow thrusters, I swung the nearly sixty-foot boat in a zero-foot radius, slammed the throttles forward, and launched us along the surface of the water. Seconds later, Bones ran up alongside and held up his phone, which meant he was tracking his orange case. A half mile later, Bones retrieved the watertight box.

As the boat skimmed across the surface with little more than the prop in the water, ten girls stared at me through eyes the size of Oreos while the flames behind us became an orange ball that turned night into day and sent that yacht splintering through the stratosphere.

The barge had cut off our return home, but we knew that in advance and turned east into the calm waters of the Atlantic, skirted around Little St. Simons and Sea Island, then headed west into Gould's Inlet, past Rainbow Island, and finally into the docks at the Cloister at Sea Island where we were met by a coordinated team of DHS and FBI. While they knew about the thirteen boys, they did not know about the eleven girls. Compounding the problem was the fact that it would take time to figure out who these kids belonged to and how to get those people to some prearranged location. Not to mention the fact that everything we did from now until the moment we passed these children to their parents would have to take place under tight security.

It was nearly daylight by the time we docked at the Sea Island Resort and Spa. The Cloister is a world-famous beyond-five-star resort located on Sea Island. It's a who's who of the rich and famous with a storied history, including everyone from the Hollywood elite to the world powers at the G8 Summit. The resort is known for world-class service, and the accommodations aren't bad either.

We pulled into the dock beneath the flash of multiple red lights and the sound of several ambulance and fire truck sirens. Bones quickly got on the horn, and within seconds, all were doused and muted. The kids were scared enough without adding all that to it.

Climbing onto the dock, I looked at all these scared children hugging one another and said, "Might take a while to get this sorted out."

Bones studied one wing of the resort and said, "Wonder if they'd rent that."

By midafternoon, local doctors had triaged the kids, all of whom were quietly tucked away in rooms literally fit for kings. The parents of all twenty-four kids were en route. Most from overseas, which presented a problem. It would take a few days for many to arrive. We thought it better not to move all twenty-four until they'd had at least one good night's sleep, so Bones made flight arrangements for the following day. FLETC, the Federal Law Enforcement Training Center, sits just around the corner, and when they heard of our arrival and with whom we'd arrived, they came out of the woodwork. The White House wasn't this well guarded.

Given that none of these kids had been victims of long-term trafficking, but rather victims of kidnapping, we didn't think they'd need long-term care so much as a safe place to reunite and rest with family. Freetown obviously fit the bill, but moving nearly two dozen kids, who'd already been moved enough, presented its own set of difficulties. I'm not downplaying the horror of having been kidnapped, but in my experience, the horror of one week is less impacting to the soul than the horror of two years. Each of these kids had been with their families a little over a week ago. Most of them just wanted to get back home. Consequently, we decided to wait it out at the Cloister—and judging by the looks on the kids' faces, along with the pool, the ice cream hut, the candy store, and the twenty-four-hour room service, they agreed.

The following afternoon, seventy-two hours after we'd flown out of Freetown, Bones, Gunner, and I sat at a poolside cabana as the kids waited on parents and swam in the pool or ordered grilled cheese, all while security monitored our location. Bones sat legs crossed, wearing a Hawaiian shirt he'd just bought at the beach store. He was smiling and seemed to relish the sight of so much good walking about him. Resting on the table between us sat his orange Pelican case. Having traveled well over a million miles, if the scuffs and scars could talk, that case could write several trilogies. Unlocking the watertight latches, he set four small hard drives on the table, then lifted out a bottle of wine. Speaking matter-of-factly, he said, "Ulysses. 2015."

That meant little to me, but judging by the look on his face, a good bit to him. He poured two glasses and amid the sounds of laughter and

"Marco Polo" and Gunner sniffing about, we sat and soaked in the atmosphere. A good day. After a few minutes, he noticed the stitches in my arm and above my eye. "How many?"

I'd lost count. I shook my head. "No idea. You?"

He chuckled. "Same." Then he whispered, almost to himself, as he stared out across the sea of innocence, "The price we pay."

It would be tomorrow before the last few sets of parents flew in from around the world, so we wouldn't be returning home tonight to Summer and the girls. With a few hours of afternoon daylight remaining and an exceptionally nice boat at our disposal, Bones looked at me and smiled. "You got any plans this afternoon?"

"You mean other than not getting shot or stabbed or attacked by a silverback gorilla?"

He laughed.

I shrugged. "I'm all yours."

Gazing around, we saw that most of the kids' faces were smeared with ice cream and more than a few were chewing the gummy bears they'd piled on top of the ice cream. "Their parents probably won't appreciate us feeding them all that sugar."

Bones laughed like a man who'd earned it. "They'll forgive us this once."

We stood along the edge of the pool, taking in the faces. A minute passed. This time my tone was more serious. "We're going to need a bigger town."

Bones turned his attention north. Up the coast. His mind three steps ahead. "Working on it."

I pointed at the small river where we'd just stashed the *Daemon Deux*. "And your brother?"

This time his answer was slower in coming, but when he spoke, his eyes caught mine and there was pain in them. "Working on that too."

CHAPTER 8

W e returned in the demon boat to the relatively calm waters of the Atlantic and
turned north. All my life, I'd respected the ocean.
One minute she's calm and smooth as ice. The
next she's raging, pulling you down. And there
can be very little notice between those two
minutes. As I scanned the horizon, she gave no
notice of minute two overtaking minute one.

The coastal islands of Georgia and North
Florida are not islands in the same sense that
Hawaii or Bimini are. The coastal islands sit a
stone's throw off the mainland and are separated
by marsh. Sometimes the Intracoastal. Many are
connected by short bridges. We call them islands
because "marshy extension" isn't as romantic
and doesn't help sell. Most all of them were
inhabited by Native Americans at some point
given the access to an ample food source such
as fish or oysters. At the turn of the twentieth
century, many of those islands were turned into
wealthy country clubs for the uber elite such as
the Morgans and Rockefellers—Sea Island and
Jekyll being two notable examples.

I had grown up a few islands south on a small

pitch of land adjacent to Fort George Island. It, too, is not really an island. But it was there, during one summer of my childhood, that I'd met Marie and shown her my secret island just across the Fort George River. Beneath a cathedral of majestic oaks, I'd walked her through the ruins of the chapel that I would later rebuild and watched in wonder as she ran her fingers across the grooves of the names and dates carved into the walls, coming to realize that those who'd etched their names into the tabby had known freedom there. That island had been a declaration. A stake driven into the surface of the earth. Both an ending and a beginning. Above the names, someone had carved, "Even the Rocks Cry Out." And they did. I remember walking home late that summer, holding her hand as we stood in the knee-deep water where I told her I was going to buy that island.

And I did.

In the following summers, we'd found megalodon sharks' teeth and spent our days digging to China. When sweat and innocence were all we knew. It was there, digging one afternoon, that I'd come upon the grave of what I had to assume was a Native American. He'd been encased in what today we would call coquina. A combination of shell and cement. The Indians made their own version, not quite as stout, but strong enough to preserve the body.

I don't know how he'd died. His bones were all intact and he'd been buried wearing something on his head, a fishhook in one hand, a small knife in the other, with a rather primitive bow and arrows lying across his chest. The bow was well worn, maybe three feet long, and the string must have been something like catgut. It was very tough and spun, or twisted, to stretch and thin it. The arrows were surprisingly straight and flint-tipped. Sharp enough to penetrate hide. They had been fletched with what looked to be feathers that had disintegrated over time.

When we'd found him, we pulled away the rocks, uncovering him but not disturbing his rest beyond that. We didn't poke at him. Didn't lift him. Didn't steal anything. We just sat staring at him. A warrior from another age. I don't know if he was young or old, but I'd always hoped he had been old. In my mind my island had once been his island. I'd like to think we shared that in common. Maybe he liked to fish like me. Late that afternoon, we quietly covered him back up. Returning the stones. To make sure the dirt held in place and wouldn't erode too quickly, we transplanted several ferns and two lemon and two lime trees to mark the four corners. Citrus trees covered my island, and they had to have come from somewhere. Given the fact that the warrior still had many of his teeth, I wondered if citrus had been a staple in his diet. Whatever the case, it was a staple now as the four trees literally stapled the corners of his grave into the earth. A fitting tribute, we thought.

In the months that passed, the memory of that old guy would return to me. Especially the image of him holding that bow. The way his fingers rested on it. That winter, I began researching handmade bows and made several, learning quickly it's more difficult than it looks—that some people are blessed with that creative gene and I was not one of them. So I bought a recurve. Then another. Soon I gravitated to compound bows. First Bear. Then Mathews. I became fascinated with them. A bow is simply stored energy. That's all. Somewhere in the riser, limbs, and string, energy is held, and when called upon—or when the string is pulled back—all that energy is released. If an arrow is nocked to the string, then the energy is transferred to the arrow, sending it downrange. If no arrow, the energy is returned back into the limbs, where it usually cracks them.

Some bows harness energy better and with more consistency than others. Better replication. Better multiplication. Mathews does this maybe better than anyone. But no matter how sophisticated, at the end of the day, a bow creates energy that is transferred to a stick of some sort. Filled with that energy, the stick is propelled forward at three hundred–plus feet per second and will fly several hundred yards if angled correctly. I shot them through high school and during my time at the Academy. When Bones found me, I would later capitalize on my own affection for archery and use its benefits in our rescue missions. While primitive, a bow is quiet—and quiet mixed with deadly is often vital to survival.

In the first two decades of working with Bones, I'd collected dozens of bows and arrows from different countries and continents. Each had its own personality and use and context and culture, and each was designed in a unique way. But no matter how different they might be, they were all the same in one regard: they stored energy until called upon. Energy that could be replicated. Indefinitely. Or at least until you got tired of pulling back the string. I carried them back from all corners of the globe and hung them in neat rows along the chapel wall on my island. Just feet from where my Native American friend was buried. Of course, that was before someone blew up my island. And me.

Standing in the demon boat, the scar tissue on my back and stomach roared to life. A searing hot poker. I guess my wrestling match with the gorilla in this same boat thirty-six hours prior had stretched or torn it. Whatever the case, the pain reminded me of the bolt that had sliced through me. That someone had sent through me. With intention to hurt and kill me.

While regular bows store energy well, a cross-bow stores it extremely well, often in a smaller package. The discomfort returned my thoughts to what started this mess in the first place. And to the fact that it wasn't over. While the adrenaline of yesterday had dumped and faded, we were no closer to finding who blew up my island, who blew up Freetown, who kidnapped the girls, and who shot me.

Gunner stood alongside me, letting the wind pull at his ears and tongue. Bones pushed the throttle forward half, and within seconds we were traveling 93 mph. It was hands down the finest vessel I'd ever been aboard.

We returned across the mouth of the Altahama, around Wolf Island and Queens Island and across the Doboy Sound where the land curves northeast along the shoulders of Sapelo Island and the Blackbeard Island National Wildlife Refuge. On the north end of the refuge, we turned west into the Sapelo Sound and up the Sapelo River, running along the western side of St. Catherines Island. Bones navigated with an uncanny knowledge, putting the large vessel in skinny waters I'd not thought possible. He was threading the needle between oyster bed and sandbar and doing so at a fast rate of speed. When he did throttle down and brought us off plane, I found myself looking at a protective high bluff canopied in ancient live oaks, all draped in Spanish moss.

Bones cut the engine, and we tied up at what was once a dock. He looked over his shoulder. "Feel like walking?"

Some hurricane had long ago separated dock from land, so we hopped down onto the beach. Bones led, leaving an imprint in the soft sand much like the one he'd left in most everyone who'd ever met him. Something that lingered.

I followed. Something I'd been doing for close to twenty-five years.

He kept most of his equipment in pristine condition, especially his weapons, routinely trading old for new. Never letting the possibility of age-assisted failure—or what I'd call worn-out stuff—limit his ability on a mission. But the same could not be said of his boots. This pair was nearing a decade old, just a few months from needing a third resole, and there's no telling how many times they and he had climbed to the Eagle's Nest. At the Academy, he had told me that boots were like a warm blanket on a snow-swept night. They provided comfort when little else did. He also said that about his Sig.

As I wound along behind him, his imprint in the sand had not changed. Slightly worn on the outside of the heel, suggesting slight pronation. He was still very much a heel-to-toe runner while I was more midfoot-to-toe. And while we wore the same size 12, I did not fill his prints.

We climbed the bluff and stood staring. Me

across a beautiful landscape and Bones back into what I would soon learn was a painful history. Knowing he had brought me up here for a reason, I tried to jump-start the conversation. "Something on your mind?"

Bones scratched his chin. "Did you know the first sin outside the garden was one brother killing another?"

I nodded, not quite sure where this was going.

He continued to press his question. "Does that strike you as strange? I mean, really. Brothers."

Gunner walked in circles around me. Sniffing everything. And peeing on everything else. "Given my experience with you, not really."

He spoke matter-of-factly. "As best I can determine, my brother is responsible, either directly or indirectly, for kidnapping and attempting to traffic Angel; kidnapping Summer; blowing up Freetown, your island, your boat, and you; kidnapping the girls; and shooting you with your own crossbow. Although I doubt he actually pulled the trigger. Probably paid someone instead. It's not that he's unwilling to get his hands dirty. At this point in his life, they're permanently stained. It's just that he seldom ventures out. Oh, and that head count doesn't begin to include the more than one hundred names now inscribed on your back that at one time belonged to him."

It struck me as strange that Bones would have anything to do with someone so evil. One hundred names was more than a third of the two hundred fifty. That meant his brother had been personally responsible for much.

"You actually grew up with this jackwagon?"

"Shared the womb."

That explained why the bad guy looked so familiar in Montana. "He's your twin?!"

"Came out first."

"This just keeps getting better." We continued moving through the trees. "When were you going to tell me this?"

"Figured it would come up at some point."

"You didn't think I needed this information prior to this moment?"

"I planned to tell you when you needed to know."

"Which was?"

He checked his watch. "Right about now."

"Have you lost your ever-loving—"

He cut me off. "It wouldn't change anything."

"Of course it—"

His tone changed and pain echoed beneath the surface. He shook his head once. "Bishop . . . he's not like you. Or me."

Bones rarely called me by my real name. When he did, he was trying to get my attention. Or make a point. Usually both. "Then why in the world did you pluck me out of the Academy to take on trafficking if you're not going to tell me who the bad guy is?"

"I didn't choose you to take on trafficking."

"What?"

"Trafficking's part of it." Bones was resolute. "I chose you to find lost sheep and kill wolves."

"One of whom just happens to be your brother."

A painful nod. "Correct."

"Before we go any further, have you got any more secrets I need to know about?"

"No." He chuckled. "Between Marie and Frank, I've kept all the secrets I want for one lifetime."

"Frank?"

"Yep."

"That's his name? I was thinking it was something more like Adolf or Osama."

"Well . . . that's the name the priests gave him. It's short for Francis. As in Saint Francis, which always struck me as comical."

"What's his real name?"

Bones shook his head once and chuckled again. "That's the question, isn't it?"

"What do you mean?"

"He's been asking me the same thing for most of his life."

Bones saw the confused look on my face and decided he'd back up and start from the beginning. "For a long time Frank and I didn't know where we came from. Who bore us. Or where. We knew nothing. Only when I went to work for the government was I able to do some digging and discover bits and pieces. Even now, we don't know our real names."

"But what about birth certificates?"

"According to record, Frank and I were born to a single mother"—he pointed—"in a trailer a few miles that way. From what we can piece together, which included more than one arrest for prostitution, Mom was trying to pay the bills and got us in the process, proving there's a blurry line between prostitution and trafficking. Local paper said she died the week after our birth with a needle stuck in her arm and enough heroin to kill a cow.

"From the hospital nursery, a nearby parish priest and his wife took us in. Good people. Faithful. Kind. He had a small rural church and even smaller flock, but unlike many who preach it, he actually believed and did what he read. She played piano and I have faint memories of hymns echoing off pine walls, of Frank singing and laughing, a fireplace, and a stained glass window depicting, I think, the story of the prodigal. I also think I remember the sound of church bells. Even today, real bells are the sound of home."

That would explain why he had them installed in Freetown. We turned a corner around a row of trees and the remains of a building came into view. Surrounded by hedges, pierced by trees, choked with vines, and with a tower that had caved in on itself, the small formerly white structure suggested it had once been a church. All the windows were gone, most of the roof had rotted, and the porch had become disconnected from the building, causing those who would enter to jump across a three-foot chasm.

Bones and I climbed the stone steps onto an uneven porch and through where the front door, now missing, had hung. Like the roof, the floor had rotted and taken many of the pews down with it. Three remained. The others sat at odd angles, having disappeared through the floorboards like sinking ships in a sea of ice. Bones sat staring at the wall where the altar had once stood. He pointed at the nail holes. "I think there was a cross."

The sound of creaking boards flushed out several pigeons and sent two cats and one opossum scurrying. Judging by the droppings on the floor, this place had rats aplenty.

Bones sat running his fingers across a well-worn, hand-oiled pew. "Frank and I stayed here, I think, with this man and his wife until maybe five or six." Bones paused and sucked through his teeth. "Memory is tough to recall when doing so brings pain. Not long after, he, too, died, and the church"—he gestured to where the other pews would have sat—"figuring it wasn't worth the effort or they'd never find another who would put forth the effort, closed the parish, condemned the property, and moved us from the safety of the only warm bosom we'd ever known to the cold, frigid, and very infertile womb of an upstate New York convent. Upon his death, his wife returned home to New York, but the trail grows cold at an asylum. I'd like to think she was heartbroken. Evidently we were taken from her when she could no longer care for us."

He paused and shook his head. "When I sit here, something in me breathes more deeply than anywhere else on the planet, causing me to think my roots must sink into and out of this earth." For several minutes he sat breathing. "The property has changed hands several times, selling years ago off the courthouse steps. A company out of New York bought it. At the time, there were rumors of an uber-elite waterfront golf community."

Finally, he stood and wound his way to a back door. We stepped beneath limbs and through vines. Once outside, we walked into a larger canopy of even older oaks whose limbs arched up, turned horizontal like a roller coaster, then swooped down to kiss the earth, only to rise up again. He pointed north. "The convent was the first place I ever knew, or experienced, favoritism. Of the two of us, Frank has always been better looking. So if someone gave us a turn on the swing or handed us a toy, they chose him first. He had then, and has now, a presence that draws people. A magnetism. Somewhere near the age of six they moved us to an orphanage. Run by priests. And while the nuns favored Frank, the priests favored me—but for different reasons. It was the first time I remember knowing cold. And pain."

He paused.

When he continued, his voice had softened and he spoke as much to himself as to me. "If you don't know something is wrong, and don't know what to call it, and if it's all you've ever known, then it's difficult to know for certain that it shouldn't be happening to you. I once explained abuse like growing up in a world without hot water. If cold was all you ever knew, then a cold shower was normal. All you ever took. You had no choice. That doesn't mean you liked it, but you didn't complain. You could imagine something else, but what good would it do? The dial you were given read On-Off, not Warm-Cold." Bones sipped from his water bottle and then offered me some. "So a cold life with these men who called themselves servants of God was all we knew. Until . . . we must have been seven. Maybe eight. They made us serve as acolytes. White robes. Reverent faces. We'd sit up front, holding a cross or candle, staring out across the congregation, and over time, familiar faces began to register. As in, we recognized them. Which is the thing about physical abuse. It's face-to-face. These were men of standing, successful, powerful, who bought what they wanted, when they wanted. Sitting properly next to their wives and kids. Completing the act. But our bodies told a different drama. Our bodies were keeping score.

"During Communion, the priest would offer the body—the wafer—to the penitent, along with a whisper detailing time and place." Bones shook his head and stared at his right hand. "Took me a long time to understand how they offered the body of Christ with one hand and us with the other." Another long pause. "Of the two of us, I was stronger. When I rebelled, they beat me until I couldn't."

A longer pause.

"As soon as we were able, Frank and I gravitated to sports. Wrestling. Weight lifting. Track. Soccer. Anything to get us outside and make us stronger and faster. Somewhere in there I learned the value of a push-up and pull-up. And I did them by the hundreds. Then the thousands."

Even today, Bones could rattle off fifty to sixty pull-ups without stopping.

"By the age of ten I had become totally non-compliant. I fought at the first hint of somebody putting a finger on me." He paused. A single shake of the head. "One night they drugged me and brought me to one of their . . . parties. I didn't realize it at the time, but the fact that I was feisty and not interested made me all the more desired.

"When the drugs wore off and I figured out where I was, what was going on, and most importantly what had been happening to me . . . I flipped a switch. You might think a ten-year-old kid can do little harm to grown men, but that was the night I learned rage can be a weapon. Along with a brass lamp. And your teeth. Took them a while to corral me. When they did, they wouldn't take me to a hospital because they were afraid of both what I might say and the questions regarding the nature of my injuries, so they patched me up and somebody set my arm—broken at the elbow. The rest of the story of my injuries and how they occurred was either snuffed or blamed on me. Who was going to believe the word of a troubled orphan against a few well-respected priests who had been charged with my care, protection, and provision?

"Their problem was that my face and neck were a purple mess, one eye was completely swollen shut, and there was nothing wrong with my ability to speak. So the next day Frank and I found ourselves on a private plane. Our first time. I remember waking up and seeing the ocean shimmering beneath us. Strange.

"We landed on the Spanish island of Majorca, floating smack in the middle of the Balearic Sea—the northeast corner of the Mediterranean. Africa lay due south. Spain west. About here it registered with Frank and me that we were a long way from nowhere and the message was clear—if you scream, no one will hear you. We also discovered that whatever official record had traveled with us from Georgia to New York had not made the trip to Spain. By design and decision, we had been separated from our identity, from the only thing that linked us to something beyond ourselves. A birth certificate. The effect on both of us was profound. Maybe only an orphan can understand this, but we had been cut free from our anchor and the blow was crushing. We didn't know who we were, and more importantly, we didn't know whose we were—forever proving that identity precedes purpose. You can't know who you are until you've settled whose you are. Whoever flew us across the pond knew that if we had no record, then we didn't exist. And if we didn't exist, then they could do what they wanted to us because no one would care enough to come looking. Which allowed actions without consequences. Before you're rescued, you first have to be lost, and to be lost you have to be someone. Otherwise, what's lost? It's an age-old tactic. Hitler did the same with the Jews. We had become 'unborn.'

"We were driven to what I can only describe as a Roman-walled city high on a massive granite cliff several hundred feet above the shore. The stone walls were some twenty-plus feet high and ten or fifteen feet thick. The place was a fortress. A thousand years ago, it was impenetrable. No one getting in. No one getting out. Inside the walls we found a quiet, penitent farming community with a beautiful church and even more beautiful bells, all wrapped in the rather unloving arms of a backstabbing hierarchy and power structure populated with tight-lipped, sadistic, conniving, sex-craved priests. After a soup dinner, they walked us to a door and more stone stairs. Leading down. To the bowels of not only the church or the walled city, but the entire island. Sixty steps down, they walked me through giant metal doors and into a cavernous place where they stored stuff. Including people. Evidence that they didn't trust me to run free inside the city. Frank and I affectionately called it 'Hell Squared.'

"It wasn't just twice as bad as what we'd known, it was exponentially worse." Bones closed his eyes and extended his hands. "The bars became my companion. I held on to them. Along with the rats. Both of which, after days and weeks in near total darkness, told me I was alive.

"Save a rope cot, my entire world was stone. No books. No light. I had to learn to see with my hands. In one far corner sat a hole. Maybe six feet in diameter. I found it by mistake. A wooden bucket and pulley system hung above. I dropped a pebble and counted several seconds before I heard the muffled splash. In the coming days I'd learn the well would rise and fall every six hours. Driven by the tide. The hole had been bored, by God or man I didn't know, but it descended out of my prison cell nearly a hundred feet where I could only imagine it opened up inside a saltwater cavern below the cliffs that lined the ocean's edge. Interestingly, given the absence of daylight in my world, the water level became my only access to the passing of time.

"They fed me, allowed Frank to visit every few days, and dragged me topside once a week to the confessional where they force-marched me to confess my sins. I told them I had none." Another pause. "But, I told them, if they ever unlocked that door, I'd break the sixth commandment." He chuckled again. "In truth they wanted to know what I remembered and what I was prepared to tell. Which was everything. So . . . I didn't see the sun much.

"I had been there a few days when I heard the whisper of another boy. Down the hall. Until then I thought I'd been alone. I soon learned that other boys filled other rooms. Students from the boys' school up top. Fellow orphans under the 'care' of the brothers. Brought below for disciplinary infractions. Some stayed a day. Some two. A few of the older ones stayed three. Frank would later tell me that a month or so in I'd reached legend status with the surface crowd, and he overheard the brothers remarking in jest that I had single-handedly done more for reducing boyhood foolishness and outright defiance than all of their disciplinary actions combined. Regardless, we were not allowed to talk, tap the wall, or communicate in any way. That said, I found ways around it, which kept me from losing my mind.

"Despite my history and my willingness to throw down at the sound of heels on stone, that didn't stop the most depraved among the brethren from unlocking my door. And while I was a scrapper, I was no match for several frustrated priests wanting to 'educate' me. A pattern developed, so when I heard them coming, I'd crouch, listen for the squeak of the hinge, and then launch myself as soon as they cleared the massive iron frame. My hope was twofold: either escape, albeit unlikely, or fight so hard that one of them would knock me out, allowing me to ride out my torture in the bliss of sleep. Eventually, they graduated to chloroform." He laughed heartily this time. "Chloroform only works if you breathe, so I learned not to. Or at least, to hold my breath for a very long time. I tapped out at five minutes. After they'd gone and the drugs wore off, I'd wake, drop the bucket into the salt water below, and wash my wounds. Then I'd brace for the next night's round of footsteps. Somewhere in there I learned the intent of man's heart was evil continually, and if that wasn't bad enough, it did so masquerading as good. As servants of God."

I stopped him. "Why haven't you ever told me any of this?"

He shrugged. "Would you?"

I didn't answer.

He continued, "Six stories above me, Frank had different problems. Two to be exact. While better looking and possibly smarter, he was not as strong as me—at least not yet—and he witnessed what they were doing to me. Which he did not want them to do to him. Not to mention the fact that he was dreadfully afraid of the dark. So he adopted another tactic. Possibly the better of the two. Silent compliance." He held up a finger. "Interestingly, somewhere in here, he started what would become his lifelong obsession. Painting. He began with sketches. They weren't bad, but he kept at it. Drawing all the time. Anything. Everything. If he could see it, he attempted to place it on paper. Then, when he could scrounge together oil, he'd paint. Crude at first, but he got better over time.

"At some point Frank smuggled in a flashlight and, oddly, a pew Bible. Strange when you think that what he smuggles now found its root in that dungeon we called Hell Squared. Given that they wouldn't let us talk—for fear of what we might concoct—we devised a way to communicate using our fingers. Numbers. And the . . ."

I stopped him. Creating numbers with my fingers. "This started there?"

"Word for word."

"I had no idea."

He laughed. "My only signal that it was daytime was when, by some merciful act of God, the sun would rise to about ten thirty and hit a window and reflect off the stained glass at the far end of the cavern. For almost an hour I could see the faint hint of crimson-tinted daylight. I would later learn that glass was part of an underground prayer sanctuary—once dug by persecuted Christians escaping the Moors.

"In the absence of daylight, my bodily clock adapted to the water level in the well, so I had no idea what time it was. Unless they woke me, I slept twenty hours a day. I'm told people on death row do the same. Another month or so in, Frank slid a knife into my hands, and I started crying and laughing at the same time."

We walked another ten minutes while Bones wrestled the memory. When he spoke again, his tone was lower. "Given the stone steps, I heard them coming. Heel scuffs. Shuffling robes. Sadistic, hyena-like whispers. Not to mention the fact that my eyes had adjusted to the dark. Theirs had not. Which was only made worse by their flashlight. One night, three young priests unlocked my door. They were drunk. High as kites. Fat and slow. I had decided I was not going to live that way any longer. I was going to either fight my way out or take a swan dive into the well. When they unlocked my door, I pounced, and they were too drunk to counter. I didn't know it, but centuries earlier a ventilation shaft had been drilled through the rock above my head—helping keep me alive. The shaft exited in what was now an unused storage room in the rear of the church. A priest, walking the prayer maze in the contemplation garden, heard the faint echoes of their screams rising up through that shaft and brought help. Which they needed. By the time help arrived, not a one of them could stand. From that moment, nobody wanted anything to do with me, which fed a rather heated discussion that I found comical. They had no problem imprisoning me under lock and key, then abusing me like chattel to their hearts' content, often daily. But somewhere, some priest grew a soul and drew the line at murder. How sick is that? In the meantime I'm sitting there thinking, *No, just shoot me, feed me to the fish, and be done with me. Death is better than this any day.*"

Bones shrugged. "The problem they had was that I'd done a pretty good job of dissuading anyone from ever wanting to unlock that door again, so, unable to come to a consensus, everybody soon lost interest in me.

"A few days later, I was blindfolded, brought to a car, and driven to a plane. Only after takeoff did I learn Frank was sitting across from me. We were flown to another coast. I have no idea where. But once again, they were attempting to separate us from our history. I was malnourished, gaunt, and couldn't open my eyes for very long given the sunlight. Not to mention the headache. My body was in a bad place. Getting off the plane, Frank locked his hand beneath my arm and lifted me when I fell. Frank was fit, tan, angry, and held a look in his eyes I'd never seen. While I'd been below in darkness, Frank had taken a liking to things that lit up—like computers. And planes. I've never met anyone with a mind like Frank's. He could watch something performed once and then replicate it. Perfectly. Even complicated things.

"Frank has a photographic memory, which, among other things, allowed him to impersonate. Comedians. Actors. Politicians. News anchors. It also allowed him to fly planes and program computers, but that would come later. He grew quite good at impersonations. Voices. Slight intonations. Bodily actions. When they threatened him or made advances, he'd respond with an impersonation—which made them laugh. It was emotional sleight of hand. A deflection. Often it held off the impending abuse as they somehow saw him as something other than chattel in that moment. It was genius. His art changed too. What was once innocent turned violent. The images themselves spoke horror. Every scene depicted some sort of death, and red was hands down his favorite color. If art is an outward expression of an inward condition, then along in here I picked up on the fact that Frank was in trouble.

"Having moved us to a different coast, our new"—Bones made quotation marks with his fingers—" 'fathers' put us in a plush suite overlooking some body of water. Two large rooms. Separate bathrooms. Marble. Granite. Stocked refrigerators. Miles of church grounds. For a long time I thought this move was their form of an apology." Bones shook his head. "I was wrong."

I waited.

Bones pursed his lips. "On the surface, it appeared Frank had convinced them we would be no trouble. Silent as church mice. Just give us daylight and grass. 'We don't want no trouble.' So they locked us in a different type of prison. An anklet. And then showed us the stone walls. The message was clear. What they didn't realize is that Frank is Mensa smart. And if Mensa is the top two percent of all people, then Frank is in the top two percent of the top two percent.

"The story of my surgical skills had preceded us, so everybody left us alone. Including the brothers. Who only let us eat with plastic utensils. While I recovered and strengthened, which would take months, Frank was working them, and they never saw it coming. To his credit, neither did I.

"My time in the dungeon had wreaked havoc on my system, and my bodily clock had all but disappeared. I had no concept of a circadian rhythm. Conversely, Frank's never stopped. While I slept constantly, he could go three or four days, sometimes a week, and never close his eyes. He painted constantly. Then, when he did let himself sleep, he'd only do so an hour or two at best. I started calling him 'the Giraffe.'

"Frank fought sleep for fear of what might happen when he did, so he developed a taste for things that kept him awake. Drugs that sped up both his heart rate and his mind, and films that scared him or enticed him. Horror and adult. All three had the same effect. I, on the other hand, had been forced to make friends with the dark and could sleep through a hurricane.

"Apart from art, Frank grew more addicted to video games, drugs, and porn, and Frank as I knew him faded. As did the light behind his eyes. He was still my brother, we'd grown tough and would fight anyone, but given that we were both well into the changes of puberty, we were no longer as desirable from a physical standpoint. After several months in solitude, they moved us again. This time, Monaco."

Bones was quiet several minutes. "I've never spoken of what occurred there." He shook his head.

"Most of our time was spent at a rolling estate

in the country. Winery. Thousands of acres. Armed guards. Monaco was the convergence of wealth and power. A perfect place for a church that cared nothing for God. Took us a while to learn that the priests had bugged every hallway, every room, every bathroom—anyplace a human might speak or reveal something hidden. And given that some of the most powerful men and women in Europe graced their doors, the powers that be listened to and recorded every conversation, every interaction. Including video. Those in power were gathering more power, and what better way than to record the sins of others. Then leverage it. So they lured the wealthy, gave them what they wanted, satisfied their fetishes, then held the evidence in cold storage until needed. They did this with priests, businessmen, actors, politicians. No one was off-limits. All were fair game. Somewhere in there, Frank and I learned the power of both fear and shame. Turns out our"—Bones again made signs with his fingers—"method of communicating became invaluable. Saved us, really. They were oblivious."

CHAPTER 9

Bones and I returned to the shoreline and stood staring at the demon boat.

"Our worlds changed dramatically. Since we were no longer desirable from a physical standpoint, they put us to work. Often working twenty-two-hour days. Frank had reached his tipping point, so not long after we arrived, he shut down. Emotively. Facial expressions and any intonation in his voice ceased almost altogether. And, strangely, his eyes physically changed color. From blue to amber. What once looked like the Pacific now looked like a lava flow. I have no explanation for that.

"Somewhere in there I began hearing Frank recite a list of names. They didn't register at first. Then . . . they did. Frank had kept a mental record of all the men that had abused us. Every one. By name. And not only had he remembered their names, his photographic memory had remembered their faces—which he continued to attempt to sketch and paint. His problem was that his anger and the horror they'd inflicted prevented him from accurately depicting them. As a result, they were heinous. Quite often I'd find last week's painting torn into a thousand pieces, stabbed in the eye, or throat slit.

"On the surface, the group in Italy were the most pious. Reverent. And seemingly holy. They were also without a doubt the most emotionally manipulative bunch of miscreants we'd ever encountered. Given their geography, they had access to leadership, power, and money. From religious to political to professional, all types passed through the doors. During the day, we worked odd jobs. But never together. They knew better. I worked facilities and helped maintain the grounds. Frank was all over. Primarily organization and record keeping. I seldom saw him. We would go weeks without speaking to each other. At night the priests lit the church with candles, dressed all the prepubescent kids in red robes, and made them sing. Beautiful, angelic, tormented voices. The older kids—like us—they busied with tasks that created what would be perceived as a holy atmosphere in this epicenter of hell. When we weren't working, they required we kneel at the altar. Create an impression of the devout. And it worked. The effect on the congregants was revealing. The penitent would enter the church, hear the sound of heaven come to earth, breathe in the 'holiness' of the moment, then enter the confessional where they'd bare their souls. Over the coming trust-earning months, the father would listen empathetically and, when

111

appropriate, ask probing questions to get at the 'root' of the sin, the skeleton in the closet, the thing they were taking to the grave. When he had what he wanted, he'd offer absolution, and then well-trained girls with excellent typing skills would transcribe the recordings. Building résumés on congregants.

"Others, who knew what went on behind the curtains, would pay for that information. The church was a revolving door. Confession was made. Absolution given. Transcription sold to the highest bidder.

"As tactics go, it was genius. Money in. Information out. Power obtained. Fortunes changed. Whoever sat atop this food chain was more devious than anyone we'd encountered. He, or they, knew man's greatest need is forgiveness while his greatest desire is power. To obtain the first he confesses his sin. Where do a lot of people do that? The confessional. Which presents a problem. Certainly you can bug a confessional. It's pretty easy. But if you do that, chances are good you'll only get bits or scraps or half-truths and possibly not the whole story. They needed more certainty. They needed the assistance of someone who would intentionally guide the confessor through specific questions to tell the whole truth and nothing but. To unearth the totality of the sin. Complete absolution came under the guise of complete truthfulness. All while under the protection and forgiveness of the church itself.

"But how do you do that? I mean, really? Well, to start with, you'd need the cooperation of the priests, who by definition are idealists. In theory they work for no man. They work for God. And they hold the sanctity of the confessional above everything else. How do you upend that? How do you convince them to betray their God and their sacred vows?"

I interrupted him. "Shame."

Bones nodded. "Exactly. And to do that, you'd ingratiate yourself to them. Earn their trust. Then you'd empathetically provide what they wanted. To ease their tension-filled existence. Take their mind off the difficulties of the priesthood. Let the steam out of the cooker. This meant you'd come alongside and convince the priests, young and old, that you, of all people, understood the difficulties of the celibate life. A difficult burden. And it's here that the separation occurs. Between the resolute, the true. And the waffling, the weak. And this is where the real skill occurred. Determining who could be swayed— and turned—and those who could not. And not getting caught in the process. Months were spent studying, baiting, manipulating, toying with, and offering insinuated invitations. A touch here. A comment there. Nothing was rushed.

"There were good men of the priesthood. True

servants of God. Those who could not and would never be turned. They didn't hang around long. They were scattered on the outskirts of the realm, given churches in faraway parishes and dioceses that mattered little. The rest, well . . . once the weak were identified, bait taken, hook set, they were made an offer: 'Come spend a relaxing, soul-recharging week with other like-minded servants who understand the burdens you carry, where, if you so desire, you can unmask the real you in protection and secrecy.' And maybe most importantly, empathy, understanding, a judgment-free zone. 'Come experience forgiveness like you've never known.' "

Bones fell quiet a moment. Lost in memory. "Seldom, if ever, has the civilized world seen such . . ." He shook his head. "Maybe Rome." Minutes passed. He continued. "Every fetish was supplied. But before they returned home, being the penitent priests they were, they would confess their sins—to those with whom they'd sinned— grant one another absolution, and then step on a plane bound for home. Guilt-free. Ready to face the future, come what may.

"And about here is where reality set in. As they stepped off the plane, they were given a nicely packaged, professionally edited video 'to remember their weekend.' What they didn't know was that through sophisticated, cutting-edge technology, everything they'd done from the time they first set foot on the plane to the time they stepped off had been recorded. Every conversation. Every interaction. Every breath. It highlighted multiple camera angles, views, and audio-recording technology that made Watergate look like something out of *Romper Room*. The message was clear. Join us, or . . . Their close rate was 100 percent. To lessen the sting of getting caught literally with their pants down, they were encouraged to recruit their own. Which they did with much enthusiasm. Hence, the circle expanded organically. And exponentially.

"The goal was information. Secrets. Whatever miscreant ran the show was a psychological master at obtaining it, using it, and then convincing you to do the same. Deceive someone else in order to obtain their secrets. And once you had those secrets, you'd leverage them, employ that complicit person, and expand the reach. Who would then expand the reach by deceiving someone else who would join in. And so on. It is the most genius pyramid scheme in the history of pyramid schemes. Fueled by deceit, manipulation, and fear. The longer the downline, the more secrets you had and could leverage and the more power you wielded within the 'organization.'

"All that information had a purpose. It was used for something. And to the someone in charge, that something was more important than money or prestige or fame. The goal was control. Of people. Get them to do what you want them to do. Not only now, but forever. Frank and I were just expendable cogs in the machine. All of us were.

"The problem with a system like this is that it inherently breeds distrust. It has to. It's built upon it. And distrust is a shaky foundation. Sooner or later, the walls will come crumbling down.

"Their problem was that nobody trusted anybody. At all. Everyone was afraid of everyone else. Factions and infighting were commonplace, but given the iron hand that ruled, all rebellion and mutiny were quickly snuffed out. During our time in Monaco, Frank and I began looking for a way to exploit the cracks.

"One afternoon, I was taken underground and beaten senseless. For twenty-four hours. Then the beating turned to torture. They wanted something, but I had no idea what. Eventually, Frank appeared next to me. He looked to be in worse shape than me. Evidently they thought we had something. Turns out we did. Frank had just failed to tell me.

"Sometime during the previous week, Frank had found a few tapes lying on a desk. The video camera above him—which he had not seen—recorded the theft, but not what he did with them. They were hoping to extract that information because the tapes contained images of a sensitive nature. From that day, we didn't see the surface or the sun. 'Call us when you want to talk.'

"A month or so in, we overheard a conversation between two bitter priests who had been passed over for promotion. They were serving at a place with little that excited them. Further, they hadn't been invited to the upcoming party. Rather big party. People were flying in from all over. Live entertainment. Somebody from Vegas. Several nights. It promised to be memorable. We, along with a dozen or more boys and girls the same age as us or younger, would be the underground entertainment. Or at least part of it.

"By this point, Frank and I were done. Done with this place and these sick people. We didn't care if we lived or died. So what do two boys do who don't want to join the fun?"

I shrugged.

"Once the party started and we could hear the concert above, we set fire to everything and brought their playhouse to the ground. Literally, ashes. We had every intention of just dying in the fire, but a propane tank blew a hole in the wall and we walked out free men. Staring at a line of fancy Mercedes. So we picked the nicest one and drove it empty. Then started walking. White-capped mountains. Switzerland. Somewhere in a snowstorm, a farmer and his wife took us in. Which was surprising given our visible condition. They fed us. Clothed us. Didn't ask us too many questions and nursed us back to health. That man and his wife were reminders that the intent of man's heart was not always evil. Until then, I'd forgotten.

"I liked farm life. It agreed with me. The old man was a sheep herder. Sold the wool. Flock of a couple hundred. On two occasions I saw him leave in the middle of the night only to return in the morning with a wolf draped over his shoulder. More times than I could count, I saw him leave the safety of the flock to go find the one dumb sheep that got itself lost. And when he found it, he'd feed it, care for its wounds, and return it to the flock—teaching me more about life in three months than any human before or since.

"When the snow melted, motivated by the fact that we didn't trust anyone—no matter how nice or kind—we left quietly in the middle of the night. We hadn't gotten very far when the farmer appeared in front of us. Turns out, sheep weren't the only thing he was good at finding. He invited us back but we declined. Asked us if he and his wife had done something wrong. When we shook our heads, he reached in his pocket and handed us each an engraved silver coin."

I reached into my pocket and pulled out the silver coin Bones had given me at the café more than twenty-five years ago. The years in my pocket along with the oil from my fingers had polished the coin to a bright shine. I turned it over in my hands. "This coin?"

He nodded.

"If it meant that much to you, why'd you give it to me?"

He looked at me out of the corner of his eye. "Giving it to you didn't make it mean any less."

I had never thought of it that way.

"We thanked him, pocketed the coins, and kept walking. Ended up outside Lucerne. We avoided main roads, slept in barns, and ate what we could steal. A week later we stumbled upon the barn and the girls. I was fourteen."

We climbed into the demon boat and began idling out of the creek. "Farm country. Walking through this high alpine meadow. Dilapidated barn in the distance. We were trying to find some eggs to steal or cows to milk. Started poking around. Heard what sounded like a fight in the barn. A man and girl. We pushed open the door and an old guy had a girl tied up. Neither were dressed. Her wrists were bloody and she was in a bad way, but she wasn't having anything to do with him, and from the looks of his ear she'd already bit him. He was pretty good and drunk, and somehow in that moment, everything I'd suppressed, everything pent up in me, all my hate, anger, and rage, decided it would stay buried no longer. Frank had to pull me off him. When we untied her, she scurried into the basement of the barn. Which surprised us. Why not run away? Her instincts were more animal than human.

"We lit a lantern, followed, and saw nothing but eyes staring back at us. Four more girls. Each in various states of bad. We cut them loose and the four of them pounced on him. Not a pretty sight, but we figured he deserved it. A while later, they led us to the man's house. Not much to show for his life. Rather sparse existence. The girls rifled through his stuff, ate what little food he kept, and disappeared without a word. I have no idea whatever happened to them. Meanwhile, Frank and I were in no hurry, so we kept digging around. Wrapped in an oilcloth beneath a board under his bed, we found a dozen sequentially numbered keys. All the same size, shape, and model. We knew we couldn't just walk into any bank, show them the keys, and expect them to open the safe-deposit vault—but it was Switzerland, and we'd heard the stories. That said, while we were world-wise and could pass as older than our age, we could not pass for twenty-one. Or whatever age was needed to open those boxes. So we decided to put on a little charm and rent a box—at each bank. Turns out there were four.

"The plan was genius, and Frank's ability to deceive was uncanny. The ladies at the bank took to Frank like a puppy in the park and we scored bingo at bank number three. When they handed me the key, Frank smiled. They led us to the vault, shut the privacy door, and we began unlocking boxes. If the first one raised our eyebrows, the second through the twelfth put our jaws on the floor. Interestingly, the last two boxes contained keys—for other banks."

Bones paused, sipped, and nodded, his complexion changing. "That was the moment. When Frank became who he'd become.

"We opened boxes at other banks, transferred all the contents out of the first, as well as the second and third banks, and split the keys. The whole process took days, as we could only fit so much in school-size backpacks without attracting attention and . . . the contents were heavy. A week later, we walked out into the street and sat quietly at a café, sipping espresso. New clothes. Haircuts. Cash in our pockets. Our own hotel rooms. The world at our feet."

Bones paused. "Most of the time, when I think back, I wish the story ended there. Happily ever after. A wife. Couple of kids. Cul-de-sac. Volvo. Wine cellar. White picket fence." He sucked through his teeth. "But it didn't and we didn't."

CHAPTER 10

Bones stood at the helm and navigated through these shallow waters by muscle memory. He was home, evidenced by the fact that he didn't even have to think about it. He turned, skirted an oyster bed, and continued. "The following week, a newspaper reported that a man had been found lying in a nearby barn with severe wounds to his face, chest cavity, and groin. Along with severe dehydration. Article said the man was Russian but they had few details. Several months later, he died a in a freak motorcycle wreck. Hit-and-run. Witnesses spotted a couple girls in the other car."

I pressed him. "And?"

"From what we could piece together, he was a Russian banker who left Moscow in a hurry after he'd been discovered skimming off his customers' deposits."

"By 'customers,' you mean mafia."

Bones nodded. Then chuckled. "Oh, you wanted to know what was in the boxes?"

I laughed. "Seems important."

"Gold bars, coins . . . and loose stones. Lots of stones. Rubies, emeralds, and lots of diamonds. Many uncut. But the most valuable item came in the form of canvas. Oil on canvas, to be specific.

"Frank and I found ourselves sitting at a corner café. Absolutely no idea what to do next. Our options were endless and yet we could not wrap our heads around the enormity of it. One moment, we had been imprisoned in hell. The next we were sipping espresso, wealthy beyond our dreams. Answerable to no one. Truth was, neither of us could answer our own question, having never had the freedom to ask it. 'Just what do we do now?' Unable to make a decision, Frank frequented the red-light district while I wandered the small town, letting my mind think through possibilities. When we'd meet, Frank kept repeating his list of names. Like a nervous twitch. He wasn't even conscious he was doing it. But as I listened to him, I realized I was not the only one carrying anger, and neither of us could let it go.

"We also knew we couldn't simply march up to the gates, demand to be let in, and exact our revenge. So, again, Frank's conniving paid off. With unlimited resources and new identities, we began four years of what I like to call our 'training' period. While I could pass for competent and even excel, Frank was a natural in all things warfare. We spent a year in Brazil studying Jiu Jitsu, rolling six to eight hours a day. In Israel we studied Krav Maga and, through a chance meeting with a Mossad member, weapons training, intel, and countersurveillance tactics. To keep our edge, wherever we found ourselves we'd search out the local street fights, where I never saw Frank lose. Interestingly, that got us noticed by what today we would call a terrorist organization. So we traveled to the desert of North Africa, fought our way to the top, and learned weapons craft. Mainly explosives."

"Which"—I interrupted Bones—"Frank still seems to remember, given that"—I pointed—"he blew up half of Freetown."

Bones nodded. "Evidently. By the time we were nineteen, we were scared of no one and could turn most any man into a whimpering Cinderella at short notice using whatever we found at our disposal. Including something as simple as a spoon.

"When we weren't training, I'd get out and see the sights. Drink the wine. Taste the food. I quietly sat on hotel porches wondering about the rest of my life. Was this all? Would revenge satisfy me? Frank"—Bones shook his head—"not so much. He kept to himself, or back alleys, still didn't sleep much, if at all, and was never far from a computer or those paintings. I've never seen someone so obsessed with something as Frank became with those pieces of canvas. He would stare at them, study them, for days. He kept them rolled up in a tube, which he never let out of his sight. It was as if by owning them they could somehow transfer their beauty to his own work. Which . . . never occurred.

"Thinking we were ready and tired of planning and waiting, we started with the first name on the list. Chose the day, the place, the time. Perfectly planned. Father Bill never stood a chance. Frank wanted to kill him slowly. I thought we should just maim him. Change the rest of his life. Which we did. Quite successfully. From there we moved on to names two through nine or ten. I lost count. We picked them off one by one. Early in the morning. Late at night. Leaving the church. After a service. During Communion. Our favorite was from inside the confessional. Over the months, while Frank was licking his chops, gorging on the bloodshed, I discovered that each measured revenge only served to deepen my emptiness. Each of these men had done unspeakable things to us, things that should never be done to another human—and they did so with smug and cavalier indifference—yet I gained no satisfaction from hurting them.

"One of the trademarks of all of our training was submission. To inflict such severe pain that our subject would submit, tap out. Beg for mercy. I tested this theory with one priest who, on more than one occasion, had been particularly evil in his treatment of me in the dungeon. To refresh his memory I dislocated every joint he possessed. Arms, shoulders, ankles, all of them.

It was a long time before he would walk, go to the bathroom, or feed himself. I mangled the arms and hands that had abused me and left him forever dependent upon the mercy of another to accomplish even menial tasks. That afternoon, while Frank relived the carnage, stuffing himself on the memory, I took a look at the hole in my chest. Vengeance had not filled me. Only left a bitter taste. Further, if there was good in me, anything remotely resembling kindness, much less love, I felt it slipping away. Draining out. I was becoming as dark inside as those we hunted. Frank had no such response. He drank from it like a cup, never getting his fill.

"Frank was making plans to drive down to Italy for what he liked to call 'stage two' when I said, 'Nope, I'm finished.' He didn't believe me until I said I was flying back to the States to try my hand at college. He laughed. He couldn't understand why I'd go to college when I already had more money than I could spend in a lifetime. The structure, the requirements, this made no sense to him.

"What I didn't realize was that, for both of us, our deepest wound—inflicted at birth and reinforced every day since—was rejection. And in that moment, I was adding to his. I don't blame him. And I don't blame me. It is what it is. Frank's primary question in life had become, 'What is my name? Who am I?' He had vowed that after we'd made it through the list, we'd get to work on solving that mystery. Frank was obsessed with holding his birth certificate. To him the most priceless work of art in the entire world was the piece of paper that spoke his name.

"He saw my leaving as one more rejection, so he raged. When he came at me, I realized my brother was not in there. Some other demon now controlled his body. He couldn't understand my betrayal. It was a painful fight, and I knew that if I was to get away, I had to hurt him. So I did. Left him on the floor of the hotel room. Crying. Begging me not to go."

Bones paused and was not proud of the admission. "He still walks with a slight limp."

"So . . . you beat your brother, who you'd never seen lose?"

Bones nodded and said no more about it. "I flew back to the States. Not quite sure what to do. Entered and won a few Jiu Jitsu tournaments. Then won a national championship. Then another. This was pre-MMA, so these things served as a feeder for the Olympics. Which I cared nothing about. I began thinking I wanted to fly planes. Something about the freedom attracted me. The ability to leave here and go way up there—total freedom. Something I'd never really known. So I walked into a recruiting office, and they looked at me with dubious curiosity. Weren't sure I could pass the physical. When I broke their record, or rather all of them, they sat me down and gave me a series of tests. Aptitude. Problem solving. I never really knew my test scores, but evidently they were good because somebody somewhere pulled some strings and got me a backdoor appointment to the Academy, where I put my nose down and tried to forget my past. Which I found difficult to do.

"Some days I managed not to think about Frank. Most days I thought about my life and what I might do with the rest of it. In the beginning of my senior year, a man visited me. Didn't wear a uniform. Didn't tell me his name. All he said was, 'Tell me what you know about sheep.' Thanks to that old man in Switzerland, I knew a good bit. I shrugged and said, 'They're dumb. Hunted constantly. No match for the wolf. And totally lost without their shepherd.'

" 'So what do you do to help them?'

"My response was quick. 'Kill the wolf.'

"He considered this. 'You thought about life after graduation?'

"I pointed to the sky.

"He weighed his head side to side and then nodded. 'You can do that. And you'll be good at it. Probably have a long career. But what if I could offer you a chance to stop bad men from doing bad things to people who can't defend themselves?'

"In the weeks that followed, he opened up to me

128

and I to him. Aside from you and Frank, he's the only person on the planet to hear me talk about me. Upon graduation, while everyone around me was scurrying off to jets or carriers or intelligence or some desk job, he flew me to DC, walked me below the city streets, and showed me what few had ever seen. An organization with no name. No official designation. Immune from government bureaucracy. Handpicked staff. All with one goal: making bad men pay for their sins. As a unit, they targeted specific people. Not countries. Not regimes. Not factions or movements. But individuals. Primarily individuals who enslaved others. He sat me down at a conference table and said, 'We have one goal: to find the snake and cut off its head.' I signed up right there.

"That took me on quite a ride. A hundred and fifty plus countries. Millions of miles on planes—all of which I learned to fly—and hundreds of operations around the globe. The years flew by as we racked up success after success. I cannot count on two hands the number of times I've been brought into the Oval Office for a thank-you or commendation or medal—most of which I had to return the moment after receiving them because the op was classified and we weren't supposed to be where they said I'd been."

Bones shook his head and laughed. "I think they're all in some shoebox in the Library of Congress waiting for the statute of limitations to expire—which will occur twenty or thirty years after I'm gone. Some grad student will stumble across them, blow the dust off, and footnote them in his dissertation.

"Several years in, I used my government contacts to track down Frank. At the time, he could still be found. Hadn't gone underground yet. He was living in Paris. I surprised him at a coffee shop. He looked so different. Almost unrecognizable. His hatred for me was palpable. You could cut it. I just wanted to reestablish connection. Let him know I was alive. See his face. Hear his voice. He said little. I left my card. A month later, someone broke into my home and stole the two paintings. I let them go. I guess if I'm honest, I was tired of looking at them. Let Frank keep them. I returned to my work and tried to forget my past. The farther I traveled and the more I rescued others, the more I buried the parts of me that hurt.

"But a decade in, I knew I was burning out and needed to replicate myself. My body wouldn't let me do this much longer at the current pace, but the work was necessary. So I began thinking I needed to find another me. Train up somebody to do what I did. But how? There were very few of us who had my skill and thought like me. How do I find another me? Then I bumped into you on that riverboat."

I laughed. "If memory serves me, it was a forty-plus-foot dilapidated troller tied up to a forgotten dock attached to a deserted house, where Jack tried to rip my head from my shoulders."

"Good for you I showed when I did."

"But I was eleven. How'd you know then I had what I'd need now?"

Bones shrugged. "I didn't, but you fought back when you had no chance of winning, and then I watched you run—only to turn around when you heard the two more tied up down below that you hadn't seen. Plus, the next day at the diner, you didn't leverage your rescue of those girls as a chance to get something from them, when many would."

I scratched my chin. "Honestly, I was hoping for a free cheeseburger. Maybe some fries."

Bones chuckled and returned to the story of Frank. "As best I could piece together, Frank continued checking names off his list until the head of the snake tracked him down and offered him the world."

"The demented guy who ran the weird pyramid scheme and filmed videos of the world's elite?"

"The very same."

"Why?"

"Not sure. And I'm not sure I ever will know, but despite his attempts to suggest the contrary, Frank is still human. Still has needs."

"Like?"

"Sleep and power. Both of which were tough

to find." Another pause. "He had money, anonymity, he could have lived out his life however he wanted. Walked off into the sunset. Bought a beach. Flown in caviar. I'm not sure what was dangled, but all I can guess is that the offer included something Frank couldn't buy. Frank loves nothing and no one, so you can't leverage what he loves against him. And little tempts him because no one has what he needs. Save one thing. In many ways, Frank is still the scared boy who won't let himself sleep for fear of what will happen if he does. Every time he closes his eyes, the memories return. And memories are the one thing he can't kill, outrun, bribe, or lock up. They control him. The only way he can rest, much less sleep, is if he controls every aspect of his world. And the only way to do that is to own your enemies. So he became the very thing he hunted—working for the puppeteer who'd created him."

I sat dumbstruck.

"I don't know the extent of his wealth, but I imagine he'd make *Forbes*'s top ten. 'Course, all of it is hidden. Only he knows. He has enough to do what he wants, when he wants, however he wants, and he asks no one's permission. Through shell companies several layers deep, he doesn't just own buildings or skyscrapers so much as he owns multiple city blocks in multiple cities and all of the buildings that exist on those blocks.

Including several in New York City. He doesn't own homes so much as he owns counties. And he doesn't own beachfront so much as entire islands. He never sleeps in the same place two nights in a row, and much of the time he sleeps on a plane because it's only there he can ensure that he's alone and safe and no one can get to him. He does have secure vaults spaced around the globe, but he uses them less and less. I think he's grown paranoid that someone will find him and lock him inside.

"If you need evidence of his paranoia, four out of seven nights a week he boards one of his dozen or so jets and takes off. By himself. No pilot. Somewhere around forty thousand feet, he sets it on autopilot en route to some destination on another coast or in another country—all in an effort to get a few hours of sleep. Each flight costs him eighty to a hundred twenty thousand. But that's not the half of it. At the same time he's taking off, he sends up several decoy planes. Each is empty save the pilot who's been instructed not to land until a designated time the following day. Do the math. What is sleep worth to you?

"That's an expensive shell game." I shook my head. "I write fiction for a living, and even I'm having trouble believing this one."

"The other three nights he doesn't sleep. Occasionally he will sleep on land, and when he does . . ." Bones paused to consider his words.

133

"Think Fort Knox. If a cockroach moves within a thousand feet, he knows it. Frank's every decision is predicated on his own safety, exit, and control. He will not allow himself to be put in a cage or come under another man's authority. If those three don't exist, you won't find him. And everyone, and I do mean everyone, is expendable when it comes to achieving that. In the last few years, we discovered he would prefer to sleep on a boat rather than land for much the same reason he likes to sleep on planes."

"Does this guy do anything for fun?"

"Golf. Almost daily. Always alone. Multiple locations around the world. He plays private courses under one of his many aliases—which might or might not include makeup and a disguise. He owns many of the courses. Can shoot par on a good day.

"To keep everybody guessing and to make him as unpredictable as possible, he has at least six different teams of assistants who plan six to twelve possible itineraries for each day. Meals. Tee times. Locations. He chooses the itinerary at the start of the day, and nobody knows which he's going to choose until he does. The choice appears completely random. The unchosen five complete their assigned tasks anyway—acting as if he chose that itinerary. They fix meals. Set tables. Regardless of whether he's in the country or not. Given that he's a computer and programming genius and nobody has better security, he makes sure. If they fail to set out his lunch or his 3:00 p.m. tonic water or the 4:30 masseur, they're gone.

"He's been known to 'jump' from one itinerary to the next without notice. He'll start the day on itinerary number one, jump to number four at lunch, and finish on six. Only to further confuse everyone the following day. Random is his friend. The only thing predictable about him is that he is unpredictable.

"The fact that you saw him in Montana is a miracle. Because if he doesn't want you to see him, you won't—which means he wanted you to. Face-to-face meetings are rare. His own staff rarely see him. It's also thought that he's a master of disguise, traveling freely around the world as any number of characters. Man or woman matters not. He could be sitting next to you at a bus stop or movie theater and you'd never know it. He pays his people exceedingly well, so they are loyal. An office assistant will take home a million dollars a year. Tax-free. He keeps much of the details of his kingdom filed away in his head, but he's grown so large now that I suspect that's becoming more difficult. It's thought—"

I interrupted him. "By whom?"

"The underground folks in DC. It's thought that he's set up computer banks. Or systems. Comprising his own closed Internet. His own cloud. Where he stores the information he uses to leverage those below and around him. He is a voracious reader and can read several thousand pages or files in an evening. Retaining ninety-nine percent. He's the most unhuman human I've ever met. When he drinks, he drinks only very expensive wine. Does not do drugs. Is a strict vegetarian. And interestingly enough has no romantic inclination of any kind. Nor does he sample his own menu. By some accounts, Frank is thought to enslave several hundred thousand people, and yet he touches no one.

"Oddly, and as his brother I find this interesting, he collects art. Mostly black market. Has a thing for Rembrandt and Monet. Rumor suggests he may well be the owner of Rembrandt's *Storm on the Sea of Galilee*."

"How do you know all this?"

Bones paused. "It's taken some time. Over the years, he's brought in what you might call generals. Top-tier men to whom he's given some measure of authority. And power. These are men without remorse. Without feeling. Godless. Who see flesh as a commodity. He grooms them over a period of years and then sets them up as kings of their own kingdoms. None of them know each other, and they've never been in the same room at the same time. It's doubtful they've ever been in the same city." Bones laughed. "Mutiny is easier to prevent if all the sailors never sail on the same ship at the same time. Frank safeguards his own position atop the food chain since anonymity breeds suspicion. Which breeds loyalty—albeit perverted. The keys to Frank's kingdom are a better-kept secret than the Coca-Cola recipe.

"We've been almost two decades collecting what I just told you. Our problem is that, at best, we're always several steps behind him. And we can't seem to get any closer. We've reached a wall. In return he toys with us. He's hacked and crashed our system multiple times. Deleting everything. Leaving smug little messages that only I understand. At this point we're entertainment. Sport, even. Which would be consistent with the Frank I know."

The demon boat idled beneath us. He pointed at my stomach—where the crossbow bolt had exited. "I'm not getting any younger. Neither are you. In my youth I thought maybe I could remove Frank from the equation, whatever that looked like, and maybe make a dent in this whole trafficking thing. Now . . . I'm not so sure. It's bigger than me. There are more people enslaved today—women, children, girls and boys—than in the history of the world. And there will always be demand."

I nodded. "The intent of man's heart."

"Exactly. But maybe we can affect the supply side. And in order to affect supply, we have to cut the head off the snake."

"So what's the holdup?"

"In many ways he's just better than us. The reason we're talking in his boat is because I'm reasonably certain he hasn't bugged it. We have found dozens of devices in Freetown. None placed by us. Not only is he listening to us, but he's watching us. We're his Netflix. If you're in a room with electrical outlets or any type of high-speed wiring, and there's a computer or a cell phone in someone's pocket—regardless of whether it's yours or not—he's listening. And recording. He probably has a dozen people assigned to you alone."

"Only a dozen?" I asked.

Bones smiled. "We have to change tactics. Get smarter. In some ways—we have to out-evil evil."

"Got any ideas?"

"We need to build a team of hackers who are better at his game than he is and bring his playhouse crumbling down. Disrupt his supply, or his ability to administer it, and force him out of hiding."

"Then what?"

Bones hesitated. "Help me hunt the wolf."

"You want me to hunt him? Or kill him?"

Bones looked at me but made no response.

CHAPTER 11

Las Vegas

From Cornell to Princeton, MIT, Stanford, and Harvard, we had handpicked twenty. Sent personal invites. All but three agreed. From there, we rolled out the red carpet. All expenses paid. Give us forty-eight hours to wine and dine you and make you an offer tough to refuse. Then we'll send you home $2,500 richer just for listening. These were people who thought in code, zeroes and ones and languages spoken by a select few. Who possessed special skills. And minds. Given that the best hackers often avoided college, Eddie helped us cast another net into the non-college, not-so-legitimate world. Guys who broke the law for fun and, often, for anonymous fame. We focused specifically on individuals who had been questioned by a federal agency and who may or may not have actually hacked into or stolen information from the government.

By design there was not a single female in the group. Certainly there are talented female hackers and programmers. Some better than the guys we'd brought in. But we needed guys who, for lack of a better explanation, thought like guys. An inherent trait, not something we had to train. We didn't have the time. While Frank might be different from most, those who worked for him were not. And we were going to use their carnal desires against them.

Bones had hatched this plan, along with input from Eddie, during my long nap. When I woke up, he filled me in. The general idea was that we needed a team of brilliant minds to first find and then hack and get behind the impenetrable technical walls of Frank's world. Our first problem was that neither of us was all that technologically savvy. And we knew this. It's why we leaned on Eddie, and when we did, he had floated his idea.

"To outsmart the smartest, you need to hire smarter people." When we pressed him, he asked, "You ever see the Gene Wilder version of *Willy Wonka*?"

We both nodded.

Eddie continued, "We need to create a process—an attractive process—whereby we bring in the best, whittle them down test by test, and find the one or two worthy of the chocolate factory."

This made good sense. So Eddie hacked the recruiting systems of Google, Facebook, Insta-gram, Apple, and Microsoft and 'discovered' this year's top picks. Every year, the tech giants receive tens of thousands of applications from the brightest minds on the planet. They then task about a hundred people with sifting through the résumés to find the diamonds in the rough. The ones they would hire. They range from programming opportunists selling themselves and their services to the highest bidder to green-world idealists hoping to make their dent in the universe, along with every gradation in between. Rather than reinvent the wheel, we opted to let them do the heavy lifting. The overlap was insightful. We then sifted them ourselves. Narrowing the herd to twenty.

Each was transported by limo and flown first class. They arrived on a Friday afternoon, where they were met at baggage and escorted by beautiful women—hired out of a modeling and talent agency. They were then immediately herded into a small bus with no air-conditioning and made to wait while expected arrivals were delayed and delayed again.

Within five minutes, we lost one thanks to the heated-sardine-can tactic.

We then drove them to the Ritz-Carlton where, upon disembarking the hot box, they learned someone had bungled their reservations. No vacancy. Add to that the UFC fight tomorrow night, and there would be no vacancy anywhere. While the grumbling grew, we played incompetent. They made calls to recruiters registering their discontent and who-else-can-I-meet-with-while-I'm-out-here exasperation, while rooms were booked at a nearby Holiday Inn Express. Which included free breakfast and a stale cookie upon arrival.

Bones gathered the troops and expressed the itinerary change with almost laughable innocence.

As the bus loaded, we lost two more. Fourteen remained. Pulling out of the parking lot, the youngest in the group pulled me aside. "You want rooms here?" Meaning the Ritz.

From an early age, Ben "BP" Potterfield was uncoordinated on a level seldom seen. Absolutely could not walk and chew gum. He also had a problem with acne that severely limited his social life, so he had gravitated toward computers. He worked his way through high school by building computers and hooking up his buddies to get free HBO and cable. In his early teens he won a Microsoft programming contest and used his winnings to put himself through community college, after which he applied for and earned a hardship scholarship to Harvard. Given his genius, he had blossomed. During his tenure in Boston, he consulted and programmed for several video game companies. Now, weeks from graduating, he was exploring his possibilities. He wore Coke-bottle glasses and seemed to have conquered the acne situation, although not necessarily the coordination.

Under the collective grumbling of the group not excited about a move to a lesser hotel, BP pulled me aside and lifted a device that looked like a phone. Again, in our planning, we thought this might happen. Although we didn't know who might offer it. So a contingency was made.

Interestingly, when he asked me, "You want rooms here?" he didn't ask loudly enough for the others to hear. Which told me something about him. I nodded and shrugged. Forty seconds later, he looked at me over the top of his glasses. "How many?"

"Fifteen."

His fingers moved at the speed of hummingbird wings. Ten seconds later, he closed his phone. "Reservation's under the name of Shepherd."

"Why Shepherd?"

He spoke with no emotion. "Stole it off your credit card."

I wasn't sure how he did that, but I liked him immediately. "How old are you?"

"Does it matter?"

"Not really."

"Nineteen."

We returned to the Ritz where our reservation was miraculously "found." Club floor, no less. Incidentally, BP put himself in a suite. A nice touch. The others never knew.

Which, again, spoke volumes.

In our preplanning Bones suggested we narrow

the gap again by doubling the candidates up in shared rooms, but I shook my head. Force me to share a room and I don't care if you're Mother Teresa, I'm gone. I don't do shared rooms with strangers. Too weird. We were trying them, testing them, hoping to get at their motivations, not get rid of all of them. We also needed to know what they did in their spare time. Alone. We wanted them comfortable. Isolated. Walls down.

The group disappeared into their rooms while Bones and I joined Eddie in his room, which became command central. Eddie's desk was covered in several numbered screens corresponding with room numbers, which mirrored what each person was watching on TV and/or their personal computer, phone, or tablet. Most were hacking into the hotel's system to get free movies and whatever else they could find.

Twenty minutes later, Bones welcomed them in the conference center. "Tomorrow morning we will talk business and offers and money and—"

A well-dressed kid, maybe twenty-three, wearing a custom sport coat, oxford shirt, and designer running shoes, interrupted him. The kid was tan, fit, and spoke with a measure of authority. "If it's all the same to you, I'd prefer to skip whatever entertainment you're offering and talk package." He tapped his watch. "I'm evaluating several offers."

We knew this was true, but we wanted to know if the self-appointed alpha male had the ability to listen. Which, he had just proven, he did not. Instead, he was letting everyone in the room know his value—which, in his mind, was greater than theirs.

Or so he thought. In truth, he was lower third.

Roger Peeking was Ivy League bred and silver spoon fed. Father ran a hedge fund. Yet that isn't to say he hadn't worked hard. To his credit, Roger had. He was also off-the-charts smart and had already been questioned by the FBI for possibly hacking several government agencies. Which made him all the more attractive to the Silicon crowd. Roger's hiccup was that he vacillated between entitlement and hard work. After we'd dug into his file, our concern was that his hard work, when coupled with pedigree, may have only served to reinforce the idea that someone owed him something. So that, ultimately, he could return home and show Daddy what he'd made of himself. Allowing him to sit atop Daddy's kingdom and play with other people's money. The flip side could also be true—that he was not responsible for where he was born or to whom he was born, and that his hard work was his attempt to lose the silver-spoon image, something that had dogged him his entire life. No easy task. Clay suggested a third possibility—that Roger was an unpredictable loose cannon who, no matter how brilliant and talented, couldn't be trusted. I posited he had a Napoleon complex.

Bones was currently targeting all four theories. I had my suspicions when he interrupted Bones and tapped his watch, but it was his tone of voice that confirmed he had no place with us. You don't speak to Bones like that. I don't care who you are or who your daddy is.

Bones played dumb and gestured to a side door. "Roger—"

Roger interrupted him. "Mr. Peeking."

Bones nodded apologetically. "Your credentials speak for you. We will make you wait no longer, but for your benefit, we'd rather do that individually." Bones chose his word here carefully. *Individually.* If Roger bit, we'd know he might not play well with others. Granted, we had to be careful here because not everyone who jumps at an "individual" package explanation is off the team. I work well alone, but I also know the value of a team. The question we were trying to answer was, Did Roger, or anyone else in this room, value himself more than others? It's one thing to think you're better or more talented than another. It's a fact that some of us are better than some of the rest of us. Take music. Or art. There's no argument here. The motive at hand had to do with value. And at root, if Roger valued himself more than everyone else in the room, and his stuff was more important than anyone else's

146

stuff, then we had to question why he would ever leave the ninety-nine to find the one.

Bones continued, "If you will please follow me, my team will give you the particulars. I'm sure you won't be disappointed."

Roger stood and followed Bones, who led him to an exit door and a shiny black 600 Series Mercedes.

Roger sat in the back seat while I drove slowly in circles. Heat on. Looking for an address that did not exist. Playing the village idiot. You might say I was trying to give Roger a second chance and see how long he could accommodate me and put up with my weaknesses. My failures. Certainly he deserved that. What if we had judged him too quickly? What if he was actually just an introvert who didn't like crowds? Certainly I could empathize. But while an argument could be made that I was, in effect, giving Roger the benefit of the doubt, truth was, I didn't like Roger and I didn't like the way he spoke to Bones, so I was just trying to make him as physically uncomfortable and mentally frustrated as possible.

Over the next six minutes, Roger huffed and sweated and made himself look important by pounding out texts to any number of people, all of whom I was sure waited with bated breath. At minute seven—and frankly, I'm surprised he made it that long—Roger cussed and demanded answers. When I continued to play dumb, he blew his stack. Or what was left of it. He cursed Bones, me, my mother, and the camel-leather seat upon which he fidgeted. Two blocks later, at his spit-filled and expletive-laced request, I quietly deposited him on a street miles from nowhere with spotty cell coverage. No worse for wear. I was sure Roger would make Daddy proud. Right after he walked a few blocks to summon an Uber.

When I returned to the conference center, Bones explained, "If any of you, like Roger, would prefer to skip the party and know your particulars, we will be happy to oblige. In short, we are looking to hire the best programmers in the country for one job. It might last six months. A year. Possibly two. Depends on how good you are." Laughter rippled around the room. "When complete, we will pay you a bonus that could reach seven figures." The laughter ceased.

Here, we were poking at motivation. Did money alone drive them? There's nothing wrong with money in and of itself, but if it was their sole motivation, they would be better served elsewhere. When Bones said "seven figures," every face in the room smiled save three.

Bones continued, "In the meantime you keep what you kill and the target is on the *Forbes* list."

Both *kill* and *target* were specific word choices. As was the unspoken suggestion of going after a specific someone—without knowing the reason why. Were they turned off or on or indifferent at the idea of specifically targeting a "someone"? Also, they were not told why or if he deserved it. Much was left hanging.

Prior to our entrance, Eddie had fitted the room with nearly a dozen cameras. As Bones spoke, Eddie was busy analyzing facial movements and what they told us. Most were intrigued, save five who did not seem quite so enthusiastic as they had moments before. We needed to know if they had the stomach for a fight. This word test began that examination.

When Bones said *"Forbes* list," every face in the room smiled save one. A quiet, reserved guy in the rear of the room. Jay Middlecamp. Known to his friends as Camp.

Camp was ex-military. Navy SEAL. Active duty until an IED detonated beneath the vehicle in which he was riding—which detached both retinas and rattled his noggin. Surgery repaired both retinas and his vision, but between that and the concussion, he had been medically discharged. Mind you, against his wishes. So he used the military's money, went back to school, and floundered in business school until he took a basic computer class and discovered his second set of skills. From there he dove into languages and took to them like a fish to water. Ever since, he could get into and behind anyone's computer. Including the president's. Which he had. Leaving him an electronic yellow sticky plastered in the middle of his screen. The note read, "I'm keeping my promise. Your security needs some work. Almost as much as your golf game." Then Camp signed his name, rank, and phone number.

Since the president had hung a few medals around his neck, they didn't bury him beneath the prison. Instead, after a rather lengthy interview, they thanked him for the heads-up and hired him to work in cybersecurity. After eight years, and bored with the political arena and the new administration, Camp was now late twenties and looking for the excitement he was robbed of when the bomb went off. He was unmarried, lived alone save a dog, and visited his grandmother on the weekends. Not to mention his security clearance went to the top. Of course, he didn't know we knew any of this.

Bones continued, "If you're willing to wait until tomorrow for those details and would like to enjoy yourself in the interim, this is Las Vegas. The possibilities are endless. If you have need of anything, please call our private concierge. The details of which you can find in your welcome packet in your room." With that, he said, "Any questions?"

As there were none, he stepped aside and said, "Enjoy your evening."

The test started when they found themselves alone in their rooms with nothing but time in Vegas. What would they do with time and anonymity in Sin City? Bones and I returned to Eddie's control room, where the next two hours proved to be revealing.

Calls were made to discreet escort services with several asking for "younger" girls. And one for a young boy. A quarter of our guests quickly scoured the dark net and put in a delivery request for various types of medication—including several of the powder variety. One Cornell graduate bypassed his room completely and landed at the roulette table, where he was four drinks in and losing his shirt. Four had made in-room massage appointments that included rather detailed and specific requests. Several had made untruthful and misleading calls to girlfriends back home. All of them had hacked their in-room TV provider and were watching porn.

Save two.

BP was playing a war-based, futuristic video game. His partner was some kid in South Africa, and they were competing against a team in Zurich. They were winning. By a lot. Camp had returned from ninety minutes in the fitness center, which included a phone call with his grand-mother, who lived in a nursing home. Her air conditioner was broken. Now back in his room, he'd made arrangements, at considerable cost to himself, with a twenty-four-hour repairman to make an after-hours call to his grandmother's room. Currently he was eating a cheeseburger, drinking a beer, and watching the Braves game.

To turn up the heat, we paid the bellman to deliver personalized notes to both their rooms, further emphasizing the opportunities available to them. When neither bit, we sent a girl. Or woman, rather. At six foot two, Sylvia Thacker had once worked the strip on Vegas as a showgirl. With a dancer's legs and runway model's face, she'd performed the world over. But after having seen the true side of Vegas, she retired, applied to the police academy, and had spent the last ten years working as part of a sex crimes unit in Nevada. Her specialty was running sting operations on sex trafficking. Bones and I had helped her with a few cases over the years, and when we told her what we needed, she quickly volunteered. Sylvia is crazy beautiful, enticing, a black belt in Jiu Jitsu, and loves her job.

None of us were too crazy about hiring a woman to proposition either of these guys—it seemed rather disingenuous. But we did need to test them, and Sylvia offered a way to get at their motivations without actually hiring someone in that line of work. Not to mention, Sylvia was overseeing an operation at a hotel four blocks away where she and her team had sold thirty-minute time slots with kids through Facebook and Craigslist and a few other apps. Using several rooms on several floors, staffed by several teams, she had filled all but a few of her ninety time slots, meaning tomorrow would prove to be an eventful day—with a full jail and a lot of arrests.

Given the noise-canceling ear phones he was wearing to communicate with his South African partner, BP never heard Sylvia's knock. So Sylvia let herself in and propositioned the wide-eyed young man, who dropped his hand controller—killing his on-screen character—spilled his two-liter Mountain Dew, and lost the ability to speak English. Mind you, she was dressed. He'd just never seen anyone dressed like that. When he didn't respond to Sylvia's advances, she asked a second time. When he declined a second time, using the words, "No thank you, ma'am," she laughed and let herself out, telling Bones and me, "He's perfect."

Ten minutes later, she knocked on Camp's door. One look through the peephole told him it wasn't room service. He opened the door and, judging by his expression, was not impressed. "You've got to be kidding me."

When Sylvia assured him she was not and that his future employer thought he might enjoy some time with her, Camp responded with, "Lady, go put some clothes on."

Feeling rather self-conscious that she was losing her touch, Sylvia doubled down and sweetened her offer, including her willingness to add a younger woman to their party—with an emphasis on "girl." The offer, while cryptic, was clear.

Camp considered this. "Are you actually offering to bring a girl to my room?"

Sylvia smiled and nodded.

"What age?"

"Whatever."

"So"—Camp leaned against the doorframe—"if I told you I wanted a ten-year-old girl in my room in thirty minutes, you could arrange that?"

"Absolutely."

With that, Camp threw Sylvia over his shoulder and carried her to the glass elevator, where he rode down ten floors and strode through the lobby—with Sylvia kicking and screaming from his shoulder—and sat her on the front desk.

When the manager began asking him, "Just what do you think you're doing?" Camp played the voice memo recording of his conversation with Sylvia. The manager, Matt Kemp, was, in reality, Sylvia's sergeant and a nearly thirty-year veteran of law enforcement. Apologizing profusely, he offered to comp Camp's room and buy him dinner. Even offered free tickets to any show he desired.

Camp, tired and wanting to get back to his baseball game, refused and began walking toward the elevator. The manager, not to be outdone, wasn't finished. And this, I think, showed the mastery of Bones's plan. Kemp met Camp at the elevator and spoke in hushed tones. At which point Camp picked him up and dumped him, headfirst, into a trash can.

CHAPTER 12

As we stood watching the festivities projected through one of the many hotel cameras and onto Eddie's screen, someone knocked on the door. Loudly. Bones answered. An attractive, athletic-looking girl stood outside with a wrinkled brow. A backpack over one shoulder. Laptop under one arm. Hair pulled back in a single ponytail. She was sweating slightly and looked like she'd been running.

She pursed her lips. "You all are a bunch of chauvinists."

Bones almost laughed. "Excuse me?"

She slipped past Bones and stood in the room, pointing at each of us. Jessica Peterson would have been top three on our list had she not been a girl. Problem was, she was. That said, she also had a short temper and a track record of making room for herself in places in which she was not welcome. Eddie had informed us three days ago that she'd booked a flight and rented a car. We also knew that after BP had booked our rooms, her reservation had quickly followed.

We had all placed bets as to when she'd make her entrance. Clay won.

Jessica continued, "I don't know why you're doing what you're doing, but I know you've been through a lot of trouble to do it, and I know I was left out of it when I can run circles around"—she pointed at the screens showing the rooms of all our prospects—"these idiots." She stepped closer and we didn't prevent her. "Not to mention the fact that you"—she pointed at Eddie—"have been inside my phone and computer for a week but you've done nothing but watch and I can't figure out how you got in there." She studied the screens. "All idiots. 'Cept those two." She gestured toward BP and Camp. "BP is young but he knows his stuff. And the other guy is a bit of a ghost, but I've bumped into him before. And"— she smiled as the screen mirrored the Uber app on his phone—"looks like you're about to lose him."

Bones nodded at me while Eddie responded to Camp's order. He'd also booked a return flight home on the red-eye. I guess he'd had enough of us.

I pulled around front where Camp stood waiting. When my car and tag lined up with what Eddie, I mean, Uber, had sent Camp, he opened the door and said, "Airport."

I asked in return, "You mind if we pick someone else up on our way?" I shrugged. "Doubling up helps me out."

Camp responded, "No problem."

Two blocks later, I pulled to the side where Clay stood with a walker and a suitcase. While I grabbed the case, Camp helped Clay navigate the curb and gave him his seat up front. The smirk on Clay's face told me he was enjoying playing the crippled old man routine. The airport was only ten minutes, so we had to work quickly. Clay started in. "Where you headed, young man?"

"Home."

"Kind of late. Can't it wait?"

Camp looked with disdain out the window. "I've had my fill. Besides, my grandma's A/C is out."

Clay slapped his leg and laughed. "If Gran-mama ain't happy, ain't nobody happy."

Camp laughed. "That's a fact."

"You here on business?"

"Thought I was."

"What happened?"

Camp weighed this. "Bait and switch."

Clay's face showed confusion.

Camp continued, "Couple of guys pretending to be one thing when in reality they're another."

Old men can sometimes get away with pressing personal questions, so Clay did. "Who you work for?"

Camp showed good judgment in not answering. "I work for myself."

Clay again. "You out here interviewing with

this Silicon crowd? Hoping to make a little money?"

Camp thumbed behind us. "I got suckered. Turns out they're just a bunch of incompetent hacks. Couple of government guys gone rogue." This meant he'd penetrated our firewall, which Eddie had been expecting, so he left an electronic paper trail making us look like low-level government wannabes with an ax to grind. Camp continued, "And yeah, I'd like to make some money. Just not interested in what they had to offer."

"You got a plan B?"

Camp shook his head. "Not really." Then a laugh. "But neither do they."

Clay chuckled. "Sounds ominous."

"The barrier to entry is too easy. Anybody with a laptop thinks they're the next Zuckerberg. These guys need to quit before they get taken to the woodshed. I tried to help them."

Clay pretended interest. "Yeah?"

Camp was staring out the window. Relaxed. "They'll soon discover that all their files have been deleted and I control their phones." Camp checked his watch. "Right about now, they should start receiving more spam calls than they thought possible."

As he finished speaking, our phones started vibrating. Nonstop. One call after another. I held up my phone. Clay did likewise. I said, "You mean like this?"

Camp frowned. "What do you guys want?" When he said it, he was not the least bit rattled, afraid, or impressed.

Clay spoke. "Honestly? Help. But we needed to thin the herd. Separate the real from the counterfeit. You mind giving us an hour?"

Camp folded his hands in his lap. "Does this involve me taking my clothes off, dressing up like Little Bo Peep, or violating my oath to my government?"

Clay weighed his head side to side. "Well"— Clay thumbed at me without looking—"if I know this guy, he will definitely press the boundaries of what's legal."

I glanced at him in the rearview. "I took the same oath."

"Yeah, but from your files—"

I interrupted him. "If you were us, what would you have let you know about us?"

Somewhere in here, he began to see the bigger picture and just how greatly he'd been played. And for what reason. "And the woman at my door?"

"She runs the anti-trafficking unit here in Vegas."

"And the manager?"

"Her boss."

"Well played." He laughed. "I'm listening."

I made a one-eighty while Clay spoke to Bones, who was listening through the car's Bluetooth. "Bones, we are inbound."

Camp looked at me and then Clay. "So all this . . . was a test?"

Bones spoke over the speakers. "And, Mr. Middlecamp, you passed with flying colors."

"You should probably call me Camp."

"Good enough."

CHAPTER 13

When we returned, Bones and Eddie were sitting in Eddie's suite while Jessica stared at the computer screens. She did not look happy. "So you're letting these other jackwagons off the hook?"

"They're of no further interest to us."

That wasn't entirely true, but Bones was baiting her. "So"—she almost smiled—"you don't care what happens to them from here on out?"

"Not really."

She gestured to Eddie's keyboard. "May I?"

After a few minutes and a bunch of clicks, she spun around and sat quietly. Eddie stood with his arms crossed, laughing. As did Camp and BP.

Every few seconds, the computer would ding and she'd type a few clicks in confirmation. After five minutes, she sat back and crossed her arms.

Bones asked what neither he, nor Clay, nor I knew. "You want to let us in on the secret?"

Eddie pointed to the screens and spoke for her. "She sent all of them personalized invites to Sylvia's remaining time slots. Courtesy of you. Those dings are their acceptance."

Bones shook his head and turned to Jess. He

knew the answer but he asked anyway. "Were you raised with brothers?"

"Five." She smirked. "But you already knew that."

"You'll fit right in."

Then he turned to everyone and said, "Folks, if you'll follow me."

Bones took us to the rooftop restaurant and a private room where Clay closed the sliding doors and Bones wasted no more time. "I apologize for the circuitous route each of you took to this room, but it was necessary. Thank you for your patience. We have a problem and we need help. But before we could invite you to join us, we needed to know what drove you. Or, at least, what didn't. It really doesn't have anything to do with any of us making a lot of money, although you will. If you join us and you succeed—as a team—people will live who won't otherwise. If you fail, they'll die. Lives—people with real names, mothers, daughters, children—all hang in the balance. What I'm about to tell you is highly classified, so please speak now if you want out. If you do, I'll buy your dinner, give you some cash for your trouble, and we will part friends."

Bones waited. No one moved. Evidence that he had their attention and that the buildup, while tedious, was necessary.

"Going once . . ."

Still no takers.

"We work for an organization out of DC with no name." He glanced at Camp. "And our security clearance travels above yours."

Camp thought for a moment. Then whispered Bones's name out loud, more to himself than anyone else, then turned to me and smiled. "That would make you . . . Murphy Shepherd."

I extended my hand. "You can call me Murph."

Camp sat back. "So the rumors are true."

Bones again. "Depends on the rumors."

Jess crossed her arms. "Great. Another good-old-boy network. Anybody care to explain?"

Clay smiled. "I like her."

Bones started, "Ms. Peterson—"

She interrupted him. "Let's just stick with Jess."

Bones nodded in agreement and turned to me. "You mind?"

I lifted my shirt and waited as each of them read the names across my back. Bones pointed. "Virginia Appleton. Seventeen years at the time. Number 187. Met her date online, agreed to meet him at a bar where he slipped a Mickey in her drink. She woke up twelve hours later. In Canada. Locked in a hotel room. We found her two weeks later. By that time she'd serviced more than a hundred clients." He pointed to another name. "Jacob Feinberg. Eleven. Kidnapped from the basement of his synagogue where he was practicing the trumpet. Transported via tractor trailer to Orlando where he was offered to high-paying clients who wanted a 'young Jewish boy.' We found him eight days later. Took him six months before he'd talk again."

He pointed again but waited while Eddie read aloud his own name. I let down my shirt, and Eddie told his story.

"I was playing video games at a movie arcade. Sneaking into my second showing of one of the Star Wars films. Somebody pressed a rag to my face, laced with chloroform, and I went to sleep. I woke in a shipping container. Seasick. When my exploiters learned my dad was the CEO of a solar company worth a couple hundred million, the first ransom note came in at five million. Which my parents quickly paid. That was followed by a second. Which they also paid. When the third demand appeared and I did not"—Eddie pointed at Bones—"my folks called and"—he glanced at me—"put Murph on a plane. His last words to my folks were, 'Don't pay it.' A few days later, I heard a ruckus, then bones breaking and men screaming. A few minutes later, Murph lifted me out of a warehouse, flew me overnight to DC, and handed me to my inconsolable mom and step-dad.

"My ordeal had taken a toll. Weeks passed but I was in a daze. When I finally started to cry, I couldn't stop. Couldn't shake the fear. I didn't eat, sleep, speak, or hug. I'd been muted, save the tears and the nighttime terrors. So . . ." Eddie paused while the memory returned. Another point at me. A tear welled in Eddie's eye and broke loose, trailing down his cheek. "He came to see me. Sat me up at the kitchen table. Lifted his shirt. Which scared me. Then he turned slightly and asked me, 'Can you read?' I nodded. 'Can you read the last one?' I studied the names on his back, finally reading the last. 'E-E-Eddie F-Fisher.' Then Murph asked me to read it again. 'E-Eddie Fisher.' The second time I read it, it hit me and I whispered, 'Eddie Fisher. That's my name.' Then the man with the tattooed back told me, 'Wherever I go, I carry you with me.' And at the sound of this, I almost smiled. I liked the thought of that. I said, 'F-f-forever?' The man nodded. Then he asked me if I could count to a hundred. 'Y-yes.' Then he said, 'Two hundred?' And when I nodded, he said—" Eddie looked at me and waited for me to finish the story.

I picked up where he left off. " 'If you were to count all the names before yours, you'd find 173. That means there are 173 kids like you. Many of whom now live at a place called Freetown."

" 'Wh-where's th-that?' " Eddie mimicked his childhood self.

" 'The mountains of Colorado. Would you like to go there?' And when I said this, Eddie looked at his parents, who nodded. So Eddie asked me . . ."

Eddie was smiling at the memory. "Are you there?"

"Sometimes."

Eddie and I tossed the memory ball back and forth. "Wh-wh-where do you g-go?"

"To find kids like you."

"Do you c-c-come back?"

I had laughed out loud. "Yes."

"Always?"

"Until now, yes."

"Ca-can I h-h-help you?"

"What do you mean?"

"F-f-find k-k-kids like m-m-me."

I studied the three candidates. Jess. BP. Camp. "It was the first time the rescued had ever asked to rescue. And it had come out of the mouth of a scared kid. I didn't know quite what to do, so I glanced at his parents, who quickly said, 'Anything you need.' Which explains why much of Freetown runs on solar power and why Eddie here, now twenty, is enrolled in distance learning at MIT and runs our communications department. But"—I made quotation marks with my fingers—" 'communications' is a cover. He runs anything and everything having to do with IT and all countersurveillance. If it's computer in nature, be it something as complicated as our security system or programming a satellite to find a needle in a haystack, or something as seemingly simple as an iPad, Eddie runs the team that oversees it."

When Jess spoke, her tone was kind. "What happened to the stutter?"

Eddie shook his head. "Don't know. I moved to Freetown, found my place in the world, and when I turned around, it was gone. I can't explain that."

Camp raised a hand. "I'm in. I don't care what you folks are doing. I want in."

BP followed. "Ditto. Sign me up."

Bones looked at Jess, who raised a finger. "Okay, but I have a thing about needles, so if tattoos are mandatory, you guys can count me out."

I laughed. "Truth be told, Jess, I hate needles."

Camp nodded at me. "What's Appoll—"

Eddie finished it for him. "Apollumi."

Bones spoke for the team. " 'That which was lost.' And the operative word there is 'was.' "

Now that we had their attention, Bones laid it out: "We'd like to continue this conversation where it matters. So let's order, eat up, and pack your bags. Wheels up in an hour."

CHAPTER 14

Just prior to midnight, we landed just outside of Freetown where we were met by Summer, Ellie, and Gunner in one Range Rover and Casey and Angel in another. Gunner gave everyone the sniff test, and then they drove us to Main Street, where we bypassed all the public venues and unloaded in the trees just beyond Bones's house. Before we exited the vehicle, Bones took his phone out of his pocket and placed it in a bag held by Clay. I did likewise, followed by everyone else. He then pointed, without speaking, to the backpacks of laptops and other electronic devices shouldered by each member of our new team and shook his head, motioning to leave them in the car. Having "cleaned" us of our devices, Bones led us down a short path and punched his code in a keypad. The large vault-looking door cracked open, allowing us entrance into the rabbit hole that led into the tunnels beneath our homes. Jess, BP, and Camp followed while Gunner and I brought up the rear. The tunnel came to a T-intersection. Left led to my vault. Weapons room. And underground range. Right led to Bones's photography room and his wine cellars.

We turned right and took our seats amid the many slides hanging in glass cases on Bones's wall. Eddie had stopped the projector from showing Bones's slides and instead uploaded the video of the events that occurred the night of Summer's and my wedding. Once we were comfortable, Eddie pressed play.

I'd seen the montage. Beautiful moments. Our first dance. Summer's beauty. Clay's speech. Ellie's laughter. The dreamy sequences melted one into another.

Then the flames. Running down Main Street. Into and out of the hospital. Followed by the girls running in and never running out. Followed, finally, by Clay running in and then a fireball and the video going black.

The team was silent.

I picked up the narrative. "The following day, Gunner smelled a handkerchief from a quarter mile away and led us to some clues that let us know they were alive. After a bit of a chase, we were able to bring them home."

Ellie, who was sitting in my lap, spoke over me. "Yeah . . . and then you died."

After a couple of days' absence, Gunner was happy to see me and was currently trying to lick my face off. I wrestled him to his back where he let me rub his tummy. "There was that too."

Bones turned on the lights. "I'll save the backstory for another day. But a few years ago, Murph interrupted a trafficking operation moving up and down the Intracoastal Waterway. Sophisticated. Many players. Several vessels. Homes. A couple dozen girls. Some high-profile customers and a lot of money at risk. Further, on one of those vessels, he took a couple hard drives that we didn't think too much about until after it was all over."

Summer raised a finger and interrupted Bones. "In truth I carried those drives off the boat." She thumbed at me. "Then left him to mop up the mess."

I nodded in affirmation. "That is correct."

Bones knew this but played along. "On one of those boats, Summer took a couple of hard drives. A couple things resulted from this. One, between lost boats and lost income on people, we cost somebody a couple million dollars. Not the end of their world but not pocket change either. That got their attention. Two, the hard drives. Initially, we scanned them for what they told us in the present tense. And they were useful. But in the last several months, Eddie has dissected the drives to find out what they might tell us about themselves.

"The drives are solid state, so they're extremely fast and have no moving parts, which makes them durable—to a point. From what we can tell, they're collection drives programmed to transfer their data every few hours. Eddie can explain later what he's found, but here's the big picture and why we need you all.

"First, we're really good at what we do, and because of this we have a target on our backs. All the time. This was not such a problem when it was just our backs, but that changed when a bomb went off in Freetown."

Camp spoke up. "You know who's responsible?"

"One man. He traffics thousands of people and Murph has cost him a lot of money. Which would explain why he blew up Freetown and tried to kill Murph. Until now we've focused our energies on rescuing the trafficked. The slaves. But it would be naive to do that now. We can no longer be content to rescue sheep. Or sit here and protect the flock. We need to hunt the wolf. Which brings us to you."

Bones told them bits and pieces of the longer story he'd told me, but in doing so, he spoke as an outsider, giving them enough to fill in their understanding while skipping the personal connection. He continued, "I don't know how to rate hackers and programmers, but he's been doing it since before any of you were born, and I'd say he could go toe-to-toe with any of you."

Jess took issue with this. "He's that good?"

Bones shrugged and pointed at Eddie. "Eddie got in your computers and phone and you can't figure out how or how to get rid of him?"

The admission was almost painful. "Correct."

"Well"—Bones pointed to the screenshot frozen on the moment of the explosion—"he's in every area of our system, and as good as Eddie is, we can't figure out how he keeps getting in or how to get him out."

She nodded.

Bones continued. "This is not a video game to him. He's not in this for kicks and giggles. He's in this for him. Period. The reason we're meeting in here is because"—Bones tapped the granite walls—"we're as certain as we can be that he's not. Also, you should know, the moment you say yes to this job—if you say yes to this job—the bull's-eye is on you too. He will attack all your fancy electronics, and Eddie tells me that if it has a processor, he'll own it. Frank's problem—"

BP raised a finger. "I'm sorry, did you say Frank?"

"It's short for Francis."

"Okay."

Bones continued, "His problem, or at least we hope his problem, is that while he's smart and has both a photographic and encyclopedic memory, his organization has grown beyond his ability to keep it all in one place. Information is both his advantage and his Achilles' heel.

"Further, he's paranoid, so he doesn't trust anyone to know all that he knows. Which is why he spends so much time and energy listening to us. From what we can piece together, he's got seven generals beneath him who actually run his empire, but nobody knows anybody else and nobody knows what everybody else knows. Or what they don't know."

Camp nodded. "It's easier to prevent a mutiny if the shipmates never meet."

"Exactly. Further, Frank has no succession plan and no interest in what happens after he dies. He couldn't care less. He's not building for the future or trying to pass a healthy empire down to his children or second in command. That said, he does have one problem. His ability to exist is built on information. Information about other people. He's not just selling flesh. He's selling the 4K recording of that transaction—that sold flesh—to bribe those who bought it. Interestingly, very powerful men with a lot of money do that all the time. They can have anything they want. Women throw themselves at them. And yet they'd rather pay to play."

BP articulated the question voiced by the wrinkle on his forehead. "Why?"

"Power," Jess answered for Bones.

Bones nodded in agreement.

Jess, showing that growing up with brothers had not been lost on her, continued. "Unbridled, uncontested, and unaccountable power. Their money allows them to do things to and with people they could never do otherwise."

Bones picked it up again. "That amount of video of that number of people requires a massive amount of storage. Secondly, he has so much money coming in from so many sources, there's no way he can keep it all straight. Not to mention all the account numbers, banks, and countries. Even he has limitations. Thirdly, those sources of income represent people being trafficked. Locations. Calendars. Activity. So how do you collect, assimilate, organize, and keep safe all that data?"

One of the team interrupted him. "What about his own cloud? Maybe an IP address only he knows. Somewhere on the dark net."

"Possibly, but we don't think so. Historically, the reason for a cloud is to allow you, or many people like you, to upload or access information from anywhere—provided there's an Internet connection. They also help keep that data safe from physical hazards such as fire, theft, etcetera. And make it available anywhere—again, provided there's a connection. We don't think he can risk being connected to the Internet because that means he's susceptible to folks like you. Forgive me if I have my terminology wrong, but couldn't you all send out a 'bot' that would search for patterns and possibly find where he's hiding if you had the time and resources?"

They all nodded.

"Eddie suggests, and I tend to agree with him,

that all this data is transmitted by the low men on the totem pole. The men on the boats. Or in the hotel rooms. Houses. There are hundreds of these men. Maybe a thousand. The data is never stored where the trafficking occurs. Only uploaded. And from what I understand, it's pretty tough to hack an upload. Plus, why would you? It's one interaction out of thousands."

More nodding.

"By not storing it where the trafficking occurs, Frank keeps the hands on the ground off the data. Not only does he keep them off the data, he keeps their hands off the money. He only takes electronic currency. Sure, some of these low men will skim via cash discounts, but again, Frank incentivizes those up the line to make sure those on the ground are charging for every encounter. These 'collectors,' let's call them, simply maintain a physical site and handle the monetary transactions. From there, the data is uploaded up the chain. Not to a cloud but to larger, for lack of a better word, servers. Physical computers. Maybe there's one in each city. Or each smaller geographic area. We suppose there are hundreds."

Camp raised a finger. "These would need to be connected to the Internet."

Bones nodded again. "Yes. Based on what we've seen firsthand through the years, they are. It's an efficient and quick way to gather real-time data."

"Isn't that risky?"

"Yes, but to lose one wouldn't bring his playhouse down. For him it'd be like losing a platoon from an entire army. Think economies of scale. He's got so much coming in, he's got to funnel it somewhere. And this is the mouth of the funnel. Maintained by middlemen who capture the data and store it on portable drives, which they then disconnect from the Internet. From what we can tell, all of it is encrypted, so those middlemen probably have no idea what they're handling. And they don't care, because they're paid really well. These folks could be anyone from an executive assistant sitting at a desk all day to a UPS driver. They don't need to understand computers. They just need fingers and hands. And the ability to pull one out and replace it with another.

"Speaking of drivers, these drives—which are about the size of a Pop-Tart—are then placed in overnight bags and sent to one of seven, again for lack of a better word, 'commanders,' who replicate the process. Assimilating dozens of drives into one. I'm sure Frank would like to do away with all these people, but he can't. He's got to keep someone to do his dirty work. Like when someone steals from him. These guys are the heavy, the muscle with guns, and they know where the bodies are buried. Which distances Frank. They collect all their data onto one drive, which is then delivered to Frank. But never by hand or in person. It's always dropped. Frank picks it up in the normal course of his day, and unless you're watching him like a hawk, you'd never notice it. Think magician sleight of hand. It could be taped inside his golf cart. The underside of a massage table. A restaurant bathroom. Tucked inside his dry cleaning. Or room service. The possibilities are endless. Whatever the case, those drives end up in Frank's possession every fourteen days. Which presents him with a problem twice a month."

Camp spoke next. "He has to do something with them."

Bones continued, "And right about here you need to start thinking Fort Knox, because when those seven drives are turned into one, its value is priceless."

Jess again. "But why would he risk just one copy? Fire or tornado or flood or whatever is a real problem if you don't let yourself use the cloud technology."

"Which is why we think he has three, possibly four locations."

BP asked the obvious. "Any idea where they are?"

Bones shook his head. "None whatsoever."

Jess completed his thought. "Needle in a haystack."

"Exactly."

Camp again. "Let's back up. How does he

keep the folks below him from stealing the data themselves? Leveraging it against him?"

"They're cogs in a wheel. The folks at the bottom have no idea what data they're transferring. The folks higher up do know, but they're not about to betray Frank."

"Why?"

"Think about it."

Camp nodded. "He's got something on them."

"Let's say you ran a company, maybe a Fortune 500 company, and someone had detailed video of you sexually abusing a seven-year-old boy. What would you do? My guess is that Frank's seven generals, the ones at the top of the food chain, are not hardened criminals but CEOs and politicians and actors who don't want to go to jail. Prison is not kind to men like that."

Jess again. "Then what motivates him?"

"On the surface, power. Beneath the surface, a deep-seated fear of what you might do to him if you could."

"Sounds exhausting."

"Which is why we think there might be an eighth member of the team. We think he's brought in someone to handle the bookkeeping."

Jess spoke. "You mean an accountant?"

"Exactly."

Jess laughed. "It's how they took down Capone."

"Frank spends his energies keeping his record

179

safe. As long as his record is safe, he's safe. So my theory is if such an accountant exists, Frank uses him like he uses everyone else, and I doubt Frank trusts him. My guess is that he's got something on him and the accountant has to work for Frank or face personal ruin. Or prison. Or worse. It'd fit Frank's modus operandi. Same is true with his generals. Frank only employs people he can manipulate. And the way he does that is to entice and record and then hold that against you while you do what he wants, when he wants, however he wants, for as long as he wants."

Camp again. "Sounds lonely. Doesn't he have an inner circle?"

Bones shook his head. "He is the circle. If our theory is correct, Frank has thousands, even tens of thousands, of files on people around the world. Nicely organized files with detailed videos of their sins. It's his lifeblood, and he will do anything to protect that. We think, given the attempt on Murph's life and the explosion here at Freetown, Frank must have something important on those drives that Summer and Murph lifted off the yacht. Problem is, we don't know what that is. We're hoping you three can help with that. There's the thought that buried somewhere in that data bank is a real-time record of where his people are holding and trafficking people. If we get our hands on that information, and work with law enforcement around the world, we could possibly free not just one but hundreds, maybe even thousands, of sex slaves." Bones snapped his fingers. "Overnight." He paused and then shook his head. "It would be an exodus."

Camp raised a hand. "You've considered the possibility that he must be constantly adding drives. Daisy chains. And he can't risk a corrupted drive, so he continually changes the drives long before they fail. Certainly he can't do this all by himself. He's got to have help."

Oddly, when he said that, Clay looked at him. Then pursed his lips and stared out the window.

Bones responded, "Yes, we have. Which only makes our job that much more difficult."

Camp spoke again. This time I heard his military training. "Not to be Debbie Downer, but have you thought through the logistics of freeing that many people at one time? Like, what will you do with them all? You can't simply set them back on the street, and from what little I've seen, you can't house and rehabilitate them here."

He was right, and I had the same question. Bones nodded. "Working on that. Until then . . . walk first. Then run."

Jess was the next to speak up. "And while we hunt him?"

Bones paused, knowing he had their attention. "Protect those we love." A single shake of his head. "Because he loves no one."

"How do you know so much about him?"

Bones folded his hands. "He's my brother."

BP shook his head. "And I thought my family was screwed up."

"He's a shell of his former self. There is very little resemblance to the kid I knew. I haven't seen him since he tried to kill me."

"Kill you?" Jess asked.

"The world he chose has three enemies: One, law enforcement. But they can't wrap their head around him. They think he's three to six people. So they're constantly looking in the wrong place. Two, his competition. They want their share of the pie. But honestly, they can't hang with him. They don't possess his mental and cognitive abilities, and he's just better. It's like racing Secretariat. You're going to lose. By a lot. Not to mention that he roams invisible and no one will ever find him. He's a chameleon. His third problem is the one he can't outsmart or outhide, and there is only one solution, which he will never accept. Immersion. He's like a man in a gas chamber. There is no corner of the room, or his world, where the air won't kill you. Just breathing is like drinking gasoline. It eats you from the inside out. There's nothing you can do about it. The clock is ticking and he can hear it.

"And before any of you get idealistic . . . there's not a shred of good in him. He loves nothing and no one and alternates between two emotions.

Both of which are insatiable; fear and hatred. He only wants one thing: power. Which gives him control." Bones shrugged. "For the simple reason that we grew up without any."

Camp raised a finger. "How'd you turn out so different?"

Bones smiled. "You're assuming I'm different."

Camp looked around him. "Yes."

Bones shook his head. Maybe the first real look behind the curtain. "I don't know. When I look at my scars, I should be worse."

"If he's such a ghost, how do you know so much? And how come no one has ever caught him?"

"I've spent thousands of hours. I know my opponent. And my brother. Sometimes when he thinks, the thought turns up in my head. I can't explain that."

CHAPTER 15

New York City

The lights of New York City mirrored the sky above it. Too numerous to count. Every time I stared down on the Big Apple, I marveled at the power needed to light it. Fifty floors down, Central Park sprawled like a carpet beneath us. I pressed my face to the glass, wondering if I could feel the building swaying. I could not. On the streets and sidewalks, people and cyclists darted to and fro like ants in a game of chicken with yellow cars.

After the bomb went off in Freetown, Casey's book tour came to an abrupt halt, but the media followed her capture. Her book sales caught fire and shot to the moon. You couldn't ask for better publicity. When Bones found me in that cave and my condition worsened, Casey quit talking altogether. To everyone. Including Angel, Ellie, and Summer. If I didn't make it, they were afraid what she'd do. Bones put her under twenty-four-seven watch—although she didn't know it.

When I opened my eyes, Casey had been standing at the foot of my bed. Dressed in white.

She saw my eyes open, sucked in a breath of air, then let it out. Along with a lot of pain. At the time, I hadn't known she'd been holding both for weeks. Since then, like me, she'd been slow to return to the land of the living. Every morning, aside from Summer and Gunner, she'd been the first to check in on me.

"How's he doing?" or "Race you to the Eagle's Nest?" She was the Energizer Bunny. I was more AARP.

We landed a few hours ago. All of us. To celebrate Casey Girl and the massive achievement that is her book. Multiple weeks at number one. Soon to be several million copies printed. Soon to be printed in over fifty languages and some seventy-five countries. Multiple companies bidding for the chance to make the movie. The world had wrapped their arms around her and, in many ways, Casey had become the voice of the voiceless.

With my return to health, Casey agreed to return to the limelight. Albeit briefly. One showing only.

The venue was standing room only. We came to New York out of necessity because it was simply not feasible to host all these people at Freetown. Too much construction. Everyone wanted to get a glimpse of Casey Girl and her record-breaking book, not to mention her incomparable and unconquerable smile.

My publisher was beaming.

When I was at my lowest, Karen Mixer sat at my bar in Key West. Asked, "What're you writing?" as I scribbled on a pad at the end of the bar. I didn't know it at the time, but Marie had been to see her. Twisted her arm. Karen and I had been friends ever since. When I first agreed to publish, I told her I would do so under one condition: "Nobody ever knows my name. Period." She had agreed and, to her great credit, she'd kept my secret. Especially when so many were willing to pay her a lot of money not to. Together we'd produced a career. Now she was in the process of producing another. Albeit of a different sort. She had pulled out all the stops and all her leverage for Casey. And it had worked.

I stood with my face pressed to the window, watching my breath fog the glass only to dissipate before I fogged it once more. Standing five hundred feet off the earth's face, nothing between me and falling but glass. A kid at the circus. Casey appeared next to me. Watching me. Then she leaned in and began fogging up the glass herself. Standing there with our heads pressed to the glass, she watched the ants below us. "Seems so peaceful from up here."

I nodded.

Casey was one of the smartest people I'd ever met. She rarely small-talked. I waited. "You think he's down there?"

I turned and waited for the remainder of the question.

She studied the streets. "The man who trafficked me?"

I nodded.

She stared back through the window and chose her words. "Is he the same man who blew up Freetown?"

For weeks she'd been hammering me to help find him. Another nod.

"Is he the reason you just returned from Georgia?"

"Yes."

"You know who he is?"

"I do."

"Will you tell me?"

"No."

"You going after him?"

"I am."

She leaned closer. Her shoulder pressed to mine. She had become as much my daughter as Ellie. I saw no difference. Neither did she. "Can I come?"

"No. And not just like 'sort of no,' but 'completely no.'"

"What if you need a translator?" A legitimate question, as Casey spoke a half dozen languages.

"I'll hire one."

"What if you need someone to . . . drag you out of a burning building?"

I pointed at Gunner.

"Funny."

Then at Clay.

She rolled her eyes. "You're really not going to let me help you?"

"Nope."

"What if I can be helpful?"

"I want you free of him, not consumed by him."

"What about you?"

It was a fair question, so I dodged it. "I've been free of him. Now I'm going to bring his playhouse down."

"But consumed?"

I laughed. "One of us has to be."

"That's not fair."

I turned. "Casey . . . don't let him hold you captive from a distance. He's just a man."

She nodded. "And when I close my eyes, I remember what that man did to me." Having voiced her fear, she turned and walked off.

Karen slid her arm in mine. She was skinnier. Pale. Looked as if she'd aged. I wondered if she'd been working too hard. Her arm was trembling slightly. She whispered with a smile, "Before you leave, can I get five minutes?"

"Sure."

"I'd like you to meet someone."

Her mischievous smile betrayed her. "New man in your life?"

She weighed her head side to side as Clay

stepped to the microphone. "Ladies and gentlemen, if I could please have your attention." Clay had survived being blown up and burned over half his body. Undeterred, and with the help of most every woman at Freetown, he'd taught himself to walk again. Not to mention dance. Although I think he could walk long before he actually did. If ever I saw someone milk an injury . . . But given the fact that he'd spent five decades in prison, he'd earned the right. Clay had absolutely no trouble whatsoever being the center of attention.

"Folks, if you'll take your seat." The room hushed as Clay cleared his throat. "I know you all didn't come here to hear me, so I'll be brief." Clay smiled and chose his words. "Prior to the fireworks show at Freetown that got a little out of hand"—laughter rippled across the room— "Casey had educated much of the civilized world on trafficking. On being trafficked. Since that time, she has become the voice of the voiceless. And while she and Ms. Karen have set publishing records, she has done one thing that can never be measured. Maybe more than any other. She's given hope to the hopeless. Speaking as one who was once hopeless, I can attest that there is no value you can place on hope. Please welcome Casey Girl."

Whenever Casey spoke publicly, she never spoke alone. Angel always stood alongside her.

A shoulder against the memories. An arm to hold her when she stumbled. Casey, shadowed by Angel, stepped to the microphone but paused as the applause held her at bay. Summer and I watched in wonder as she stood. Confident. Having shed her shell. Casey had become comfortable in her own skin.

When she did speak, you could hear a pin drop. And she was looking at me. "I was lying on the floor of a shower. Some house in South Florida. Have no memory of how I got there. In the week prior I'd"—Casey held up her fingers like quotation marks—" 'serviced' more than a hundred clients. Which in English means I'd been raped for profit fifteen times a day. One after another. To keep me busy, or rather get the most money for my time, my traffickers had put my available schedule on the dark web. Sold thirty-minute slots. I'm told I was profitable. But that 'profit' "—more quotation marks—"I never saw a dime. Selling flesh is different than selling drugs. Drugs you sell once. Flesh you sell a thousand times over. To help me forget, to transport my mind out of the hell in which my body lived, I did a lot of drugs. Anything I could. Whenever I could. Because of that, I don't know how long I'd been on that ship. A year. Maybe two. Anyway, they brought in some new girls. Fresher. Less mileage. They relegated me to a closet. Truth was, they'd had complaints.

Said I was no longer desirable. Which makes me wonder, what had they done to me that even the worst of the perverted and whacked human beings on the planet couldn't satisfy themselves with what was left of me?"

Casey paused and shook her head. "I know you're here because you have heard my story. Or read it. And you are amazed at what you call my 'courage.' But here's the thing . . . if I tell you my story, like all of it, half of you will throw up. You'll never print it and I will find myself speaking to an empty room because none of you have the stomach for it. I certainly didn't. Hence the drugs. Truth is, I am anything but brave."

Casey studied her hand. "I once 'worked' on a cattle farm, and during a break between clients, I saw a man shoot a horse he'd ridden ten years because the horse had grown old and blind and the cowboy didn't want to pay to feed it." She paused. "They made sure I saw that. The visual served as a deterrent. To make sure I didn't run off.

"So . . . back to the shower. In the tradition of shooting horses, my traffickers fed me a cocktail intended to make my heart explode. Or my brain. Didn't matter to them. Just as long as one did. Then they packed up the desirables, moved the party, and left me . . . on the floor of that shower. So I lay there. Counting the drumbeats in my ear. Just waiting for the boom.

191

"Then I heard a whisper. Felt a body. One of the new girls found me." Casey pointed across her body to Angel. "Pretty girl. They were gushing over her. I'd seen her on the ship and we'd talked. A little. She didn't know it, but they'd posted her picture on the dark web and were hosting an auction. She was forty-eight hours from being air-lifted to the highest bidder—currently a guy in Russia. No one would ever see her again. Take one look at her and you can see why the numbers were impressive." The audience squirmed as they didn't know how to respond. So they didn't.

"I was seconds from eternity. And freedom. She? Just hours from a living hell. One I'd been living. We? Brought together in some sadistic plot." Casey studied the audience. "She knew none of this when she found me in the shower. And for some reason, in the first act of kindness I'd known in . . . years, she stole some ice, a bunch of it, and packed me in it. Talking to me all the time. Telling me to hang in there. 'You're gonna be okay.' I was too high to tell her that I didn't want to be okay. The ice countered the drugs, lowered my heart rate, and kept me alive. When I woke, the ice had melted and I was a Popsicle but somehow still alive. Sort of. Some sort of weird drug-induced coma. Alone. Dying a slow death. No voice. No hope. But I was shivering so hard I thought my teeth would crack, so I climbed out and turned on the shower before fading off again. Somewhere in that haze, I decided I hated all men. And would forever. I knew with my last dying thoughts that nothing would or could change the fact that every time I looked across a room like this and saw men like you, I'd hate every one of you. And so I lay there, using my last breaths to scheme how I'd hurt men if I found any of you alone in a dark room. What I'd cut off. Because in my experience, which, to say the least, was extensive, you're all the same. You're cold, heartless, and you only care about you, which is why men like you would pay so little to do what they did to me."

Nobody moved.

Since I woke up from my Rumpelstiltskin nap, Casey had continued to improve physically. Thanks to Gunner, she'd even quit taking sleeping medication. But emotionally she was not healthy. Having grown stronger, she began fighting the memories she couldn't shake. Memories in which she constantly found herself helpless. And muted. She told us, "It's like drowning every day only to find that someone lets you up long enough to suck in a breath of air just before they shove you down again." She spent a lot of time shooting pistols in my underground range, becoming proficient with several different weapons systems, and had applied for her concealed carry permit. Don't get me wrong—I had encouraged her to do both. I wanted her both to be and to feel empowered to defend herself, but I get a little squirmy when the driving motivation is hatred bordering on rage.

And possibly revenge.

Some might cry foul and suggest that's like the pot calling the kettle black. I won't argue. For me there can be, and has been, a fine line between rescue and revenge. And to be honest, I'm not sure I can always tell you where one ends and the other begins.

Her tone changed. "I watched a TED Talk last week where a computer hacker attended a conference—of the media. Many of you were there. He used your Bluetooth connection to hack your phones. What he found was consistent with the rest of the male population—over half of you have a daily porn addiction. Yet you argue you're not hurting anybody. No big deal. Just a little peeky-boo. Nobody's the wiser. But in economics you are creating what is called 'demand.' And throughout the history of the world, wherever demand exists, someone meets it with what is called 'supply.'" Casey pointed to herself. "I.e., me."

She paused to let that sink in. "I am supply. But it doesn't end there. What starts as a porn addiction becomes pay-to-see. Then pay-to-experience. But that, too, gets old, and the pay-to-experience that used to satisfy no longer does. So now you pay-to-experience someone younger. Someone fresher. Soon the age drops. From eighteen to sixteen. Then fourteen. Twelve. Ten." Casey studied the room. Most everyone had grown uncomfortable. "A wise man once told me that a man with a theory can never argue against a man with experience. I have seen with my two eyes 'normal' men like you satisfy themselves with five- and six-year-old boys and girls. If that's not enough, they then posted the videos on the dark web and sold them so other miscreants could gorge on their carnage."

Silence.

"Do I make you uncomfortable? Oh, I'm sorry. I thought you wanted me to tell the truth."

She continued, "So there I was. Floor of the shower. Content to hate men forever. No problem. With whatever life I had left, I was going to live it hating men like you." Casey shook her head. Tears appeared. "Then I heard this voice. Through the steam. And if I'm honest, the last thing I wanted was to hear a man's voice. For a man to save me. To be beholden to a man. Men did this to me. I was lying in that shower, shot full of enough heroin to kill a moose because some man valued himself over me. But he wasn't the only one. Two days prior, they had marked me 'half price.' I remember seeing a line of men out the door. All of whom valued themselves more than me. Otherwise, why were they in that line?"

Her voice softened. "But then I felt these arms beneath me. I'd known enough men to know that these were a man's arms. More often than not, arms like these had pinned me down. Beaten me. Shoved my face into the wall. Or dirt. Or . . . caused me to do what I did not want. But not these arms. These arms were rocks. But . . . tender rocks. They lifted me. Carried me. And while this man was carrying me, I was thinking to myself that the one thing I hated most in the world, a man stronger than me, just rescued me. What's worse, I'll probably live because of this idiot. What's a girl got to do to get a break around here?

"And if that's not bad enough, when I asked him, 'Why?' he told me something I'd long failed to believe. Couldn't believe. He said"— her voice cracked—"'Because you're worth rescue.' I thought he was talking about somebody else. Maybe that new girl. Maybe he'd gotten us confused. Maybe her family had spent a bunch of money to get her back. But he kept carrying me. And he carried me out of hell. Then he got me help. Cleaned me up. Sat with me. Asked nothing of me. Took nothing from me. Moved me someplace safe. Where nobody can hurt me. And when I got there, I found a family that tended my wounds. Both outside and in. Then, because he was once someone who needed to heal, he gave me a pen and told me to 'tell the truth.'

"Somehow I found I had a voice. What's more, he wanted to hear what I had to say. I thought he'd lost his ever-loving mind. Are you kidding me? Why would he want to listen to anything I had to say? Yet he did. Every word. And somewhere in that fog of remembrance and creation, I turned around and looked in my cracked rearview and I found he'd done the one thing I believed no one could ever do. Certainly no man." The words were long in coming. "He had restored my hope."

She waved her hand across the room. "As evidenced by the fact that all of you are sitting there staring at me." A pause while she read their faces. "But now I have this problem. I can't hate all men, because he is one of you. No, he's the best of all of you. And—" She stepped to the side, pulled Clay onto the podium with her, and stood locked arm in arm. Angel on one side. Clay on the other. "Then he gave me Clay." Clay had become the face of Casey's security. Even now, walking with a cane and nursing his own burns, he stood chest puffed. Swinging his cane like a sword. The media were eating out of his hand. Casey pointed to Bones. Dressed in a suit yet wearing his collar. "Then he gave me Bones." Finally, not to be left out, Gunner jumped up onstage and, standing on two legs, put his paws on the podium, tongue dangling, tail wagging. Gunner had become the face of Freetown and his applause was louder than Clay's.

Casey laughed, but her tone was still slightly acidic to those whose ears were attuned to listen. "My world is now full of men who are nothing like those I knew, and I would trust all of me to any of them."

Clay sat back down and Gunner returned to Ellie's side. "That said, the soul is like Velcro, and when you brush up against someone else, especially when there are no clothes to separate you, part of you clings to them and part of them clings to you. Soon you find yourself carrying pieces of souls that you don't want and don't want you. But you can't help it. It's like being handcuffed to a stranger on the subway and your stop never comes."

She pointed to her book. "In your hands you hold the story of who I was. Casey Girl. Now I'm trying to figure out who I am. And yet, when I close my eyes, the faces return. The countless men. Twenty-four-seven, they play like a slideshow across my eyelids. I want to be me, whoever that is, but I'm left carrying them. I spend my days trapped inside memories I don't want with people I don't want and who don't want me." She shook her head. "The farther I travel from that hell and the healthier I become, the more my memory returns, and the more clearly I see. You should know that I'm approaching twenty-twenty. My question is this: What do I do with all those who gave so little and stole so much? What do I do with these men who live rent-free in my mind? Am I not of value? Do you not see me?"

The room was silent.

"A few weeks ago, we were talking. Me and the one who rescued me. He heard this bitter tone that you now hear in me, and he told me again, 'Write it down. Tell the truth. Let it out.' When I asked why, he pointed at my chest. 'This thing you're holding on to—this rage—is the poison we drink thinking it'll kill someone else.' So . . . once again, I am. Reminding me that those men stole pieces of my soul, and I want my pieces back." Casey paused. Making eye contact with many in the room. "Why? Because in the blurred edges of my mind, I remember . . . I'm a daughter. A friend. One day I'd like to be a wife and—if my body can—a mom." Casey was whispering now. "It's my love letter to the me I used to be. And to all those like me."

With that, Casey turned, and both she and Angel exited the stage as the salivating press jumped to their feet and applauded.

Karen watched Casey with admiration, only to whisper in my ear, "She's a publisher's dream." Karen shot a glance at me. "Almost as dreamy as you." She half smiled, then shook her head once and looked away. Staring out the window. Central Park. After a pause, she said, "I wish . . ." Karen trailed off and disappeared into the crowd.

I kept to the shadows while Casey signed books and posed for pictures. Women of all ages, and even many men, stood in a long line for just five seconds with Casey. Ever at her side stood her support team: Summer, Angel, and Clay.

Not to mention Gunner.

CHAPTER 16

An hour into the signing and picture frenzy, Karen found me in the corner. Overwatch. "Got a second?"

I followed her. Down one hallway. Along another. Through an open glass atrium and then through two huge oak doors and into the executive office of suites, where I found a young woman sitting on the floor playing Legos with a small boy. Karen sat next to the boy and watched the imaginary Star Wars world being constructed. Gunner followed me in, saw his opportunity, and seized it, licking both the woman and the boy. The kid retreated to Karen, and the girl laughed and petted Gunner, who got what he wanted. Karen sat the boy on her lap and wrapped her arms around him. He was six. Maybe seven. Small for his size. His eyes scanned the room, landing nowhere, and the vein on the side of his head told me his heart was beating fast. I knelt, picking up the now-trampled Star Wars figure, and pieced him back together, snapping the lightsaber to the hand. Then I handed Luke Skywalker to the boy.

The boy didn't move.

I placed Lego Luke in Karen's hand and she

offered it to the boy. Slowly, his hand accordioned out of his chest, grasped the action figure, and retreated once again to the safety of the space between himself and Karen. She combed his blond hair with her fingers and spoke. "Murph . . . I'd like you to meet my son." Karen looked up at me, then back at the boy. "His name is Shep."

The name was not lost on me. I extended my hand. "Hi, Shep."

He didn't respond.

"You like Star Wars?" The boy's eyes darted to me, then back to the pile of Legos on the floor.

I picked up Obi Wan Kenobi and Chewbacca and pieced them back together as the boy watched my hands. The girl next to me, midtwenties, whispered, "I'm Nat." She pointed to Karen. "Her assistant and"—she smiled—"new nanny." Her body language told me she was equally pleased with both job descriptions, and maybe the latter slightly more than the former. Karen's office was a memorial to the work she and I had done. Awards. Number of copies sold. Foreign editions. Language translations. My own private museum. Interestingly, I gathered Nat had no idea that I'd authored all of the books displayed in glass cases on Karen's wall. Which meant Karen had kept our secret. Even from those closest to her. Which brought me back to the boy.

His eyes were laser-glued to my hands as I set Obi Wan and Chewy inside the *Millennium*

Falcon, seating them next to Han Solo. Finally, I set it down on the floor next to his feet. "Good enough for another Kessel Run in twelve parsecs."

His eyes flickered to me, then back to the spaceship.

Having thoroughly mopped up Nat's face, Gunner moved on to Shep, who tucked his face in Karen's arms. Karen stood, handed Shep to Nat, and said, "Give us a few minutes?"

Nat and Shep disappeared into Karen's executive lounge, along with Gunner, where I heard a cartoon playing.

I waited.

Karen walked to the glass and stared down. Her back to me. "You remember the girl you rescued out of Nicaragua?"

"Ines Cecilia."

Karen nodded. "Remember the 'orphanage'?"

"I remember the smell."

Karen glanced at Shep then turned to me. "How long have we been working together?"

I smiled. "All my life."

She turned but this time didn't look down. She studied the skyline. "Two years ago, I started the process. Orphanage in Russia. Paperwork, interviews, money, attorneys. Then a week after they found you alive in that cave, I got the call. Flew over." She paused. "He grew up in a cage. Didn't walk until he was four.

"I'm not married." She said it with honest self-deprecation. "Have no prospects. What man could put up with me? I don't sleep. Work way too much. And yet"—she turned so she could see Shep—"I love that little guy with . . ." She turned to me. "I should have asked. I hope you don't mind. I mean, about the name."

"It's a good name. He wears it well."

"I just wanted you two to meet." Another pause. I couldn't tell if it was purposeful on her part or inflicted upon her by the emotions. Or something else. "I've been thinking of taking . . ." A laugh. "Did you know that in the last twenty years, I've not taken a single day of vacation? I've been thinking of doing that. Thought maybe we'd come to Freetown. Let you show him around. He—" She paused. Looked at me. "Will need good men. Since I know so few."

Something in her tone struck me as off, but I also knew her experience with men had been difficult and she'd not always chosen wisely. "I'll send the plane."

She brushed away a tear, patted my hand, and said nothing.

I'd never seen her so frail. "Anything you need, you know that."

She whispered, "Thank you."

"You okay?"

"Yeah. Midfifties and a first-time mom. Maybe a little overwhelmed." She shot a glance at him. "Don't want to mess it up."

I watched him fly the *Falcon* through the space. "I know of nothing more resilient than a child."

She shook her head once. "Even broke up with my one love affair."

Karen loved few things more than a good cigarette. "Say it ain't so."

"Four months, three days, seventeen hours."

"That can't be easy."

"It's nothing compared to being responsible for that little guy." As we studied him, another tear formed in her eyes. This was not my publisher speaking but the mom my publisher had become, which was beautiful to watch. "He's so small. I'm afraid people will make fun of him. And they say he might never talk." The words were difficult to speak. "Six years old and never held. What kind of world is this . . ." She trailed off. "Even when they fed him, they did so through the bars of his cage." She fought for the words. "What if . . . I can't reach him? What if . . . he won't ever hug me back?"

"Hey . . . give it time." I put my arm around her. "I've seen love do amazing things."

She leaned into me and cried. Allowing me to hold her. Something she'd never done. She looked up at me. "Can it reach through bars?"

I smiled. "Yes. It's actually really good at that."

She palmed her face. "I should've asked you about the name thing."

"I'm honored. He even looks like a Shep."

The noise down the hall returned her thoughts to Casey. "We'd better get back."

Even blown up, burnt half to death, and walking with a cane, Clay was enjoying the spotlight and, along with a little help from Bones, had the security situation covered. When I returned to the room, the line had shrunk to the last few people, and Casey was standing next to the table rather than behind it. A guy dressed in all black but wearing press credentials and carrying a camera bag stood tapping his foot. His face told me he wasn't a fan. Which made me wonder why he'd stood in line for more than an hour. Summer got my attention, nodded at the guy, and then shrugged when she pointed at Clay. As if to say, "I'm not sure he can handle it and Bones is on the wrong side of the table." I stepped closer, watching the guy's hands. When his turn arrived, he stepped onto the platform and just a little too close to Casey. I mirrored him from behind while not interfering. At least, not yet.

His tone was acidic and his smirk concealed something. "I didn't like the way you talked to us." He waved his hand across the men around him. "And unlike these perverts, I don't have a porn addiction."

Casey stood unfazed. "Can I see your phone?"

He shook his head arrogantly. "Not a chance."

Casey dismissed him. "You're hiding."

He didn't like being called out.

Bones eased closer.

Casey was locked on the man and she was unflinching. "Your eyes betray you."

Without warning, the guy reached into his backpack and pulled out what looked like a can of spray paint. Turned out to be pepper spray that backpackers use on grizzly bears. As he extended his arm, he said, "How much for thirty minutes?"

I launched and was about to dislocate his arm from his shoulder when something moving very fast flashed in front of me. I never saw it coming. It whiffed in front of my face like an airplane propeller. I felt a swish of air and then heard the distinct sound of bone snapping. At which point the punk fell to his knees and began writhing and cussing. No sooner had he fallen than the blurry fast thing again made a circle in front of me, followed by the unnatural sound of smashing teeth. The guy coughed, spat out pieces of teeth, and was in the process of uttering something unkind when the blurry thing whiffed again and turned out his lights.

The guy crumpled in a pile as all the media around him stood in silent shock. All quiet on the western front.

Bones and I stood over the man. His arm had a new elbow, his face was swollen, and one eye was shut. Not to mention his toothless grin. When I looked at Casey, I saw that Clay had stepped in front of her. A shield. No longer leaning on his cane. He now held it like a baseball bat.

I asked him, "You all right, Clay?"

He spoke calmly but never took his eyes off the idiot on the floor. "Yes, sir, Mister Murphy. Just fine."

I examined the unconscious man. "Clay, what's in that cane?"

Clay showed me the end, exposing the iron rod that ran the length of the cane.

"How much that thing weigh?"

Clay shrugged. "Nine pound."

That explained it.

Bones shook his head. "You can take the man out of prison, but it's a little tougher to take prison out of the man."

Clay sucked through his teeth and nodded, saying nothing while saying everything. As I studied him, I realized he wasn't even sweating. Clay was getting healthy and his strength was returning.

Following the signing, Karen had rented a private room at the restaurant on the top floor. It was a special moment. Summer holding my hand. Gunner at our feet. Bones and Clay telling competing stories while Casey, Angel, and Ellie laughed. Life was good. Summer leaned in and wrapped her ankle around mine like a vine, which had become her custom. She placed her hand on my chest and whispered, "You good?"

"Honestly?"

She nodded.

"I don't know if I've ever been this good in my whole life."

She kissed me. "Me too."

Bones looked at me and then nodded at Karen's empty chair. "Want to call her?"

"She said she just had to do one thing."

We waited a few more minutes and Bones again looked at the empty chair. I dialed Karen but no answer. Which was not unusual. A few minutes later, I told Summer, "Be right back."

I rode the elevator down to the fifty-fifth floor and wound my way to her office, where I found the door cracked open but no sound of a nanny and no sound of Shep. Gunner walked around me to a far corner of the room and stood whining.

Over Karen's body.

CHAPTER 17

The waiting room was empty save us. The sounds of monitors and alarms and a ticking clock above me were little comfort. None of us talked but rather sat staring at the doors leading to the trauma center. Willing the surgeon to exit with good news.

An hour after we arrived, the doctor walked out and took off his mask. "You Murphy Shepherd?"

His green scrubs were covered in red puree. "I am."

"Karen's final directive says I'm to speak with you. And only you. You comfortable with all these people hearing what I have to say?"

I nodded.

He shook his head. "I'm sorry."

Summer wrapped her arm around mine as I tried to digest this. "What . . . ?"

"She didn't make it."

How could this be possible? We were just talking. She was a new mom. Just adopted Shep. A whole new life in front of her.

He continued, "Cerebral aneurysm." A pause. "I know it doesn't help, but she did not suffer. Never knew it was happening."

I could not process this. It made no sense.

"Would you like to see her?"

The lights were bright and the room cold. All the monitors had been turned off and medical personnel were working to clean the room, which was not clean.

Karen lay on the table, her body covered by a sheet. Someone had wiped the blood from her nose but not her cheek. I stood next to the table, and Summer stood next to me.

Karen's hand was still warm.

I didn't know what to say.

Summer leaned in and whispered, "Just talk to her."

I swallowed. The memories flooding. How did we get from that bar twenty years ago to this room? I held her hand in both of mine. "You were a friend . . . when I didn't have any. You believed in me when I didn't. You kept me alive . . . when I didn't want to live." I shook my head. "You made me . . . me."

I could see her sitting at the bar. Sunglasses. Martini. Cigarette in hand. I didn't know it at the time, but she would change my life forever following that moment. She alone was the reason I published. That I made more money than I could spend in several lifetimes.

Summer kissed my cheek and locked her arm inside mine.

I tried to speak again but could not.

Summer held my hand while I held Karen's. I tried again. "Without you, there is no Freetown. No Murphy Shepherd. No . . . David . . ." I whispered, "Bishop."

Bones appeared across from me. Ashen.

The pain in my chest was growing and I couldn't shut it down. Couldn't escape it. I leaned over and kissed Karen on her now-cold forehead.

The waiting room had filled with distraught people. Including Karen's assistant, Nat, who stood hugging Clay. She, too, was a mess. A tired Shep crouched in a corner clinging to a worn tiger–teddy bear thing and a dirty blanket. Something I guessed had made the trip from Russia to here. Something normal. He sat expressionless.

Nat stood leaning further into Clay, her shoulders shaking.

How do you make sense of the nonsensical? Explain the inexplicable? I don't know. I can't. She was here. Now she wasn't. And how in the world could we help a six-year-old boy understand this?

Nat composed herself, wiped her face, and approached Summer and me. She was clutching an envelope but hesitant to give it to me. When she did, she said, "We should probably go somewhere quiet."

Summer, Nat, and I retreated to the chapel

where she extended the letter. "At Karen's request."

The envelope read "David." And had been written in Karen's handwriting, which, after her having edited so many of my books, I knew quite well.

I unfolded the letter.

Dearest David—

After so many years of calling you Murph, David seems strange, but you are both to me—which is good. You've always been twice the man of any man I ever knew.

If you're reading this, then the "thing" in my head must have broken loose and I am gone. They will probably call it some sort of aneurysm and I am sure my doctors will tell you more about it, but it was inoperable, making me a walking time bomb. Writing you this letter, I have but one regret—that I didn't learn about it sooner.

I remember our first meeting. You were tending bar. A shell. A broken man. Wishing the earth would open up, swallow you whole, and bury you alongside Marie, and yet somehow you managed to do something with your pen that I, in all my years of publishing, had never seen.

From the first page, I knew you were the one. Maybe the only one. I would have given anything to publish you, and yet you were so easy on me. In all my professional life, I have loved nothing more than giving your beautiful, innocent, powerful words to the world. To this day I don't know how you do it. How you string them together and suck us all in.

I used to get so excited when I'd open my email and find your manuscript sitting unread in my inbox. I'd sit down and relish every word. The first of your fans to read the new work before anyone else. A delectable luxury. I'd usually read it two or three times before I came up for air. I am and always will be your biggest fan. Self-nominated president of the club. For years I'd scratch my head and wonder, *Where do these words come from? What power drives them?* I'm a tough New York City girl with an acrid experience with men, but I am not so jaded that I cannot conclude there can be only one answer. Love. And not the kind we see sold around us. The kind played out on the screen and through the airwaves. I'm talking about the real kind. The kind that, in your words, leaves the ninety-nine to find the one. Oh, how I needed that. How many times did your words rescue me and return me from the brink? I cannot count.

Like the boys and girls you rescue, I did not have a good experience with men. Hated them, actually. Always taking. Never giving. I closed off my heart years ago. Let it become covered and callous. Prided myself on being so impregnable. "You can't touch me." But then I "discovered" you tending bar. I must admit I read your words that night with a bit of skepticism. You can't be this true. This beautiful. Magnificent. Unassuming.

And yet you are. And your words . . . oh my. Your words reached down into a place in me that I'd closed off long ago. Unlike my history, you gave and took nothing. You defied my every experience.

And for that I'm forever grateful. For that I love you. For that I will always love you.

Which is why I'm writing this letter. This is going to catch you off guard, but I'm asking you to dig down into that love of yours one more time and do something for me. It's a big ask. I know. But one thing I've noticed about you—as the number of people you carry has grown, your shoulders have only broadened, and your heart . . . well, it's bottomless.

I am giving Shep to you. To be his father. I know of no better. I am asking you and Summer to make him your own and raise him with the same love with which you love one another—and have loved a crusty cynic like me. Had I known about my possible aneurysm, I would not have adopted him. But I didn't start having seizures and blurry vision until my return. Incidentally, my doctor said the long flight over and back probably brought about its early onset. Ironic, don't you think?

Shep is now alone. Again. He's been abandoned by everyone he's ever known. Including me. I realize what I'm asking you will be an uphill battle. I know this. He has night terrors, wets his bed constantly, eats little, and communicates almost not at all. Attached to this letter is my Last Will and Testament. You will find in there that I have given him everything that is mine and given you control over all that. To help you in whatever way you need. Not that you need the money. But it's there if you ever do.

I may not have given birth to him, but a strange thing has happened in the few months that we've had each other. He stole my heart and made me feel like a mom.

Something I thought could never happen.

Because he was afraid, I have let him sleep with me at night. Every night. And every morning, I've had to change the sheets. But often at night when he shook and kicked and screamed, his tiny little hand would reach through the covers and find mine. Completely asleep and yet reaching out. I think that's what broken hearts do.

You showed me that.

My mama heart tells me he needs a father. Now more than ever. Please. Please do this for me.

One more thing. One day, when you tell him the story of me—as I know only you can—please tell him that I love him with my whole heart and the greatest joy of my life was being his mom even if just for a few short months.

I love you.

Yours always,

Karen

P.S. It's probably too soon for this, but I have been, am now, and always will be your publisher, and you need to hear it: there's never been one like you, and I highly doubt there will be when you're gone. The world needs your words.

David—the world needs your words.

Don't keep them all to yourself. And don't let my death silence them. They have rescued countless millions.

Like me.

CHAPTER 18

I sat with the letter. Reading. And rereading. Summer sat quietly. Shoulder to shoulder. Her heart was hurting too.

When we returned to the waiting room, I handed the letter to Bones and found Shep crumpled in the corner, eyes closed but not asleep. Gunner lay on the ground next to him, watching him.

I have little experience with little people, but my guess is that he was trying to keep the world from hurting him anymore, and closing his eyes was his only weapon. I sat on the floor next to him and just waited. Sensing me next to him, he opened his eyes, blinked a dozen times, scanned the room, noticed everyone huddled around Bones reading the letter, and then took in the lights and all the sounds and beeps and monitor alarms down the hall. Then his eyes darted to me, flickered around the room once again, and finally returned to me. Surprisingly, he whispered, "I don't belong here." It struck me as I listened to his beautiful words that, in all my life, in over two hundred fifty rescues, I'd never seen some-one more afraid. Or more alone on planet Earth.

I patted my lap. "It's okay." When he didn't

move, I extended my arms, and he let me lift him so I sat him on my lap. He leaned his head against my chest, and I could feel his heart beating. I counted. One hundred fifty beats a minute. Gunner laid his head across my legs.

As I held him, Summer sat alongside me. Followed by Casey, Angel, and Ellie. Then Clay and Bones. When they did, I heard my own echo: *Love shows up.*

I wrapped an arm around him, held his hand in mine, and whispered, "I know, buddy. Me too."

I had asked the doctor if I could escort Karen's body to the morgue. She had no family. No siblings. No ex-husband. She had her work, she had Shep, and she had me. I didn't want her to go there alone. When the doctor returned, he beckoned and Bones and I followed. I rolled her out of the now-sterile trauma room, down a long hallway, and into an elevator that took us down. On the bottom floor, the door opened and I pushed her the length of another long hallway and through two large electronic doors labeled Morgue. The doctor stepped aside and spoke reverently. "Take all the time you need," he said, leaving us alone in the empty wing.

The temperature gauge on the wall read fifty degrees, and as the large doors closed behind us, I felt a page turn. In my mind I saw "The End."

Bones pulled a vial of oil from his pocket,

dabbed his fingers, and touched her forehead. Making the sign of the cross. His voice was little more than a whisper. "In the name of the Father . . . the Son . . ."

As Bones prayed, the slideshow played across my mind's eye. All the images of our life together. A minute later, Bones whispered, "Father, into your care we release your daughter Karen . . ." Then he pulled the sheet back over her face.

Silence blanketed the room—until, from an unlit corner, an indifferent voice sounded, tinged with sarcasm. "It's probably for the best."

Bones turned and folded his hands. Staring into the darkness. Saying nothing.

The voice sounded again, its owner crawling out of the shadows. He shook his head but there was no feeling in it. "Shame about Karen."

Bones didn't move. "I wondered when you'd show."

"Oh." The man waved his hand across the room. "I wouldn't miss this for the world." He pointed at Karen. "The woman who discovered"—he pointed at me—"David Bishop. Put him on the map."

Bones's tone was measured. "Why?"

The man stepped closer. A slight limp. His amber eyes flickering like two candles. His face a mirror image of Bones's. He wore black robes and the collar of a priest. He glanced at Karen, then me, and shrugged dismissively. "Why not?"

My mind raced to assemble the pieces. A half second later, they clicked into place.

Frank.

He stepped even closer, only the table separating us. Staring down at Karen, he ripped the sheet off her now chalky white body. Exposing her, dead and naked. He studied her. "Amazing what modern medicine can do these days." He placed his hand on her head and tapped her temple with his index finger. "How it can mask itself. Make one thing look like another." When he spoke, he was looking at me. "Although"—he shrugged as a smile spread, and then he tapped his heart—"this one worked much faster."

I leaned onto my toes, a half second from pouncing, when Bones put his hand on my arm and pointed to the shadows where I found the muzzle of a suppressed MK4 pointed at my chest. The red laser was visible and held at my sternum. Bones never took his eyes off his brother. "What do you want?"

The man was a strange mixture of masculine with touches of the effeminate, and he alternated with ease between both. "I'm surprised you have to ask."

"I wasn't really asking."

Frank laughed. "Same thing I've always wanted."

"You have everything you need."

Frank sucked through his teeth, nodding. "God

has been very good to me, yes. But everything?" He raised a single finger into the air. "Hmm?" His robes were immaculate. He gestured to me, letting his eyes walk up and down me. "You taught him well."

Bones didn't take the bait. "I'm surprised you still believe."

Frank laughed and adjusted his collar. "My hypocrisy knows no bounds."

Bones pressed him. "Why'd you do it?"

Frank glanced at me. Then Karen. Then back at me. "Simple. I enjoy watching him suffer." Another feigned smile. "And he is so predictable and such a glutton for punishment. It reminds me . . . of you."

Frank shifted his weight. Bones didn't even blink. "How's the hip?"

"Oh, that." Frank waved him off. "Let's just say it keeps you on my mind." Frank beckoned to the man in the shadows who slowly stepped forward. Wearing a dark shirt and dark suit, he was shorter than me but stockier. Catlike in step and reflexes, he stood more tree trunk than man. He had almost no neck as his head seemed to grow out of the muscles that comprised his shoulders, and several tattoos climbed up his neck and out along both wrists. Finger resting on the trigger, the man leveled the rifle and never took his eyes off me. He was calm and not the least bit threatened. "Bishop, I would introduce you, but"—

he tapped his left rib cage—"you've already met."

The man bowed ever so slightly but made no facial expression whatsoever. The rhythmic pulse of the vein on his temple suggested his resting heart rate was in the low forties.

So that's who pulled the trigger. I'll bet the same guy blew up my boat.

Frank continued, "So, about that—"

Bones shook his head and began pulling the sheet back across Karen's body. Adjusting the wrinkles. "Just can't let it go, huh?"

Frank shook his head once. "Not likely." Then he snapped his fingers. "Oh, and nice work on *Sonshine*. Impressive." He pulled a mint out of his pocket, unwrapped it, and stuck it in his mouth. "I watched it live with some close friends. Felt like I was watching a UFC fight. It made for great entertainment."

Bones chuckled. "You don't have any friends."

Frank looked at me and waved his brother off. "The way you carried those boys. And kept coming back." He shook his head. "Reminded me of . . ." he studied the ceiling. "A hospital somewhere."

Frank was trying to get a rise out of me, and he was close to getting it. He clapped his hands together and looked at Bones. "Well, Brother, last chance." He held up his gloved hands. They were black leather. "The gloves are off. I'm coming at what you love."

Bones hadn't taken his eyes off Karen. "You haven't worn gloves since Brazil."

The memory stopped Frank, who smiled and nodded.

Bones continued, "And you've been coming at what I love for twenty years."

In a flash the speed of which I'd seldom, if ever, seen, Frank struck at his brother. The blow was the most difficult to see coming—straight on. This was no haymaker. No hook. No upper-cut. This was a punch intended to remove all of Bones's teeth from his mouth. But in matching speed, Bones's left hand came up and caught the punch. Doing so caught Frank off guard and off balance as his weight was moving forward, so Bones used that, pulling his brother to him. As he did, the laser moved from my chest to his. Bones registered the red dot and let go of his brother's hand. But in a move that matched or exceeded Frank's speed, Bones ripped the collar from around Frank's neck. Judging from the look in Frank's eyes, he'd not thought that possible.

Frank raised both eyebrows and nodded. "Nicely done."

Above us, alarms sounded. Followed by sirens. Frank smiled. "I tend to think you'll change your mind."

At some point it occurred to me that this entire exchange was a head fake. Frank was buying time, keeping us occupied while his goons worked upstairs.

I turned to Bones. "Watch my back."

He smiled. "Always."

I bolted for the door and bypassed the elevator in favor of the stairs, bounding two and three at a time. Exiting onto the main floor, I found myself surrounded by a sea of screaming people, girls crying, and a puddle of blood followed by drag marks that led out the main entrance. I searched the room but recognized no one. Following the smeared blood on the floor, I ran through the main entrance where a group of people huddled around a body. In the center, a head taller than everyone else, stood Clay. A bloody cane leaning on his right shoulder like Babe Ruth's bat. In his other hand he held an automatic weapon like the one that had just been pointed at me in the morgue. At his feet lay a man who used to have a nose. Better said, he used to have a face. And judging by the blood covering his groin, and the blood on Gunner's muzzle, the man used to have something else. Casey, Angel, and Ellie stood in a circle around Summer, who was sitting on a bench clutching Shep and rocking back and forth. Summer's nose was bleeding, one eye was swollen, her lip was cut, and her clothes were torn. Shep sat unmoving. Devoid of emotion.

All looked to be shaken but alive.

I knelt next to Summer. "You okay?"

She nodded, but there was little comfort in it.

I turned to Clay. "What happened?"

"You and Bones escorted Miss Karen downstairs. 'Bout the time the elevator close"—with his toe Clay nudged the guy on the ground, who moaned but didn't move—"this dumb fool show up waving this thing around." He lifted the automatic weapon. "He told Mrs. Summer to let go the boy or he was gone blow her face off. She told him she wasn't 'bout to let go the boy, and so he started beating her. At which point I introduced him to my cane and your dog." He nodded toward Shep and his voice lowered. "They were here for the boy."

"They?"

"There were two. The second ran, but not before I broke his left arm above the wrist and his right collarbone." He thought for a second. "And I might have gotten a few of his teeth." Clay was bad news with that cane. He shrugged. "Prison justice."

My mind was swirling. *How did they know about Shep so quickly?*

Within moments, the place was crawling with police, a SWAT team, and enough flashing lights to entertain a circus. I sat with Summer a few minutes, answering questions and making sure she and the girls were okay.

That's about when it hit me. Bones.

I studied the crowd. Bones was not here.

I launched myself off the bench, through the doors, down the stairs, and back into the much colder air of the morgue where I'd last stood with Bones as we faced his brother and the miscreant who'd shot me.

The room was empty, save Karen's body.

Written in black ink on the sheet that covered her face, someone had left the words, "I'll be in touch." Wrapped up in its own straps lay Bones's shoulder holster containing his Sig. Across the room, near the shadows, I found a single spent 5.56 shell casing. Bones had been shot and disarmed. His Sig was something he would not have given up willingly.

I fell to my knees. Bones was gone. I'd failed him. Based on twenty-plus years of doing life with Bones, my guess was that he saw what was happening and made a move to distract Frank and his assassin. Buying us time. Buying me time.

I saw no sign of a struggle and no blood until I opened the back door that led out of the hospital and found handwriting on the wall. Written in blood at knee level—which meant Bones must have written it from his back. I studied them, but the characters were indecipherable.

I took a picture because I knew Bones was trying to tell me something, but no matter how I studied it, I could not decipher the code. The larger question, for which I had no answer, was more difficult to stomach.

PART 2

CHAPTER 19

Day 1 Without Bones

We landed just after noon. I spent the flight staring at Bones's empty seat. His orange Pelican case resting right where he left it. I was spinning and felt like I was walking around without a heart in my chest. No matter how I tried, I could not wrap my head around how I'd failed him. How I'd let them take him. How I'd not thought it through. How did I not see that coming? Why did I leave him? Why didn't he come with me? I thought he'd been right behind me.

Summer tried to comfort me, but she knew I was hurting and words wouldn't help.

Shep slept in my lap for most of the flight. Just prior to touchdown, I felt warm liquid seeping into my clothes and lap. A lot of warm liquid. Draining down my legs. A moment later, Shep woke, realized he'd peed all over me, and began shaking. Afraid to look at me. I pretended to just be waking up. I smiled. "Hey, big guy. How'd you sleep?"

He didn't respond. He was shaking so hard his teeth were chattering.

"You all right?"

No response. I appeared to "just realize" my clothes were wet. When he realized that I realized what he'd already realized, he began to whimper slightly. Twitching. I tried not to react. "Hey, no big deal. I don't really like flying either. You hungry?"

He looked at me like I'd lost my mind.

Summer opened the door. I stood, picking Shep up with me, and tried not to cringe as one bladder's worth of pee descended down my pants and into my shoes. Exiting the plane, the air was cooler. He was still shaking. "You cold?"

Still no response.

Summer handed me a blanket and I wrapped it around him as we walked into the private airport. Minutes later, she and Shep returned from the bathroom where she'd gotten him changed into dry clothes. He was afraid to look at me and clutching his tiger to brace against the blow his experience told him was coming.

I knelt. "Can I tell you a secret?"

Still no eye contact.

"Just between us." I leaned in and lowered my voice to a whisper. "I wet the bed sometimes too."

He shot me a glance.

"You can ask Mama Summer."

Summer looked down at me. Primarily for the "Mama Summer" label. But also for the lie I'd just told. Not wanting to make a bigger deal of it, I began walking to the parking lot. Shep was uncertain. Should he follow? Stand still? Gunner nudged him, and the two of them walked along behind me. Tiger in tow. I continued, "It's true. I got sho—" I was in the process of lifting my shirt to show him the scar caused by the exiting crossbow bolt when Summer caught my attention. The look on her face said, "What do you think you're doing?" So I rethought my decision-making paradigm. Something she was good at. "I mean, a few months ago, I got sho—short of breath and real sick. Had to stay in bed like two months, and I peed in my bed every night and every day. Several times a day." I shrugged it off. "Sometimes it just happens." It wasn't a complete lie. I just didn't explain the whole bit about doing so through a catheter. What I said was true. From a certain perspective.

The look on his face told me he'd never heard this about an adult. That it was possible. Or that an adult would admit that it was. His face also suggested he wasn't sure what to do with this revelation.

Over the next several minutes, he quit shaking, his teeth stopped chattering, and he released his death clutch on his tiger. Halfway across the parking lot, Gunner circled Shep, sniffed him, then slowed alongside and nudged him with his shoulder. Shep studied Gunner, then extended his right hand and hooked a finger inside Gunner's collar.

CHAPTER 20

G unner lay flat on his stomach, paws out, tail wagging, nose pointed at the plate. Saliva dripping out his mouth.

"We need to talk."

He did that forward tilt thing with his ears and whined slightly.

"I need you to do something for me."

Gunner's eyes darted from the steak, to me, and back to the steak.

"No, I'm serious. No funning."

Another whine. I lifted his chin. "Listen. Eyes on me."

Gunner looked up at me.

"I need you to watch over Shep."

Gunner grumbled and lay his head flat on the ground.

I cut a bite of steak, held it in front of his nose, and said nothing. His eyes were glued on the steam coming off it. Finally, I turned my palm up and nodded. Gunner gently lifted the bite off my hand and inhaled it. Without chewing. At which point he assumed the same begging posture.

I spoke as I cut. "He's afraid. Scared of his own

shadow." I pointed the knife at him. "I need you to stand overwatch."

He tilted his head sideways and grumbled.

I extended another bite. Saliva spilled from his muzzle. After a few seconds, I turned my hand, nodded, and he inhaled the steak. Tail wagging faster.

More cutting. But this time I pointed at him with the fork. "And you can't make a scene if he wets his bed. Okay? No sniffing around. No doing that thing you do with your ears that will let him know you know. You can't let him know. You gotta run the play like it's completely normal. No big deal."

At this point he started crawling closer to the plate. Whining.

I gave him another bite. And was in the process of extending another when I pulled it back. "And if he gets lost, you bring him home. But"—I gave him the bite—"he should never get lost because you'll be watching him."

More crawling.

"Wherever he goes, you go. You're his shadow."

Gunner stared at me.

"If he starts shaking and closes his eyes, especially if he squats down, you lie down with him. I don't care if his pants are wet or not. You just put your head under his hand. Just let him feel you breathe."

Gunner looked at me, the plate, then back at me. When he did, he tilted his head and pointed his ears forward.

"Are you listening to me?"

He barked once.

"You sure?"

Another bark. Not quite as loud.

I pointed the knife at him. "Lastly, if anybody, and I do mean anybody, tries to take his tiger or hurt him or take him somewhere he doesn't want to go, I want you to chew their face off and turn them into a eunuch. Deal?"

Gunner rubbed his muzzle with his left paw and licked his chops.

"I'm not kidding. Eunuch."

Gunner's tail quit wagging and he lifted his head. Staring at me. Then, without notice, he walked toward the table where I'd set Bones's orange Pelican case. Gunner nudged it with his muzzle, licked it, pushed it with his paw, and then returned to sit next to me where I rubbed his head. The emotion was overwhelming.

"I know, buddy." I choked back a sob. "Me too."

Finally, I released him, slid the plate toward him, and watched him inhale the rib eye.

CHAPTER 21

Eddie and the team wasted no time creating a "clean" room for us to work in. No sooner had we landed than they went to work. From scanning walls to floor to machines that block radio waves to scanning for listening devices to no personal phones to satellite imagery and drone surveillance, they did everything they knew to do to make us as invisible as possible to Frank. With the all clear and the clock ticking, I assembled the team and figured I'd cut to the chase.

"Bones has been gone twenty-four hours. Anybody got any ideas?"

Crickets.

After my excursion into the cave, Bones placed locators on his person and gear. Just in case. After I woke up, he did the same with me. In deciding locations, we'd tried to think of things we were never without. Bones soldered one to the back of his cross, which he wore around his neck. Wedged another inside his pocket knife—which he was never without. Screwed a third inside the guide rod of his Sig P220. And wedged a fourth inside his wallet—which he was prone to misplace. The fifth had been placed inside his orange Pelican case—which was on the plane when he was taken.

Eddie set four GPS locators on the table. "Found these in a room next to the morgue where you last saw Bones. Laid out like they wanted us to find them. Like somebody was making a statement."

"Which means Frank knew not only to look for them, but where to look for them. And removed them from Bones before they left the hospital."

Eddie nodded.

I looked at the team. Camp, BP, and Jess all stared at me. "I need you all to figure out how Frank knows what we're going to do before we do it."

Eddie nodded. "Working on it."

Jess raised a hand. "That's a waste of time."

Camp nodded in agreement.

"How so?" I asked.

"We're spending energy on defense. We don't have time. Finding Frank's entrance into us won't find Bones. We need to focus all our energy on that one thing."

"Got any ideas?"

"The bookkeeper."

"I'm game, but how—and where does that get us?"

Camp spoke next. "Trade him for Bones."

Behind me, I heard the unmistakable step-step-tap of Clay's cane-assisted walk. Although I was pretty sure the cane was for show. "Mister Murphy?"

I turned. "Clay, you're killing me. We've known each other long enough now. You can get rid of the 'Mister.' "

"Yes, sir, my head knows that. But like I told you, in prison everyone is 'Mister' and I was in prison a long time. Just 'cause I'm out here doesn't mean my mouth is."

I knew what was coming, but I asked anyway. I just liked how he said it. "Meaning?"

"Meaning, if 'Murphy' is in my mouth, then 'Mister' is coming before it."

The team chuckled.

He sat at the table and folded his hands. "Remember how I once told you I needed to tell you a story?"

I nodded.

"Given everything that's happened, between Freetown and the island and you being laid up, seems like we never really had time. To be honest, I was starting to think maybe it wasn't all that important anymore, but now maybe . . ."

We waited.

He waved his hand across all of us. "I think I might can be of help."

"Please."

"Several years ago, I was moved to an old prison in Alabama. No A/C. No nothing. It was old school. Hot as hell. Used to have the lynchings in the yard where all us could see. Right before I come to live there, they'd built this new prison next door. State of the art. But they had a problem. The old prison cemetery was surrounded by an old stone wall, and since they had war heroes and such in the cemetery, it was made a historical place. Big plaque and everything. Which meant they couldn't tear the wall down. Which meant they couldn't get a backhoe or Bobcat through the gate. Which meant all graves were dug by hand. And since they didn't trust too many of us with a pick and shovel, they used to send me and another old boy, Larry Rogers, out there to dig holes. Which was fine with us. We didn't mind. We liked the exercise, plus it got us outside and we got to smell the air and stretch a bit. They didn't push us too hard, so we took our time. Dug slow. Talked a lot. Me and Big Rog' made a pretty good team. I don't know how many holes we dug, but it was a couple dozen 'cause every prison in Alabama buried their dead in our yard. Big Rog' told me a story one day I think you should hear."

"You want to give me the CliffsNotes?"

"I think you better hear it for yourself."

CHAPTER 22

Day 2 Without Bones

The plane touched down in Nowhere, Alabama. A few miles from the prison. When we parked, Clay stared at the two rows of chain link topped with concertina wire and the opposing guard towers—and the armed men who stood there.

He touched my arm. "Mister Murphy?"

I studied him.

Clay's black skin wasn't quite so black. "You promise me they're going to let me back out?"

I nodded. "I promise."

"And if they don't?"

"I won't leave without you."

Clay's eyes traveled the length of the fence and stopped at the guard studying us through binoculars. "You promise?"

"I do."

Clay put his hand on the door handle, bit his lip, and never took his eyes off the tower. "You ever broken a promise?"

I shook my head.

"You plan to start today?"

"No."

Clay spoke more to the memory than me. "This place ain't kind to Black men who kill white men."

I put my hand on his arm. "Clay?"

He looked at me. As I was about to speak, my phone rang. I recognized the number, answered, and put him on speakerphone. "Yes, sir."

A female voice responded. "Captain Shepherd, please hold for the vice president."

Clay looked at me and his eyes grew wide. A second later, a man's voice resonated across the line. "Murph, just heard about Bones. You need to know we're doing everything we can."

"Yes, sir, Mr. Vice President. I know that."

His voice strengthened. "I will personally turn hell inside out to find him. You know that, right?"

I didn't bother to tell him that Frank was probably listening to our conversation. "Yes, sir."

Clay looked at my phone as the voice of the vice president matched the one he'd heard on the news. He smiled and his shoulders relaxed.

The vice president continued. "You got any leads?"

"Sir, we know very little. It's pretty thin."

"Anything I can do to help?"

"Ask your team to assist Eddie in any way he needs. He's heading up our team. I'm chasing a lead in Alabama as we speak."

"Alabama?"

"Yes, sir."

"Mr. Pettybone with you?"

"Yes, sir. He was once a guest here."

"Mm-hmm. Bones told me about Clay and his help both in Key West and at Freetown during the fire. Showed me the video of him running back into that inferno. We sent a burn specialist down to help with his recovery following the explosion."

"Thank you, sir."

"You give him my best regards, and you two be careful."

"Yes, sir."

The phone clicked dead and I glanced at Clay, who was smiling wide enough to display most of the teeth in his mouth. I pointed at the security checkpoint. "You ready?"

Clay opened the door. "I never been more ready in my whole life." Clay buttoned his top button, exited the car, and we walked up the sidewalk to the window. They buzzed us in, and when the security guard saw Clay, he stood and extended his hand. "Clay, it's good to see you, sir."

Clay bowed slightly and shook the man's hand. "Mike. Good to see you, sir. How you and Cheryl? And . . . I guess Sam must be—"

The guard smiled. "Sixteen. A junior now. Just started driving."

Clay laughed an easy laugh that rose up out of his belly. The kind of laugh that had been earned. "Lord have mercy. Time flies."

"Yes, sir, it does. Seems like five minutes ago I was changing his diaper."

"Seems like five minutes ago you were running around here showing off a picture of a squishy, red-faced kid with no hair. Eight pounds and something."

Mike nodded, smiling at the memory. "You good, sir? We heard you'd been hurt rescuing some kids in a hospital. Folks around here were asking about you."

Clay nodded. "I got a little smoky, but I'm all good."

Mike looked at me. "You must be Mister Murphy?"

"I am."

"Sir, I know who you are, but anytime you meet with a lifer"—his tone was apologetic—"I have to search you."

"No problem. Do what you've got to do."

"Thank you, sir."

Twenty minutes later, they placed us in a concrete room with several steel tables. I watched Clay staring at the walls, and I wondered what memories they evoked. He pointed. "This used to be the hospital. Maybe 'triage' is a better word. They'd bring us here if we got cut or . . ." He trailed off. "One night, I got jumped by two men. Bad dudes. They'd taken a toothbrush and sharpened one end." He lifted his shirt, showing several scars in and around his rib cage. Another point to the corner. "They put me over there." He chuckled. "You look hard enough and you'll find my bloodstains on that floor."

About that time, we heard the unmistakable sound of electronic locks unlocking and doors swinging open, followed by the sound of guard commands and shuffling feet. When the last door opened, two guards escorted a big, hardened-looking man chained hand and foot. The man saw Clay, smiled, and stood silently while Clay rose and the two studied each other. The guard, who did not know Clay, pointed at the two of us. "You may not touch or pass anything to the inmate." Then he pointed to the cameras. "Understand?"

I nodded. "Understood."

CHAPTER 23

The huge man sat, folded his hands on the table, and asked Clay, "How you doing? You look good."

"It's what freedom do to you."

The man smiled. His face was kind and movements slow. Like a man with all the time in the world. Clay asked him, "You remember when they had us on grave detail?"

The man nodded.

Clay looked at the man but thumbed at me. "You mind telling him what you told me?"

The man spoke deliberately. "I been here a long time. And there were a lot of lifers like me—"

I held up my hand. "I'm Murphy Shepherd."

Another smile. "Mister Murphy, I'm Larry Rogers. 'Round here they call me R273469518, or Stumps for short."

"Thanks for meeting with us."

He glanced over his shoulder. "Anytime." He continued, "Stay here long enough and you serve your sentence. Your life runs out." A shrug. "Prison ain't easy on a body. Especially when you get old. So they send me and Clay out to dig the holes. Cemetery was old and they couldn't get a Bobcat through the wall. We got pretty good at it too. Prided ourselves on square corners, and sometimes that ain't easy in Alabama clay. Anyway, the cemetery ran alongside the road that led to the new high-tech prison. It's got more barbed wire, lights, cameras, and armed guards than a POW camp. It's where they put the most evil of us. Had one whole block of nothing but solitary, but whoever built that place was smart 'cause they put it several stories underground. Which was true of much of the prison."

He pointed in the direction of the prison. "You can see a couple floors up top, but there's far more below. While the old prison was a state prison, the new one was privately owned. Prison for profit. Anyway, they liked us old-timers. Thought we were harmless. And since they were private and always cutting costs, they brought us over to do menial stuff. Empty the trash. Mop. Whatever. We didn't mind. Got us out of our cells. Plus, they had A/C. So they put us on trash detail. Which, personally, I kind of liked. Let me stretch my legs. We just pulled out the old bag and put a new one in its place. Nothing to it. And we got to ride the elevator. Seven floors total.

"On the bottom floor, they had this glass room filled with computers. The glass was three to four inches thick and outside sat an armed guard. Which I always thought strange. Who in their right mind was going to try to break in down here? Never made no sense to me. Anyway, me and Clay kept to ourselves. Minding our own business. Did what they told us. Once a week, they opened the glass door and slid out this cart filled with these thick, black plastic bags and cardboard boxes. We never dug through it 'cause much of the trash was either soiled linens or medical, and I don't like needles. Once we collected it, all the trash went into the incinerator. They burned everything. And I do mean everything. Anyhow, me and Clay would divide and conquer. He'd take one hallway. I'd take the other.

"One day, they opened that glass door and passed me the cart filled with all those black bags, and when they did, I noticed one of those bags wasn't sealed. So what'd I do? I looked. Of course. I was curious. Wanted to know what they were throwing away. What I found was strange. All these little silver boxes. Dozens of them. All the same. I had no idea what they were used for, and they didn't mean nothing to me. Didn't have no screen. No On-Off button. Just a funny place on one side where it looked like you plugged it in. So I kept my head down and just kept pushing and didn't bother nothing, all the way to the incinerator, which was good because I learned quickly they always counted those boxes. Every week. Without fail.

"After a few months, I got to thinking about

those boxes and wondering why they counted them only to burn them. They treated them like Gillette razors. Use 'em once or twice and pitch 'em. It seemed to me that by burning them, they were hiding something. I talked to Clay about it, and he said he thought they were something that might have been important. It was a for-profit prison. They didn't throw out nothing. They stretched a dollar till it screamed. But not those drives. All shiny. They still looked good to me. And all of them had the date they were installed written in black ink on the outside of the drive. Each was only a few months old. Some only a few weeks. Why not reuse them? Seemed like a waste of money.

"Around about in there, something else happened." He nodded toward Clay. "Clay got out. His time ended before his life did, so he left me. I guess he'd been in so long that the state reevaluated his sentence and figured he was too old to do any harm."

Clay nodded. "Never thought I'd see the day."

Larry continued, enjoying the easy, measured pace of the story. "Prison gives you a lot of time to think and not a lot to think about, so naturally I got to thinking about those drives. Couldn't figure it out. So one day, I switched one of those silver boxes to another bag and just went about my business. I dropped the trash off at the incinerator, checked my cart, and started making my way out of the prison. I heard the first alarm on the elevator, and by the time I got to the surface and the door opened, there were four guards pointing guns at me. To be honest, I liked the attention. But I played dumb anyway. I wanted to see what all the fuss was about. So they search me up one side and down the other, then turn me around and march me back to the incinerator where they start asking me a bunch of questions. All of which I answered truthfully, save one. 'Did I tamper with the bags?'

"Well, they knew I didn't have the silver box tucked under my shirt, so they made me rifle through all my trash. Empty every bag. And sure enough, when I got to that last bag, there was that silver box. Big as Christmas. They looked foolish and tried to cover it up, but most days after that, whenever I emptied the trash, they made sure to slip a few glazed donuts into a Ziploc and place it on the cart. They didn't intend for the donuts to get incinerated. They meant those for me. Which was nice 'cause I'd lost a good bit of weight in prison and those donuts helped me put on a pound or two."

I couldn't quite figure out where this was going, but Larry was enjoying telling the story so much that I just let him finish.

"So a year passed. I dug graves when they needed me to dig, and I emptied trash when it needed emptying. Then a funny thing happened.

They brought me down to the morgue one day to show me some young guy who'd died in the new prison. Which was unusual, but every now and then, somebody'd get in a fight and kill somebody else, and I just figured that's what happened. But not this guy. This guy had died of heart disease and asked to be cremated. Which made the coffin a lot smaller. Which they needed me to measure. Actually, it was just a small square box that we then sealed inside this other weathertight thing, which they then set inside a concrete crypt. So they brought me down to measure the box 'cause the hole in the dirt needed to be a lot smaller; so I measured it and was about to leave when it got interesting.

"The walkway to the morgue was also the walkway to the incinerator, and both were behind the desk where the guard counted the drives. Meaning, the drives I could see had already been accounted for and were only minutes from being burned. Plus, I was on my own. The hall was empty. I guess they figured I couldn't hurt nobody seven floors down.

"For some reason"—a chuckle—"and I'm still not quite sure why, I grabbed a bag of those drives and put them inside that box under the ashes. Nobody would ever notice a few extra pounds. Then I just went about my business digging the hole. When I finished, they rolled the box out and left it with me. I sealed the container, using almost a whole tube of sealant, laid it in the ground, and shoveled the dirt on top. I don't know why I did it other than I wanted to get something by them. Get away with something. Which I did. Those drives were in there when I put that old boy in the ground. I know—I looked. And until now, I never told anyone 'cept Clay."

Clay interrupted him. "Think they're still down there?"

"Can't say. All I know is I ain't dug 'em up."

I studied Clay but asked both of them, "What does all that have to do with me?"

Larry continued. "Prison guard is one of the worst jobs on the planet. Nobody likes you, and even if you do your job perfectly, nobody likes you. It's thankless. They have no one to talk to but a bunch of old guys like me. So they talk. And they don't have much of a filter because who am I going to tell? Plus, they want somebody to think they have at least some value—and in prison, information is value. So, over time, they talk about what they know. Makes them feel important. To know something others don't. Eventually, I figured out that they had no idea what was on those drives except that the guy who owned the prison used to come down there himself and swap out the drives. Every couple of weeks, he'd come in a side entrance, not through the front of the prison like all the rest of us but down some other tunnel way, and he'd work a little while. Then he'd disappear. I never saw him, but I heard one of the guards say he had the strangest eyes. They looked like fire. Then he started sending somebody else. A new guy. Not quite as sure of himself. Kind of uncertain."

I cut to the chase. "You remember the dead guy's name?"

He nodded. Smiled. And held the answer for just a second on the tip of his tongue. Then he let it out. Exercising the only remaining power he held in this world. "Webster Mays."

"Think you could find his grave?"

"Don't have to." He turned to Clay. "You remember where we laid Lester."

"Surely do."

"He's in between Lester and the wall. Under the shade of that ol' tree. A good spot too."

Clay nodded. "I can find it."

"How long ago was this?" I asked.

"Time is funny in prison. Gets away from you 'cause the more you focus on it, the slower it goes. I'd say three years. Maybe two and a half. Not four."

I turned to Clay. "Think you can find it in the dark?"

He smiled. "Yes, sir."

I asked them both, "Can the prison guards see you?"

Larry smiled. "They don't care about the dead inmates. Only the live ones."

I stood to leave.

"Mister Murph?"

I turned.

"There's something else."

I sat back down.

"My cell sits pretty far down in the earth. It's like they're burying me before they bury me. It's pretty quiet, because the walls are concrete and steel, but they do transmit some sound. My bed is next to the wall, so at night I lay my head against it 'cause the buzzing sound helps me sleep. White noise. Like bees in the distance. Every two weeks, 'round midnight, that noise stops and I can hear other random noises. Can't pick them out 'cause the walls are too thick, but if I had to guess, I'd say they were human. Like somebody doing something on the other side of the wall. Now, I never finished school and I've never been accused of being a smart man, but I think that buzzing is computers, and I think that sound every two weeks is somebody messing with them."

"Every two weeks? You sure?"

"May sound crazy to you, but knowing there's another human being a few feet from me who can walk in and out of this place at will—" He shook his head. "The thought of that impossibility is what I have to look forward to. So yes. I'm certain."

"Thanks, Larry. You need anything?"

He studied his hands, and his answer was a long time coming. "Not anything you can give me."

I needed to phone Eddie. Which presented a problem. We knew Frank was in our communications. We didn't know how, just that he was. Hence, we assumed he was listening to every conversation. With that in mind, we'd agreed to revert to one of the lessons I'd learned from Bones at the Academy. An expensive workaround, but it worked. Eddie's team had secured multiple burner phones. Single-use cell phones. If used rightly, they could eliminate the problem we might be having. Or at least frustrate Frank and his team long enough to give Eddie and me space to communicate. The challenge came in telling Eddie the new number without using a known one.

The tactic was simple and required three new and unused phones. Turn on the first phone and text him the number—with one difference. The number texted was the actual number $+ 1 + 2 + 3 + 4$ and so on. So a 904 area code was actually 027. This is where it got tricky. Because Eddie had to leave his burner on twenty-four-seven, we assumed it was already compromised. So when Eddie called me back, we knew someone else was listening. I'd then verbally give him the number of the second burner, using the $1+2+3$ code, and then throw away the first. He would do the same and call me on a second unused burner.

Using a third phone, we repeated the process. If someone was in our communication to the extent Frank was, they might follow us from first phone to second, but deciphering the real phone number from the one given would take some time—and by then we'd be well into the third phone.

Doing all this required six new phones between the two of us. Paranoid? Maybe. But it worked. At least in the short term.

I turned on my first burner phone, texted Eddie the number, and waited. When it rang, I gave Eddie the number of the second burner and then removed the SIM and battery from the first. One second later, the second phone rang and I repeated the process. Clay watched all of this with amused curiosity. When the third phone rang, I wasted no time. I also assumed Eddie had me on speaker and the team was listening.

"Team, can you guys hack into this prison?"

Eddie spoke for the team. "Been working on that. What do you need?"

"I know we can't access the computers since they're a closed loop, but what about the power supply? And the HVAC?"

Seconds passed as the sound of keystrokes echoed through the phone. Eddie spoke again. "Yep, we can arrange that."

"I need you to spike the temperature. Reverse the A/C. Run the heat. And I need a power surge. Enough to fry some drives while not killing everything. I need it to look natural. Something that would require immediate attention but not necessarily the fire department."

More keystrokes. "What time?"

"Immediately. And I need you to monitor the video feeds including the gates and all the back doors. I need to know who they send to fix the problem."

"Keep your phone on."

"Check."

CHAPTER 24

The nearest hardware store was forty-five minutes, so with a lot of daylight to burn, Clay schooled me on the proper pick and shovel, and then we ate until the sun went down. Larry told us the guard changed at eleven, so we parked in the woods and wound our way through the trees to the far side of the cemetery.

At one point I caught Clay shaking his head. "Never thought I'd be sneaking back here."

We approached the southeast corner under the shadow of trees and then crept along the stone wall. We entered the cemetery at the only wrought-iron gate, and I followed Clay to the final resting place of Lester Copperton. Lying three feet to his right, alongside the wall, sat a stone that read "Webster Mays."

Clay and I took turns swinging the pick and shoveling the dirt, and for an eighty-five-year-old man, he could no doubt outwork me. Clay was smooth and powerful, and where my hands blistered, his showed no sign of wear. Two feet down, soaked with sweat, I asked him, "How many of these you dig?"

He leaned on the shovel handle and stared across the cemetery. "North of fifty."

After an hour of digging, Clay figured we were getting close so he started poking around with the pick and found the top of the concrete crypt. We cleared the dirt around the edge and then used the crowbar to lift it off. Inside sat an ivory-colored PVC cube. Almost looked like a cooler. Clay lifted the box, I slid the concrete lid back into place, and Clay set it on top. Doing so allowed us to work with a flashlight inside the hole. Using a box cutter, he loosed the seal and removed the lid. Inside rested a small wooden urn.

But no drives.

Clay lifted the urn containing Webster's ashes, revealing nothing beneath it. If there had been drives at one time, they were gone.

I looked at Clay. "You think Larry lied?"

Clay considered this. "Could have. Wouldn't be the first time."

"But did he lie about this?"

Clay shook his head once. "I tend to think not."

"What makes you say that?"

"Other than some perverse satisfaction of knowing we dug up Webster's ashes, what does he gain? Nothing. Only our distrust. And a man in his position can't afford to be losing friends. He doesn't have many to begin with."

"I agree. So somebody beat us to it?"

Clay nodded.

"Which would suggest that even used, dis-carded, and buried, they were valuable enough to be dug up and retrieved."

Another nod.

We replaced the box inside the crypt and began filling in our hole. After a few shovelfuls, Clay stopped, leaned on his shovel again, and stared across the cemetery. For three minutes he stood staring. Finally, he said, "Mister Murphy?"

When I turned to him, tears had streaked his face. "Yes."

He wiped his face on his shirtsleeve. "When you were laid up, body fighting infection, I spent a lot of time with Mister Bones. He's a good man. Maybe the best of men. He told me a story. We were talking about him being White and me being Black, and he said that when Jesus was carrying his cross up that hill, he stumbled 'cause they'd beat him so bad. When he did, the soldiers grabbed a man out of the crowd and said, 'Carry that.' So this man named Simon shouldered that crossbar and, although the Book don't say it, Bones think he lifted Jesus. And the two of them walked up that hill. One man carrying a crossbar and maybe helping Jesus when he stumble and Jesus carrying, well . . . everything else.

"Bones told me that man was from Cyrene." Clay looked at me. "That's North Africa." He paused. Wiped his forehead with his handkerchief. "That means, according to Bones, the last man to touch Jesus in kindness was a Black man from North Africa. 'Cause the next to touch him drove nails through him." He nodded as another tear cascaded. "I like the thought of that." He swallowed and waved his hand across both the prison and the cemetery. " 'Round here, you don't think about it much when you're young, but as you age, you start to thinking that the end is closer than the beginning, and one thing all us old guys think about a good bit is who's going to lay us to rest. A friend, or just some guy sent to dig a hole?"

He nodded toward the cemetery. "All them men I laid low, no matter what they did, I spoke words over all of them. Tried to lay them down easy. Cover them slowly. And I asked God to have mercy." He shook his head. " 'Cause we all got it coming. Every last one of us." Clay blinked and turned to face the prison. He spoke both to me and to someone I couldn't see. "I killed one man on the outside. Six on the in." A pause. "When my time comes, I'd be obliged if you'd dig my hole. Put me in the ground. Maybe help me walk from here to there." A final pause. Clay stared at me. His lip trembling. "Walk me home."

Standing alongside that grave, in the shadow of the prison walls, I hugged that old man. I held him while he cried on my shoulder. I don't know what was released in that space, but something got let go. Something came off. I held his hand in mine and nodded. "I'd be honored."

He smiled. "When I walked out of here, the state paid me $527 for my time. The sum value of my life. When we arrived in Key West, I went to the funeral home. The people that sell the plots. And I paid off the rest. So they couldn't put anybody else in there." A chuckle. "After a lifetime, the only thing I own on planet Earth is that dirt." His eyes found mine. "If it's not too much trouble, I'd like to be laid to rest next to my wife."

I marveled at him. How much had been stolen? And yet six decades behind bars had not hardened him. "It's not too much trouble."

"Thank you . . . Mister Murphy."

About then my phone rang. Given that Eddie was the only one who knew the number, I didn't need to check caller ID. "Give me some good news."

"Prison security put in a call to a cell phone in Queens, New York. Told him they had a power surge. Internal thermometers show possible over-heating. They asked him if he wanted them to check the room. He declined. Said he'd check it. We're tracking him. He's on a plane. Lands in an hour."

"Good work. We'll be ready. Let me know when he gets close."

CHAPTER 25

Hidden in the woods a half mile away, Clay and I sat in the front seat of the Suburban watching the prison, which was lit like a runway. Clay wore sunglasses. He crossed his arms and pointed. "The sun ain't that bright."

A few minutes after midnight, my phone rang. A dark sedan had pulled up to the rear employee entrance, paused briefly, and sped inside the gate. We wanted the appearance of a legitimate power surge and not a cyberattack, so in the time since our first phone call, Eddie had restored the temperature in the computer vault to a brisk sixty degrees but kept sending micro surges just in case. We had him on the line. Now we needed to land him.

As soon as the man's face appeared in the monitor feed, Eddie began running facial recognition. Moments later, he called me. "Bernie Gomez."

"Interesting name."

"Jewish mother. Mexican father."

"What do you know?"

"Thirty-six. Harvard MBA. Cut his teeth in Silicon Valley. Now consults for several banks on Wall Street. Handles some heavy hitters."

"Area of specialty?"

"Cybersecurity and data protection."

"Thought so."

"Any priors?"

Eddie laughed. "Twice arrested in Vegas. Record expunged. But if you look deep enough, it smells like he has a thing for kids."

"Married?"

A second passed in silence as Eddie continued looking. "Yep. Two kids. Seven and eight. Boy and girl."

"Can you make him out?"

"Blind. No cameras inside the vault, but BP got inside his phone, so we're listening."

"Let me know when he leaves."

An hour later, Eddie phoned again. "In the car. Headed to the gate."

"He bring anything out with him?"

"Not that we could see. But we've got his phone, so don't get on his bumper."

"Check."

The sedan cleared the gate and sped from the prison. Looked like he was in a hurry. I followed a mile back with turn-by-turn directions from Eddie. Twenty minutes later, Eddie sounded over the phone. "You're not going to believe this."

I waited.

"Dude just pulled into a strip club."

By the time we arrived, Bernie had gone inside,

so we parked across the street with a view of his car. In my way of thinking, one of two things was happening. I based this on the assumption that Bernie was in town every two weeks, away from wife and kids, and he seemed to know exactly where he was going. Either Bernie was here for the entertainment and had bellied up to the stage, or he was here to secure entertainment at his hotel. I had my money on the latter.

Five minutes later, Bernie walked out. A little swagger in his step. He climbed into his car, stopped at the "Always Open" liquor store along with a drive-thru burger joint that closed at 2:00 a.m., and finally came to a stop in front of room 117 at the Sweet Home Alabama Motel. Again, we parked across the street.

Fifteen minutes later, a van pulled into the parking lot. I wanted this on video, so I opened my smartphone, zoomed, and began recording. The van parked next to Bernie's sedan, and the driver—a woman in her fifties—let two people out of the passenger side. One boy. One girl. I doubted they were thirteen. The driver spoke something harsh to them, smacked the boy in the head, then herded them to the door where she knocked. Bernie answered, apparently having showered, wearing only a towel and his watch. He smiled and let the kids in, but not before handing them each a bag from the burger joint. He then gave something to the driver—which I assumed was money—and shut the door. The driver tapped her watch, said something to Bernie, and drove around the motel and parked on the opposite side, where she leaned her seat back and lit either a cigarette or a joint.

I turned to Clay. "I've seen enough."

He hefted his cane. "I'll take the driver."

"You don't want me to—?"

Clay was out of the car and heading toward the sidewalk. Looking like a man in search of a beer. Watching him saunter over, I thought, *Gray hair, cane, slight limp. She'll never suspect him.*

Crossing the parking lot, I called Eddie and told him what I needed and that I needed it quick. Approaching the door, I heard cartoons in the background along with a man's voice. Sounded like he was talking to children.

I was tired and Bones seemed a long way away. My water boiled.

I knew if I knocked down the door, I'd scare the kids, but with video still running, I did just that. The door flew off the hinges and landed next to a screaming and naked Bernie, who looked to be acting out something. The only thing he was wearing was his watch. The girl sat on the bed on the left, boy on the right. Neither was dressed. Bernie began cussing me, so I reached into memory and turned out his lights, smearing his nose across his face.

Both the children pulled their knees to their

chests and started crying. I handed them each a blanket and their clothes and said, "Are you afraid?"

The boy looked to the girl, and when she nodded, he followed.

I pointed to the parking lot. "Is that woman making you do something you don't want to do?"

Two more nods.

"Do you have families that are looking for you?"

They both shook their heads.

"Is she related to you?"

Two nods.

"Your mom?"

The girl shook her head. "Mom's mom."

I could not believe their grandmother was pimping them out. I heard a commotion behind me. When I turned, Clay leaned against the doorframe, pulled out his handkerchief, and wiped his brow. He looked like he'd gone to check the mail.

I said, "You good?"

He refolded his handkerchief. "Spectacular." At his feet lay the woman. Hog-tied, gagged, and unconscious. Impressive.

I returned to the kids but pointed to Bernie. "Do either of you want to be here with this guy?"

Their body language was a resounding "No." Bernie still had not moved, and one leg was awkwardly folded beneath the other. "Does your mom work at the strip club?"

Two nods.

"Does she know you're here?"

Two head shakes.

"So your grandmother brought you here when your mom is working?"

Both nodded.

I was in a bit of a pickle because I needed to extricate Bernie and take him with me. I had a few questions for him, but I couldn't very well leave the kids. Not to mention the fact that the grandmother needed to pay for her sins.

I turned to the girl. "What's your mom's name?"

"Ocean."

"Ocean?"

Two head nods.

"What's her real name?"

The daughter spoke. "Phyllis."

"Phyllis?"

A single nod.

I dialed the strip club. The music was loud and receptionist rude. All he said was, "Yeah."

"I need to speak with Ocean, please."

"She's dancing."

"It's an emergency."

"So."

"It's about her kids."

He shouted something to someone not nearby. Three minutes later, a female voice answered. "Hello?" She sounded young and high.

"Ocean?"

"Who's asking?"

"Phyllis?"

Her tone softened. "Yes."

I tried to explain. When I'd finished, she was screaming hysterically at both me and someone nearby who owned a car. As best as I could decipher, his name was Brutus.

Seven minutes later, a mostly dressed Phyllis and a ginormous tattooed man exited a Burt Reynolds Trans Am. Phyllis jumped over her mother who lay facedown across the threshold, ran into the room, and hugged her children, who were both wide-eyed and crying. As I studied them, I wondered how it had all come to this. I imagined that when Phyllis was young, if that was in fact her name, she hadn't envisioned her life turning out this way.

The ginormous man stood holding a revolver with which he kept rubbing his groin. Behind me, Phyllis was screaming, "What is going on here?"

I handed Phyllis the video, which she watched in tears. When finished, she rose and kicked her mother in the face, then spat on her. Then kicked her again. This time in the rib cage. The impact was accompanied by the sound of expelling air. Seeing Phyllis in apparent distress and trying to impress her, the ginormous man stepped into the room and pointed the Smith and Wesson in my face—which I took from him. I then climbed on top of him and, despite his verbal objections, choked him out. When he came to, I was sitting on top of him, his revolver in my hand and resting on his temple. His eyes crossed looking at me.

I spoke softly. "I work for the federal government. You tracking with me? Nod once if yes."

A single nod.

"I am going to stand up, but you're not. You're going to stay right where you are. Agreed?"

Another nod.

"If you move, I'll turn your head into a canoe. Got it?"

A slow single nod and a long exhale as the vinegar drained out of Brutus.

I turned to Phyllis, who sat with both arms around her kids. Every few minutes, she'd sling a profanity at her mom, who was spitting blood and teeth. Phyllis's face was ashen, and I was pretty sure she was coming off something.

I pulled up a chair. And this was where it got interesting. The girl had a backpack I hadn't seen. The backpack sat on the floor, zipper open. Inside sat a book. A familiar book. I lifted out *The Resurrection of Casey Girl* and turned to the daughter.

"You read this?"

She nodded.

Next I spoke to Phyllis. "You read this?"

She averted her eyes and shook her head,

finally saying, "I don't read too well, but she reads it to me."

I cut to the chase. "Do you want out of this life you're in?"

Phyllis nodded. As did the kids. I pointed to the book. "Can you keep a secret?"

They nodded.

I whispered, "I'm Wilby."

It took a second, but the little girl's eyes grew even wider, and when she made the connection, she catapulted off the bed and hung her arms around my neck. Which caught me a bit off guard. I tried to gently pry her off me, but she wasn't budging. Finally, I handed her to Clay, who said, "What you want me to do with her?"

In the meantime naked Bernie started to come around. When he cussed and looked like he was going to try to sit up, Clay put him back to sleep with his cane. That's when it registered in the little girl's eyes that Clay was actually the man in the picture on the back of the book standing next to Casey.

Needless to say, it didn't take long to convince them.

I pointed to Brutus and asked Phyllis, "Is he part of this?"

"No. He just works the door. He don't know nothing."

I let him up, opened the cylinder on his revolver, and spilled the shells onto the ground.

Then I held it out. "If I have to come back here, you will not see it coming, and you won't enjoy it. Capiche?"

He nodded.

"Get out of here."

Finally, I shut the door so her mom could not hear and turned to Phyllis. My voice was little more than a whisper. "Phyllis, here's the deal. I'm going to take Bernie with me. He's going for a plane ride. He's about to pay for his sins. I don't want to leave you here, so I'm offering you three a chance out of here, but you've got to decide right now."

Her daughter clutched the book and spoke up. "Are you taking us to Freetown?"

"If you'll let me."

I turned back to Phyllis. "They'll give you a place to live, get you clean, and start working on a future."

She looked dubious. "What's it cost?"

"Nothing."

She studied me. "What do you want?"

"Nothing." I pointed at her daughter as I ripped the phone cord off the wall and started wrapping it around Bernie's hands and feet. "Ask her."

Phyllis looked at her daughter. "Is it true?"

Her daughter opened the book and began reading Casey's description of Freetown. Of Clay. And of me. When I heard them, I almost teared up.

Bernie protested, but I threw him in the back of the Suburban as Clay dragged Grandma into the motel room and left a note for the ATF and Homeland Security—both of whom were en route. I uploaded the video to Eddie to maintain a copy of it, and so that he could send it ahead to the officer who was about to be in charge of this scene. He could come to Colorado to interview Phyllis.

Twenty minutes later, the six of us boarded the plane—and no, I did not let Bernie dress. Instead, I laid him facedown on the floor of the plane, hog-tied and gagged. The last thing I heard him say was something along the lines of, "Do you know who I am?" I did spread a small blanket across his hairy butt because I didn't want to see it, but I needed Bernie to *feel* naked—because if he felt undressed now, he had another thing coming. In about two hours he would learn the definition of naked.

I got on the phone after takeoff. Eddie answered. "Inbound. ETA is an hour forty-seven. Tell Summer and Casey to meet me at the runway. I'm plus three and I need a book signed."

"You need a what?"

I hung up only to find Clay sitting in his chair, smiling at me.

I didn't have time to wait for better surroundings with less of an audience. I needed to interrogate Bernie now. So I flipped him over and squatted next to him. Given that his arms and feet were tied behind his back, he was not comfortable.

"Bernie." I clicked play on the video. When it had finished, I said, "I have some questions about the prison, the computers, and the drives. You ready to talk?"

He nodded slowly.

CHAPTER 26

Day 3 Without Bones

After my rather informative conversation with Bernie, I called Eddie and told him what I'd learned and what I needed. When we landed at almost 4:00 a.m., he met me on the runway. He was holding a lead-lined bag. I slid my phones into it, and we walked away from the plane.

"Frank can hear us because he owns the companies that supply our telecommunications. Everything from cable to cellular to satellite; his shell companies own them. If we speak, he can hear us because he owns the framework."

"This guy really did not like his brother."

"It gets better."

"I'm listening."

"The drives that Bones pulled from *Sonshine* weren't ordinary hard drives. They were actually processors for the navigation system, which also happen to store information about routes, locations, etcetera. That means while they have a lot of video you don't ever want to see, they also leave something like digital bread crumbs that show precisely where they've been. Like a smart-phone—even though most don't know it and aren't aware, it records your every step. These drives function the same way. It's inherent in the software. It has to track itself; otherwise it doesn't know where it is. Meaning, it can't navigate."

I knew this was going somewhere, but I wasn't quite tracking. "So?"

"So, boats float on water, but these drives took a detour. Several blocks inland. Which means either that big boat sprouted wheels or somebody lifted them off and transferred them by hand to another location, dumped their data, and then returned to the ship. And this happened not just once or twice, but three times. It's systematic. Somebody is transferring data by hand."

Eddie's discovery agreed nicely with Bernie's confession. "How certain are you?"

"The drives contain a time stamp along with location. Like geo-mapping. They moved off the ship, not stopping, then they arrived at a location where they sat still for over four hours, then immediately returned to the ship."

"Can you pinpoint the locations?"

He nodded slightly. "Within one or two feet."

I looked at the plane, then my watch. "Can you route me there?"

"Done."

Thinking through logistics, I asked, "You didn't happen to—"

Eddie motioned to the passenger inside the vehicle. The door opened, and Camp appeared, dressed in black tactical gear, carrying two arm-loads of gear and a couple of Pelican cases. "Summer let me in your toy room. I like your password." He set down the bags. "I took some liberties 'cause you're old school, but we can make do."

"We?"

He was wearing a Glock 17 mounted with a Trijicon RMR in a thigh holster. The Trijicon is an incredibly durable red-dot sight mounted atop a handheld platform. It's new technology com-pared to my Sig, but you can drop one out of a helicopter and chances are good it will function when you pick it up. With his left hand, Camp pulled a magazine from his left pocket, topped it off with a few rounds from a handful in his right, and then inserted the magazine into the magwell of the Glock until I heard the click. He did this without unholstering. It's easy enough to do, but he did it without looking and while he was talking to me. Suggesting he'd done it a few hundred times.

I could use the help, and I knew he knew what he was doing, but if I'm taking a man to what might be his death, he should be given the chance to speak his intention. "What makes you think you're going with me?"

He spoke while loading an AR magazine. "I've

conducted multiple missions in countries around the globe extracting high-value targets while protecting my team." He slid the AR magazine in his vest. "And I've never left anyone behind. Be it man or woman." He dropped the bags at my feet. "Trust me, you want me with you."

"I work alone."

He lifted his suppressed MK4, inserted a magazine, turned on his Aimpoint, adjusting for brightness, then transitioned from right hand to left, cycled the bolt, and closed the ejection port cover. He hung the single-point sling over his head and let the weapon rest against his chest. "I understand. I would, too, were I you. So I'm asking to come along. Besides, you're all thumbs when it comes to computers."

He had a point. And I was glad to have the company. Especially since I was going on four days with no sleep. I pointed at the jet. "It's kind of like Southwest. Just pick the seat you like."

He laughed and began loading gear.

Eddie handed me a satellite phone. "Jess encrypted this. If Frank discovers it, it'll keep him busy awhile. I've programmed all the new numbers." He pointed to Bernie. "We sent a team to pick up his family. They're scared but safe."

Turning to the plane, I said, "Eddie?"

"Yes, sir."

I tapped my Omega—the watch Summer gave me since I gave my Rolex to Ellie. "Seventy-two hours and counting. Bones is out there some-where. Right now he's thinking about it. And trusting us. Don't let the trail get cold."

"Yes, sir."

"Oh, and, Eddie."

"Yes, sir."

"If Frank is watching us, you can bet he's monitoring all eyes at the prison. Which means he just saw me and Clay walk in and talk to an inmate. He's no dummy. He'll be one step ahead of us."

"Yes, sir."

"Oh, and, Eddie?"

"Sir?"

"Thanks."

CHAPTER 27

Day 4 Without Bones

The thought of Bones being alone and needing me kept me awake. During my training at the Academy, he'd sometimes pull me out of class, hand me an eighty-pound pack, and point to the mountain. Rain, snow, sun, the end of the age, or the zombie apocalypse mattered not. If he pointed, we were headed up.

This addition to my training produced a few things in me. It forced me never to get comfortable because at any second Bones might appear and cause me great discomfort. I was always just thirty seconds away from extreme physical and mental hardship. It also forged in me an ability to push myself past my mental limits, because Bones accepted no argument. No excuse. I could have been at death's door, but it didn't matter. It wasn't that he didn't care. He did. It's just that he cared more about something else. He wanted to see if that trait did or could exist in me. Did I care about something more than me? Because if I didn't, he was wasting his time.

One week during exams, he opened my door

and dropped a pack on the floor. It was snowing. Icy. And he chose the straight-up route. The one that included ropes. I hadn't slept in a few days, and I needed to. When I objected, he stared at the pack, the mountain, then me. He didn't say anything. He didn't need to. The choice was clear. The rest of my life swaying in the balance. Either pick up the pack and haul it atop that rock, or he'd close that door and I'd never see him again. Not to mention this was the third day in a row he'd done this. In the last forty-eight hours, I'd not only climbed his stupid mountain twice but taken three exams, with one remaining.

To this day I can't really tell you why I picked it up.

A couple hours later, half frozen and needing sleep, I made a mistake and slipped. A couple hundred feet below me lay a carpet of earth. Textured with rock face, treetops, and more than a foot of snow—which would do little to break my fall. If my ropes held, they'd stop my fall, but the thirty-foot drop may well have snapped my neck given the weight of the pack. And that was only if the ropes held. If they didn't, I would either be impaled on a spiraling fir tree or experience blunt-force trauma when my face impacted the rocks at fifty-five feet per second.

As this thought was passing through my mind, a hand appeared from above me and grabbed the pack. I didn't know he was there, as I always climbed alone. He caught me and returned me to the rock.

"Thought you looked a little tired."

Oh, you think? What gave it away?

Despite the fact that all I wanted to do was punch him in the teeth and then curl up in a fetal ball and get some sleep, he kept his hand on my shoulder. Steadying me. Four hours later we reached the top. The snow was coming down heavy. A total whiteout. I pulled myself up over the ledge, crawled under the overhang that formed a small cave, but couldn't pull myself into a seated position. I was drenched, cold, couldn't feel my fingers or toes, and didn't have the strength to do anything about it. Whatever my limit had been, I'd reached it. My body shut down. I guess the third time was the charm. Fading off into la-la land, I heard Bones chuckle. He lit a fire, got me out of my wet clothes, slid me inside my sleeping bag, and poured me a cup of something hot. Chicken broth, I think. When I woke, I sat up, stared at my watch, tried to make sense of the time, and then realized I'd not only slept through the day but missed my final exam. Which did not bode well for me.

He was sitting cross-legged with his shirt off. Mind you, the temperature was near zero. I rubbed my eyes and tried to sit up. Only then did I notice his bandage. Right shoulder. Just below his collarbone. He was in the process of peeling off the bloody one and replacing it with a clean one. His skin had been sutured. Front and back.

"What happened?"

My question caused him to pause. He raised an eyebrow, applied the dressing, and chuckled, proceeding to pull on his shirt, fleece, and down jacket. Then he leaned back against the stone wall, crossed his legs, and sipped his wine as a crimson sun spilled off the side of the planet.

"Shoulders don't react well to bullets."

I guess that's when it hit me. He'd returned a week ago from Central America, and we hadn't talked about his trip. Since then, we'd climbed this stupid mountain three times and finally, tonight, or rather early this morning, as I'd slipped and started falling, he'd mustered the strength and gumption to reach out with his right arm—the one that had been shot—and not only pull me back but place me safely on the rock. To this day I have no idea how he did that. Having now been shot several times myself, I've found myself completely unable to function. I turn into a boy with a man cold and start crying like a teenage girl watching *The Notebook*. You can ask Summer. It's ugly. But not Bones. He was on the mountain with me. Who does that? I know of only one man.

The insanity of it struck me. So I asked him, "You mind telling me what we're doing up here?"

He stared into his wine as a cold wind washed

across us. When he spoke, he did so from both memory and experience. "People who steal people, and then line up a train of miscreants and perverts deserving only of a single bullet, don't think like you and me. Their business model is rape for profit. Twenty times a day. They open the door. 'Please, come in.' Then they sit at the table and count the dollars or smoke a Marlboro as some little girl or little boy's spirit slowly exits their body beneath a blanket or another's sweat. The only way you and I ever catch those people, the only way they ever pay for their sin, is when we learn to think more like them and less like us."

He held up a finger. "Notice I didn't say 'become like.' I said 'think like.' There's a difference. And one way we force ourselves to do that is to override what our body is telling us. Pain is a signal. That's all. The body's response to discomfort. We are here learning to mute it. Because if we don't . . ." He waved his hand across Colorado and the earth beyond. "We can't hear the cries of the dying and those who wish they were dead."

While he was sitting there with his legs crossed, I could see the bottom of his right boot. On the Vibram sole he'd used something like a knife tip to carve two bones between the flat space of the arch and the heel. Normally that area of the sole wouldn't touch hard-packed ground, but in snow and soft sand it would leave an imprint. As I studied the snow around me, I realized we were surrounded by bone impressions.

I pointed. "What's with the bones?"

He nodded, leaned his head back, and closed his eyes. For the last two years I'd asked him the same question. Every time, he'd shake his head. "You haven't earned that."

By that time, I'd broken every known record he held at the Academy. "When will I?"

"If you have to ask when, then you haven't."

Finally, lying on the side of that mountain, face blistered, having worn the skin off my fingertips, "when" had come. I simply pointed.

He stared into his wine and then at me. For a long time much of what he said on that mountain was a mystery. But Bones's recent revelations put it all in a new light. "I'll tell you the full story some other time, but I was in Majorca. In a dungeon. Called it 'Hell Squared.' There's more to this story, but this part will suffice. I'd lost count of the months, had named all the rats, and was pretty sure I'd die in that grave." A pause.

"Whenever the priests"—he made quotation marks with his fingers—" 'visited,' they'd bring a lantern, but I was too busy fighting for my life to see my surroundings. Plus, a lantern shoots light downward. It doesn't shine up, so I never really got a good look with my eyes. I'd walked around feeling the walls, but that only allowed me to 'see' what I could reach. It wasn't until someone smuggled in a flashlight that I saw what I'd been missing. And it was a lot."

He sipped his wine. "I knew my ceilings were taller than I could reach, and based on the echo, they were a good bit taller, but how much I couldn't guess. Enter the flashlight, and I couldn't believe my eyes. Someone slipped that thing in my hand and I began scouring the world around me. It nearly took my breath away. I wasn't in a dungeon, and the bars weren't prison bars. The entire cavern was an underground chapel, and I was living in a crypt whose bars separated it from the altar. It blew my mind. This entire time I thought I was just in some dank cell, but in reality, I'd been living in a thousand-year-old tomb. Prior to the flashlight, my hands told me there were these holes in the stone. I thought people had put candles in there. But the flashlight allowed me to see they were a ladder cut into the rock that led up to where the body had been laid. The entire time, some old guy had been lying in a tomb. Shield. Sword. The works.

"The story etched into the wall said he'd saved more than a thousand people after the Moors invaded. Lived underground for a couple of years but somehow managed topside raids at night. No one could ever discover how he got out. Night after night. He rescued countless people from untold horror, getting them out of the city. And yet when I studied the walls, no one had written his name. The only inscription I found was a single word."

He paused. "Study Scripture, and the word *bones* is equated with the person. There's no difference between this hard thing"—he tapped his leg—"and me. I am that. That is me. So there I was. Stuck down in that hole in the earth with this pile of bones, and that's when it hit me. I am . . ."

I finished his sentence. "Bones."

A nod. "I've always liked the name. Just seemed to fit. Maybe I was half crazy, but I felt like that old guy spoke it over me. So that night I took my knife and carved a set of bones into my shoe. I would have carved it into me like a tattoo or brand, but I was tired of people hurting me and didn't want to add to my pain. Something about putting my mark on the sole of my shoe meant I left an imprint wherever I went. Like, 'This is me. I was here.' Which as a boy living in that dungeon, I thought impossible. In the years following, wherever I traveled, I took that old guy with me. And maybe what he did for me, in some small way, I've done for others."

He sipped. Nodded. "Least I'd like to think I have." He studied his boot. "When others saw the crude carving, the name stuck." He paused. "Maybe it was my way of telling the world, 'You may stick me down here in the bowels of this earth, abuse me, forget me, treat me like an animal, and strip me of my hopes and dreams, but you can't take my name." He tapped himself in the chest. "I'm Bones. That's me. You can take everything else but not that. And I'll be here long after you"—he waved his hand above him in the air, signifying the priests who lived in the world above him—"sick miscreants are gone and burning in hell."

The falling snow muted the world around us. "My name became a knowingness. An understanding. I knew that I knew that I knew that a reckoning was coming. That's what it was. My name was a reckoning. There in that hell, all I had were my words. And there and then I gave myself one. A name. It was the only thing I could give me. Because I had nothing else." He raised a finger. "In the years since, I've come to understand, no . . . to know . . . through the hundreds of people I've rescued, that nothing matters more than a name. It's why it's always been the first thing I've asked them. Because no matter what hell they've endured, a name can call them back out. A name establishes a record. Drives a stake in the ground. Shouts across the stratosphere, 'I'm here! I matter! I'm not invisible!' And while you may think very little of me, God himself actually thought me up. What you see in the lens of your eye, this thing we call 'me,' started in his mind. He actually took the time to think me up. Imagine." Another leg tap. "God thought of me. Molded my bones like a potter. And if that's true, and he thought of me, and then made me, and then named me, then there's a record of my existence. Evidence that I'm real." He was quiet a moment, slowly swirling his wine.

After several minutes, he said, "When you're in hell, slavery, nothing matters more than a name. Because with it, someone can walk up to the bars that shackle you, point at you among the many, and call you out—by name. A name is the singular thing that separates us from the ninety-nine. A name makes us the one." The look in Bones's eyes was one of longing. Of remembrance. And of pain. "Without a name . . . there is no record."

I tried to sleep on the plane, but every time I closed my eyes, I saw the imprint of his boot in front of me. The reason it was always in front of me is that all across the world, no matter where we'd traveled, and no matter how dangerous, he'd always gone first. I hadn't lived theory. It was tangible. There in front of me. I could touch it. Wipe my fingertips through the imprint. Size 12. Vibram. How many times had he bailed me out? How many times had he found me when I'd gotten myself lost? How many times had he led me into battle? How many times had I heard him turn to a child, scared out of their mind, and whisper through a smile, "Tell me your name"? In every single case, they had.

I couldn't count.

I didn't know Frank, but based on my limited experience with him and Bones's retelling of their history, I had no doubt he'd use Bones as leverage to get what he wanted. I just had no idea what that was. He hadn't said. Frank loved nobody. Not even Bones. So all bets were off. Frank was betting that after we'd seen enough of those videos and understood just how helpless we really were, he'd be able to reveal what he wanted and structure a trade. Bones for something. I knew two things: it would be an impossible trade and Bones would never agree to it.

Four days had passed, and we were no closer. My only hope was to find Bones before Frank made that demand. Given our present situation, I calculated our chances at maybe one in ten. Maybe one in a hundred.

Camp, Bernie, and I landed in New York City in the early hours of the morning. My least favorite city. Too many people. Too much concrete. Which, if I had to guess, was the very reason Frank had chosen it. Bernie led us through the streets, pointing at each turn. He explained that *Sonshine* had docked somewhere along the island and handed off the drives to him, and then he drove several blocks inland to an SVL—a safe vault location. And copied the data. That meant

Frank was hiding—or sometimes hiding—in plain sight.

Smart. Doing so allowed him to blend in. One eccentric among many.

We offloaded the plane, transferring the gear into the Suburban and breaking every New York City firearms law in the process. If caught, I was hoping my get-out-of-jail-free card—the vice president's number saved in speed dial—would prove helpful. At least, that's what I told myself as I routed my way to the building with an AR-15 pressed against my leg. If confronted, I wasn't taking any chances and I had no intention of implementing the subtle tactic. My hope was to arrive and get in and out before the workday started. According to Bernie, the eighty-five-floor building housed both offices and homes, and while eighty-five floors wasn't the tip of the skyline, it was a very tall building. Loosely, offices filled the bottom forty floors, whereas multimillion-dollar townhomes and ridiculously expensive apartments filled the rest. The top few floors had been saved for a few high-end restaurants, two private clubs, three fitness centers, and some sort of Asian spa.

Bernie told us the parking lot gate combination changed daily, so Camp hacked it with his phone. I have no idea how and I didn't ask, but when the gate lifted, he stepped to the side like a matador and let me in. I still hadn't let Bernie dress. I needed his subconscious telling him he wasn't in control. Because he wasn't. We drove through the gate into the underground parking garage with memories of *Die Hard* flashing in my mind's eye. Bruce Willis's portrayal of New York City cop John McClane had long been one of Bones's favorite. Get two glasses of wine in him and he can quote most of the movie.

We spiraled down farther into the earth, stopping on level three just a few spaces from a door marked Laundry. We couldn't very well go walking into a New York City high-rise looking like a couple of SWAT team members dragging a nude man without raising a few eyebrows, so we rummaged through a cart filled with dirty laundry from both the restaurant and fitness center and wrapped ourselves in a couple of towels, which, save black boots, made it look like we'd just finished a workout and were en route to the steam room. Bernie looked like a barefoot man going to the spa. We loaded on the elevator and soon saw the effectiveness of our disguises when the doors opened at the seventh floor to a guy wearing a suit, carrying a briefcase and a cup of coffee, and talking into a pair of earpods. He stepped into the elevator, took one whiff, gagged, then stepped out and never looked back.

Evidently our clothes had been sweated in. Yesterday. We were ripe.

I asked Bernie what floor and he punched 55.

Interestingly, Eddie confirmed that floors fifty to sixty were owned by one company and not presently occupied. *Ten unoccupied floors in New York City?* There's no telling what that cost. It reminded me of Bones's statement about sleep. *"What would you pay for a few hours?"* Of course, the cost would be easier to absorb if you owned the building.

We unloaded at forty-nine and walked up the stairs to fifty. Every room was locked, but we didn't need to actually see inside. We just needed to be close enough to scan through the door with Camp's thermal imager, which we did. From fifty to fifty-four, we found not a soul. Nor a computer. Nothing. Exiting fifty-four, we climbed two more flights to fifty-six, and over the next hour scanned every room up through sixty—but netted nothing. Bernie followed and told us what to expect. Turned out he was correct.

All that changed when we returned to fifty-five.

We descended the final step, and I pressed Bernie's face and eye to the retinal scanner. He protested. "I do this and he knows I'm here."

"Good."

The first door unlocked, followed by a second requiring both palm and retina. Bernie complied, the door slid open, and the rush of cold air swept across us. With a clear view of the room, Camp's thermal imager lit up like Christmas. Registering heat signatures everywhere. The entire floor was unfinished, complete with steel beams, concrete floor, metal framing—and totally empty. Like the others, not a piece of furniture to be found. But unlike the other floors, which had been broken up into individual suites, each with several rooms and bathrooms, floor fifty-five was one giant expanse. The only construction was a room in the middle encased in thick glass and equipped with a halon fire-extinguishing system. Not to mention a rather elaborate 128-bit encryption security system. Bernie approached the vault door and held his hand over a keypad. "May I?"

I nodded. He punched in a twenty-seven symbol code, and the door of the giant air-sealed vault clicked and swung open. Stepping through the door, I noticed the walls were every bit a foot thick.

Inside we stared through thick glass at what can only be described as a room full of computers. Or what looked like computers. Several metal racks housed multiple processors and, at one time, several daisy chain hard drives. Now all that remained were empty spaces where the drives had connected. A quick count proved there would have been more than a hundred.

Bernie spoke out loud. "They beat us here."

"They were in and out of here fifteen minutes after they dispatched you to the prison."

"So they knew I'd get caught."

I nodded.

Camp shook his head and whispered, "I've never seen that many terabyte drives in one place."

"You sure they were terabyte?"

Bernie nodded. "They were."

"Is there any outside electronic access to that room?"

Bernie shook his head. "None. By design."

I noted the cold. It must have been fifty degrees. "You could hang meat in here."

Camp nodded. "I'll bet his electrical bill is something."

Bernie gestured to the empty daisy chains. "The drives are constantly transferring massive amounts of video data. It's cold now, but"—he pointed—"when they're running, it'll heat the room."

I studied our surroundings. We'd now struck out twice, but despite failure something was bugging me. Something unusual. Camp picked up on it, so I asked him, "You smell that?"

He nodded. "Yeah. Smells like . . . Old Spice."

I studied the air vents. "Given this system, how long you think that would linger?"

"Not long."

"He's still in the building."

Camp voiced his question out loud. "How would you get this many drives out of here?"

I answered him. "Elevator to laundry or helicopter from the rooftop."

Camp nodded. "I don't hear a helicopter."

We ran to the service elevator where the sign above read P3. I slammed open the door, and we began bounding down the steps. Four at a time. A floor every two to three seconds. We would have traveled faster were it not for Bernie. I doubted he'd done any physical fitness in a decade. Ten floors in and Bernie hurled. Again at fifteen. Thirty floors and he was staggering and dry heaving. Forty-two floors down, he was gurgling and begging for mercy.

We landed in P3 just as a decked-out, black Mercedes Sprinter van began easing up the ramp. I tossed the Suburban keys to Camp and began running. I reached the ramp, spiraled upward to the second level, and when I cleared level ground, the Sprinter had accelerated, reached the end of the parking lot, and was in the process of turning left up the next ramp. My only advantage was the concrete wall. As in, it gave me a solid backstop. Meaning, bullets wouldn't pass through it. I leveled the suppressed MK4 and emptied four rounds at each rear tire before it disappeared around the next upramp. Two seconds later, I heard the crash. Followed by twisting metal and frantic cussing.

I sprinted, climbed again, and rounded the corner to find a man on his knees, hands raised, begging for mercy. Measuring the level of fear on his face and fresh urine soaking his pants, it didn't take a genius to realize he had no idea what was going on. I kept the muzzle trained on his face, opened the back of the Sprinter, and found the laundry cart sitting in the back. Full of drives.

While the gun was suppressed, I was certain we'd draw some attention as cars began pulling in for the day's work. When Camp appeared behind me with the Suburban, I slid the cart out, passed it to Camp, and told my new friend Guido to get in. Camp opened the rear doors where we found Bernie facedown and wearing only his birthday suit along with that ridiculous collar. Bernie's position did not encourage Guido, who tried to back up, but I nudged him with my muzzle and he climbed in, lying on his stomach next to Bernie.

Three seconds later, the four of us drove out of the parking garage.

I nudged Guido with my barrel. "Who are you?"

Like Bernie, he had his face pressed to the carpet, but I could read his body language. His eyes kept darting toward his hands, and he was blinking profusely.

That's when I noticed he wore a watch identical to Bernie's. Clever. At first glance it looked like an ordinary smartwatch. Only problem was, it wasn't. A smartwatch you can take off. This you could not. The band was woven stainless steel with no clasp, although the USB-C port on the side suggested it could be charged. Somebody was not only keeping track; they were listening. Constantly. I surmised the only way to remove it was to break the electronic connection, and I had a pretty strong feeling that would not bode well for either man or his family. Camp handed me a roll of duct tape from his pack, and I wrapped both watches several times. I doubted doing so would hinder the GPS tracking, but it might mute the microphone. Having done so, I motioned to Guido to continue. Which he did—albeit in a weak whisper.

"Please. They have my family."

"Who has your family?"

"Don't know his name."

"How do you know he has your family?"

The man pulled out his phone and showed me a picture of a woman and three kids, all wearing black hoods and tied up.

"How do I know you didn't stage this?"

Guido might have weighed a hundred and thirty pounds and never lifted a weight in his life. He stuttered. "Do I look like I staged that?"

"Who are you?"

More whispering. "Juseppe Vincenzo."

"Where do you work?"

He nodded. "Financial district."

"What do you do?"

"I . . . man—"

I didn't have time for stalling. Another nudge with my muzzle.

"Manage large accounts with oversight into lessening tax liability per statute."

"What's that mean in English?"

"I help people pay less tax."

"So you help people cheat the government?"

He shrugged. "Yes. Although I—"

My BS-meter was dinging. "What else?"

"I moonlight as a programmer."

"Programmer or hacker?"

"Yes."

These people didn't just target some finance nerd to help them move some drives. There was more. "How'd you get involved in this?"

Guido turned away.

I turned him back. "Nope. I want the whites of your eyes."

"I got caught."

"Doing what?"

I could tell the admission was painful. Maybe even embarrassing. I doubted it had anything to do with finances. "Something I should not have."

From the bloody floor of the Suburban, Bernie chimed in: "Tell me about it."

Camp laughed behind me.

I moved closer. "You don't say. Continue."

Guido clammed up and bit his lip until I threatened to rip off his earlobe. "I paid for some time with . . . these boys."

My reaction must have been subconscious because the next thing I knew my hand hurt and his nose had exploded like a tomato across his face. Much like Bernie's. Both men's noses now pointed to 7:30 rather than 6:00. Camp meanwhile had parked in a lot not far from the lights of Times Square, which flashed a psychedelic disco effect inside the Suburban.

I poked Guido in the face with my muzzle. "Talk."

His voice had grown nasal. "I used to leave work and visit this"—he made invisible quotation marks with his fingers—" 'massage parlor.' Every Friday. My job is very stressful and my wife is not very—"

"I really don't care."

"One day I returned to my office and found a video in my inbox. The next day a second. And so on."

"And the videos were of?" Another poke.

He looked down. "Me and . . ." He trailed off.

"So whoever captured this video of you is using it as leverage. And now you're a runner."

Guido nodded. "Among other things." Here was the first twinge of bitterness.

"What else do you do?"

He paused and then whispered lower. "If I tell you, I'll never see my family again."

This might have been the first truthful thing

he'd said. "And if you don't, you won't. Pick your poison."

He considered this. "I manage the data."

"Define manage."

"I deliver the drives and manually transfer the data."

I nudged Bernie. "That what you do?"

He nodded. "Yes, but I've never met this guy."

"I'd guess that's on purpose." In my ear I heard Bones: *"Mutiny is easier to prevent if all the sailors never sail on the same ship at the same time."* I turned to Camp. "You get the feeling he's not telling us the truth, the whole truth, and nothing but the truth?"

Camp nodded. "More song. Less dance."

About here, Bernie chimed in. "You should just come clean, man."

Guido looked to Bernie and his naked body. "Oh, so that's working out pretty well for you?"

I leaned in closer to Camp. "What if one of these guys is more important than he's letting on?"

Camp considered this. "Anything's possible."

I returned to Guido. "Strip."

"What?"

From his French cuffs to his gold cufflinks to his matching Italian leather belt and shoes, Guido dressed with intention. And suggestion. He also wore a lot of jewelry, and I wasn't sure if he did so to mask the watch he couldn't take off or because he wanted to look flashy. Either way, I was pretty sure he wanted those around him to think a certain way about him. So, as with Bernie, I intended to take that away.

"Take 'em off."

"But—"

I met him across the chin with the butt of my MK4, splattering blood across his custom shirt. "You or me. What's it going to be?"

Guido stripped to his birthday suit, which reminded him that he was vulnerable and not in charge, which I gathered was a new emotion. I pointed to all his jewelry. "All of it."

He protested. "You know what this is worth?"

I thought about educating him on the value of my friend Bones or the value of the tens of thousands of trafficked people under Frank's control but figured it'd take too long. "Do I look like I care?"

He dropped the jewelry. Except the watch.

"You wear that because you want to?"

He shook his head once, and his facial expression changed. It was the first time I noted a measure of sincerity.

I figured the owner of that watch was tracking both Guido and Bernie, so I zip-tied them to each other. Watch to watch. Pragmatically, doing so would make any attempted escape comical to witness. At a minimum it would need to be coordinated. But in truth, my motive was a bit deeper. I wanted the ear on the other end to know I had two of his people. And two of his locations. And his drives. And I wanted him to have a front-row seat to our conversation. If one started talking, both watches would pick it up. Maybe it wasn't much, and maybe the owner didn't care that I had two of his minions, but it made me feel better. I also thought if we could play one off the other, they'd sell each other out.

I was right. Ten seconds in to being strapped to Guido, Bernie read the writing on the wall and started singing like a canary.

"He's the book—" Bernie only got the word "book" out of his mouth before Guido started pummeling him with his free fist. Which did little to stop "account" from coming out of Bernie's mouth. Watching them spin in circles, each swinging their one free hand, convinced me we were on to something. Soon the two men looked like fighting cats rolling around the back of the Suburban.

Unlike the drives and the computer vaults, these watches had to be connected to some Wi-Fi, satellite, cell signal, or all three, because whoever put them there had to be able to track and listen. I turned to Camp, who was typing keystrokes into a tablet. "Can you get into these things?"

Camp didn't look up. "Working on it."

Bernie had Guido in a headlock, but both men were so winded neither could hurt the other.

I tapped Guido in the temple. "How does he communicate with you?"

Bernie spoke first. "If you don't tell him, I will."

Guido was about to open his mouth when Bernie clamped down on the headlock. "The truth, man." The additional applied pressure would have worked had he not held his other arm in front of Guido's mouth. Evidently Bernie had never been in a fight but had watched his fair share of WWF. Guido seized the opportunity, biting through the skin, and Bernie let go.

Guido sat up, kicked at Bernie's face with his heel, and then leaned against the rear window, trying to catch his breath while still connected via zip tie to Bernie's left hand. After a few seconds he motioned with his right hand like he wanted to write something. I handed him a black Sharpie and he wrote "Google doc" on the window.

"Take me there."

He nodded to his watch, covered in duct tape. Clever. The watch held the address for the document, which was also where he received his instructions and communications. I unwrapped his watch but did not cut the zip tie, leaving the two connected.

Guido manipulated his watch and, when directed, positioned it in front of his face, allowing it to perform a facial scan. Once finished, the document opened up. Guido scrolled through it, causing his eyes to narrow and creating a wrinkle above his nose. After a few frantic seconds, he held up the watch for me to read.

It was empty. I motioned to Bernie, who completed the same sequence. When finished, he held up the watch, allowing me to view the document. It, too, had been deleted.

Camp tapped me on the shoulder and displayed his tablet. The word "Disconnect" sat in the middle of a button with the cursor hovering over it. He was asking me. I nodded, he clicked on it, and the two watches unlocked themselves, falling onto the floor of the Suburban. I opened the door, set them in the gutter, and returned to my two friends. Both of whom did not look happy that we'd freed them from their tethers.

Guido was on the verge of crying. "My family is dead."

Which got me to wondering, so I stepped outside the vehicle and called Eddie. "Eddie, we think Guido is married with children because that's what we read. But this guy doesn't seem like the marrying type, and I'm pretty sure he's not interested in women. Can you do some checking? I think his whole bio may be fabricated."

"On it."

I returned to the car to find Bernie and Guido fighting once again, with Guido trying to scratch out Bernie's eyes. I had just closed the door when the sat phone rang. It was Eddie. "You're good. Juseppe is not what he seems. If the medical records Jess dug up are correct, he had a vasectomy a decade ago. Somebody somewhere is lying."

I tapped Guido on the shoulder. "I'm losing patience. How old are your kids?"

He thought for a second. "Seven and eight."

"And yet you had a vasectomy a decade ago."

He considered this. "It didn't work."

I'd had enough. I'd never really considered torture something I'd entertain. I just figured I'd either kill them or arrest them or leave them to be arrested by someone else—but for Guido I made an exception.

The human eyeball is literally a bundle of nerves. Some two million of them. They can sense a single speck of dirt. So I grabbed Guido by the hair and shoved my right thumb into his eye. Applying sufficient pressure.

Guido didn't like pain. "Okay, I'm not married. Never have been. Don't have kids."

"Thought so."

"And the videos?"

"That part is actually true."

"Thought so."

I turned to Bernie. "Why'd you say he's the accountant? You ever met him?"

"No. Just heard rumors."

Back to Guido. "You handle his books?"

"I doubt anyone handles all of his books, but of those that are handled, I handle some."

"How far is your reach?"

"This hemisphere."

"North, South, and Central America?"

He nodded.

"Brazil?"

"Yes."

"Europe?"

Another nod.

"You have an interesting definition of hemisphere. Asia?"

He shook his head. "No. That's somebody else."

"You ever met them?"

"We don't meet anyone." He thumbed to Bernie. "He's the first I've ever met. It's by design."

"Does he keep books like you?"

Guido shook his head. "No. He's a runner. We use them a little while . . ." He looked to Bernie and shrugged. "Then we don't."

Bernie kicked him square in the gut with his heel, knocking all the air out of Guido's lungs.

When he sat up and began breathing again, I pressed the muzzle against his left shoulder and said, "I'm short on time, and because of that, so are you. You're going to tell me exactly what you do and where you do it."

He began crying. "But they'll kill—"

Before "me" could come out of his mouth, I pulled the trigger, sending the bullet through the flesh of his right shoulder. Just beneath his collarbone. He'd live but he'd need rehab. Since it was the first time Guido had ever been shot, he didn't know that. Guido screamed and flopped like a line-caught fish. When I leveled the muzzle at his left shoulder, he started singing like a canary, proving that confession is good for the soul.

Guido explained he managed data at three sites. The high-rise in New York and two private penitentiaries. One in Atlanta. The second in Alabama."

"That all?"

The sight of blood was making him queasy and he was having trouble formulating the words. "Once a year, I make a drop to an oceanfront home on Amelia Island."

"They all set up like this one?"

By now he was lying down on the floor of the Suburban, and Bernie was screaming at me to get medical attention. I leveled the muzzle at him and he shut up. Camp dumped some clotting powder on the wound and pressed a gauze in the hole. Guido was only seconds from passing out. Finally, he managed, "Identical. They all are."

"You have any personal encounters with any-body?"

Guido's face was sheet white, and he kept screaming something about how he was dying. I waited. "One guy . . . one time. Two years ago. Haven't seen him since."

I pulled out a picture of Bones. Given that he and Frank were twins, I figured it was close enough. "Look like him?"

He nodded. "Yes."

"Where's the house?"

He gave me the address.

"You recall that from memory?"

He nodded. "I'm photographic."

Now we were getting somewhere. I pointed to the drives. "What's on them?"

"Videos."

"Any financial?"

"No."

"Where's that?"

He tapped his temple.

I pulled out a laptop and offered it to him. "Take me there."

He held up bloody hands.

I pointed to Camp. "Speak it. He'll type."

Over the next fifteen minutes, Guido walked Camp through eight different banks with forty-eight accounts. Bernie, obviously much lower on the totem pole, listened with rapt attention. And while Guido knew the information and had been depositing into these accounts often, he was surprised by the new account balances.

Zero.

All the accounts had been emptied in the last twenty minutes.

"Tell me about the Amelia home. Did you meet somewhere there?"

"Yes, but I never saw his face. He spoke through a telecom."

"Anybody else in the home?"

"Not that I could see."

"Anything strange about the home?"

"It'd been built around a cement vault. Only time I ever walked by, the door was open—only it'd been reversed and only locked from the inside."

"Anything in the vault?"

He held up a single finger. "One thing."

I had a pretty good idea, but I waited.

"A bed."

Behind me I heard Camp say, "Uh-oh."

"What do you mean, 'Uh-oh'?"

He pointed at his tablet. "I've been hacked. I can get it back, but it'll take a minute."

While Camp typed source code, the screen flickered black, then switched to a live-feed video. The camera angle had been blurred on purpose, but I was able to make out the side of someone's head. It was Bones. The face was his. His profile. Oddly, there were no marks. No sign of beating. Only dark circles below his eyes suggesting he'd not slept. As the camera moved forward, I got a better picture of Bones's face, and while he didn't appear to have been beaten or tortured, he was in pain. Evidenced by a single tear hanging just below his eye. Bones was focused on something in front of him. Something that hurt to look at. As the camera circled in front of him, his eyes focused on the lens. Staring directly at me. Then the video went black.

I suppressed my emotions, rewound the video, and studied it. Carefully staged, it gave away nothing.

Camp spoke quickly while his fingers typed at the speed of hummingbird wings. "The GPS signature of the video is from the coast of Florida. If you believe it."

I put the car in drive. We were flying to Florida—via Colorado.

CHAPTER 28

Day 5 Without Bones

I spoke over the comms and asked Eddie not to wake Summer, but no sooner had I said it than she responded in my ear, "You really think I'm sleeping?"

Nothing on planet Earth soothed me more than Summer's voice. And the thought that she'd been listening to my every word since I'd left was medicine to my soul. "I guess not. You good?"

"Be better when we get him back."

"Me too. I think I could use your help."

"Name it."

"Meet me at the plane?"

"Done."

"Oh, and . . ."

"Yeah?"

"Bring Angel."

When I stepped onto the tarmac, she was standing there. A backpack over one shoulder. Gunner at her side. Seeing me, Gunner tackled me and attempted to lick the skin off my face, eliciting involuntary laughter. Which I needed. "Hey, boy, I missed you too."

His tail was wagging at warp speed.

I rubbed behind both ears, at which point he closed his eyes, leaned his shoulder into me, and started that guttural moan thing he does. Eventually he lay on the tarmac and put his limp paws in the air, reminding me of Disney's *Jungle Book* and the lovable Baloo. I spoke as I rubbed. "I need your help."

More moaning. His tail wag had slowed to intermittent wiper speed. Living in a town populated almost entirely by dog-loving women had spoiled him rotten.

"Bones is in trouble and we need to go get him."

He let out a long moan.

"Are you even listening to me? I said Bones needs us."

Gunner rolled over and tilted his head.

"Bad men took him."

He sat up. Trained on me.

"That's better. They're holding him in a house, and I need you to put on your game face." I pointed to the steps leading up to the plane. "Now are you in or out?"

Gunner turned, bounded twice, and disappeared into the plane.

Summer stood in front of me. I wasn't sure which one of us was more tired. Evidence of that love I couldn't stop thinking about. "Hey, you."

She placed her palm on my cheek. "You look tired."

I half smiled and shrugged. "I hadn't noticed."

She smiled. "Liar."

I held her hands. Conflicted. Because I didn't want to bring her into it, but I'd seen her pursue her daughter down the Intracoastal when she couldn't swim. In many ways Summer was tougher than me. She had no quit. And no fear. "I need a favor."

"Anything."

"Come with me. Probably have you back here this evening, but if I'm right, you'll be needed and I won't have time to hang around."

Summer grabbed my hand and faced me like the dancer she is. She twirled on her toes, spinning three times, then wrapped herself in my arms, where she paused and placed her cheek to mine. Then, having said what she wanted to say, she untwirled and faced me once again. Classic Summer. Still on Broadway. Bowing, she curtsied and stepped onto the plane without another comment.

We couldn't very well turn Bernie and Guido over to the police because they had info we needed, but I also didn't have time to sift it out of them, so I passed them to Eddie and his team, who were eager to start their own questioning.

I opened the car door and found Angel staring at me. Shep was asleep in her lap. She yawned, wanting to make sure I knew that she woke from a dead sleep for this little meeting. "Hey, Padre."

"Hey." I'd asked Summer to bring Angel because Casey was still too fragile and needed time. Ellie was still a girl and I needed to just let her be one. Angel was in the best place of all. She was also tough, and I needed tough.

I stared at the plane. Then back at her. "Need a favor."

She gestured to Shep. "I know that."

"You do?"

"Of course. Why else would you drag me out here in the cold when other civilized people are sleeping?"

"Good point."

When I pointed at Shep and tried to whisper, she held up her hand like a stop sign and nodded as if she already had this covered. "Padre, seriously. Give me some credit. I know what you need."

"You do?"

"Of course. I'm a woman. You're a man. I swear, sometimes you're dumb as a bag of hammers."

I was tired and most of this was going right over my head. "I thought—"

She chuckled. "That's always where you make your first mistake. Thinking." She ran her fingers through his hair, her tone changing. Seriousness replacing humor. "Little man is safe. I got him. Don't worry."

"I left my Glock 19 and several magazines on the top shelf just inside the safe."

She patted the backpack at her feet. "Way ahead of you." A slight grin. "Again."

"Don't hesitate. These guys are playing for keeps, so shoot first and ask questions la—"

She straightened the blanket around Shep's shoulder, her tone sounding almost motherly as she responded, "Padre, I told you. I got him. Now—" She shooed me off, smiled again, and her tone changed a third time. Tenderness replacing the others. "Go find Bones."

I nodded and quietly shut the door. "Working on it."

Three hours later, as the sun rose over the Atlantic, the G5 landed at a private airfield in Fernandina Beach. Three miles west of the coast. For the first time in several days, I'd slept an hour. When Camp shook me and said we were two minutes out, I had been dreaming of a night on the mountain with Bones, Summer, Casey, Angel, and Ellie. How we'd made s'mores. How we'd laughed at Ellie's marshmallow-and-chocolate-covered face. How Ellie and Angel had slept on either side of Casey, and how we all listened to her tortured sleep. How Bones had sat sentinel-like, strapped with his Sig and sipping the fruit of the earth. A wrinkle between his eyes. The final image was Summer. The look on her face. A look that both carried and defended. It was one of the things I loved most about her. Maybe the most. How she loved. She never halved her love. She multiplied it. Exponentially. As a result, she never ran out of room. Which was why she was on the plane.

When we landed three hours later, I held Bones's orange Pelican case under Gunner's nose and let him sniff the handle. "Find Bones," I told him. Then I asked Summer to stay near the radio. She tapped her earpiece in response.

The coastal house was massive and suggested Frank did here what he did in NYC—hid in plain sight. Camp told me I should wait and study the house. I told him he was right but I was going in the front door. Given my tone, he held on to Gunner's collar and didn't argue. "We've got your six."

With four rounds of 00 buck from the Benelli M4, I shot the massive front door off its hinges. This disturbance was met with return rifle fire, but I'd caught them off guard as they hadn't expected me to be so brazen—their response was sporadic and their aim poor. I found one in the kitchen and the second on the balcony. Both were inexperienced and ineffective. Camp found the third who tried to be cute and hide in a huge vase. Gunner sniffed out a fourth in the pantry.

In the basement we found the first sign of a struggle. Upturned furniture and a trail of blood leading to the swimming pool where a body floated. I had a feeling Bones had been kept here but no longer. My suspicion turned to certainty when Gunner found a man in the next room. The man was stretched out on his back, and a cursory scan proved somebody had worked him over. One shoulder had been dislocated, accompanied by a broken clavicle, and one forearm had been snapped in two. He was taking shallow breaths, suggesting trouble breathing, and one leg was lying at an unnatural angle with a wooden table leg sticking out of the thigh. Gunner latched his mouth on the man's neck and held him until I pressed the muzzle of my M4 to his chest.

He was floating in and out of consciousness, so I knelt and rested my left hand on the table leg. When his eyes opened and focused on me, I wiggled the leg slightly. He moaned.

"How'd you get this peg leg?"

He shook his head, attempting some sort of macho refusal. Looking at his condition, I could see he was done; he just didn't know it yet. Bones would call it confusing stupidity with courage.

Eventually he swallowed and managed, "Some old dude."

I chuckled. "That old dude called Bones?"

"Don't know his name."

"Where is he?"

He stared at the ceiling and shrugged. More stupidity.

"Looks like he worked you over pretty good."

318

"I've known worse."

I shook my head and wiggled the peg. "I doubt it."

The man moaned, exposing a snapped femur. "Second time. Where is he?"

He glanced at his leg and his macho facade faded. When he spoke, he did so through gritted teeth. "*Hotel California*."

"Explain."

The man was pale as a sheet and sweating. "It's a boat."

I spoke into my comms. "Eddie?"

He responded, "On it."

Back to the man. "Like the Eagles song. You can check out but you can never leave?"

He whispered, "Something like that."

Behind me, Gunner sat whining and scratching at a closed door. Camp opened it, cleared the room, and motioned. I left the bleeding man to reconsider his life's choices and stepped into the darkened room alongside Camp. A girl lay curled up in the corner. Eyes open. Knees pulled to her chest. She, like so many others I'd discovered, was hugging herself in the absence of anyone else to do it. I clicked on the light and watched her shoulders wince as she realized she'd been found but didn't know our intentions.

Camp knelt, said, "I'm not going to hurt you," then gently sank his arms beneath her, lifted her off the concrete, and carried her to a couch where he covered her with a blanket. She blinked, pulled the blanket up around her shoulders, and studied us. Trying to suppress the coming flood, she looked at me and whispered, "Murph?"

She might have been a freshman in college. "Yes."

"He"—she let out a deep breath and retreated to the memory—"told me to wait. Promised me you'd be coming."

"He's good about that." I wanted to put a hand on her shoulder but thought better of it, not knowing what she'd suffered. "What happened?"

She pointed to the bleeding man in the adjacent room. "He was trying to . . . and then this older man pulled him off me. They got in a fight, and then the older man carried me in here and told me to stay put until you opened the door. That I'd know it was you because you'd have a yellow dog with you that would probably lick my face." True to form, Gunner had.

I nodded. "How'd you end up in this house?"

She stared at the ceiling, then back at me. "Got a job offer to model. Said they'd pay a thousand dollars cash for the day."

"How'd they communicate?"

"Everything came through social media."

Most traffickers use image recognition software to troll Instagram, Facebook, and TikTok accounts and then recruit naive school-aged boys and girls, based largely on selfies. The desire for likes and followers drowns out any common sense when it comes to posting online, but in my experience most kids don't care. *It'll never happen to me.* The girl in front of me now knew otherwise. "Model what?"

"Jewelry. Bathing suits. Furs." She shrugged. "Even a few expensive cars." Another retreat. "When we arrived . . ."

"How many of you were there?"

She shrugged. "A dozen? I don't know. We were never all in the same room." She calculated. "Maybe eighteen. Everything looked above-board. Professional photographers. Expensive cameras. Makeup artists. Spray-on tan. Nobody laid a finger on us. After work, they invited us to stay for the party. Dancing. Music . . . I don't remember much after that."

I needed more information. "When my friend placed you in this room, did anyone else know?"

She pointed again at the bleeding man. "Other than him?"

"Yes."

She shook her head. "I don't think so."

"I know this is the last thing you want to do right now, but"—I held up my phone—"will you let me take your picture? I need to search for you online. It might help us find the others."

This made her uncomfortable. "What do you mean?"

I waved my hand across the house. "These guys baited you under the guise of professional work. Once they'd convinced you they were legit, they casually lured you to the party. Which was the intention from the beginning. Once you were comfortable, they slipped something in your drink and took the real pictures."

"What do you mean, 'real pictures'?"

"The ones they took while you were passed out—the ones they're currently using to advertise and sell you."

She pulled the blanket higher up around her shoulders. "Sell me. Sell what?"

"Your body."

In her innocence she was having trouble connecting the dots. Textbook prey for guys like these. "Where?" she managed.

"The dark web. You probably have your own auction—provided they don't know you're missing."

"The dark what?"

"Web. It's an Internet for sick and twisted people." I held up my phone. "May I? Please. It'll help us."

"Us?"

I pointed at my radio and the earpiece.

She looked concerned. "Am I in trouble?"

This time I did put my hand gently on her shoulder. "No. You're not in trouble and you've done nothing wrong."

She was crying now. "What'd I do?"

"You were born beautiful."

The girl was in shock at the thought of having been undressed, posed, and photographed without her consent or knowledge. Through tears, she nodded, so I snapped a close-up of her face, then handed my phone to Camp and spoke to Eddie. "Eddie, file incoming. My guess is that where we find her, we'll find the others."

Eddie sounded over the radio. "Check."

Thirty seconds later, Eddie returned. "Murph, it's cryptic but she's listed. Pics attached. She was right about the furs and the cars. Time slots start tonight, but they give no location."

"They send that after you've 'won' the auction. How often are the time slots? What are the intervals?"

A pause. "Looks like you buy segments of eight hours."

Now I understood the reason for Bones's tears. Frank could torture his brother, but it wouldn't hurt as much as forcing him to watch the worst miscreants on the planet gather around the auction block and buy the innocent of the world. Why sell a body once when you could sell it a hundred times? Frank had probably made Bones watch them bring in these girls, then drug them and photograph them.

"How many bidders?"

"A lot."

"Where are they from?"

"Where are they not from?"

"What's the starting bid?"

"Twenty-five thousand. But there's a drop-down menu where you can select certain fetishes. The current bid is seventy-eight for three segments. Uh . . . nope. Scratch that. Eighty-two. No, three. Now ninety. She's popular. Looks like two guys driving the bidding." A pause followed by more clicks. "The other girls are tracking the same. And . . ." Another pause. "Looks like whoever is running the show requires a fifty-thousand buy-in before you ever bid."

"Their business model is much like Amazon Prime, though slightly more expensive. You buy in with a yearly membership fee, and then they notify you when they have something you might like. The fee gives you the right to bid but no guarantee of winning. It simply gives you a seat at the table. It also weeds out the posers." I stared out across the Atlantic. "What's the weather forecast for the coast of Florida?"

"Clear. Wind out of the southwest at two. Seas one to two."

I returned to my half-conscious friend in the other room and wiggled the wooden spike Bones had impaled through his leg. He moaned. "Where's that boat going?"

He didn't answer.

I twisted the spike.

He writhed under the pain. "Don't know."

Given his current level of discomfort, I tended to believe him. "You overhear anything?"

He nodded.

"Explain."

"Didn't make sense. They were talking about low fence, potcake, and sipping something."

While this made no sense to me, Camp asked the guy, "They say 'sip'?"

Another nod with no explanation.

Camp explained, " 'Low fence' is Bahamian for pushover. 'Potcake' is a stray dog or something you'd feed scraps. And 'sip-sip' is gossip or news you heard through the grapevine."

I raised an eyebrow.

He shrugged, not feeling the need to explain, which was one of the things I liked about him.

"Eddie?"

"On it." Keystrokes echoed in the background. As did Jess's voice. She was saying something about satellite. Eddie again. "Murph, Jess found a yacht on satellite. Two hundred feet. Traveling fourteen knots. Pretty decked out, too, including a helicopter pad. Just north of you. It's just come through the mouth of the St. Mary's and is heading toward open water."

I returned to the bleeding man and wiggled the peg to let him know he wasn't allowed to pass out yet and that I was still there. "The man that did this . . . How'd he leave here?"

He shook his head. "Don't know for sure, but I heard a helicopter."

"Eddie?"

"Check."

"You see a helicopter on that boat?"

A pause. "Yep. And heat signatures are bright red. Meaning—"

I finished his thought. "It just landed."

"Check."

Time was the slave traders' problem. Guys trafficking flesh were constantly caught in the tension between too little and too much. They needed to let the auction play out in order to attract the highest bidder, but the longer they waited, the higher the chance that something could go wrong. As in, they could get caught. Not to mention that they only made money when they sold something. Hence, short time limits on the auctions. They could get around this problem if they had a ready-made country club paying audience that had "enrolled in membership" and was awaiting the next sale. They'd send notification of the auction through some sort of social media with self-destructing data and end-to-end encryption. Like Snapchat, Telegram, or Wickr.

Of the three, Eddie and team confirmed Wickr was the best—or worst, depending on your perspective. Most self-destructive apps used a single encryption key on both the sender's and receiver's end that converted the data to unreadable texts—until encrypted by the right key. Wickr was different in that it used five end-to-end encryption keys, making it one of the safest and most secure apps in the world, as evidenced by the number of terrorist groups and government agencies using it. I'd never claim any technology was unhackable, but until now Wickr had been.

With little else to go on, I looked at Camp. "We need to get on that boat."

I spoke over the radio. "Summer?"

She responded quickly. "Be there in ten."

Camp, Gunner, and I shot out of Sapelo Sound in the demon boat, *Daemon Deux*. Turning south and then east, we crossed the Intracoastal and cleared the jetties, and then I pushed the throttle forward. In a few seconds we passed eighty miles an hour. Then ninety. And when I looked down, given clear seas, we were skimming across the water doing 114 mph with plenty of throttle remaining. Gunner was lying on his stomach, bracing himself between my legs. Radar on the demon boat showed *Hotel California* traveling on a bearing of 142 degrees south. Provided she maintained her current course, the system estimated we'd intersect her in about nineteen minutes. Give or take.

Eleven minutes in, Eddie sounded over the radio. "Murph, satellite just picked up an explosion onboard the *California*." I studied the horizon for smoke, but we were still eight minutes out. Eddie continued, "Judging by the size of the fireball and now the smoke column, they're in trouble."

I slammed the throttle to full, and the two Mercury engines roared to life. Carrying us to the insane on-the-water speed of 142 mph. "Check."

Gunner barked below me.

We crossed the remaining miles with little more than the propellers in the water. It wasn't long until the spiral of smoke came into view. Then the *California*.

Our first problem became immediately apparent. We couldn't tie up to a sinking boat. Not to mention the fact that those on the boat were highly motivated not to allow us. My hope was that they'd be too distracted getting off or fighting an engine fire to shoot at us. I gave the helm to Camp. "Bring me alongside. Then stay close. We might have to get off in a hurry."

Camp nodded.

Smoke poured from the bow and a second blast hole on the upper deck. If I had to guess, I'd say Bones had everything to do with both. We approached from the stern, in what would have been her wake save the fact that her engines were as silent as was she. Dead in the water and listing slightly to starboard. It was also obvious that her nose was dipping. Meaning, she was in the process of taking on water, which would eventually sink her. As for time, I didn't think we had long. I had one goal: get on, get Bones, and get out. I doubted Frank was aboard, but if so, I'd very much like to send him down with his ship.

Camp ran us alongside just as someone leaned over the upper bridge railing and leveled a rifle at us. Camp saw him first, steered with his left hand, and shot with his right. The body spilled off the railing and into the water just as Gunner and I jumped from bow to stern. We ran across the pool deck and into a gym that ended in a stairwell. We descended the stairs into an empty galley where steam poured out of a pot on the stove and bread was burning in the oven. I cleared the galley and ran to a second spiral stairwell that led both up and down. Sound and smoke rose up the stairs from the engine room, and somewhere above me echoed the report of a rifle. We climbed the stairs, passed the corridor to the cabins, and entered what, prior to the blast, had been a ballroom and bar.

About the time we cleared the doorway, a muscled man came at me from my left. He looked like a brick wall with no neck, cauliflower ears, and Popeye forearms. He was covered in soot and ash and his face was busted up and bleeding. His right elbow was angled the wrong direction. Given that he wasn't wielding a weapon and that I might have to talk to him for information,

I tapped him in the leg with a round from my M4. The round missed his femoral but shattered his femur. He spilled to the ground and began screaming at me in Russian. To my right was a pool table. I wrapped the eight-ball in a towel and turned out his lights. Two seconds later, Gunner's ears pointed toward the corridor in front of us. Then the hair stood up on his back and he started growling. At the far end of the main lounge, a stairwell led up.

My approach to finding Bones was simple—if he was on this boat and he was able, he'd move to either the bridge or comms room. Gunner growled again, jumped past me on the stairs, sniffed his way through the bridge, and disappeared through the door on the opposite side. I followed, finding the bridge empty but sounding with every possible alarm, the control panels lit up like Christmas trees flashing red. I rounded a corner and headed toward medical and the stairway that led up to the comms room, where I heard someone talking. Unlike anything else on this boat, the voice sounded calm.

I climbed the stairs, bounded into the comms room, leveled my rifle, and found Gunner standing over the body of a man. Licking his face.

It was Bones.

He'd been worked over pretty good, his face was more black than blue, both of his eyes were nearly swollen shut, and there was a reason he wasn't standing. His right knee was problematic, as were his left shoulder and arm. Something about the bone between his shoulder and elbow looked unnatural.

It took me a second to recognize him. To realize I'd found him.

He looked up at me while his right hand rubbed Gunner's ears. " 'Bout time you got here. What took you so long?"

I knelt and started assessing his wounds. "Next time I won't come at all."

Before I had a chance to figure out if I could move him, he said, "Never mind me." He pointed. "Take the elevator shaft. Exit at the water storage and make your way below into the ballast rooms. They're probably flooded, but it's where they're keeping them."

"Keeping who?"

"Seventeen girls. Three boys."

"I'm not leaving you. You can't move."

"I've been hurt worse."

"Bones, do you—"

He grabbed me by the collar and pulled my face inches from his. He was in more pain than he let on and his breaths were short. Brick-wall man must have broken a few ribs before he came at me. Bones spoke through gritted teeth. "This! . . . is what we do." Another short breath. "You've got about ninety seconds. What are you going to do?"

I tried to lift him.

He slapped me across the face. "Not listening! Eighty-five." He pointed at the ship's intercom just above him. "The water is rising. They're locked inside."

I didn't care what he said or who was about to die, I tried one last time to lift him. I was not going to leave him behind.

Finally, he put his hand on my shoulder. "Murph."

I made it to my knees, but he was deadweight.

His voice was calm and tender. My friend was speaking. "Bishop."

I set him on the ground and he shook his head. "Don't do this. Eighty seconds." Speaking was difficult, and something I couldn't see was causing him pain. "That's somebody's daughter. Sister. Son." He grabbed my vest and pounded me in the heart. "I was once them. I remember. Being alone. Praying for rescue, and nobody came. I used to wonder why." He shook his head. "Not anymore. This is what we do. It's why God put us on planet Earth. Everything else is gravy."

I was about to argue with him when he held up a finger. "I trained you for one purpose." With the same finger he pointed below us. "And that purpose is seventy seconds from drowning. Now choose."

I turned to Gunner and held out my hand. "Stay. If anybody but me comes in that door, eat their face off." I turned to run when I heard Bones laugh. "Oh, and one more thing."

I stopped and looked at him like he'd lost his mind.

"Your training is officially over. Congratulations. You've graduated."

I turned, shaking my head, and hit the elevator shaft at a dead run. I slammed open the doors, jumped for the cables, and fireman slid to the bottom, which was knee deep in water. I pulled open the exit door and stared at a long corridor of what must have been crew cabins as the doors were smaller, not so ornate, and spaced more closely together. One by one I kicked them open but they were empty. Then I heard the screaming. Below me was a hatch. I lifted it to reveal a steel stairway and a labyrinth filled with pipes, gauges, and various pumps and tanks. The stairwell led to a smaller hatch door with a round glass window four inches in diameter. The door looked to be thick steel locked by a single lever.

As I studied the door, I heard screaming erupt from inside. Then a girl's face flashed across the glass as a movement of water pressed her against it. I grabbed the ax, hit the lever square, and the pressure behind the door slammed it open. The massive flow of water slammed me against the stairwell and ripped my M4 out of my hands as the wall of water and pile of bodies buried me beneath the surface.

For what felt like several minutes, one body after another pummeled me, pressing me farther into the bowels of pipes and gauges. Though muted by the water, I could hear both boys and girls screaming for help above me. Needing air, I fought through the pipes and the darkness to the light above where arms and legs thrashed and fought for the exit hatch. When my head broke the surface of the water, I found myself in a sea of screaming children climbing over one another and clamoring for the exit. I knew I was of no help if I got tangled up in that mess, so I swam to the wall, climbed the pipes, pushed open a second hatch, and pulled my water-soaked frame through the hole. Then I crawled through several inches of water to the first hatch. One by one, I grabbed each hand and lifted the body attached to it through the hole. One, two, three . . . nine, ten.

Where were the other ten?

I turned to the nearest girl. "Where are the others?"

She pointed to a door at the end of the corridor. As she did, the boat listed farther, suggesting that while my opening the hatch door freed those inside, it also hastened the sinking of the ship. She was taking on massive amounts of water, and this two-hundred-foot superyacht was soon to join the *Titanic*. I knelt. She looked scared and maybe sixteen. "Can you get these kids upstairs?" She was scattered and not hearing me. I set my hand on her shoulder. Her eyes found mine. I spoke calmly. "What's your name?"

"S . . ." Her teeth were chattering because she'd been in the water so long. "Sage."

"Sage." I held her hand and eyed the mass of writhing and shivering bodies around us. "I need help. Can you get these kids up those stairs and to the back of the boat?"

She nodded.

"Good girl. I'll be up shortly." I took off at a dead run down the corridor that spanned the length of the boat. Knowing that many boats like this store their fuel in tanks in the rear and away from the engines in the mid and fore sections, I found the door that read Fuel, but the lever wouldn't budge, so I slammed the ax-head square into the middle of the lever. Under more pressure than the previous entrance, the door swung open and a wave of water rolled me backward head over boots. When I came to a stop, more bodies lay around me. These were younger. And in worse shape. Two at a time, I began lifting them and carrying them up the stairs as the bow of the ship pointed more toward the ocean's floor. One trip. Two trips. Three. Finally, I appeared in the stairwell and found Camp carrying a child over each shoulder. I had no idea what he'd done with the *Daemon Deux*, but I didn't argue.

On my fifth trip, I returned, waded through the

water that was now waist deep, and climbed into the hole where I found a boy clinging to a pipe. He was shaking, and fear had gripped him. Entirely. I pulled on him, but he wouldn't budge. The water had risen to my chest and was soon to close off the hatch door. I pulled again, but he resisted me more strongly. The water closed off the hatch and began rising in the room. Our only exit now was swimming. I pulled myself up because I needed him to come willingly. I could not fight him and the water. I found his eyes, his eyes found mine, and I said, "You wanna get out of here?"

He nodded.

"Can you swim?"

Another nod.

I lifted my collar. "Can you hold on to this while I"—I pointed at the submerged hatch—"swim through that?"

A final nod.

"Take a deep breath."

He did. I did. And I submerged while he clung to my neck.

The flow of cold water was akin to a current inside the hold. I grasped pipes, latches, even the steel grate of the walkway to claw my way back to the hatch door while the water pulled on us. Once through, I kicked off the sides of the door and we surfaced alongside the others. They were younger, scared, and didn't know who to trust. The boat was listing, making noises consistent with metal bending, and based on the water up to my chest, we didn't have long. I pointed and began herding kids to the stairwell. Camp met me, naked children scurried up, and Gunner led them to the demon boat.

Above me I heard a helicopter winding up. I hollered at Camp, "I'm going for Bones."

I mounted the stairs, climbing three at a time, drawn to Gunner's bark. I reached the bridge and hollered, but Bones did not respond. The whirring blades of the helicopter were drowning out Gunner's more rapid bark. I turned the corner, bolted past medical, and then bounded up one final flight to the comms room where I'd left them both. I was speaking to Bones as I entered the room: "Time to get up, old man. We got to get off this—"

But the room was empty. Bones was gone. So was Gunner.

That's when I noticed the trail of blood that led out of the comms room, down the corridor, and out onto the helipad. Like someone was dragged. I exited the comms room and sprinted down the corridor to the helipad, where the helicopter had wound up and was hovering about three feet off the deck a second or two before takeoff. I could see the pilot through the glass, and his face was mangled and disproportionate. Gunner was bouncing around on the helipad, attention trained on the pilot but unable to get to him.

I ran through the doors and threw myself at the nearest skid. The pilot saw me, yanked up on the collective with his left hand, straight back on the cyclic with his right hand, and countered both with the pedals. The only thing I had going for me was that the comms tower blocked his forward movement. All he could do now was back up. Which he did. The bird vaulted skyward and I caught the left skid with both hands and struggled for purchase. Having cleared the tower and the antennas, the pilot slammed the collective down and pulled hard right on the cyclic. The bird dropped, turned hard right, and slammed me against the skid. This pilot must have flown combat, because he wasn't messing around. The skid was several inches thick, requiring me to wrap an arm around it instead of a hand. Oddly, my two thoughts were how the movies made this look much easier and how Gunner's bark was fading away.

The pilot swooped the helicopter low over the water, then pulled hard on the collective and straight back on the cyclic. When he did, the helicopter shot skyward like a rocket. No sooner had he done this than he slammed the collective down and the cyclic straight forward. This created negative Gs, shook one hand loose, and threated to toss me into the rotor. Below me, the yacht was getting smaller. As was the demon boat. The pilot's unexpected maneuver had upended me, pointing my feet at the sky, which gave me an upside-down view of Bones. He'd been hog-tied and still seemed to be taking shallow breaths. Blood across his chest and face.

Bones looked at me through one eye, attempted a painful smile, and shook his head as the pilot reversed his movements one more time, once again creating negative Gs. Just as my feet were about to be blended off my body by the rotors, he pulled up, back, and hard right, shed me like a flea, and left me suspended in space, staring at Frank. Who was smiling and enjoying the Cirque du Soleil act outside his window.

When my horizontal movement stopped, gravity took over. My last view of the helicopter was Frank's smiling face—those smug amber eyes and the resident evil behind them. As he faded off into a beautiful blue sky, I lamented I'd not shot him in Montana when I'd had the chance. I didn't know how far I was going to fall or which part of me was going to hit first because my short ride on the bird had turned up into down and down into up, but I had a pretty good feeling I wouldn't enjoy it. Strange that while I could not see him, I could hear Gunner. Evidently he was still hopping around the helipad following my progress. Or better yet, lack thereof. Two seconds later, I contacted the surface.

I couldn't help but think about those videos of the world-champion cliff divers who, dressed in a Speedo, launch themselves off some high ledge, spin, flip, turn, and then gracefully enter the water a hundred feet below with little to no splash, only to swim gracefully to the edge, climb out, and begin walking up the cliff once again. That wasn't anything like my descent to the water. I flailed, screamed like a girl, and tried to turn but could not. For the record, water is not a soft surface when encountered from ten stories up. The impact knocked me unconscious and, while I did not realize it at the time, also knocked all the air out of me.

Which, in turn, caused me to sink. Like a rock. In several hundred feet of water.

I don't remember having conscious thought. Only that a cold darkness surrounded me. Maybe *cocoon* is a better word. I tried to fight it, but my arms and legs wouldn't respond. My last physical sensation was pressure on my chest, and when I fought for air, I found none. My last emotional sensation was something akin to heartbreak. And it was piercing.

The last picture to flash across my mind's eye was Marie. Not because I didn't love Summer. I did. But because when I'd rescued Marie in the ocean in high school, she'd been floating for hours before I found her. Literally washed out to sea. I wondered how many times in those fearful hours she thought about getting too tired to tread water and being unable to fight any longer. At what point do your arms and legs quit and the water pulls you down? What is that second? The last second.

Whatever the case, I couldn't fight. The impact had rendered me unable. And now the water pulled me down. I did have one sensation. I was incredibly aware of one thing.

The quiet.

It was like standing in the snow. The whole world was not just muted, but silent. Almost in reverence.

One of the things I loved about my island, before Frank blew up my boat and set everything on fire, was waking to the quiet in the mornings. Before daylight, after the crickets and the frogs quit, there was a momentary pause. Often several minutes. When all the world stood in silence and you wondered if your ears worked at all. It was as if all of creation just stopped and stared in wonder at what was about to happen. That the sun was about to rise. That light would once again pierce the darkness, and the darkness would roll back like a scroll. Many mornings I would walk out of my home and around the chapel and walk to either the beach or the dock. Geography mattered not. I'd stare over a mug of coffee, close my eyes, and listen for it. That singular sound that started the day. Many times I've thought it's the sound of heaven. It must be. Any other description holds no value. If heaven has a frequency, it must be this one. It's both a lonely echo and a magnificent cry. Made by a singular creature. And while I don't pretend to understand frequencies, this one travels. I don't mean it's loud. I mean it travels. There's a difference. You have to listen to hear it, and if you're not paying attention, you'll miss it. It almost slips by you.

It's the song of the mourning dove. Calling to its mate. For me it has long been the cry of heaven, and I've wondered, more than once, if that is the sound of angels. In my life I've taught Bones very few things. While we are friends, he's the tutor. I'm the student. It has always been this way, but one morning he visited me on my island. And like every other morning, he found me standing on the beach. Coffee. Listening. He stood alongside and asked without asking. Then it sounded. Then again. That quiet coo. That shout-out across the stratosphere. One lover calling to another.

It's the cry of the human heart. And every one of us knows it.

As the water pulled me down, I had a singular desire. To hear that cry one more time.

CHAPTER 29

Day 6 Without Bones

I don't know if I gave in to the water or accepted the fact that I couldn't do anything about it, but about the time I figured my ticket had been punched, I felt an arm wrap around my neck and someone pull me toward the light. Which was good. About the time my head cleared water, my lungs woke up and remembered how to do what they were meant to do, and I started sucking in air. Camp dragged me into the boat and flipped me on my side, spilling the water out of me. Which also was good. I lay there hacking and sputtering a few minutes as reality slowly returned and Gunner licked my face off.

While I was alive, my situation had not improved all that much. Bones was gone, and unlike the previous six days during which we had some inkling of where he might be, we now had none. Zero. Frank had lifted Bones without a trace. And even if he'd left a trace, it was soon to rest on the ocean floor several hundred feet below.

That's when it hit me: it wasn't sunk. Not yet.

Sitting up, I hollered, "Camp, put me back on the *California*."

He looked at me like I'd lost my mind.

I pointed. "Right now."

"You almost died."

"Bones'll die if you don't get me back on that boat."

The *California* had turned almost forty-five degrees, with its bow totally submerged and its comms room and pool deck the only two remaining visible parts still above the waterline.

Camp spun us around, throttled up, and came alongside the comms room. He hollered above the roar of the engines, "If you're in there when it goes down, the suck will take you down with it."

I nodded. *Get off before it goes under. Check.*

I stood on the bow, timed my jump, and launched myself at the door of the comms room, landing on what was once a secondary control panel that mirrored the controls in the bridge. Most of the floor where Bones had been lying was underwater, or would be soon. The only thing I could still see were the walls that supported the door. The same walls that you'd try to hold on to if someone were dragging you out of the room and you didn't want to go with them. The reason I'd come back was because of what I'd seen there. Which was the same thing I saw in the hospital when Frank had first taken Bones.

Something on the wall. An imprint smeared in blood.

Below me, the boat was moving. Coming apart. I didn't have long. I snapped a picture with my phone, and then a second closer up. That's when I saw it. The tablet mounted to the wall. It hadn't been there when I first left Bones. If so, I'd have hit it with my head when I left. That meant Frank had left it when he took Bones. Left it just for me. As I stared at it, the screen flickered on and I saw Frank's face. I was looking at Frank as Frank was looking at me. Live and in person.

Frank was no longer in the helicopter. His surroundings were plush camel leather, high-back reclining seats, and small tinted windows. He was in his jet. One of them. He spoke without introduction, as if he knew me. "Well done." He nodded. "Really. Swimming through that hatch with that kid tattooed to your back was impressive. And it took some strength. I'd like to think I could've done it, but"—he shook his head—"I'm older now." He angled the phone down. Bones on the carpet. Either unconscious or pretending to be. "I want something and you're going to find it for me. And bring it to me." He half smiled. "I'll be in touch."

The screen went black. I didn't have time to think of something cool, menacing, or tough to say because he was gone just as quickly as he'd appeared. But if I'd had time, I would have told him I was coming for him. That I was going to tear down his playhouse and that his meeting with God would happen on my terms and sooner than he thought. Lastly, I'd have told him that if he hurt my friend Bones, then our meeting would be painful for him.

The ship moved beneath me. A life measured in seconds now and not minutes. Climbing onto what was once the roof of the superyacht, I clung to a useless antennae, fought the waves, and steadied myself as Camp moved in close, proving that he was equally as good a captain as me. I tested my footing, felt the boat sliding, timed my jump, and then launched myself as far as I was able, landing on the bow of the demon boat as *Hotel California* disappeared, torpedoing downward, leaving froth and bubble in its wake.

How did I lose him? Again? Why did I leave him alone? Why didn't I realize Frank would never let me take him? Gunner, too, felt his loss. He stayed close by, pressing his chest to my leg.

By the time we arrived on land, Summer, along with local officials, had established a triage using teams of Child Protective Services, law enforcement, and medical staff. Unable to sit still, I returned alone to the house at Amelia.

As a kid, I'd spent a lot of time on my island digging and trying to unearth history. Truth was, I wasn't the only one. Feral hogs were a problem in our part of the world, and they seemed to travel in groups of thirty or forty. They'd forage into an area, destroy it by uprooting everything in sight, and then move on, having laid waste to the landscape. My island was no different. Hogs came and went, hopping from one island to the next. No matter what anyone tells you, they're excellent swimmers. In high school Marie and I had increased our digging efforts to find megalodon teeth and Indian ruins. We spent every waking second pretending to be Indiana Jones brushing our way through an archaeological dig. Unearthing fragments of history and dreaming about the stories behind them.

Summer of my junior year we discovered an area of mounds along the marsh with a large collection of discarded shells. Akin to a three-hundred-year-old trash heap. So we sank in a shovel and spent the summer removing layer after layer. Digging to China. In many ways it became the motherload of arrowheads and shards of pottery. We were some four feet down when we returned one morning to find that the hogs had returned during the night and destroyed our dig. It looked like a bomb had gone off. Everything we'd uncovered had been chomped, chewed, or rooted by the pigs.

A sow can reproduce three times a year and birth eight or more piglets each time, proving to me that they're just overgrown rats. So I traveled inland to an archery store, bought a compound bow, and began shooting. With the hogs continuing to eviscerate my island, I built platforms in several trees, and since hogs eat mainly at night, I started sleeping up there. If I didn't hate mosquitoes before then, I did after.

One night under a full moon, the sounder group returned. I picked out the largest body among all of them, drew my bow, set my pin just behind her shoulder, and let the arrow fly. I heard a squeal, and then about forty pigs vacated my island rapidly.

I crawled down at daylight, recovered my arrow, which, judging by the red paint covering the shaft, had passed completely through her, and began tracking. Looking for blood. It wasn't difficult to find.

A drop here. Three drops there. More there. I walked from blood sign to blood sign. In a few places it looked like she stopped and stood, indicated by blood on both sides of the trail. I walked slowly, listening and watching. At the time I had no idea I'd later follow this same pattern as I hunted men.

The sow had run a giant circle and eventually returned to water, but that's where I lost the trail. The water's edge. So I backtracked, studied the trail again, and realized I'd lost it. Which made no sense. It was so strong a trail just a few feet ago, how could I lose it?

For several minutes I stood studying where

she'd come from and where I thought she was going—but that's where I made my mistake. A past blood trail had no bearing on where a wounded and dying pig would run. None whatsoever. Her path was illogical. Instinct driven. Erratic. And unplanned. That meant I could not impose my conclusions. I simply had to follow the sign. So I turned around, found the sign, and retraced my steps.

The process was valuable as I learned to follow sign and hold off assigning assumptions to the red drops splattered below me. The path returned me to the water, but where I assumed she'd entered the water, she had not. Given that she weighed several hundred pounds, her footprints weren't tough to follow beneath the surface of the water. But that was the key. Shifting my search from blood to footprint. Obviously she'd continued to bleed, but she did so in the water, where the blood dissipated and disappeared. Once I made the adjustment, I followed her around the edge of the marsh to another game trail where she exited the water and returned inland. Once again I picked up blood. Slowly, I followed. Drop to drop. The process was painstaking as I searched for minute specks of blood on leaves, dirt, the sides of grass. For whatever reason she began to bleed less. I would later learn that pigs clot rapidly. After three hours of looking, I found that the trail had gone cold and all the blood had dried up. She'd stopped. I had no explanation for this.

Finally, I sat beneath an oak tree, laid my bow across my lap, and tried to think like a pig. *Where would I go if I was wounded?* I had no answer, but as a human I thought I'd return to water. Especially if I was wounded and thirsty.

So I turned back toward the water. And that's where I found her. Laid up beneath a palmetto bush. We ate bacon and pork chops for the remainder of the summer.

Staring at the hastily erected triage, and at Summer who had quickly checked into "mother mode," I found myself parked beneath a giant, sprawling oak. I was spent. I'd been running on fumes for six days, hadn't slept in over four, and could barely keep my eyes open. I don't know if it was my thought of Bones, Bones's voice himself, the memory of that pig, or the delusion of sleep deprivation—but somehow I knew I needed to return to the water.

So I did.

I borrowed a car and drove to the Amelia house. Turns out it was once owned by some famous reclusive writer who paid a premium for privacy, so the driveway was long, fence high, and house massive. The front door was ajar when I arrived, and everything inside was as I'd last seen it. In disarray.

I knew Bones had been here. As with the pig,

this was one of the last places I saw blood. And if he'd been here, he'd have left me a signal. I just needed to find it. Gunner and I roamed the house, room to room, staring quietly at each, leaning heavily on Gunner's nose. I tried to look at each room through Bones's eyes, wondering if anything was out of place. Unnaturally. Did any one thing look like it had been set alone, apart from other things? Had a lamp been left on when it should be off? Had a chair or table been set at an odd angle from other furniture in the room? Had a blind been left half open, and if so, what was revealed through the window?

We spent four hours walking through the house, finally ending in the kitchen. The pantry was empty. Cleaned out. As was the fridge. There was no evidence that anyone had ever been here. The stove and ovens were clean. Unused. Maybe never used. And the dishwasher was empty and in like-new condition. The only thing in the kitchen that had been used was a single burner on the stove, as evidenced by the water kettle still sitting on it. The kettle was cold and mostly empty, but next to it stood a French press with the press fully depressed and grounds lying in the bottom. Someone had used it. Probably today. Behind me stood a granite-topped island with barstools. Two were pulled out. A cup of coffee in front of each. One empty. The other half full. Some sort of coastal birds had been painted on the mugs. Next to the half-full cup sat an orange.

I had no idea if Frank had poured his brother a cup of coffee in this kitchen and, if so, who sat where, but I wouldn't put it past him. He was crazy. *Let's talk about the good old days.* I studied the mugs. The position. Then the chairs. I moved around the room, but nothing made sense. Finally, I leaned against the wall and stared out over the ocean, which was calm. Gunner lay on the floor in front of me. Head up, paws crossed. Smelling.

Light flickered, and something akin to a blue haze caught my attention. I turned and found Frank standing in the kitchen. Eight feet away. I drew my Sig and was in the process of squeezing the trigger when it struck me that looking at Frank was like looking at him through glass. Or a screen. Gunner stood in front of me, and the hair on his back stood on end as he, too, stared at Frank. Growling. Frank was not armed, just smiling smugly, so I stepped closer. Then closer still. Finally, I pressed my muzzle to Frank's chest—but his chest wasn't there.

That's when he spoke to me. He looked down at the muzzle, then at me, but he didn't move. "You like my sleight of hand?" He shook his head. "I've always loved Star Wars. I own a company in Israel, and they perfected this hologram technology a few years back. It's how I conduct business around the world without having to actually be there." One hand came up, and he pressed the end of his finger into the muzzle of my pistol. "Safer too. Although you would not believe the number of people who do not share your restraint." The realness of the image was astonishing. Any further distance, and I would be unable to tell he was actually a projection.

Frank smiled, walked across the kitchen, and sat at the table. He gestured to a chair. "Please."

Set into the ceiling were projectors I'd not seen. They were made to look like recessed lights, so if you weren't looking for them, or if you weren't trained to see them, you wouldn't. Given the cost of such technology and his comfort with "sitting" in his surroundings in a room in which he was not actually sitting, I gathered Frank had conducted many meetings here, causing me to wonder how much flesh had been bought and sold right here. I walked around behind him and stared down. Looking down on his head, exposing the weakness of the technology. He was nearly identical in size and shape to Bones. Maybe thinner. Not as much muscle. But wiry. Unlike Bones, all his hair was silver-white. And there was something about his movements. Nothing was wasted. Each was practiced. Measured. And had been for a long time.

"David, I've been watching you for some time. My brother trained you well. You have a remarkable skill set."

I moved around in front of him, conscious that his prolonged interaction with me might simply be a head-fake to occupy my attention while some team of goons snuck in behind me and shot me in the leg. I also did not miss his use of the name "David." I scanned my six, listened, and then completed my circle around the kitchen, still studying the mugs, the orange, and him.

Frank gestured to the coffee. "The beans are from Nicaragua. I own the farm. They're quite good."

When I didn't respond, he crossed his legs and pointed again. This time at me. "I'd like to make you a proposition."

I said nothing as I figured he was going to talk to me whether I responded or not. I don't think he was used to people not responding to him, so he said it a second time. This time with a twist. "I'd like to make you a proposition . . . David."

There it was again. I turned and stared at the image in front of me.

He smiled. "Your books are quite good. Such a shame about your editor. What was it, a brain hemorrhage? So strange how certain toxins can bypass the blood-brain barrier and set up shop inside our"—he tapped his head—"medulla oblongata." He held up a finger. "Research has shown that cigarettes are a perfect delivery system. Just goes straight through the sinuses."

He continued, "Even with much persuasion,

my brother isn't much help." That meant they were beating Bones. "Despite our best attempts, he's not talking. So I'm moving on to plan B." He pointed at me. "You."

"What have you done to Bones?"

He thumbed over his shoulder. "He was always the stoic one, so he can sit and think about his future, or not, while you can find it for me. And before you tell me you won't do anything I request, or some such thing, just realize that you roam freely around the planet attempting to be this savior of humanity only because humanity doesn't yet know you are also the hopeless romantic who writes the books they can't live without. If only they knew . . ." He smiled and then uncrossed and recrossed his legs. "So, David, you're going to find and bring me my birth certificate, which my brother has kept in hiding. A small thing, I know, but you worry about you. I have my own reasons."

He stood. "Here's where we are." He walked around some barrier to Bones, who was hanging from ropes. "Truth be told, I hated doing this. But he's pretty thickheaded, always has been, and this is about the only way to get through to him. So . . . my birth certificate. You'll find it. And of course, when you do, I'll be watching and I'll be in touch. If you don't find it, then the whole world will know that David Bishop and Murphy Shepherd are one and the same, and you won't be able to buy gas without attracting a crowd, much less find what you call the Apollumi." A sick smile as he tapped his back between the shoulders. "Just think of how many people I'll profit from in your absence."

He moved again. This time behind Bones. Allowing Bones's face to come into view alongside him. His face was swollen, and he was unconscious. Gunner saw it and barked. Frank continued, "I know how much you love this pile of Bones, but if you want to see him again, then you'll turn your attention to my request. If not, I'll ship what remains of him to you in a box. Oh, and just in case you need any more incentive, you might want to check in with all those fine folks in Colorado." Another sick smile. "Maybe Freetown isn't so free."

He smiled, snapped his fingers, and the video disappeared as quickly as it had appeared. I slid down the wall and sat on the floor, and only then did I hear footsteps behind me. Summer sat alongside me, locked her left arm inside my right, and said nothing. Camp stood across from us. An MK4 hanging from a single-point sling. Neither spoke. Then my phone rang.

CHAPTER 30

Day 7 Without Bones

The three-hour flight to Colorado seemed infinite. Clay met us on the tarmac, and his face was not happy. Nor did he speak. He opened the door, we sat down, and he drove. Quickly. Which was unlike a man who'd learned to live with time. At midnight we drove onto Main Street to lights and a mob of people. Many crying. Most looked shell-shocked.

Angel stood in the center of the street, flanked by Casey. Both were carrying rifles lifted from my safe. Spent shell casings littered the road. Three men dressed in black tactical gear, tied hand and foot, lay on the ground behind them. Someone had pulled off their masks, but I didn't recognize them, and all three were bleeding from various holes. I doubted they knew much.

We exited the vehicle as Ellie ran through the crowd and launched herself into my arms. One eye was puffy, and there were bruises on her neck and powder burns alongside one cheek. Closer inspection of Angel, Casey, and Clay proved the same. They'd been in it. A firefight

357

on Main Street. The truth didn't take long to set in. Frank had sent a team of people here while he was yapping it up with me, and somehow our security team, along with the girls, had defended Freetown. Eddie stood off to one side talking with our on-site commander. Both were carrying rifles.

Eddie was out of breath, but he spoke first. "We caught movement on the sensors. And we did what you told us. They never knew what hit them."

Angel stood just a feet away. "You okay?"

A nod.

"Anybody hurt?"

She shook her head.

I turned to Casey, who was holding Shep. "They take anybody?"

Another shake.

Ellie clung to me, pressing her cheek to my stomach. Her hair smelled of gunsmoke. I scanned the world around me, and one thing was apparent. No, glaring. I was losing. Frank was winning. And Bones's life hung in the balance.

We gathered everyone in the Planetarium, including newcomers Phyllis and her two kids, who seemed to like the excitement. My fatigue had not relented, but I needed to circle the wagons. Rally the troops. They looked at me, and their faces all said the same thing—I was their hope. Yet I was growing hopeless. I stood and knew I couldn't let my face say what my heart felt. Six members of our security team surrounded the Planetarium, providing a show of force. The three unmasked goons lay on the ground just outside in full sight.

I started with the obvious. "Anybody hurt?"

I scanned a room full of shaking heads.

Then I feigned a smile. "Anybody scared?"

Most every hand rose.

"That's okay. Me too." I studied their faces, and they were. All scared. I was too tired to be crafty, so I decided to shoot straight. "As I look across your faces, I'm reminded. Each of you, every single one of you, has one thing in common with me. I found you, lifted you out of that place, and then offered to bring you here. To heal. Forget. Remember. Start over." I slowly studied the eyes of many. "You remember?"

They nodded.

"I don't want to resurface bad stuff, but if you'll let me, do you remember how you felt? How you prayed for someone, anyone, to break down the door?"

More nods. Even smiles.

"Right now . . ." My emotions surfaced and I was unable to choke them back. I paused, gathered myself. "My best pal on the planet needs me to find him and bring him home. He's in that place where you were. And the guy holding him, his brother"—I waved my hand across Freetown—"is the reason for all this. Everything. From the explosion to"—I pointed to the guys hog-tied on the ground outside—"them, to my island, to"—I gestured to Clay—"Clay, to my being shot. I thought about moving all of you to our summer getaway up in the mountains. You've heard us talk about it. It's an old converted bunker. You'd be safe there and probably enjoy the excursion, but I'm not doing that. I'm not moving all of you to a hole in the ground because of him. I'm not doing that to your hearts. We're bringing in some more tattooed and jacked guys from DC. Most will be current military on leave, wanting to make some extra money for Christmas, so we thought we'd help them out." I feigned a laugh and pointed to Camp, who'd been the source of more than one googly-eyed whisper since he arrived. "Not to mention some of them are single."

Laughter rippled through the room.

"I'm not moving you and I'm not changing your routines. Tomorrow morning the shops will be open and we're getting on with our lives, albeit with a few more guys circling the perimeter." I had a feeling my pep talk was falling short. I also knew I was way past tired. So I pulled up a chair, sat, and scanned the crowd. Making eye contact.

"Jeanie, you remember the Harley we used to get out of Vegas?"

She nodded and smiled.

"Pamela, you remember when I opened the door and said, 'Tell me what you need'?"

She smiled and spoke loud enough for the room to hear. "I need a pizza. Right now."

The room laughed.

"And Jacqueline, what was the first thing you did when you arrived here?"

She lifted up one foot. "New shoes."

"Katy, you remember how I got you out of Brazil?"

She nodded. "You stole a plane."

More laughter.

"Well, let's just say I borrowed it. And Becca, did I sit with you in court the day you testified against your exploiter?"

A nod.

"And is he spending the rest of his life in jail?"

A second nod.

I studied the room. "It's not always clean. Sometimes it's messy. Sometimes we take one step forward and maybe one back, but this is what we do." I waved my hand over them as they wrapped arms around shoulders. "For one another." I looked out through the windows. Down Main Street. "I'm sorry about tonight. I'd like to tell you it'll never happen again, but I didn't think it would happen the first time. I do know this—there's a bad man out there who wishes us harm, and I'm going to find him. I'm going to make it so he can't do that anymore.

And I'm going to do what I can, the same way I did with all of you, to bring Bones home. Now, I need to ask one favor."

They waited.

"I need you all—I'm asking you all—to lean on each other. Be a wall for one another. A shield against the world. You can be. Every one of you is tougher than you think, as evidenced by the fact that you survived. You made it. You're here." I paused. "After the explosion here, I told you I wasn't rebuilding Freetown. You were. You all thought I was talking about buildings and hospitals." I shook my head. "I was talking about you. You are Freetown. You matter more than bricks and mortar. You are of priceless value. And every single magnificent one of you is worth rescue. Again. And again. The one who taught me that needs rescue right now, so if you don't see me for a little while, just know I'm"—my emotions surfaced again—"trying to bring him home."

I looked at Eddie, who nodded, and then at Summer, who had the concession stand up and running. "Now I think it'd be a good idea, since we have all these armed men currently circling our town, if you would spend some time remembering. Not the bad, but the good." Eddie clicked Play and Bones's slideshow started. "Eat some popcorn—"

Pamela spoke over me. "And pizza."

The room laughed.

I slid out the side door and spoke to myself. "In the meantime I need to find the one who taught me to find you."

Summer found me. In the basement. Sitting in Bones's photo lab, in his chair, staring at the wall. Every few seconds another picture flashed. Someone we'd rescued. Another reminder that I hadn't protected him. She stood behind me, arms wrapped around my neck. In my lap I held his orange case. Pelican cases are made out of the same stuff with which they make kayaks, so they can take a beating. Which his box had. I ran my fingers across the deep scars in the plastic. If only they could talk, what story would they tell me? How many grooves had been made chasing me around the planet? How many had I caused?

I could not count.

Summer ran her fingers through my hair and thumbed away my tear. Finally, she set the box on the ground next to us and sat in my lap, wrapping her arms around my neck. "How you doing?"

I shook my head, but no words came.

She waited.

A few minutes later, I spoke. "I was at the Academy. Had a long week. Hadn't slept in three days. Bones got one of his wild hairs, and with me at my weakest and most tired, he decided to test me. So he pulls me out of class, it's snowing, he hands me some gear, a pack, points to a snowcapped mountain, and says, 'Start walking.' So I did.

"He wanted to see what was on the edge of my plate. How far he could push me before my body quit. About twelve hours later, I was climbing through a snowstorm at thirteen thousand feet. En route to a cabin where he'd conducted some of my mountain training. I was well outside my limit. Starting to shut down. Wasn't processing. Not making good decisions. Fatigue. Altitude. Hunger. He had found the edge of me. The snow became a whiteout. Couldn't see my hand. I just kept walking. Somewhere in there I fell and couldn't get up. I just physically could not pick my body up. I passed out facedown in the snow.

"When I woke, I was sitting in the cabin. Fire. Dry clothes. Smell of coffee. He was sitting across from me. Sipping Cabernet. I found out later he'd carried me—and both our packs—nearly a half mile along a ridgeline. When I asked him how he found me, he just shrugged and smiled." I shook my head. "Bones has a gift. I do not. He's part bloodhound. Finding him is beyond a needle in a haystack. I don't even know where to begin."

She hugged my neck several seconds. Saying "All the world will be right" without saying it. Finally, she let out a deep breath, stood, and pulled me up alongside her.

"Okay, cowboy. Pity party over. He chose you.

He trained you. Shared the best parts of himself with you. And sitting here whining is doing nothing. So let's get to work. What would he do?"

I shrugged. "He could be anywhere. Think needle and haystack."

"I'm pretty sure if you were missing, he wouldn't be sitting in this basement staring at the walls. He'd be turning over every—"

"Summer!" My frustration and failure flared. "I don't know where to look. I have no idea where he is. Frank could have taken him anywhere. I have no lead. Nothing. Zero."

She held my hand. "I know. Me neither. But we can't sit here, and we've got to start somewhere. What about Eddie and the team?"

"They're doing everything they know to do."

She kissed me. "Think like Bones."

We assembled in the basement. No phones. No electronics. No Frank. Summer sat on my left, Shep on her lap. Gunner on the floor. Clay on my right. Camp, BP, Jess, Angel, Casey, and Ellie sat around the table.

I fought the weariness. "Anybody got anything?"

Nobody spoke.

"Any leads whatsoever?"

Still no one spoke. I rubbed my face. "I have nothing. Bones could be anywhere in the world."

Eddie broke the silence as he projected the

pictures I'd taken at the hospital in New York City and the comms room of the *Hotel California* onto the screen. "Our assumption is that Bones made this symbol or letter or something as he was being dragged out the door. So he made it in haste. Probably less than a second. We have to assume that if he's trying to tell us something, then whatever we're looking at is a shell of the larger version."

Both symbols were three lines. One horizontal across the top. And one vertical down the right side that connected to the horizontal. The two made one half of a square. A third curved line started at the intersection of the two lines, swooped left several inches, and then swooped back right, where it connected at the bottom of the right vertical line. It looked like a left parenthesis. But a wider arc. There was a fourth mark, but the team couldn't come to an agreement on whether it was an unintentional smear or purposeful dot. An inch to the right of the intersection of the vertical and horizontal lines, we found a single fingerprint. It was clearer in the comms room than the hospital but both contained the same mark. Had it been in only one, it certainly could have been a mistake, but the fact that it appeared in both suggested it was purposeful.

While I originally thought the marking in the hospital could have been a number, we all agreed, when compared with the comms room, it was not. Bones had rapidly drawn a symbol in blood. Was that purposeful or was he using available resources? In both cases it looked as if his last brushstroke was to dot the horizontal "i." But in both cases, the dot was directly to the right of the horizontal line but two inches down the vertical. To make matters worse, both horizontal lines that ran across the top were smeared, with the New York City symbol being the worse of the two. Almost as if after Bones had painted it, he used his forearm to brace against whoever was pulling him and had smeared it on his way out. It was the angle of the smear that suggested this. It started at four o'clock and finished at ten o'clock, swiping right to left across the horizontal.

My eyes were tired and I was starting to see double. Summer handed me a coffee and sat rubbing my neck.

I'd never felt so useless. So utterly incapable.

The rest of the team sat silently as we stared at the screen and compared the two pictures side by side. After fifteen minutes, I had to stand up because I was about to fall asleep in my chair, so I started pacing. Trying to wrack my brain. When I vacated my seat, Shep took an interest in the screen and sat cross-legged in my chair. He studied it, turned his head sideways, then stood and walked around the table to the wall, staring up at the picture.

Then he turned to look at all of us. The look on

his face was calm and matter-of-fact. *Don't you see?*

When we made no response to him, he walked to my safe room and stood at the door—which I'd locked after I'd dumped all my and Camp's gear. Not to mention the girls' rifles. Then he just stood there, looking at me and waiting.

"You all right?" I asked.

He knocked on the door.

"You want in?"

He made no response. Summer motioned for me to open the door, so I punched in the code, LOVESHOWSUP, and turned on the light, and we followed him into the room where he slowly circled the table in the middle. That he was looking for something was obvious. What he was looking for was not. He circled the table once along with the pile of wet, dirty, and disorganized gear lying just where I'd left it when I dumped it there thinking, *I'll deal with this later when I can think.* Shep circled the table a second time. Halfway around he used his finger to lift my vest, and a second time he lifted a small duffel to look beneath it. On his third trip around, something higher up caught his eyes, so he turned to his left and stared up at Bones's weathered and worn million-mile Pelican case resting on top of my safe. I'd set it up there when I walked into the room because that's where Bones kept it.

Shep looked at the case. Then at me. Then back

at the case. Then at everyone else. His matter-of-fact look had morphed into *Don't you get it?* As he did this, Gunner came to stand alongside him. With his left hand, Shep hooked a finger inside Gunner's collar, and with his right hand he pointed at the case, saying in a broken voice, "Pelican." Then he pointed back to the screen where the two pictures projected in contrast and said it again: "Pelican."

Every one of us turned our heads and stared at the screen from inside my safe vault. And almost in unison we tilted our heads as he'd done when he stood in front of the screen. Making three o'clock the top of the drawing—which it would have been if Bones was lying on his side. After a minute, I turned back to Shep, who pointed one last time to the case and then to the screen. "Pelican."

Suddenly my tired brain started to make the connections. The drawing had been made with blood. How many times had I seen him serve Communion with the wine inside? When we made three o'clock the top of the drawing, I could make an argument for a pelican. From the left parenthesis representing the mouth, to the thumbprint for the eye, to the smear across the horizontal representing feathers, I began to think that Bones had drawn a picture of a pelican. Then I remembered Bones's coffee mug at the Amelia house—how it was sitting next to an orange.

Had I really been carrying some clue with me all along?

It can't be that simple.

I pulled the box down, and we returned to the basement conference room where I set the box on the table. Shep sat in my chair, crossed his legs, patted the box, and pointed at the picture, this time saying nothing.

I spun the box, clicked open the latches, lifted the lid, and stared inside, where I found several things. A bottle of wine, an opener, loaded spare magazines for his Sig, his satellite tracker, a first aid kit, a knife, a lighter, a pair of reading glasses, three canisters of unused Kodak film, a compass, paracord, a pair of Costa sunglasses, a small package of fishhooks with fishing line, a ballpoint pen, and a worn Bible. Taped to the underside of the lid was a picture of two identical suntanned, towheaded boys fishing out of a small johnboat. One standing in the front throwing a cast net. The other sitting in the rear with his hand on the tiller of the outboard. They might have been eight years old. The bottom of the boat was piled three high with mullet.

But the most striking item in the case was the envelope lying across the middle. Across it, Bones had written "Murph."

Everyone leaned in, focusing on that envelope, and I discovered that I was no longer sleepy.

I opened the envelope and read these words:

Dear Murph—

Well, if you're reading this, I'd bet Frank took me and you're fumbling around without a clue as to how to find me. Don't blame yourself. He's like that. Nobody thinks like him. It's evidence of his genius and his demented and evil nature, both of which he is, so don't be too tough on yourself. It's a good thing you don't think like him.

Let me help you out. Chances are near a hundred percent that I'm in Majorca. I'd bet the bottle in this case, which is a good one by the way, that Frank has taken me back to where it all started, and he's stuck me down in my dungeon home. Years ago, he converted it into a home of sorts. It's one of the only places on earth where he can sleep, even if just a few hours. It's also where he can lock me up in the dark with my painful memories and leave me to rot. He will do all this because he knows he can't make me talk, so he'll use me as leverage to get you to bring him what he wants—probably his birth certificate. Which I don't have. Haven't for a long time. His obsession with that small piece of paper proves that identity precedes purpose. Whose you are matters more to the soul than who you are or what you are. I have my reasons for keeping it from him.

There is hope. The attached map should help. Follow the instructions. Closely. Don't deviate. See you soon.

Bones

I read it again, out loud. Then a third time. That was it. Just a simple here's-where-to-find-me letter. It had been there all along. And he wrote it in advance, which meant he knew we'd find ourselves in this position—which either meant he couldn't or didn't prevent it.

I knelt next to Shep and smiled for the first time in eight days. "Nice job, big guy. Thank you." I wasn't certain, but I think he cracked a smile. That said, he wasn't looking at me. He was looking at my Omega. Mesmerized by the second hand.

Ellie had once done the same thing.

I clicked the latch, then slid it off my wrist and onto his, locking it. His eyes grew wide, and judging by the look on his face, you'd have thought I'd just given him all the tea in China. I said, "I set it five minutes fast, because if I don't"—I thumbed over my shoulder to Summer—"I have a tendency to be late and . . ."

He was studying the reflection of light on the blue face.

"Never mind. It'll make more sense when

you get older." He nodded slightly, then turned and walked about the room like C-3PO, his arm elevated.

In less than an hour, the team had gotten to work and built a file on the stronghold in Majorca. Once a Catholic church, then a Crusader stronghold, a Muslim stronghold, a village, another church, and several iterations beyond that. The team pulled multiple live satellite images, thermal images, and several hundred years' worth of detailed drawings of the grounds, including the underground—which neatly agreed with Bones's detailed drawing. There was, however, one difference that only could have been etched by someone who'd lived there.

Imagery also confirmed that Frank was one of the most heavily guarded people on the planet. Getting in would not be easy. Getting out much less so.

The team also started digging for that birth certificate.

I needed to clear my head, so I climbed the stairs and left the team to strategize without me. Gunner and I wound through town, weaving among the streetlights and aspens. I poked my head in the Planetarium, which was now empty. Gunner and I stood while the facial recognition software registered us and began adjusting the slideshow to portray a larger percentage of pictures that included us. Within seconds, pictures of me and Bones flashed on the wall. As they did, one thing struck me. While he was always smiling, Bones was never in the forefront. The pictures were never about him. In many he was carrying his camera, recording others' lives. Replacing past pain with present tense.

I walked past the pet shop. Salon. Spa. Candy shop. Movie theater. Not a corner in Freetown could be found where Bones's fingerprint wasn't visible. He was everywhere and yet somehow invisible. My walk took me to the trailhead of the Eagle's Nest, where I stood wondering how many times he'd led me up and down. It was a good picture of our relationship. How many times had I stepped foot on a piece of dirt—anywhere in the world—and found that his boot print had preceded mine? That he'd cleared the ground prior to my landing?

Below me sat Freetown. As much as others had given me credit, had given David Bishop credit, Freetown existed because of Bones. Bones had found me at my lowest, put a pen and pad in front of me, and said, "Tell me what you know about sheep." Out of that rescue, David Bishop wrote books that caught fire that funded Freetown that gave Murphy Shepherd a reason for living. I'd found my place in this world because of Bones. Why? One simple reason: I'd mattered more to Bones than Bones mattered to Bones.

The needs of the one . . .

My tutor was still taking me to school.

As for Frank, I didn't believe him. The only thing I knew to be true about Frank was that he was a pathological liar hell-bent on pleasing himself. Even if he was telling the truth and did, in fact, want me to find his birth certificate, he'd never give up Bones. No matter what was offered. Frank lived under the grip of one constant emotion. Fear. Fear of not being able to control every situation he encountered. The reasons for this fear might have been valid. Granted, he grew up in horrible situations, but so had Bones—and Bones was Frank's antithesis. He didn't live in fear and never had. Ever. He lived in freedom. Something Frank couldn't buy no matter how much money he made or people he enslaved. My gut told me that Frank hated Bones because Bones didn't end up like Frank. Frank had no power over his fear, and Bones not only had conquered his fear but had none. At continual risk to his own life, Bones walked into and out of hell on countless occasions, freeing those held captive and shouldering those long held behind bars.

The Apollumi.

In contrast, Frank cowered in the shadows. Blockaded himself behind that which crippled him. Frank insulated himself behind money, power, protection, pretense, and piercing betrayal. Consequently, whatever came out of that maniac's mouth could not be trusted. Including the conversation with the hologram. The bottom line was simple: no matter how smart he'd become, Frank could not understand how Bones had escaped what Frank could not. Frank despised Bones because at his root, Frank was a coward. Bones was not. And Frank hated him for it.

I knew Eddie and the team, primarily with Camp's input, would put together a plan to extract Bones. But whatever the plan and however well executed, carrying it out would risk their lives. Neither Bones nor I wanted that. If it was true that Frank was holding Bones in the dungeon in Majorca, I knew everything I needed. I knew his location and, thanks to Bones's drawing, how to get in undetected. A team could not do this.

The basement was empty when I returned, so I packed some gear, including a weapon for Bones, climbing rope and gear, and a harness for Gunner that would allow me to attach him to me when climbing. Among other items. I loaded the gear into the truck and stood staring at my home, where the light was on in the bedroom. Summer was waiting on me. I had not slept more than an hour in over a week, and I knew if I walked up there I'd let her welcome me and comfort me and I'd sleep. Chances were good I'd sleep twenty-four hours. But what would happen to Bones while I slept? I also knew I could not tell her goodbye. Not this time. It would hurt too much.

I walked around the bed of the truck and ran directly into Clay, who was staring down on me. I didn't figure lying to him would do any good, so I didn't. He tilted his head slightly. "You going alone?"

I nodded.

"Thought so. You wouldn't want to risk nobody else's life." He stared up at the house and the light in the bedroom, then put his hand on my shoulder. "Don't worry. I'll talk to her." I held out my hand, which he shook—and only then did the light from the cab reflect off the moisture in his eyes. When he spoke, his voice had fallen to a hoarse whisper. "Mister Murphy?"

I looked up.

"Bring Mister Bones home."

I nodded, Gunner jumped up into the truck, and we drove through the night to the airstrip.

PART 3

CHAPTER 31

Day 8 Without Bones

I slept most of the flight. Every hour or so, Gunner sniffed my face, then licked the dried salt off my skin and lay back down. It was Gunner-speak for "I'm worried about you, old man."

Thirty minutes to touchdown, the pilot woke me, handed me a cup of coffee, and told me Summer had been trying to reach me on the satellite phone. She had given him strict instructions not to let me off this plane without first talking with her. I hovered over the steam and stared at the phone. I'd never survive a conversation, and I wasn't sure she would either. Not to mention the fact that doing so would put my focus in the rearview and not the windshield. Right now I needed to be singularly focused on what lay ahead. Ten minutes later, I took out a pad and pen and wrote, "Dear Summer, I need to tell you about my friend Bones and what he taught me about sheep . . ."

Per Bones's letter, the pilot touched down on a private airstrip on the southeast coast of

381

Majorca. Evidently Bones leased space inside a dilapidated hangar. I punched in the combination and the lock clicked open. Inside I found an older Toyota truck. Gunner loaded up and we began skirting the coastline. The detail in Bones's letter surprised me. To say he'd been planning this contingency was an understatement.

We followed the one-lane road north through small coastal towns to a rocky peninsula a mile wide and several miles long on the northeast corner of Majorca. Fifteen hundred years ago, a Franciscan monk followed a vision that ended here, and he and his brothers built what five hundred years later became a thriving monastery. The brothers lived in peace until the Crusaders adopted it as one of their outposts around AD 1000. This soon attracted the attention of the Moors, who drove out the Crusaders, after which the grounds fell into disrepair and eventually became the home of a hermit. Around 1500, Christians retook the citadel and refortified it, adding on and discovering that the rocky yet fertile soil, along with requisite sunshine, grew desirable grapes.

By the time Bones and Frank were held here as entertainment for priests seeking respite from the rigors of celibate life, it was a thriving center for the church. With its monastery, vineyards, retreat center, and private conference center, priests from around the world would trek here, often walking the last fifty to a hundred miles, making the destination a pilgrimage of sorts. The narrow road led from the mainland into the peninsula, traveling along the mile-wide plateau that fell off like a table to rocky cliffs that descended a couple hundred feet into the turquoise waters of the Balearic Sea. From a defensive standpoint, it was easy to see why Frank liked it—one road in and surrounded by water on three sides. The inhospitable terrain was inhabited only with goats, burros, and short, stubby trees that looked to be constantly bracing against the wind.

Bones's map led me to a small resort village a few miles away, where oiled beachgoers lounged on bleached white sands, snorkeling lovers frolicked in gin-clear water, and kayakers and paddle boarders crisscrossed the glassy surface. It was a vacationer's paradise. It was also a strategic place to store a small boat with which to navigate the coastline.

The marina was small but seemed home to more than a hundred small yachts, center consoles, and sport fishermen. I parked, found the slip, and pulled off the cover, revealing a well-used Zodiac. As the sun dropped below the horizon, I turned on the Garmin and entered the coordinates Bones had included with his map, then dropped the boat in the water where the twin Yamahas cranked on the first try. Gunner felt as at home on the bow of a boat as he did the hearth of a fireplace in Colorado, so he circled from bow to stern and back to bow. I eased out of the marina, attempting to draw as little attention as possible. Traffic was thin, and the folks on the beach seemed to have better things to do than concern themselves with a man and his dog going for a sundowner.

Gunner and I skirted the shoreline, staying close but avoiding the massive rock formations that lay just below the surface—any one of which would remove the lower unit from either engine in short order. I couldn't help but marvel at the ancient beauty of the waves crashing into the rocks, the hidden and protected coves, and the bearded goats and hairy burros who called it home.

Bones's coordinates and description were specific. On the northern side, a small cove was protected by a curved elbow of steep rock. The entrance was only ten to twelve feet wide, bordered by steep cliffs. I brought the Zodiac off plane, trimmed the engine as far as I could while keeping the propeller in the water, and steered into the smooth rock entrance. The S-shaped opening meant no vessel longer than thirty feet could navigate in, and the water-worn walls meant no purchase could be made. I understood now why Bones had chosen the Zodiac, as the rubber inflated sides were welcome bumpers against the steep canyon walls that put us in an indefensible position, causing me to hope no one knew we were coming. The exit dumped us into a hidden pool of water larger than several Olympic swimming pools. According to the Garmin, it was thirty and forty feet deep. Our presence here was predicated upon surprise. If anyone knew of our approach, we would be sitting ducks.

We idled to the far end where a rock shelf sat just a foot below the water's surface. The water here was glass. Not a ripple other than those we made, and given the sea just beyond the canyon walls, and given the water markings on the wall, the water level rose and fell only a few inches. I cut the engines and studied Bones's map. I was looking for a crack in the rock marked by a tree growing out of the crack. It wasn't tough to find. I stepped into the water and tied off to the tree. Bones's map said this next section was a bit tricky. I was looking for an underground tunnel that exited into this cove. There was just one problem: the tunnel exited into a cavern, and the only way to get to it was to swim under the rock shelf below the crack. The swim wasn't far, but it was underwater, which meant when I exited into the cavern, my entire world would be pitch black. While I didn't mind, I had a feeling my furry partner wouldn't be too crazy about it.

Gunner stood on the bow, whining. He watched me disappear underwater only to reappear a minute later, having found what I was looking for. The fact that he was backing up with the hair on his back bristled told me he was not having fun.

I climbed back into the boat and sat at eye level with him. He inched forward, sniffed me, and licked my cheek. I pointed. "I know. I don't like it either. Trust me, if there were any other way, I would, but this is our one chance. It's our only chance. Now, you don't have to go. You can stay here. But for the record, I need you. You're the best partner I've got. And you've got about five seconds to decide."

Gunner circled me, walked to the stern, and then returned to the bow where he brushed his shoulder against mine and stood staring at me, licking my face.

I rubbed his head. "I know. I love you too."

He jerked his head sideways and made that one little Scooby-Doo sound he makes when he's hungry.

"Yes, when we get back I'll grill you a rib eye."

Excited by my promise, he made the sound again.

"Yes, a big one."

Another whine.

"Of course I'll cut it up for you."

Gunner's tail had started wagging at close to warp speed.

I climbed out of the boat and lifted him into the water next to me. Standing on the shelf, the water rose to the middle of his chest. I looked down at him. "You sure are getting high maintenance."

He barked and turned his attention to the water.

I gave him the thumbs up, slid down into the water next to him, pulled my mask down, turned on my headlamp, and fell into the bosom of a beautiful Spanish afternoon. Gunner and I swam down only two feet, then horizontal some eight feet, then up. When we did, the only light came from below us. We had popped up in an underground lake of sorts. Maybe *pond* is a better word as the area was roughly the size of an Olympic pool and the cavern roof maybe some twenty feet above our heads. We swam to a smooth rock that led up out of the water. I pushed Gunner out first, then pulled myself up. Once out of the water, I buckled on Gunner's vest and attached the lamp to the broad section between his front shoulders. I also attached a holster, along with Bones's Sig, and a first aid kit. In my pack I carried additional supplies, but if we got separated and Gunner found Bones before me, Bones would have what he needed. Or at least some of it.

In some ancient day long since past, an underground river cut these tunnels. Tall enough for a man to stand in and level enough for walking, I doubted modern machinery could have done better. Bones's map gave detailed, step-by-step instructions. Twenty-seven steps to a Y-intersection. Don't take the left. Turn right. Then two hundred fourteen steps to a T. Turn left. Four hundred seven steps up the serpentine path, which exited to another lake. The fact that Bones had discovered this as a boy, and in the dark, was the eighth wonder of the world and final proof that he was and always had been tougher than me.

Gunner walked alongside me. Hair standing up on his back. He didn't like this any more than I did.

Distance was difficult to measure, but my best guess was that we'd wound nearly a quarter mile into the heart of this rock when the tunnel emptied into a second lake. This one bigger. The ceiling was covered in stalactites that hovered some forty feet above our heads. Interestingly, when I slipped into the water, I learned this pond was made of fresh water, unlike the first. Gunner and I swam the long lake, exiting the water a hundred yards from where we entered into another tunnel, this one narrower, just wide enough for my shoulders but requiring us to stand in knee-deep water. Judging by the marks on the walls, this one had been dug or carved by hand a long time ago. I lifted my MK4, drained the water from the gas tube, and pulled slightly on the charging handle to confirm the presence of a round in the chamber. I then turned on both my Aimpoint red dot and my laser and confirmed that my suppressor was locked on tight. While the suppressor would not "silence" the blast of the rifle, it would prevent me and Gunner from going deaf inside these rock walls.

When Gunner saw me checking my weapon, he pressed his shoulder to my leg. I could feel his muscles tighten, and his ears pricked up and trained on me.

At this point I switched both Gunner's and my headlamp to a dim red. Red light, while visible to the human eye, would be less noticeable than bright white—and given that I had no idea what I was getting into, we needed stealth. Had I been alone, I'd have brought infrared. But doing so would have left my partner blind, and I had a feeling I'd need his nose more than my eyes. Not to mention the fact that if and when I found Bones, he'd need to be able to see as well.

Gunner and I crept through the cold water, which pressed against us in a current pouring from some sort of spring ahead of us. Gunner followed close behind as I wound through the rock walls. Every thirty yards or so, we encountered a small shelf just large enough for two men to sit on, causing me to guess that whoever had carved this tunnel had done so in order to lift themselves out of this cold water while they worked. I couldn't imagine working down here in the dark or with candlelight. This was a world that was not just dark; it was devoid of light. Your eyes would never adjust because there was nothing to adjust to.

Two hours after we left the Zodiac, the narrow tunnel ended in another cave. This one mostly dry. Stalactites dripping minerals from above. Stalagmites rising up from the deposits raining down. The current of water we'd been walking up flowed from a spring pouring out of the rock in front of us, and while I don't know the volumetric flow, I'd guess it was in the thousands of gallons a minute. The underground river caused by the spring flowed along the left side of the cave, allowing us to walk on dry land on the right. Which we did.

Gunner shook, sniffed the sandy ground, and stared at the underground world in which we'd found ourselves. We walked through and around the stalagmites again on carved and level ground. When the river disappeared underground, the path continued. Through the rock.

Gunner followed me only to jerk to a sudden stop and sniff the air. I don't know what he was smelling, but something told me it was familiar. We followed the tunnel, which was remarkably straight, for another fifty or sixty feet until it ended at what I could only imagine were the headwaters of the spring. The water rose like a fountain out of the rock with such force that swimming against it would prove difficult. Then, ten yards away, just as quickly as it appeared, the water ducked below a shelf and disappeared again in another ancient shaft that apparently turned into the flow we'd been walking in.

Bones's map ended with specific detail. *Once you reach the headwaters of the spring, look up.*

So I did.

Gunner and I found ourselves at the bottom of the circular shaft of a well just wide enough for a man to touch both sides. I pulled off my pack, tied one end of the hundred-foot, eight-millimeter rope to my pack, and tied the other end to me. I lifted Gunner by his harness and buckled him to my vest, which added nearly ninety pounds to my climbing weight. I slung my MK4 around to my back, slid my foot into the first carved hole on my right, then my left foot into the carved hole on my left, and began climbing.

Bones had added a PS to his map. "If you slip, don't worry—the water's deep beneath you. But it's also flowing with a force like you've never known, so hold your breath because it's about to take you on an underwater ride that not even Disney could imagine, and it will either drown you or save you."

Gunner whined as I climbed, and I could feel his heart pounding through both his and my vest. When I stopped to rest as my legs started shaking, he looked at me. I nodded and kept climbing. "Don't worry. I don't like this any more than you do."

He whined quietly.

"I don't know. I'm hoping there's an exit"—I pointed up—"that way, but I have a bad feeling we've got to go out of this place"—I pointed down—"the same way we're walking in. Or swimming. Or walking and swimming. Or swimming, walking, and climbing."

When the rope began to tighten below me, I knew I'd climbed nearly a hundred feet. Which also told me I was getting close. One advantage of climbing in a dark world, lit only by the dim red headlamp, was that I couldn't see below me—which was good. I climbed three more steps and heard an echo, telling me we were about to exit into a larger chamber.

To my left I felt a worn iron rod. I latched hold of it and lifted us out of the well. I unbuckled Gunner, set him to my left, then lifted the pack, pulling up the hundred feet of rope. I returned the pack to my back and then secured one end of the rope to the iron rod while allowing the rest to fall free back into the well in the event I needed to rappel quickly out of here.

I turned to Gunner. "Bones. Find Bones." My headlamp lit the high cavernous walls where the remains of frescoes shimmered under the red wavelengths of light. Carved handholds, similar to what I'd just climbed up, had been set into the wall, leading up to a shelf where a crypt lay horizontal. Dark, dusty, and unmoving. Studying the walls, I realized Bones was right. Someone, at some time long ago, had created an underground chapel and then buried their patron saint where no one could find or bother him.

Gunner sniffed around me, his own lamp revealing the outlines of the crypt. The bar doors had been left open, so Gunner walked out into the larger open cavern, sniffing every corner, tunnel, and cell of this underground church turned prison of hell.

Finding no sign of Bones, I followed Gunner and we walked along the corridor that led into and through an underground cave the size of a European cathedral. It was massive. Smoke markings showed where constant cook fires once burned as well as rock collections demarcating one space from another. Judging from the ruins, along with the size, it was feasible that several thousand people once lived down here. And given the fresh supply of water, along with the channels carved in the rock that looked like they served as drains, conditions down here could maintain some measure of cleanliness if the people were of a mind to do so. At the far end, a wide section of stone steps led up into the world of sunlight above.

Bones's letter said he was certain Frank would hold him down here, thinking it some sort of punishment or incentive to jog Bones's memory. Bones wrote that while that had been the case early in his life, this hole in the ground had become more briar patch than prison, and maybe not even Br'er Rabbit was more at home. When Gunner returned to me, having not found Bones, I scratched my head and returned inside the bars.

That's when I thought about the crypt. Sitting up there, empty save some bones.

Using the handholds, I ascended to the cement crypt. I reached the shelf, pulled myself onto it, and stood, the crypt in front of me. Only then did I notice the lid had been slid a foot off center. Walking around the crypt, I stared inside, expecting to find bones. Which I did. Just not the kind I was looking for.

When my light bathed him, his eyes cracked open. Little more than slits. He feigned a smile and managed, "Hey, Murph."

His sense of humor was gone. No doubt beaten out of him. Bruises covered his face, which was puffy, leaving his eyes mostly swollen shut. His breathing was shallow and painful, suggesting broken ribs. I pushed the lid farther to the side and slid my hand in, holding his. My friend and brother.

Bones. I'd found him. I wanted to scream at the top of my lungs.

I leaned in.

He smiled. "Thanks for coming."

"Can you move?"

"Not much."

I noticed then that his mouth was dry and cracked and covered in blood, meaning internal injuries.

I gave him a sip of water. "How'd you get up here?"

"Same as you."

"And Frank?"

Bones sipped and shook his head. "Has no idea about this place. Always been afraid. I figured either you'd find me or I'd die"—he attempted a smile—"already buried."

I sat him up. "Can I move you?"

"You can try."

I returned down to the well, retrieved the rope, climbed back up, secured it around the crypt, and then tried to move Bones. That's when I knew we were in trouble. When I tried again, he gritted his teeth, spit up blood, and spilled out of the crypt. Getting him down was not going to be fun, and we both knew this. He more than I. I secured the rope around his shoulders, swung it around the crypt, and nodded. When I did, he began climbing down. One hold. Then two. On the third, his grip failed and he slipped, falling against the wall. The rope snapped tight and he slammed against the rock wall. I braced and began feeding the line out as fast as I could while knowing I couldn't just let him drop. When the rope slackened, I slowed the feed and laid him on the ground, then threw the rope down and descended. I found Gunner next to him, standing guard. Every other second, Gunner would turn, check him, lick him, then face the prison bars and the darkness beyond.

Bones lay still, focused on his breathing. "You found . . . my map."

A question posed as a statement. I knelt. "Sorry I didn't get here sooner. Frank . . . kept me busy."

He grabbed my hand. "He's like that."

His grip was weak, and only then did I realize there was no way Bones could exit the way I entered. The swimming would kill him. Not to mention the current, which he could not fight. Bones had to go out the front.

"I gotta get you up and out of here, but it's gonna hurt."

He nodded.

"Bones." I laid my hand across his heart, both checking his pulse and letting him know I was here. "I'm sorry it took so—"

He tried to smile and shook his head once. "There's nothing to forgive."

The clock was ticking. Bones needed medical attention three days ago. "You ready?"

He wasn't, but he nodded anyway.

I stood him up. "Drape your arms over my shoulders."

Bones did as directed, and I lifted him, grabbing a leg in each hand. Some would call it piggyback. I'd call it rescue. Bones would call it ugly. I lifted him to a deep moan of pain and began walking, carrying his two hundred pounds plus my gear. I made it through the bars and back down the corridor inside the massive cavern. We made it to the stairs and I willed myself to think of the Eagle's Nest. *You've done this a hundred times. Just put one foot in front of the other . . . and dig deep.*

The stairs were three car lengths wide and not tall. Only a few inches. I made it three flights before I had to lean against the wall and rest. Bones was deadweight. At the base of the fourth flight, Gunner began growling, and when I turned the corner, he shot up the stairs, jumped, and latched his mouth on the face of a man pointing a rifle at us. The man screamed, shot wildly into the air, and then dropped his weapon and tried to peel Gunner off him. A second man appeared to my left, holding a handgun, but he never made it into the stairwell as Bones lifted my suppressed MK4 and fired three quick rounds over my shoulder. The first man was on the ground, writhing, unable to make any progress with Gunner. When Gunner let go, Bones rid the man of his misery. Gunfire would draw attention, so I knew our time was limited. I attempted to hurry, but it was no use. Voices thundered above me, as did footsteps.

Bones whispered, "Better make a stand here. The top of this stairwell is bad for us. Like shooting fish in a barrel."

I set him down and dragged him behind a column as footsteps approached. Four men. Gunner returned and circled behind us, and Bones drew his Sig from the holster attached to Gunner's vest and screwed on the suppressor. The four men misjudged our position, and as they turned the corner, we greeted them with a wall of lead. The exertion taxed Bones, proving that his internal injuries were severe. I needed to get him medical attention as soon as possible.

I turned to him. "Stay here. I'll be back."

He shook his head. "You go up there, you won't come back." He stood. "Follow me."

He stepped behind the column, pushed against the stone wall, and then leaned against it, breathing heavy. He motioned to the stone. "Help." The two of us put our weight into it, and the stone budged. When I saw it moving, I pressed my hip into it, and the wall became a door on some sort of hinge. When it swung open, the three of us stepped inside the thin corridor, and I closed the massive door behind us. I clicked my and Gunner's headlamps to white light and showered the path in front of us. I was less worried about revealing our position and more concerned with blinding whoever was coming the other direction. The path wound upward. A spiral staircase without the stairs. Just smooth stone.

Gunner crept ahead, listening and following his nose. I followed and Bones shuffled, clinging to me. His breathing had turned to a gurgle. Beyond the stone, voices echoed, followed by angry shouts. I didn't know how many people were out there but it was more than a few.

We rose what would have been three flights, rested briefly, then ascended two more. The stonework was ancient, and I had a feeling many people had done what we were doing. Escaping. I also believed Bones had done this more than once. When we reached a T-intersection, Bones tapped my right shoulder and pointed, so I turned right where the path leveled out. Shoulder width, stone on either side, rising up fifteen feet above us. Bones motioned to my and Gunner's headlamps, so I clicked them off and we stood in the dark.

Total dark. Just as in the caverns that brought us here, we found ourselves in the absence of light. Eyes unable to adjust to what wasn't there. Blind, we stood listening. Movement beyond the wall. Bones beside me, laboring to breathe. Gunner between my legs.

Standing there, I realized something I hadn't put words to before. People in darkness don't know they're in darkness because it's all they've ever known. It's their world. They navigate primarily by bumping off things that are stronger. Immovable. They don't know darkness is darkness until someone turns on a light. Only then does the darkness roll back like a scroll. It has to. Darkness can't stand light. And it hasn't. Not since God spoke it into existence. The problem comes when you turn on a light and find those in darkness who, having seen light, prefer the dark. Who retreat into the shadows to do their deeds in secret. They are the ashen-skinned, amber-eyed, fork-tongued servants of evil. Pawns who do the devil's bidding. Who don't think twice about "owning" another person and who, without conscience, profit off another's flesh. Time after time after time. They live convinced of their independence. Their power. Their lack of accountability. Truth is, they are. Accountable. From the beginning of time, light has shone into the darkness, and since that first spark, darkness—no matter how hard it tries, no matter what sword it wields or scheme it perpetrates—has not been able to overcome it. Ever.

Which means, at the end of the day, there's an overcoming. A reckoning. And if there's a reckoning, then there's a record. Those of us who stand in the light wonder sometimes, *How much longer can it last? This onslaught. How much more can we take? This constancy.* Those of us who walk in the light grow weary. Our hope wanes. Fades. Darkness rages and threatens to drown us. We look around and wonder what happened. *Where'd it go? Where's the light?*

Behind me, Bones coughed, gurgled, and spat. He was coughing up blood. I had to get him out of here. He tapped me on the shoulder, then took my right hand and placed it on the wall in front of me. Bones was standing here dying, and yet even now he was pressing toward the light. How many had he saved? How many had he brought home? How many faces, blind and hopeless, had woken one day to find him holding a flashlight, patching their wounds, beginning to mend their broken hearts, and offering freedom? At no cost to them. He'd already paid it. How many children walked the earth, born to parents, once slaves, who were afraid to hope past the next minute but now hoped for that child's future? His skin bore the scars. The entry and exit holes of multiple bullets. Knife slices and punctures. Payment extracted.

Standing in that place devoid of light, I realized he'd taught me all of this. He'd walked up beside me, clicked it on, and showered me in it. Then he'd taught me how to read it. How to keep it. That it mattered. Bones was the record keeper. He'd kept it all along.

And yet I had a feeling he'd let his brother bring him here. He had purpose in this. Purpose in his dying.

Bones's hand pressed atop mine and the wall gave way. A cavity that became a handle. He pushed again, and cold air blew through a crack in the wall. Along with a strange yellow and blue light. Gunner pressed his nose to the crack, and the hair on his back stood on end. Bones pressed again, then fell against me. I dipped my shoulder beneath his, latched an arm around his chest, and we leaned on the door. The ancient hidden door swung open into a sea of technology and screens and flashing lights and drives.

And Frank. Sitting down, feet propped on his desk, smoking a cigar.

We stumbled into the room, Bones's weight pulling on me. As I struggled to hold him upright, Gunner lunged in front of us, eyes trained on Frank.

Frank shook his head and smiled. "You surprise me, Bishop. I have no idea how you got in here. Only that you did. Are you sure I can't convince you to work for me? Name your price. Anything."

A Glock 19 sat on the desk in front of him. "Stick that under your chin and pull the trigger and I'll consider it."

He forced a laugh. "You don't look too well, Brother."

Bones said nothing, laboring just to breathe. Only then did I notice the two men standing in the shadows pointing rifles at our chests.

Frank gestured to the screens in front of him. Wasn't difficult to figure it out. Frank was making good on his promise. He was one click away from letting the world know that Murphy Shepherd was David Bishop. Every screen in front of him showed my picture along with fabricated news stories that, when he sent them, would populate the web. Not even my hack team could undo that.

Frank drew heavily on his cigar, then sat quietly as the smoke exited his nose and mouth. Finally, he said, "You have it?"

"Doesn't exist."

Disappointed, he shook his head. "Last time. Yes or no?"

"You're a sick human being, and when I kill you, I'm going to bury you in an unmarked grave. Nameless and nobody."

He considered this, drew again, then reached up and pressed a single button on his keyboard. When he did, every screen in the room repopulated and began showing the resulting traffic. The reposting. The sharing. Within seconds, the number of hits was in the millions.

Frank sat back and smiled.

Bones crawled along the floor to a couch, pulled himself up, and sat. Eyes closed. He was pale. Fading. Frank's control room was a long hall. When I looked up, I saw stained glass windows above. Each of which had been blacked out on the other side. Preventing light from filtering through. Studying my surroundings, I realized Frank had converted a chapel into this place where he conducted the hell he commanded. At the far end, on what was once the altar, he'd created an art exhibit. His favorite pieces. Two in particular stood center stage.

Bones spoke without looking. "You've had it for years."

Frank was not amused and did not answer his brother. The look on his face was akin to sitting in a chess match and hearing "Checkmate" from your opponent.

Bones continued, "I told you. You just didn't listen." He pointed toward the altar.

Something about this suggestion caught Frank's attention and he sat up straighter, turning slowly to stare at his art.

Bones nodded. "You've had it all along."

Frank's eyes betrayed the calculating. The putting pieces together. He stood, walked to the far end of the chapel, and stared at the two main pieces in his private display.

Turning to me, he pointed at the painting on the left. "You like my Monet?"

"Not really."

He moved to the side and pointed at the second. "And this one?"

I'm not an art expert, but I knew the painting. *Storm on the Sea of Galilee.* It had been stolen years ago and never recovered, and now it was one of the most valuable paintings in the world.

Bones interrupted him. "It's more valuable than you think."

That's when the look on Frank's face suggested

he had put all the pieces together. He walked around the painting, studied the frame and the canvas. Then he turned to Bones and smiled. "Because you knew I'd steal it back. You kept it safe . . . with me."

Bones nodded.

Frank lifted the painting, broke the frame on the stone floor, and shed it from the canvas. Then he studied the canvas. A minute passed. Then a smile. Finally, he picked at one corner of the canvas, eventually peeling back a layer. A false canvas. When he'd peeled it halfway, a document emerged between the two. The real and the false.

Frank stared at his brother and smiled. Then he shook his head. "Genius." Gently, he slid the paper from between the two. An envelope.

Returning, he stood in front of Bones. Holding the envelope. Suddenly his complexion changed. He read the inscription out loud: " 'This will not help you.' "

He stared down at Bones. "How would you know? You abandoned me."

Bones lay slumped on the couch. Making no response. He was fading.

Frank opened the envelope, extracted the single page, and read it. For a second his face remained stone. Then in a moment it changed. To that of a child. He tore the document in two, then again. Then threw the pieces. He straddled Bones. "You knew and you didn't tell me!"

Bones never opened his eyes. "It changes nothing."

Frank was screaming now and punching Bones in the face. "It changes everything."

Bones deflected the blows, spun his brother, and ended up behind him. One arm around his neck. A rear naked choke. In two seconds Bones could put him to sleep. Then I'd shoot those two guys in the corner and we'd be out of here. Then, just as quickly as he'd submitted him, Bones let Frank go. Yielding the superior position.

Frank sat ghost-white. Astonishment spread across his face. The revelation was too much. Frank sat on the stone floor of the chapel and stared at his brother. "How did you not tell me?"

Bones strained to sit up. "It doesn't change who you are."

Frank laughed. " 'Male One.' My name is 'Male One.' My own mother couldn't come up with anything better than that."

Bones nodded. "Yup."

"Did she name you?"

Bones nodded again. His shallow breathing suggested speaking was too taxing.

Frank leaned in. "And what'd she name you?"

Bones lay breathing. Gathering himself. Finally, he spoke. "Male Two."

Frank laughed. "That's us. A couple of nobodies from nowhere."

Bones shook his head.

Frank, his face just inches from Bones, shouted, "What?!"

Bones was calm. "That's not who you are."

Frank was screaming now. "Then who am I?"

"You're my brother. Always have been."

Frank sat motionless. Finally, turning to me, he demanded, "How'd you get in here?"

"I climbed."

"Up what?"

"The well."

He turned to Bones. "You leave him a map?"

I answered for Bones. "Yes."

More pieces were gathering in Frank's mind. When the last piece clicked into place, he turned to Bones. He could not hide his surprise. "You found a way out?"

Bones nodded.

"And yet you stayed in this hell?"

Bones nodded again.

"Why?"

Bones opened his eyes, focused on his brother, and said, "You."

Frank shook his head. This second revelation was too much to digest. "You stayed in this hell on earth for me, even when you had a way out?"

Bones nodded.

Frank began punching Bones in the face. After the fourth or fifth time, Bones reached up, grabbed his brother's hand, flipped them both, and submitted Frank a second time. Frank couldn't move. Bones had him on his belly, his arms tucked beneath him.

I whispered, "Snap his neck."

At which point Bones rolled off him and lay breathing. "Brother. Every day I climbed down, made my way to the outside, stayed long enough to glimpse daylight, and then returned into Hell Squared. And there's only one reason."

Disbelief spread across Frank's face. "What? What could possibly make you stay?!"

Bones turned and stared at his brother. "You."

Frank shook his head. "But why?"

Bones looked at me. Then back to his brother. "Because the needs of the one outweigh those of the ninety-nine."

Frank came unglued. "But you let them do all they did to you."

Bones nodded.

The revelation was sinking in. Frank couldn't hold it anymore. "But I don't love you that much."

Bones nodded. "I know. You don't love me at all." He paused. "But that's what brothers do. They remind us."

As Bones spoke, six men broke through the door. Wielding weapons. I dropped, shot the two in the corner, and only then realized that the man closest to Gunner, a stocky wall of a man, was the guy I'd met at the morgue with Frank. The man who'd shot me with my own crossbow.

I turned to Gunner. "Choctaw!"

Gunner jumped as if shot out of a canon. He caught the man by surprise and latched onto his face, which caused the man to drop his weapon and begin wrestling with the furry thing attached to his nose and mouth. The distraction gave me the time I needed to turn my attention to the five who stood frozen. Bones had shielded himself with Frank, which gave me the second I needed. I turned, rolled again, and fired rapidly. The goons returned fire, but mine had been more accurate. They missed. I didn't. The assassin beneath Gunner managed to lift his rifle and was about to shoot Gunner—but nobody shoots my dog. Making sure to avoid Gunner, I sent a single round through the man's chest. When I did, he fell to his right, swung his rifle at me, and depressed the trigger, sending a single round grazing across the flesh of my right thigh. When the man fell limp, Gunner let go and stared at me.

As the room fell silent, I turned to Frank, whose entire world lay crumbling around him. Standing in the command center of his empire, he'd lost control. Something he'd promised himself would never happen, and yet it had. Bones had taken control. Without firing a single round. Having stood alone at the pinnacle of his pyramid scheme for so long, Frank was sent tumbling to earth by Bones's revelation. His voice took on a pleading tone. "You didn't leave . . . when you could."

Bones spoke with a shallow breath. "You're my brother . . ."

"But they . . ."

At Frank's weakness, I lunged, grabbed him by the throat, and forced every ounce of my strength, every reserve, into crushing his esophagus. My goal was to prevent him from breathing. To cause him to die slowly and painfully. And as his throat collapsed in my hand, his eyes growing wild and exhibiting fear, his life held in my palm—I felt a calm hand on my arm.

Bones.

When I turned, he shook his head.

As Frank fought my hand, which was crushing his windpipe, Bones leaned in. "Bishop . . ."

I turned.

"The needs of the one . . ."

I didn't let go. The screens behind Frank continued to update. From Google to YouTube to every news agency and social media outlet, my picture was front and center. David Bishop had been revealed. As a result, Murphy Shepherd was now dead. I'd never walk the streets in public again, and my ability to rescue in anonymity was gone. Every ounce of energy I'd ever mustered was focused in my hand. I squeezed harder and felt something being crushed. Frank's face was turning blue, and his eyes were bulging.

"But he's not—"

Bones tapped me. "Bishop."

I looked at Bones like he'd lost his mind. "He's not one."

Bones spoke softly. "You sure?"

Maybe that's when the pieces fell into place for me too. Maybe that's when, for the first time in my entire life with him, I saw the enormity that was Bones. The towering, unfathomable completeness. That while hatred had filled me and revenge consumed me, it had not filled him. And while I thought Frank had captured Bones and brought him here, the truth was Bones had come back. For one last rescue. He was here because he wanted to be.

I dropped Frank and turned to stare at the screens. My life as I knew it was over, and if I didn't get Bones medical attention fast, he'd never make it out of here. I lifted Bones and was headed for the door when I felt the burning sensation of a bullet tearing through my left shoulder. The impact spun me, I dropped Bones, and we tumbled across the floor. When I got to my feet, Frank had one arm around Bones's neck, the Glock 19 pointed at his temple, and he was leading him back into and down the secret passageway that had brought us into this room. I tried to follow, but Frank turned and fired as he shut the door.

Live security camera feeds projected onto screens that filled an entire wall. Cameras covered what looked like a hundred or more angles from inside the citadel, most of which showed armed men heading to what I could only guess was our location. I locked the office door and slid a desk in front of it, followed by another. Then I dropped the empty magazine from my Sig, inserted a new one, and repeated the same with my MK4 while trying not to think about the pain in my left shoulder. I didn't have time to dress the wound, so I felt around in there and discovered the bullet had passed through my shoulder blade and then the soft flesh just below my collarbone. I'd live. Somewhere in the wrestling match with Frank, I'd lost my headlamp, so I scoured the floor, found it, clicked it on, and then pressed on the stone door, forcing it open. Following an armed man down a spiral stairwell into enemy territory was never good, but Bones didn't have long. He'd been coughing up blood and his face and chin were covered in dark specks.

I figured I'd skip the silent, careful approach, so Gunner and I bolted through the door and began running back down into the hell from which we'd emerged. We reached the bottom, found the other door open, and continued down the wide stone stairs and through the massive underground cathedral. Oddly, a string of lights lit the walkway. At the far end, under the orange glow of an overhead light, Frank had dragged Bones's limp body back inside his childhood prison of bars. Gunner and I hurdled a stone table and bench as Frank filled the air with a wall of 9mm rounds headed in our direction. Seeing Frank pick up a rifle and level the muzzle, I grabbed Gunner by the collar and rolled behind a stone outcropping as .223 rounds showered our position. When the rifle ran empty, Frank threw it down and continued dragging Bones back into his prison.

Knowing we only had a second, I lunged from our position and we began running the length of the corridor, reaching the bars of the prison door just as Frank slammed it shut. While the door wasn't locked, I'd have to come out from cover to open it, leaving me a sitting duck, which would render me useless to Bones. Frank dragged Bones's body to the edge of the well and used Bones as a shield to protect himself from me. From behind the bars, I couldn't physically maneuver my rifle into position to get a shot. And at more than fifty feet, while I was a decent shot with a pistol, I ran the risk of hitting Bones.

For several seconds Frank knelt, staring at his brother. I knew if I didn't make a move now, I'd lose any opportunity. Just one shove, and Frank would send Bones down that well and I'd never get to him fast enough. Bones would never survive the impact with the water a hundred feet below nor the half-mile swim to the Zodiac. If I had a chance with Bones, we had to go out the front door. Not the well.

Slowly, I stepped out from behind the stone base of the bars, unlatched the prison door, and stepped inside. While my silhouette made an easy target, I was walking toward Frank, closing the distance, leveling my rifle muzzle at him. My laser held steady on his forehead. If he twitched a muscle in my direction, I was going to pull the trigger, but I doubted that'd help me since he'd fall backward, taking Bones with him. I had to separate Frank from Bones. Gunner crept along behind me, growling.

Frank sat on the edge of the well, holding Bones's body across his lap. Cradling his head and shoulders. Bones's left arm hung limp, dangling in the empty air of the well, while his right arm was wrapped around Frank's waist. I tried to will Bones's fingers to move, to send some of the signals he'd learned to make in this very room. But he made no such motion, and his fingers did not move.

Frank just stared at his brother. Then he looked at me, shook his head, and struggled to speak, proving that I'd damaged his ability to do so. He tried again but could only manage a whisper. As he spoke, a tear emerged. "You should know . . ." A long pause. "I sent a team to take you. Amelia. But Bones bargained. So I called them off."

I tried to stall, to get close enough. "What'd he bargain with?"

Frank stared down at the limp body of his

brother, and when he spoke, the tear broke loose and trailed down his face. "His life."

Realizing his brother was dead, Frank reached into his shirt pocket, pulled out what looked like a picture, and stared at it for a long moment. Then at Bones. Then at the picture again. The picture was yellowed, edges tattered and curled. The last time he looked at me, his eyes had a look I'd never seen. One I'd not thought possible. The only word I can find that comes close is *empathy.*

When I'd closed the distance to within five feet, almost close enough to close Frank's eyes forever and then lunge and grab Bones before Frank took him over the ledge with him, Frank set the picture on the ground next to him. He did so purposefully. As if he wanted to make sure I saw it. Then he pressed his forehead to his brother's, kissed his cheek, and without warning pressed the Glock beneath his own chin and pulled the trigger.

The percussion surprised me and set me on my heels. It was that surprise that cost me the time I needed to catch Bones's leg. Frank's head rocked backward, launching his body over the edge and into the blackness of the well, dragging Bones with him. One brother intertwined with the other, so that discerning who was holding who was impossible.

Then, as the echo faded off the stone walls, the two disappeared.

I lunged, reached for Bones's leg, but he was too heavy. Given the bullet that had passed through my shoulder, I couldn't hold him. I stared in shock as the indomitable man I knew as Bones disappeared into the darkness.

Seconds later, I heard the splash.

CHAPTER 32

Coastal Georgia, 24 hours later

Clay drove as I stared at Frank's photo. The one he'd left for me on the edge of the well. I didn't know it at the time, but by laying it down, Frank had left me a message. Eddie, Camp, Jess, and BP sat in the back of the van and said little. Words did not and could not console me.

After Bones and Frank disappeared, I buckled Gunner to my vest, rappelled the well, and spent eight hours searching. Until our batteries died. We walked the last hundred steps in total darkness following Gunner's nose.

Having emerged from a world of darkness, Gunner and I swam back under the stone shelf, and I hauled him with one arm into the Zodiac, where we were met by the first rays of light. The sun was rising in the east, and yet I couldn't wrap my head around my loss. I'd lost him. I'd lost Bones. I'd never lost anyone, and yet here I'd lost the one who mattered most. The pain was more than I could bear. I lay in the bottom of the boat and heard the echo of his voice. *"When light walks into a room, the darkness rolls back like a scroll. It has to. Darkness can't stand light. And while we live it in real time, it happens too fast, so we watch it in memory. To know the joy, we shut our eyes and remember having seen it."*

I closed my eyes, felt the warmth of the sun on my skin, and cried like a baby.

We'd coordinated our arrival here on the coast with my new boss in Washington. A voice on the other end of the line. Given the nature of Frank's work, our timeline was short. Once news of his death circulated through the dark world he commanded, the sharks would circle and a feeding frenzy would ensue as his generals fought for control. When that started, whatever information we had gleaned from opening Frank's third vault would be useless. I'd flown directly from Majorca to Florida and, as much as it pained me, returned to the world where Bones had grown up.

The photo showed the two of them. Suntans. Cutoff jeans. Bare feet. Not more than five or six. Healthy. Smiling. Standing knee deep in the water. Each boy held a fishing pole in one hand, his other arm wrapped around the other's shoulders. Just two boys being boys, because being a boy is what they knew. What they needed. Before their world was turned upside down, they had each other.

I flipped the photo over and read the inscription. "Brothers." Below that Frank had written GPS coordinates, which had led us here. I retraced my and Bones's footsteps beneath the oaks to the overgrown dilapidated chapel he and Frank had known as boys. Why did Frank choose this place? I really can't say, but if I had to, I'd suggest it had something to do with a peace he hadn't known since he was taken from here. I walked around back, pulled away the vines, found the keypad, and punched in the twenty-one-digit code, and the rotten, cat-infested porch slid out of the way to reveal a stone staircase leading down to a vault door. I entered the second twenty-one-digit code, and the pressurized door clicked open, accompanied by the sound of exiting and equalizing air. Then the door swung open and our team disappeared inside.

Memories of Bones flooded my heart. A tidal wave.

With the team inside, I followed the trail to the water's edge and sat with Gunner, trying to remember the name of the Spanish doctor who'd sewed up my shoulder. The weight on my chest threatened to suffocate me as I struggled to just inhale and exhale. One breath. Two. Then another. Maybe the tough part wasn't the breathing so much as the wanting to.

An hour later, my phone rang. I recognized the caller ID and answered. "Yes, sir."

The vice president's voice sounded pained. "Murph, I just heard. I can't tell you how—" He broke off. "I can't believe it. It doesn't feel real. He . . . he was the best of us. Always was."

"Yes, sir."

A pause. "I know you don't need me to tell you, but . . . anything you need. Anything at all. Don't hesitate."

"Thank you, sir."

"I'll be in touch."

The line went dead, and I realized I wasn't the only one hurting. The aftershocks of Bones's death were traveling through the ranks in DC and the hundreds of friends he'd made around the world.

Summer and the girls were en route. I told Summer I didn't want to return to Freetown right away, and she said they all thought a week or three at the beach would do us good. I didn't disagree. An hour later, Eddie found me lying on the bank with Gunner in my lap. He, too, was grieving, and he didn't know how to show it other than by placing his paw on my chest. I wiped my eyes and Eddie spoke softly. "It's all there. Names. Numbers. Addresses. Accounts. Videos." He nodded. "You're not going to believe this, but Frank gave you the truth."

The thought of this stopped me. Something else I could not process. Another breath. In. Out.

He continued, "We're going to bring in some folks from DC and coordinate with teams and agencies around the world. You can't set that many people free without some forethought and some help. The next few days will . . ."

I turned and headed for the water. Bones had done that. He'd done it all. I had not. Under the guise of capture, he'd gone back. For his brother. Something I'd never considered. Never contemplated. And I'm rather certain Frank hadn't either. Why hadn't I seen that before? My response to Frank was to crush his windpipe. Shoot him in the face. Let him burn in hell. Given the amount of evil he'd inflicted on planet Earth, why not?

But Bones?

Bones suffered beating after beating, and for what purpose? Simple really. To reveal to his brother the singular fact that while he'd known a way out of that hell on earth, he'd come back. Day after day. Why? One reason. He would not leave his brother to suffer alone. No matter how guilty. This act of selflessness was mind-blowing to Frank. A paradigm shift beyond comprehension. In the end Frank gave up the location of and codes to the closet that held his secrets. His power. The keys to his kingdom. We knew about the vault beneath the prison and the one in the New York City high-rise, but they meant nothing without the last piece of the puzzle. Now we had it. And thanks to the help of Guido and Bernie, who were now singing like canaries, we were able to unlock all of it. To make sense of it. To find the people. And the money.

In the process what we'd seen play out on the world's stage was a conflict of kingdoms.

In Frank's kingdom one man enslaved the innocent and bled profit from their flesh. A world
of darkness. Without feeling. Without empathy.
Where the one dominated the many. Concealed
in shadow and pungent with the smell of death.

A slave market.

In Bones's kingdom one man walked into the
slave market and said, "What's the price? For all
of them." And when the slave master quoted the
price, Bones never flinched. He paid it. With his
life.

The magnitude of his sacrifice was inconceiv-
able to me. Bones had known the cost going in.
I'd never contemplated it.

I could understand running through hell to
rescue the innocent. I'd done that and kept the
record on my back. A record of the undeserving.
Of the betrayed, rejected, and abandoned. But
Bones not only emptied the market, he ran back
into that same hell—hell squared—a second time,
to rescue the one who'd enslaved them. Why?

This was my problem.

As the days passed and the answer built, it
weighed me down. Pressing on my soul. Then,
when I was unable to keep it at bay any longer, it
hit me all at once. A freight train. Because Frank,
too, was enslaved. Unlike the masses, Bones
found mercy for his executioner. Whereas I'd
simply written him off.

Wanting justice, I'd kept a record of wrongs.

Payment to be exacted from the guilty. On my terms. It fueled and justified my need for revenge. Bones? Bones kept a record of hope imprinted on his heart.

In my time at the Academy, Bones and I grocery shopped on Sunday evenings. He'd park in the alley out back with a good view of a soiled sleeping bag spread beneath a cardboard shack. The woman who lived there was sun-weathered. Angry. Talked to herself. She'd stand on street corners. Eyes glazed. Palm out. Spending the proceeds on brown water and more glaze. About once a week, often on Sundays, she'd stumble into the store, fill a cart, and then argue with the manager.

One day we stood behind her in line. She was spilling stuff across the conveyor belt. The cashier spoke over the intercom. "Manager needed on four." When the manager appeared, he wasn't having any of it. He had tired of her and her constant circus. She was scaring the other shoppers. Polite society. He began ushering her out the front door.

Bones spoke up. "Excuse me, sir, what does she owe?" I can't remember what he said, but it was a couple hundred dollars. Bones handed the man cash, and then he turned to the lady. "Can I help you with that?" She was about to shout something when Bones put a hand on her shoulder. "Let me help you." The language of touch spoke something she could hear, and when she did, she nodded—and that's when I saw it. Something in her expression changed. Something replaced the anger. Something good. I witnessed one curtain lift and another fall.

For weeks we continued seeing her on the street corner, and we continued shopping on Sundays. Then one Sunday she was gone. Along with her cardboard home. Bones seemed unfazed.

I pointed in surprise. "Probably dead or in jail." As if dying was all she had left.

Bones shook his head and idled out of the parking lot. "Sisters of Mercy."

Sisters of Mercy was a private and expensive rehab facility. "What?"

He said nothing more.

Two months later, curiosity got the better of me and I rang the bell at the counter. Not sure how to phrase it, I tried the honest approach. "Excuse me, ma'am, do you have a woman here who used to live behind the Piggly Wiggly?"

She turned the clipboard around, said, "Sign here," and handed me a guest badge. "Room 119. If she's not there, try the garden."

Room 119 was empty, so I wound through the Ritz-Carlton–like facility and found the rose garden, where a woman wearing a straw hat and wielding pruning shears was tending the roses. My shadow crossed her, she stood, and I almost didn't recognize her. She pushed the hair out of her eyes, slid off a glove, and extended her hand. "Murph. Bones has told me a lot about you."

Her name was Rose, which I found fitting given the garden in which she was working. Rose was a wife. Mother. Sister. Friend. A PhD and tenured professor of romantic languages. After twenty years her high school sweetheart had an affair. That same year, her son died in a war, and disease robbed her of much that was feminine. She said she didn't remember the last straw, but when she broke, anger took over. Rage set in. Sometime later she woke up behind the grocery store having named the rats.

Rose shook her head, her eyes found mine, and she whispered two words. "Then Bones."

Once an angry woman draped in soiled clothing who created distance through the smell of urine and spit-filled obscenities, now something completely new stood before me. Smelling of roses. A reflection of the face of God. To my shame I'd written her off. Sometimes, given their depth, we become little more than the sum of our wounds, and it takes someone else to see what we can be instead of what we are.

No one was better at that than Bones.

What had found me as a boy on a river troller had gone on to carry me through the Academy. Through Roger's betrayal. Through Marie. Through Key West, tending bar, and Karen. Through more than a hundred countries

and three times as many rescues. Through gun-
shots, knives, hospitals, and infections. Through
Angel and Casey and Clay and Ellie and Summer
and Shep. Through Freetown and Frank.

Then Bones. The two words that defined my
life.

I walked down the bank and waded into the
warm water of the Intracoastal, where I stood
letting the gentle current press against me. Wash
over me. Carry my tears south. In a couple weeks
they'd be mixing with the waters around Key
West. In a year or two, or maybe a decade or a
hundred years, they'd mix with the waters of the
Balearic Sea, and maybe there I'd find my friend.

When I did, I'd hug his neck. My friend Bones.

Had Bones's last selfless act had any effect
on Frank? Did it change anything in him? If
so, was the gain worth the purchase price, or
was his sacrifice in vain? I couldn't say. In my
hand I held the picture. Frank had set it down as
I watched. A purposeful act, and unlike the rest
of his life, it was not done in secret. Standing in
the water, Gunner swimming around me, I had
more questions than answers and more pain than
joy.

Over the next few days and weeks, thousands
of prison doors would be flung wide. Ripped off
the hinges. Shackles loosed. Bones was right.
We needed a bigger town. Those who had been
slaves would walk out of the market. Sun on their

faces. Life before them. And none save me would know the price paid for their freedom.

One life for the many—starting with the one I'd written off. Who wasn't worth the cost.

I did not understand that kind of love.

But . . . *then Bones.*

EPILOGUE

It was dark when I woke. I tried not to stir as Summer was wrapped around me like a vine. Since my return, she hadn't let me out of her sight. Neither had Shep, who'd taken the news of Bones's death badly. In the days since, Summer had wanted to process, to talk about it. I could not. My anger raged at my own inadequacy. My own failure. I had thrown my phone in the ocean and silently vowed never to return to Free-town.

Her hand moved across my chest and laid flat across my heart. "Talk with me?"

I couldn't. I shook my head.

"Why?"

I said the only thing I could. "I'm in pain."

Daylight found me sitting in a chair at the water's edge. Gunner lay quietly at my side as gentle waves rolled in, bathed my toes, and then receded. With funds from one of Frank's many accounts, Eddie and the girls had made the decision to buy five thousand acres along the coast of Spellman Bluff. A purchase that included Bones's childhood playground as well as a retreat center built by the same people who owned the

Cloister. Currently the center would sleep four hundred, and given the events of the last few days and the reports from around the world, those beds would fill quickly. Summer, Eddie, and the team were already dreaming and drawing up expansion plans.

The girls voted, and the working name became Hopetown. I was silently voting for City of Bones, but after listening to myself say it a few times, I admitted it sounded a bit morbid and I was pretty sure no one would want to live there.

I flipped open the lid of Bones's million-mile orange Pelican case and stared at the dusty bottle. I lifted the wine and found a yellow sticky note written in Bones's own hand. It read "For memory."

I was working on my second glass when Casey's shadow appeared over my shoulder. Arms crossed, she studied me. "Little early to be drinking, isn't it?"

I nodded and poured a few more sips into Gunner's bowl.

She took my glass, sipped, then handed it back. "That won't numb your pain. I know. I'm a bit of an expert."

Another nod.

She leaned over, kissed my cheek, and laid a pad and pen on my lap. Then she waited until I looked at her. When I finally did, she said, "Write it out."

Casey was going to be okay. She'd made it. The rescued now caring for the rescuer.

Eddie was the next to find me. In the time since we'd returned, I hadn't looked at a screen. Hadn't listened to the radio. Had no idea what kind of conversations were swirling about me. About David Bishop. Because I didn't care and didn't want to hear them. I just knew that life, as I had known it, was over.

Eddie knelt alongside my chair, rubbing Gunner's head. His tone was soft. Gunner sighed and rolled onto his back. "Since we've been back, things have been crazy and I've wanted to tell you but never seemed to find the right moment." He shook his head. "I'm not sure this is it, but I figured you need to know. When . . . when Frank dumped your identity onto the world . . . and you watched as the hits counted into the millions, well . . . he didn't. I mean, they didn't. Not really. I mean, he thought he did, but—"

I lifted my Costas off my face and squinted at him. Only then did I notice Jess, Camp, and BP standing behind him. Angel too.

Eddie fumbled with his hands while Camp continued. "I had his machine. When he thought he was posting to the Internet, revealing the truth of you, he was really just posting into our mirror."

Evidently my eyes asked the question on my mind.

Jess held up her phone. "The world doesn't know."

Slowly, the pieces were shifting into place.

BP shrugged. "About you."

Eddie added, "Unless you want them to."

I sat up straighter and turned toward them. "What exactly are you saying?"

Jess spoke first. "Murphy Shepherd is still protecting David Bishop."

Angel knelt alongside me. "Your secret is still safe with us, Padre."

While they were speaking, I heard someone walking toward me, dragging a beach chair through the sand. When I turned, Clay stood wearing a straw hat, board shorts, and flip-flops. He held a fishing pole baited with shrimp and a lead weight that looked like Sputnik. He nodded, walked to the water's edge, cast the bait, and then hung the rod and reel in a silver stake driven into the sand. Reeling the line taut, he poured himself a glass of wine, toasted me and someone out across the ocean, who I imagined must have been Bones, and then sat alongside me, propping his feet on the orange case like a footstool.

While the nature of my reality swirled in my mind, Summer headed my way, leading a stranger wearing a suit and tie. Maybe sixty. White hair. Fit. Tanned. He extended his hand. "Mr. Shepherd, my name is Tank Witherspoon. I'm Karen Mixer's attorney."

Did he just say his name was Tank?

He continued, "As her attorney, everything she told me over twenty-plus years is privileged. Under penalty of law, I cannot reveal any of it. Ever."

The world was coming at me pretty fast, and two glasses of wine weren't helping, so rather than speak I decided to continue my current method of listening. Gunner studied the man with curiosity.

"In all that time, I handled all of her affairs. Including helping her navigate foreign publishing relationships for those she represented in the States as well as keeping those identities"—he paused, searching for the right word—"hidden." He stared at the group around him, not sure how to say what he needed to say. He gestured to an empty stretch of beach. "May we talk somewhere more private?"

Summer spoke for me. "We know all his secrets."

I nodded and shrugged.

Tank continued, "Karen's last directive to me asked me to adopt and help with a single client. Her primary client. She asked that I offer to help him continue publishing . . . if he so desired." He glanced at Casey. "She also suggested that I offer to help with her newest client, but I've yet to make that introduction."

The sun had risen and was boring holes into

my pupils. I dropped my Costas back down over my eyes and stood. "Did you say your name was Tank?"

He smiled. "My father served with General Patton at the Bulge. He named me in memory."

I drained my glass. "Seems to be a theme around here today."

He handed me his card. "If I can ever be of help to"—he gestured a second time to Casey and then back to me—"either of you."

The change in my world was akin to traveling a hundred on the interstate and throwing the gear shift into reverse. If the synapse firings of my brain could make a sound, they would have sounded like an engine transmission exploding.

I scratched my head. "Can I get back to you on that?"

"Take your time. Just needed to make the introduction." He raised a finger and smiled. "Mr. Bishop, I agree with Karen. The world needs your words. They have rescued countless millions." A purposeful pause. "Including me. But that's a story for another day."

While Clay caught dinner, I marveled at his strength. It'd be a while before I dug his hole, which was a comfort. Losing Bones was hard enough. From where I was sitting, Clay looked to be getting younger, not older.

I spent the day beneath an umbrella staring at my pad. The words were few and slow in coming.

At sundown Summer tapped my shoulder, woke me from my nap, and knelt alongside me. "It's time."

I lifted Shep onto my shoulders, and we walked along the water's edge to where everyone had gathered. My circle of friends. Those who kept my secrets as I kept theirs. Given how Bones died, we had nothing to bury. No ashes to scatter. In response we decided to bury his orange case at sea. Set it on the tide and let the waves carry it off the edge of this world and into the next. We stood arm in arm.

I wanted to speak. I just couldn't. So Clay broke the silence and spoke beautiful words over the water. Then Eddie. Followed by Casey and Angel. Final words spoken at random, while tears ran like the ocean. I stood shattered. One breath. Two. In. Out. Repeat.

Finally, Summer patted me. "Your turn."

I stared at the box. Scuffed. Scarred. One last voyage remaining. Solo. I tried to speak and could not. When I tried again, no words formed in my mouth. Then, on the wind, I heard his voice. There in that water, in that broken place of earth where the sand told the sea, "You will go no farther," Bones spoke to me. When he did, I could hear him smiling. *"Tell me what you know about sheep."*

I shook my head and spoke out loud. "No. I'll tell you about the one who keeps them."

I waded out past the breakers until the water rose above my chest and placed the orange box on the surface of the water. There I let it go.

I let Bones go.

For over an hour we stood with our arms locked, bracing ourselves against the pain, watching the tide pull it beyond the horizon. When it disappeared for good, the others returned to the house, Gunner running circles around everyone and Ellie leading Shep by the hand, the band on my Omega having been shortened to fit his arm. Clay was making low-country boil. His prison guard recipe. He'd flown in Alaskan king crab legs and Louisiana crawfish to complete the mix. Summer kissed my cheek and said, "Don't be long."

I stood on the sand, staring out across the ocean. My pad in hand. Because I wanted him to know, I read the single page out loud.

For the record.

Three miles distant, the trail of smoke spiraled upward. Thick and black, it poured from the twin supercharged diesels housed in the engine room. Orange and red flames licked the smoke against a fading blue skyline, telling me the fire was hot and growing. When the heat hit the fuel tanks, it would blow the entire multimillion-dollar yacht into a zillion pieces, sending fragments to the ocean floor.

I turned the wheel of my twenty-four-foot center console hard to starboard and slammed the throttle forward. The wind had picked up and whitecaps topped the two- to three-foot chop. I adjusted the trim tabs down to bring the stern higher in the water, and the Boston Whaler began skidding toward the sinking vessel. I crossed the distance in just over three minutes. The 244-foot *Gone to Market* sat listing on her lee side, adrift. The hundred or so bullet holes across her stern explained her loss of rudder and engine. And possibly the fire.

They also told me that Fingers had made it to the boat.

Waves crashed over the bow and water was pouring into the main-level galley and guest rooms. The stern was already lifting in the water as the bow filled, pulling her nose dangerously toward the bottom of the Atlantic. Whether by explosion or water, she wouldn't be able to take much more. I ran the Whaler up her stern, beaching it on her swim platform. I rigged a bow line loosely to a grab rail and jumped onto the main-deck lounge, where I found three bodies with multiple bullet holes. I climbed the spiral staircase up one level to the bridge-deck lounge, finding two more bodies.

No sign of Fingers.

I kicked open the ship's office door, tripped over another body, and ran into the bridge, where I was met by a wave of salt water pouring through the shattered front glass. Anyone in there had already been washed out to sea. I climbed to the top floor and onto the owner's-deck lounge. Victor's wife lay awkwardly across the floor. She'd been shot three times, telling me Fingers had gotten to her before she got to him. But the gun in her hand was empty. Which was bad. I pulled an ax off the wall and cut through the Honduran mahogany doors into Victor's stateroom. Victor, also shot three times, lay twisted with his neck forcibly broken. Suggesting he'd suffered pain on his way out. Which was good.

The vessel rocked forward, telling me she was reaching the tipping point. Telling me I only had moments to find Fingers and the girls and get off this thing before she dragged us down with her or blew us into the sky. I descended the stairs and turned aft into the engine room, but it was flooded. I waded fore through waist-deep water into the crew cabins, past Victor's prayer shrine, and toward the door of the anchor room where the water had turned red.

And there I found Fingers.

I tucked the pad next to the small of my back as Gunner and I walked along the water's edge. In my hand I turned the worn silver coin he'd given me at the café table decades ago. How much had been transferred since that moment? I walked slowly. Meandering. Winding through the woods. Past the chapel. Beneath the oaks. Walking in the paths of my mentor. My friend. My keeper.

There it was.

That might even make a good title, but could one book do him justice? No, the story was too much for one. Two even. I'd need a trilogy. Start with Water because that's where he started with me. Move on to the Letters because of what they held. End with the Record because that's what this will be. A record of my keeper.

Who left the ninety-nine . . . for me.

Like Marie, I feared being swept out to sea, so I hit my knees, dug my fingers in, and fought the riptide. *How do I breathe in a world without you? Do I still breathe in?*

I knew if my friend Bones were here, he'd hand me his phone, point to the picture, and say, "Right here. We start right here. With this one."

When I was a kid, just falling in love with Marie, I'd walked her beneath that cathedral of majestic oaks on what I had begun to call "my island." Then I'd walked her through the ruins of the chapel that I would later rebuild and watched in wonder as she ran her fingers through the grooves of the names and dates carved into the walls. I marveled as she came to realize that those who'd etched their names into the tabby had known freedom there. That the etching, the record on the wall, had been a declaration. A stake driven into the surface of the earth. Both an ending and a beginning. Above the names, someone had carved, "Even the rocks cry out." And they did. Late that summer, I walked her home, held her hand, and as we stood in the knee-deep water, I told her I was going to buy that island.

Which I did.

Gunner sat beside me, licking my face. One paw stretched across my hand. The long, slow whine told me he was hurting too. Behind me stood the chapel where Bones had grown up. Like the slave chapel on my island, I'd rebuild this one. A declaration. A stake in the ground. I made it to one knee, Gunner's muzzle pressed to my wet face. One paw on my shoulder. *Come on, old man.* As I stared up at the oaks, the wind tugging at me, the moss swaying, a dove cooed. Somewhere above.

I had but one question. I held Gunner's head in my hands, pressed my forehead to his, and voiced it: "Just how do I tell them about him?"

As the last few rays of light fell across the dunes, I returned to my chair, which was now sitting in the water as the tide had come in and risen almost to the underside of the seat. I unstuck it and began dragging it, feeling its waterlogged weight. And there on the sand, where the land met the sea and God graced the earth with shell and wonder and mystery, I looked down. Why? I cannot tell you. Maybe looking ahead hurt too much. But there, in that impressionable place where the thin water flowed like film, I saw a boot print. So I knelt and ran my finger across the imprint of the lugs. They were new. Barely worn. Size 12. Vibram. The dim light made it difficult to see, but a stride's length away, I found a second print.

That made boot prints. Plural.

They had come from the woods, so I followed them, retracing my steps and ending at the chapel where I found the prints had exited behind me. Following me. I stood staring. Scratching my head. I was tired, but . . .

Only then did I notice the second set of prints. Smaller. Not dainty but definitely a woman's foot. High arch. Tracking alongside the boots like two people holding hands.

In the darkness I lost the trail, causing me to

wonder if I'd ever really seen it at all. I stood on the beach, staring up at the house. Lit like a beacon where Gunner was barking and, oddly, Summer was twirling. And then from the house, I heard the strangest and most beautiful sound.

The sound of freedom.

Then Bones.

DISCUSSION QUESTIONS

1. At the beginning of the story, Murph is struggling between his desire to continue the work of rescuing and the exhaustion and need for physical and emotional rest. What do you think makes this struggle so difficult? Have you ever had to make a decision based on responsibility and commitment versus the need for physical and emotional rest?

2. At the end of chapter 2, Murph says that being rescued is perhaps "to be accepted in the knowing." What do you think he means by that? Do you think it's a good definition of rescue?

3. In chapter 13 we learn some of Eddie's story. In working with Murph in Freetown, "It was the first time the rescued had ever asked to rescue." Why do you think there is such power in this? Has there ever been a time you've experienced something and then later helped others through a similar situation?

4. Page 220 shares a major theme of the book: "Love shows up." Where do you see this reflected in the story? Where have you seen this theme in your own life?

5. Bones tells Murphy about the time he was in Hell Squared and only knew his surroundings by what he could touch in the dark. When someone gave him a flashlight, he was amazed to discover what he'd been missing. How is this symbolic of the rest of the book and life in general?

6. At one point, Murph mentions that Frank has lived in fear, while Bones has lived in freedom. How have those perspectives affected their lives? Have you experienced a time when you've lived in fear or freedom? How did that impact your life and decisions?

7. Chapter 31 says, "People in darkness don't know they're in darkness because it's all they've ever known . . . They don't know darkness is darkness until someone turns on a light . . . The problem comes when you turn on a light and find those in darkness who, having seen light, prefer the dark." How do you see this reflected in the book? How do you see it reflected in our world today? How can we be a light to those around us who are lost in the dark?

8. Were you surprised to learn that Bones had discovered a way out of Hell Squared but had stayed because he couldn't leave Frank? What is Frank's reaction to this news? Do you think he would have done the same as a child?

9. Bones returns to Hell Squared for one last rescue. Whose rescue was it? Do you think it was justified? What does he mean when he tells Murph "The needs of the one . . ." on page 410?

10. In remembering Bones, Murph thinks about the story of Rose, the woman who lived behind the Piggly Wiggly. What did Bones do that changed her? How does her past make you feel about where she ended up? How does her story and Bones's care for her impact how you see others? How can you live out Bones's thought that it "takes someone else to see what we can be instead of what we are"?

ABOUT THE AUTHOR

Charles Martin is a *New York Times* and *USA TODAY* bestselling author. He and his wife, Christy, live in Jacksonville, Florida. Learn more at charlesmartinbooks.com.

Instagram: @storiedcareer
Twitter: @storiedcareer
Facebook: @Author.Charles.Martin

Center Point Large Print
600 Brooks Road / PO Box 1
Thorndike, ME 04986-0001 USA

(207) 568-3717

US & Canada:
1 800 929-9108
www.centerpointlargeprint.com

4L